| **AUTHOR** | **CLASS** A FC |
| BENNETT, P. | |

TITLE
Due diligence

DUE DILIGENCE

PAUL BENNETT

WARNER BOOKS

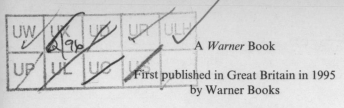

A *Warner* Book

First published in Great Britain in 1995
by Warner Books

06693565

A CIP catalogue record for this book
is available from the British Library.

ISBN 0 7515 1580 9

Typeset by M Rules
Printed and bound in Great Britain by
Clays Ltd, St. Ives plc

Warner Books
A Division of
Little, Brown and Company (UK)
Brettenham House
Lancaster Place
London WC2E 7EN

DUE
DILIGENCE

CHAPTER ONE

Friday 3rd September 1993

Later that evening I would wonder what might have happened if I had been on time. Now, as I turned off the Strand towards the Embankment, my mind focused solely on the envelope in my pocket. And the cryptic message it contained.

I had decided to walk: how strange – how cruel – that the smallest act can radiate outwards like ripples on a lake, eventually touching everything that surrounds it. The businessman would have stretched his legs in the back of a taxi; the office worker opted for the view of daylight from a bus or the swifter homecoming of the claustrophobic tunnels of the tube. In any of their shoes I'd have done the same. Then, maybe, events might have taken a different course: the dead might rise, the living become whole again. It doesn't bear thinking about. Because I had to walk.

There was freedom in walking. The freedom to choose direction and pace as it suited me – and only me. A whole world away from shuffling around in a tight circle, following the dragging footsteps of thirty brooding, silent men.

I had learnt much during seven years in prison – not the least of which was to enjoy the simple pleasures of life. So I, Nick Shannon, ex-Brixton and Chelmsford, ambled along unhurriedly, an Oxfam dinner jacket slung carelessly over my left shoulder, shirt sleeves turned over twice to hide the short, frayed cuffs.

It was that in-between time of day, that well-crafted segue by which late afternoon slips unnoticed into early evening. The sun, slanting low on my right, was casting blood-red reflections on the murky water of the Thames dead ahead.

The note was an unscratchable itch on my mind, like a broken bone healing within a plaster cast. I had thought of little else for the last few hours. The contents were indelibly stamped on my brain: the black ink that leapt up from the white paper: the two short lines of bold handwriting, flowing with eccentric loops and whorls. The meaning of the words still escaped me – the threat behind them did not.

Preoccupied with my efforts to solve the puzzle, the first shout failed to fully register.

It was the movement that caught my eye.

A young lad – unkempt, gaunt, barely sixteen – in faded jeans and a grubby T-shirt was struggling with a well-dressed woman. His pasty face began to flush with the exertion. His eyes filled with anger. Why was she resisting him, they asked? It was supposed to be quick and easy, that's what they'd told him. His brows furrowed in confusion. One half of him desperately wanted the money and credit cards inside the bag: the other half saw only her strength and determination. He had to act fast – or get caught.

I watched impotently from a distance as he dipped into the back pocket of his jeans. His hand, clenched now, reappeared. A sharp click sounded ominously in my ears. The blade of a flick knife flashed briefly in the light, then became a blur as it sliced cleanly through the thin strap of the woman's shoulder bag. One sharp tug and the thief had his prize. One last push and the woman was lying shocked and dazed on the ground.

Bag in left hand, knife in right, he ran towards the narrow alley. At its end lay the safety of the labyrinth of hiding places within Charing Cross Station. Startled pedestrians pressed back against the wall or stepped carelessly into the road, their natural fear of the knife clearing a path for the fleeing youth.

I stepped back too.

2

The boy sneered. Cowards all of you, he seemed to say: this was more like it.

Twenty yards from me he made the mistake of glancing back.

Seeing no one in pursuit, he relaxed.

He was five yards away when I sidestepped from the wall. Too close, too late, for him to change course.

I swung my right leg. The way I had been taught in Brixton.

Not low down where the trip-kick can be avoided by an agile opponent. Stomach level. Too high to jump over: try to slide under and finish up defenceless on the floor, where the next boot crashes viciously into your ribs – if you're lucky, that is.

My leg hit the target. There was so little resistance I had to work hard to keep my balance. His undernourished belly, no match for the force of the blow, formed an arrowhead as he flew up and back through the air. He landed awkwardly, lacking the knowledge to roll in mid-air or break his fall by banging down his forearm. His knees and head hit the ground with one sickening thud.

A wave of pity washed over me as I bent down to examine the damage I'd inflicted. A few bruises, broken nose, concussion too, probably: he'd live. But for what? How would he cope with the institution that would inevitably be his new home? I didn't fancy his chances up against the bully boys. They had a taste for easy meat: the small ones were always tormented first.

The woman interrupted my thoughts. And blocked my exit.

The last thing I wanted was to be there when the police arrived. I'd intended to slip quietly away from the scene, before the onlookers had a chance to gather their wits.

But the woman had an unshakeable grip on my arm. She hoisted it aloft in a triumphal salute to the small crowd that had gathered now the danger had passed.

She was in her early forties, I guessed, although the hardness in her eyes may have unkindly added five years to her appearance. Dressed for the theatre, or dinner in a smart restaurant.

Black patent high-heeled shoes. Long black skirt, slit up one leg for ease of walking. White silk blouse scooped low at the neck for a panoramic view of her ample breasts. No jacket or wrap to hide the expensive jewelled necklace, the gold bracelet or watch: rings shining brightly on both hands – she might just as well have fixed a flashing neon sign to her forehead saying 'Mug Me'.

Singling out a responsible looking man from the crowd, she summarily despatched him to call the police. I added an ambulance to his errand. She gave me a withering look that seemed to say 'no wonder the streets aren't safe'.

We stood around kicking our heels and talking – or, rather, she talked and I listened. Her system was high on adrenaline. She spoke at breakneck speed. In the space of a few minutes I learnt her life history.

Arlene Tucker. American. Some religious sounding town in New England. A 'realtor', which I took as a way of saying 'estate agent' without the connotations. Recently widowed from Cy – overweight lawyer, pillar of the community and coronary victim. On holiday in London, first stop on a European tour courtesy of the proceeds of an insurance policy. Came out of the back door of The Savoy, taken a wrong turn, finished up on the Embankment rather than at Aldwych.

She made me promise to walk her 'to the show'.

It took five minutes for the police to arrive. A further twenty before the constable had painstakingly written down names and addresses of the witnesses and details of the incident in his notebook. Waiting my turn, I watched as the young lad was stretchered away, a blanket hiding the bloodstained T-shirt but not the miserable look on his face. At least he was out of sight, if not out of mind.

Finally, we were allowed to leave.

She clamped herself onto my arm, clung on throughout the short walk as if her life depended on it. Outside the theatre she took a business card from her purse. Wrote her room number on the back. Pressed it into my hand. Gave me a long kiss. It contained plea and promise as well as gratitude.

I said I'd call her.
I didn't know whether I would.
She wasn't my type.

*

I had no option now but to take a taxi. Even then I was five minutes late.

I hated unpunctuality. Another of the side-effects of prison. To 'do time' means to become obsessed by time itself. Each punctuation mark in the unvarying daily routine – the blaze of the lights in the morning, the trayful of slops at meal-times, association, exercise – takes on a momentous significance: another step nearer the end of the sentence. And when you haven't the patience to count the hours, you tick off the minutes – each one that passes is one less to go.

The tiny mews 'cottage' was tucked away behind Victoria in one of those quiet cul-de-sacs you only discover when you're lost. I rang the bell.

No answer.

Three more times I pressed the button. Three more times I waited patiently for a reply that never came.

Giving up on the bell, I banged on the door.

It swung open.

I should have known something was wrong.

But it was all too easy to assume an innocent explanation: that John (who derided me relentlessly, among other things, for my strictness of time-keeping) was still getting ready. Left the door unlatched for me. In the shower, perhaps?

Breaking the stillness in the house, I shouted my arrival.

My voice bounced back at me, a hollow mocking echo before silence returned.

The house was unfamiliar to me – I'd always been left pacing on the pavement like a double-glazing salesman desperate to meet his monthly quota: if there had been a separate entrance for hawkers, tradesmen and servants then that would have been even better as far as John was concerned. A long, narrow corridor stretched out in front of me. There were two doors on the left, one either side of a steep flight of stairs that led up into blackness.

I entered the first room.

Big mistake.

The thick curtains were tightly drawn. Not a single chink of light intruded on the darkness of the room.

I groped around for a light switch, blinked at the sudden brightness and slowly took in the surroundings. A tall bookcase, groaning under the weight of a complex stereo system, stood opposite the door. To the left a ceremonial Samurai sword hung asymmetrically on the wall in a brass mounting. My eyes moved down to the pair of antique leather Chesterfields and the coffee table with its twin tubs of Bonsai trees at either end. Down further to the brown and cream Persian carpet.

And the body that was spreadeagled upon it.

John's highly polished black shoes.

The dark trousers of his dinner suit.

Plain white shirt, gold cufflinks with 'Ace of Spades' motif. Matching ring on right hand.

The pool of blood spreading out from the collar.

And the void where John's head should have been.

It could have been worse. Not for John, obviously. But for me. I might have bent down and picked up the sword. That's what would have happened in a film. Incriminated myself further by depositing a clear set of fingerprints on its carved handle.

The point of the sword had been thrust through the carpet and deep into the wooden floor beneath. The weapon stood upright, a thin line of blood still dribbling slowly down the outside edge of the blade. In the surface of the polished steel was a distorted fish-eye reflection of the body. I gazed open-mouthed, unable to drag my eyes away.

I could not move; my muscles frozen into immobility, my senses stunned by the horror before me.

I didn't hear the policemen enter.

Only half-felt my arms being roughly bent behind my back. And then that dreadful, forgotten chill crept into my wrists as the cold metal of the handcuffs clicked tightly shut.

CHAPTER TWO

The interview room was stark and comfortless. It smelt of cheap aftershave, the stale smoke of countless cigarettes and the nervous perspiration of the previous occupant. In the middle of the room was a heavy wooden table, its surface stained by overlapping circles from tea and coffee cups, one edge darkened over the years by the tense grip of sweating fingers. On either side of the table stood a chair. All three pieces of utilitarian furniture were bolted securely to the floor.

A downy-chinned police constable lolled against the wall, arms folded, staring without expression into the middle distance as if afraid to catch my eye.

The silence was oppressive. Even the low rhythmic hum of the tape recorder would have provided some relief to the sensory deprivation. But it had been switched off for thirty minutes now.

The two detectives had paused in their interrogation. They were checking my alibi. Giving me time to sweat, more likely.

I sat in underpants and socks, a rough grey blanket wrapped tightly around my lean body. My dinner suit, shirt and shoes had been removed on arrival and carefully packed into plastic bags ready for forensic examination. They had stripped me of my clothes – and, with them, my dignity.

I wriggled in the chair in a pointless effort to ease the pressure of its hard contours against my buttocks and hip bones. I was cold and hungry. And more than a little scared. Somewhere in the building a computer would be whirring away, retrieving my criminal record from the central files. Any moment now a print-out would tell them all they needed to know.

It wasn't difficult to imagine the reactions. Any doubts they had would vanish. It would be an open and shut case from now on.

One word would betray me.

They would find it alongside 'Previous convictions'.

'Murder'.

*

It had been eight years since I was last inside a police station. Then, after providing a brief statement, I had been taken down to the cells. The following day remanded to Brixton to await trial. I hoped that history would not repeat itself.

I was twenty-two then, a hundred years younger than now.

And Susie just sixteen.

Her life – and mine – changed one hot August evening.

I was killing time – how ironic that seems now – between finishing my degree at Sussex and returning to begin a thesis. Home again with my parents and sister in our cosy semi-detached on the outskirts of a little backwater in north-east Essex. Brimful with lethargy, I was behaving like a slob: sleeping late, enjoying second helpings of my mother's cooking, drinking too much with friends from school, reacquainting myself with the delights of several old flames.

Half watching a programme on the television, I was contemplating with self-satisfaction a safe, insulated future in the halls of academia.

'Any chance of you crawling out of that chair – or have you completely lost the use of your legs?' Susie gave me a playful kick to stir me into action. Then stood before me tapping her foot impatiently on the floor.

I had offered to give her a lift to the village disco. My car keys were dangling from between her freshly painted pale pink fingernails. As I smiled up at her she dropped them into my lap.

'Who's the lucky boyfriend tonight?' I asked.

'Wouldn't you like to know,' she replied with a blush.

Yes I would, I'd thought, but didn't press the point. Susie could deliver a fine lecture on the many faults of big brothers – 'overprotective' came about third in the list if my memory served me correctly.

I rose from the chair and walked towards the door. Instead of following hard on my heels as I had expected, Susie cast one last look in the mirror above the mantelpiece and pouted to check the outlines of her lipstick. She looked beautiful: the wonder of youth and the joys of life seemed to shine like a signal beacon from her face. The light caught the high cheekbones and emerald green eyes that were a genetic gift from our mother to both of us. I remember thinking she would break some hearts before she was much older.

The grey-bricked village hall, a stark outcrop against the background yellow ochre of the flat fields of wheat, was less than a mile away. When we arrived the incessant pounding beat of the music drew her like a powerful magnet. She skipped exuberantly from the car, more little girl than blossoming woman. Susie turned to give a last fleeting wave. Then was gone.

It was nearly midnight, Mum and Dad long abed, when the doorbell rang. I was sitting listening to the stereo, the telephone by my side. Anger rose inside me. Forgetting her key, again, was a minor irritant: walking home in the dark, despite my strict instructions to the contrary, was a different matter. All she had to do was call me!

But it wasn't Susie on the doorstep.

'Can we come in, sir?' the sergeant said gravely. He was a local man, his accent slow and slurred, certain words chosen seemingly at random for a teasingly elongated pronunciation. I knew him well, had been to school with his son. He'd never called me 'sir' before. The policewoman with him fidgeted: her eyes, intent on examining the pattern of the wallpaper, looked past me.

I motioned them inside.

'It's Susie isn't it? Something's happened.'

'P'raps you would go fetch your parents,' he replied.

Still half asleep, they stumbled down the stairs in their dressing-gowns. We sat together on the settee, Mum in the middle, holding each other's hands to bolster ourselves against what we knew could only be bad news.

The policewoman stood watching my mother. The sergeant, ill-at-ease, cleared his throat in a pointless manner. He took a deep breath, then told us all he knew.

Susie and a boy had been walking back along the main road. The car must have taken the bend too fast. The driver had lost control. Ploughed straight through them.

They hadn't stood a hope in hell.

The boy, walking like a gentleman on the outside, had been killed outright. Susie was at the hospital, her condition 'critical'. Fighting for her life that meant.

The driver – drunk beyond caring, no doubt – hadn't even stopped. Left them lying in the road, bleeding and broken.

On the way to the hospital we had to drive past the scene. The police had erected a line of cones while they measured the skid marks and searched for any clue to the make and model of the car. I told Mum and Dad not to look: the trail of blood from the boy's body stretched twenty yards up the road.

The doctor led us to a quiet room; a nurse brought us tea. He gave us the good news first – there was no brain damage. The bad news was withheld until Susie came out of the operating theatre.

Her spine was broken in three places.

She was paralysed from the neck down.

And always would be.

*

Those few months following the accident were the hardest of my life. Maybe that was why prison had seemed easy. Nothing could touch me as deeply ever again. Or cause such pain.

She was discharged into our care after eight weeks: there

was no more they could do for her at the hospital. We took her home. The only alternative was a Dickensian building that 'catered for' the paraplegic. One look at the pathetic inmates who would be her constant companions, one sniff of the ammoniac aroma of urine undefeated by disinfectant, was enough to make up our minds. How could we condemn her to that?

Mum and I formed a new bond forged out of grim necessity; Dad retreated into a shell that kept unacceptable reality tightly locked away from his sensitivities.

We became skilled at lifting her, changing sheets, rearranging her position, carrying out that multitude of routine tasks we all take for granted but that Susie could no longer accomplish herself.

For five weeks I spent all my time in her room. Talking to her, false cheer in my voice, as if it would all turn out right in the end. Listening to her sobs, gently wiping away her tears. Eating my meals without appetite as I spoon-fed a liquidised mush between her colourless lips. Sleeping fitfully on a camp bed, woken with monotonous regularity by the piercing screams of her nightmares.

Perhaps it was coincidence. Some inbuilt synchrony between siblings? Whatever, we both reached our limit at precisely the same time.

She had become more pitiful – and I more pitying – as one long day succeeded another. Each of us more downhearted, more despondent at her plight.

When she made her request I listened with understanding and relief.

I had secretly harboured identical thoughts.

I drove down to Brighton in silence, determined not to waver in my resolve. The pub off Preston Street was the same as ever. Dimly lit; warm and airless, the all-pervading hoppy smell of spilt real ale trapped inside; filled to bursting point with the youths from both town and gown. At his customary corner table, as if I had never been away, the man I sought sat negotiating his deals, handing cash to a hairy ursine minder, the pair of them getting up from time to time to go outside to retrieve a customer's order from its hiding place.

He was surprised at my request – I had only ever bought a little marijuana before, and that very infrequently.

He gave a shrug. What did he care? He took my money. Made a hurried phonecall in a whisper. Told me to lose myself; come back in an hour.

He was as good as his word.

I drove home with the extreme care of the guilty, sticking religiously to every speed limit, watching each traffic light as if red and amber were spring-loaded snares.

Susie was asleep when I entered her room. She stirred at the sound of my footsteps. Opened those green eyes for the last time. Smiled as I gave her the injection.

A syringe filled with enough morphine to kill a herd of elephants.

I kissed her lips.

Closed her eyelids.

*

My barrister said I was unlucky. Tell me something I don't know, I thought bitterly. But it wasn't his fault, he had done his best.

Throughout the trial the judge had sat stern-faced. Empathy was alien to him – it interfered with objectivity – sympathy an emotion that had atrophied a long time ago through lack of use. My frequent outbursts did little to soften his attitude or endear me to him.

The jury, under his direction, had no option but to find me guilty.

They asked for leniency.

I received none.

It was my own fault, many would later say.

The crime of murder carries a mandatory life sentence, but the judge can exercise discretion and recommend a minimum term of imprisonment. Given the extenuating circumstances of the case, we had hoped for a nominal sentence – a penal slap on the wrists and no more. The smart thing would have been to keep quiet: refuse the opportunity to say a few last words before sentence was pronounced.

But my anger got the better of me – Irish blood diluted over generations rose to the surface, a dormant volcano erupting at the injustice of life. Here was I in the dock when the true murderer of my sister was free. Free to kill again. I swore to all in the court that I would track him down. Avenge Susie. Inflict on him an equivalent death – degrading, painful, lingering.

The judge claimed he was protecting me from myself: that I needed time to consider the folly of my intentions. No one, he said, could take the law into his own hands. There can be no place in a civilised society for the vigilante. He recommended I serve seven years – one year for each of the times I had insulted the court with my undisciplined outbursts.

There was a public outcry, of course. The media, almost unanimously, took up my cause. But it made no difference. The ranks of the judiciary closed. My appeal was turned down.

Somehow, it didn't seem to matter much. Nothing did any more.

*

The door flew open, snapping me abruptly back to the present. DCI Collins and DS Baxter stepped once more inside the room. Collins had stripped off his jacket. There were dark stains under the arms of his shirt. His trousers were rumpled; his ginger hair, long and untidy, shone with that oily lustre that comes from infrequent washing. Here was a man who didn't care what people thought of him. Only results mattered: the smug look on his face told me he thought he had 'a result' now. He'd seen my record, that was for sure. Now the fun would really start.

Baxter – the comic antithesis of his superior officer – waddled across the room, juggling inexpertly with three polystyrene cups of steaming tea before placing them with relief on the table. A fat, jolly man in his forties, he had a five o'clock shadow so heavy that it probably appeared at midday. His role in this double-act had been to play the part of sympathetic confidant, jumping in to counterpoint the loud aggression of his stern-faced boss.

He produced a pack of Rothmans – there could be no other brand for a man with three stripes – and offered me a cigarette. I accepted without thinking. What was I doing? I'd given up smoking a year ago – all part of the austerity package I'd adopted on release from prison. He took one for himself – all chums together, eh? Produced a cheap disposable lighter that should have been cheaply disposed of: he had to shield the low flame as he reached across the table. He flashed me a smile. It could have been genuine – or simply the product of daily practice in front of the mirror.

I was supposed to relax my vigilance at such treatment. Lower my guard ready for the uppercut. Instead I drew deeply on the cigarette, using the unaccustomed harshness in my lungs as a focus for my concentration.

Baxter waited, as rehearsed, for his superior to speak.

The tape recorder was switched back on: primed with a mechanical recitation of 'interview resumed, officers as before'.

Collins was confident of my guilt. Had already arrived at his verdict. I had come across his type before; a good mind until it is made up, then it becomes immovable. It was easy to recognise – hadn't I been accused of possessing the same trait myself? He set his jaw pugnaciously in my direction.

'Murderers have a certain smell about them,' he said.

This was going to be good, I thought. A lecture on Advanced Aromatics from Professor Fragrant himself.

'Did you know that?' he continued. I felt like saying 'Yes' just to spoil his set speech. But I doubted that it would have made any difference.

'Shall I describe it to you? It's a burnt-out smell, like the most important fuse in a person's mind has blown and lies there black and smouldering, incapable of doing its job. You reek of it, Shannon. You made my nose twitch at twenty paces.'

I opened my mouth to say 'bullshit', then thought better of

PAUL BENNETT

it. I didn't want to antagonise him further – and maybe there was some truth in his dogma.

Collins looked at me in that disdainful way policeman have developed as shorthand for 'scum of the earth'. He produced the envelope from his pocket like a magician pulling a rabbit from out of a hat. I wasn't impressed. I'd seen the trick before. It had been his opening gambit.

Slowly, he drew out the single sheet of paper.

Placed it in front of me.

Asked the unanswerable question he had barked twenty times already.

Banged his fist down with such force that tea bounced out of the beakers, splashing onto the table to form three separate limpid pools.

'Let's go through it again,' he demanded in a bored voice. Then, abruptly, it changed to loud and threatening. 'And this time,' he boomed, 'don't piss me about.'

He moved towards me until his face was no more than inches from mine. I could smell whisky on his breath. I tried to draw away, but he grabbed the blanket. His fingers felt warm where they touched my neck. He jerked me up towards his red-rimmed staring eyes.

'He knew all about you, didn't he? Had you by the balls, squeezing them until you thought they'd burst. What was it – blackmail? Threaten to blow the lid on your murdering past, did he? Or was it something new he'd found? Caught you with your fingers in the till, maybe?' He was shaking me violently now. 'Come on, Shannon. Admit it. You couldn't stand the thought of going back to prison, could you. You had to shut him up, right?' He released his grip, letting me drop back in the chair. 'That's why you killed him,' he concluded.

I didn't even bother to answer. Whatever I said would be a waste of my breath.

I turned away and gazed down at John's note. I suddenly realised that what I had experienced on seeing John's body was shock – but not surprise.

A thought began to form in my mind as I read the words:

16

'Cheat, liar, swindler.
Prepare to unmask.'

*

If it had been left to Collins, I would have languished in the cells until, my will broken, I admitted everything – John's killing, bombing the City of London, carnal knowledge of a member of the royal family, whatever was going. His cold eyes were alive with menace. The unspoken message was unequivocal. 'There are ways around the rule book. I can send Baxter on some errand, Shannon. Then it will be just you and me. We both know you did it. What do I have to do? Beat the truth out of you?'

No way did I want to be alone with this man.

Collins knew the statistics – more than three-quarters of murders were committed by someone who knew the victim. And, as if that wasn't damning enough, the person who found the body often turned out to be the culprit. I qualified on both counts.

Besides, his instincts – and the good old fuse theory – told him that someone who had killed before wouldn't hesitate to kill again.

The questioning – on and off, Collins plus different combinations of superiors and subordinates – went on for another four hours. At the end I signed a statement. But confessed to nothing. I could see the frustration in his face as he led me back to the custody sergeant to reclaim my clothes and personal effects.

They had checked my alibi thoroughly. Three times the flap on the interview room door had slid across. First Arlene. Next the young constable who had taken my particulars on the Embankment. Finally the taxi driver. All came to identify me. In their turn, and much to the chagrin of Collins, each corroborated my timing of events.

Try as he might, he could not refute the evidence. I had arrived ten minutes after the anonymous call reporting a

17

disturbance at John's house. For this, I inwardly thanked whichever prying or public spirited neighbour had dialled 999.

Even after hearing the witnesses, my persecutor was loath to give up. Through the thin partition walls of the room I overheard a loud and heated exchange between the two detectives. Collins was desperately trying to fit the facts to conform to his pet theory. Maybe I had made the phonecall myself, before I had jumped into the taxi. Gambled that the police would not arrive immediately – it was Friday evening after all, the traffic heavy, roads difficult to negotiate even for a police car with flashing lights and blaring siren. It would have taken me no more than a few minutes to commit the murder.

Baxter's reply was polite, reasoned, and only a little sarcastic. What about the preliminary findings from SOCO, he reminded his senior officer. Apart from my fingerprints on the door handle and light switch, the only others found in the house belonged to the body. Why, if the murder was premeditated, Baxter asked, did I not take the precaution of wearing gloves? Why would I deposit two sets of prints and only then take the trouble to wrap something – and Christ knows what that was – around the handle of the sword before picking it up?

Then the clincher: what had I done with the head? Taken a leaf from Hannibal Lecter's book and eaten it, bones and all? Should we get forensic to take a stool sample?

Collins couldn't resist mumbling something unconvincing about an accomplice before grudgingly accepting his sergeant's logic. And obeying the order of a third voice which said, simply but authoritatively, 'Let him go, Chris. Now.'

As I left he gave me an unmistakable look. 'Don't think you've heard the last of this, Shannon. I'll be watching you. Like a bleeding hawk.'

I was pleased to see a friendly face in the waiting room.

Especially such a formidable ally as Arlene.

The officer at the desk looked relieved to see her go.

I doubted she had spent her time telling him, 'Your policemen are wonderful.'

CHAPTER THREE

Brixton. Eight years earlier.

With a grim finality the key turned in the lock behind me; the two heavy bolts shuddered as they slammed back into place. So this was to be my home until the trial was over. And this my cell-mate! My heart dropped into the prison-issue boots. His eyes moved reluctantly away from the game of patience on the table and examined me critically. Slowly he stood up. And up and up.

He was six feet five inches tall. He could have been the Incredible Hulk's big brother. Looked like he would think nothing of eating me in a single session – provided he had some bread and butter, a bottle of brown sauce and a mug of tea to wash it all down. The man had muscles I never even knew existed. And each one carved out of solid granite.

His powerful arms hung by his sides. He didn't bother to offer his right hand in welcome. If he had then I might never have played the piano again. His voice was deep and husky as if they fed him on gravel and he'd come back, bowl in outstretched hand, for seconds.

'Let's get a few things straight.' His jumbo sausage fingers counted off each point. 'The bottom bunk's yours. Keep your hands off my stuff. Don't snore. Don't fart.' The last finger moved up to join the others. 'And,' he warned me sternly, 'don't cause any trouble. I've got three months to go and I don't want some long streak of piss losing me any remission.'

He settled back to the cards. Realised he had missed something. Grunted a guttural 'Arfa' which I interpreted as his name.

'Nick,' I replied.

'And about the worst one there is,' he laughed.

I perched on the edge of the bunk, unpacking the few personal items I had been allowed and watching Arthur out of the corner of my eye. He tried clock patience five times – never got close to a finish. I put him down as a born optimist: the chances of winning are about two per cent.

A few hours later the diagnosis was confirmed. My first experience of 'association' was a tentative, nervous period. I felt exposed and vulnerable. The other prisoners sized me up and I, in turn, tried to draw expressionless conclusions of my own. It was made bearable only for the fact that most of the attention was on Arthur. I was grateful to stand behind him, keeping my mouth 'zipped' as ordered, while he played poker. Or, rather, while he transferred matchsticks from his pile to those of his opponents.

It was painful to watch. He was frustratingly ponderous whenever it was his turn to bet. Each time he tried to bluff he became as transparent as a glass of water (or prison tea, for that matter). He couldn't even shuffle without spraying cards in all directions.

Back in our cell, I busied myself on any small task in order to avoid conversation. I slipped off my clothes and climbed into bed. Heaved a sigh of relief when the bright light overhead snapped off with a loud clunk, leaving only the glow from the dim night-light that denied any privacy. How long, I wondered, would it be before I got on his nerves? What damage might he do if he lost his temper?

'Come on, kid. Spit it out. I won't eat you, you know.'

Stepping inside the gates of Brixton had been like entering an uncharted and threatening land: I needed a native guide to show the way round the dangers. I hoped Arthur might take that role. But if that were the case, then how could I sit idly by and watch him make a fool of himself. His daily ritual of humiliation at the card table would be more than I could bear.

'Do you always play like that?' I asked.

'What do you mean?' he snapped back at me.

'Drawing to inside straights, staying in with a pair of deuces, taking four cards to an ace?'

'And what's wrong with that? You saw me win with that run, didn't you?'

'I also saw you lose ten times that much by following exactly the same line of play. The odds were stacked against you. You'll never succeed in the long run like that.'

'You're some kind of expert on poker now, are you? Wouldn't happen to be an amateur brain surgeon as well? I don't need some snotty-nosed kid to tell me how to play.'

'It's up to you,' I said, backing off hurriedly. 'I was only trying to help. At least it was only matchsticks.'

'Christ,' he said, staring at me in utter disbelief. 'You are green, aren't you. You'll be the death of me. Bloody die laughing, I will. Did you think we were going to sit there passing money across the table? Excuse me, Mr Screw, got change for a fiver? Tomorrow I have to pay up. Which happens to be a bit of a problem.' He went broody on me. After a long pause he shrugged his shoulders. 'Still I can always work off the debt. That would suit them nicely. Thump some heads to settle a few of their old scores.'

And lose your remission in the bargain, no doubt.

'Look, Arthur, I've been playing cards since I was three. They're second nature to me. Besides, I'm a mathematician.'

'That I can believe,' he interrupted. The long streak of piss was now an egghead too.

'Just let me explain, will you? Probabilities are my speciality. I was going to spend the next three years writing a bloody thesis about the subject.' I realised he probably didn't even know what a thesis was: this was going to be more difficult than I'd imagined. Keep it simple, stupid, I told myself.

'Let's make a deal,' I said. 'I'll teach you how to win at poker. In return, you show me how to survive in here. What have you got to lose?'

Only his pride, it seemed. He took a lot of persuading but, in the end, I wore him down. 'On one condition,' he said finally, stabbing at me with his finger. 'No one, but no one, is to know. Okay?'

It was a bargain.

Well almost. I wanted one last codicil added to our agreement.

'Tomorrow,' I said, 'I'll play in your place. I want to clear your debt.'

'Too risky,' he replied. 'Here's your first lesson in survival – don't make enemies. There's nowhere to run in here. No escape from the nutters.'

'It's a chance I'm prepared to take. If I win, you'll trust me. Then, maybe, you'll listen to what I have to say.'

'You know, kid, if you weren't lippy, arrogant and pigheaded, you'd have no personality.' He gave a long sigh. 'Now, can we get some bleeding sleep?'

*

Arthur 'Dangerous' Duggan had been a professional wrestler – for a few years at least. In the ring his strength and technical skill were negated by two factors: an innate clumsiness and a brain like a Morris Minor – reliable but potteringly slow. Although he could execute the intricately choreographed moves in slow motion during the pre-match rehearsal, it was a different matter when it came to the ring. What should have been an entertaining pantomime too often turned into an unplanned slaughter of his opponent. He left a trail of black eyes, sore heads and broken limbs wherever he went. In the end no one would fight him.

Outcast from wrestling he tried his hand as a film extra, hoping to emulate the success of some of his predecessors. If Nosher Powell or Mick MacManus could play a heavy on screen then Arthur thought he could do the same. All went well for a while. He got through a bit part in an episode of *Minder*; followed that up with a cheap sci-fi film where he spent the whole time encased in the hairy costume of a yeti ('an oversized stick of candy floss', an unkind critic said); even did a commercial for chunky chocolate bars (I was only sick once, Arthur said). All without any major incident. And then the Bond movie came along.

That was when he found fame.

But not fortune.

The out-take, he told me with a shy grin, was featured on *It'll be Alright on the Night*. Had the audience rolling in the aisles: the incredulous look on the face of the poleaxed actor, his puppet-like efforts to get up off the floor before falling back unconscious. At least it was only the stand-in who had his jaw broken by Arthur's blacksmith hammer of a fist. Arthur, to this day, still claims that the man moved – or didn't move, the story varies from time to time.

He drifted into the only job for which his talents equipped him. 'Door Steward' was the grand title. Bouncer, to you and me.

Arthur found his forte standing outside London clubs and discos. Dinner jacket straining at the seams across his wide chest. Bow tie firmly wrapped around his bull-like neck.

He made a reasonable living. Enough to get by after the maintenance and putting a bit by for his kid's education. He was happy with his lot.

Until the day he was asked by his boss to collect a debt.

And found – too late – that there was nothing owing.

Arthur had been charged with 'demanding money with menaces'.

That was how he finished up in Brixton.

Whoever put us in the same cell must have had a warped sense of humour. We were chalk and cheese. Brains and brawn. Nothing in common. Except our love of cards.

And now he was finding it almost impossible to stand at my side while I occupied his regular seat at the table. He fidgeted about like an expectant father exiled to the waiting room while an old-fashioned midwife delivers the baby. How was I supposed to concentrate? I turned around and glared at him. He gave me a shamefaced smile and stuffed his itching hands deep into his pockets.

The game was important to both of us. As well as my stated motives, I hoped that by winning I might gain some respect from the other inmates. Beforehand, I spent an hour shuffling Arthur's tattered pack and dealing hands, loosening my fingers and attuning my brain. My flashy show of dexterity did nothing to ease Arthur's worries. Nor did the fact that I didn't ask him how much each matchstick was worth. It was better that I didn't know: there was enough to worry about already without the unnerving vision of debts I wouldn't be able to honour.

I cast my eyes and ears around me. Took in the surreal surroundings. Registered the hoots of laughter as a partisan group watched *The Bill* on the television; heard the hollow sounds of a ping pong ball echoing from the high ceiling; listened to the raised voices of a bunch of men discussing football as if they were in the public bar of their local.

I brought my attention back to the table. There were the same four players as the evening before. They introduced themselves by first name and crime. My opponents were Manslaughter, GBH, Armed Robbery and Burglary: a far cry from Economics, Chemistry, Sociology and Law.

I played quietly for a while. Took stock of their style, overplayed a few low-ranking hands, made sure I was found out in a cheap bluff. Waited for their confidence to grow to that point where a player becomes inattentive and injudicious.

I collected the cards with an inexpert fumble, shuffled them like a member of the Salvation Army and passed them to my right for GBH to cut. Dealt as quickly as I dared.

Manslaughter bet two, Armed Robbery raised two, Burglary folded and GBH raised again. Arthur looked despondently at my pair of threes. I pushed six matchsticks into the middle. Behind me I heard a gulp: Arthur could see the bluff coming.

I dealt the cards for the change. Manslaughter took three, Armed Robbery only one, GBH stood pat – no cards for him. I took three cards to my pair. Manslaughter made the minimum bet; Armed Robbery folded having obviously failed to make his flush or straight; GBH raised five. I covered his bet and re-raised.

It was too heavy for Manslaughter: he threw his cards deject-edly on the discard pile. The field was clear for GBH and myself. I tried not to look at him: he made me nervous.

Freddie 'GBH' Ronson was not the sort you would want to meet on a dark night – broad daylight was bad enough. At the card table he sat tall, but when he stood up his legs seemed disproportionately short for his torso. He had that classic meso-morphic shape whereby seven foot of muscular body is pounded by a pile-driver until it is only five foot six: as if to pro-vide evidence of the fact, he wore his hair in a closely cropped, sculpted style so that the top of his head was as flat – and prob-ably as hard – as an anvil. His complexion was sallow (but that is not uncommon in prison), his nose a lightning bolt of badly-set breaks.

He smiled at me. It was not a pretty sight: his teeth, gapped and crooked, were a monument to prison dentistry.

Freddie upped the stakes without a moment's hesitation. I peeped dubiously at my cards, keeping them so close to my chest that not even Arthur could see.

By now the tension was radiating from the table like the heat from an arson attack. Men drifted across from the TV and gathered round in a circle. I met the stake. Then slowly counted out twenty matchsticks and added them to the pot. Would he read the bet? Would he fold – or carry on?

'Your twenty and up another twenty,' Freddie declared. He was playing to the crowd now. A cat toying with a mouse.

His self-assurance faltered for a moment when I raised him back. But the doubt soon faded. Anyway, the spectators were egging him on. He couldn't be seen to chicken out.

'Up another twenty,' he said with a lip-licking leer.

It had gone far enough. I knew exactly how much was on the table.

'I'll see you,' I said, covering the bet.

'Full house, kings on top,' he said smugly, stretching across to rake in the pot.

'Bad luck,' I replied, trying to sound sincere. I spread my hand. 'Full house, aces on threes.'

Stunned, he slumped back in the chair. The crowd murmured. This wasn't what they expected. Behind me, Arthur braced himself. The warders, sensing the tension in the air, exchanged nods as a signal to prepare for action.

Freddie gave a wide grin for their benefit. Leaned across the table. Whispered to me in a voice so cold it could have caused ice to form on the walls of a sauna. 'You're a jammy bastard,' he whispered threateningly, 'but your luck won't last. You better watch your step from now on. Just remember this, smart-arse, we've got a score to settle. And, believe me, you'll pay in the end. One way or another.'

'Arthur,' I said nonchalantly, pushing the pile of matchsticks towards him, 'take what you need to settle your debts. Then you owe me. Understand?'

I wanted to leave immediately, but knew it would only make matters worse. It would be bad form to get up from the table without giving them a chance to get their money back. So I played slow and careful, deliberately lost a little to make it look good, until the sweet music of the bell sounded in my ears. As I walked back to the cell, I was aware of Ronson's hostile eyes on my back. It was all I could do to stop my legs from shaking.

Arthur listened to the retreating footsteps of the warder making his round of lock-up. When the sounds were sufficiently distant for his purpose he grabbed my lapels, hoisted me six inches above the ground and pinned my body against the door.

'Didn't I warn you about making enemies?' he shouted angrily in my face. 'Ronson of all people! That bastard would rape and snuff his own grandmother – grandfather, too, by all accounts – if he could sell the video for a quick profit. And didn't it ever cross your mind what they might do to you if you lost and couldn't pay up. You take some bloody chances. "Don't draw to a low pair, Arthur", you have the nerve to say. Then you do the self-same thing.'

He let me go. Watched as I dropped to the floor. Turned his back in disgust.

'You were supposed to trust me,' I said. 'Just calm down for a minute and pay attention.'

26

He spun around, eyes blazing with temper. 'Don't ever give me orders, boy,' he said.

'I'm sorry, Arthur. But there wasn't any risk. Look.'

I went across to the table. Picked up the pack of cards. Fumbled with them just as I had done earlier. Shuffled. And dealt out five cards face up. Four aces and a king.

'How the bloody hell did you do that?'

'Keep your voice down, for Christ's sake.'

I took the four aces and placed them on the bottom of the pack. Dealt the cards again. One from the top – and four from the bottom.

I was well into my party piece by this stage. I showed him one of the aces, put it on the top of the pack and dealt the card face down to him. When he turned it over it was the two of clubs. 'I can deal seconds, too,' I said proudly.

He gazed in wonder.

'Hang on a minute,' he queried. 'I saw you pass the deck to Freddie, he cut the cards. It's impossible.'

'Let me demonstrate a "crimp", Arthur.'

I had his full attention as I took the pack one more time. Gave them a hand-over-hand slap shuffle, keeping three fingers on the position of the aces. Set the deck before him, squeezing upwards midway through the pile as I did so.

I made him bend down to table level. From this angle he could see for himself. There was the crimp – a slightly raised ridge where I had put pressure on the cards.

'Cut,' I said.

Like the vast majority of card players his fingers travelled naturally to the middle of the pack.

'Now look at what's on the bottom, please.'

'You bloody conman,' he said with an ear-to-ear grin as he spied the four aces.

'Lesson one, Arthur. To avoid the crimp, always cut close to the top or bottom.'

From that point he was hooked. We became pupil and teacher. It was our secret.

At an hour or so each day, it was a long time before the

course of lessons was complete. But time was something we had in abundance.

We started with the best card game after bridge. Draw poker. The game of mathematics and psychology (although, I informed him, there is wide debate about which element is the most important).

I told him the golden rule. Whatever money is in the pot (or the 'kitty' as he insisted on calling it) belongs to the pot. Forget what you've already put in. Judge each bet on its merits. If you don't, then you're throwing good money after bad.

I made him practise counting the pot so that he knew what he stood to win. Then drummed into him the probabilities of some of the more common situations so that he could calculate if the pot made a bet worthwhile. Made him see that drawing to an inside straight was a mug's game – the odds of drawing a jack, say, to complete a run of king, queen, ten and nine are nearly eleven to one: the pot is almost never eleven times the bet you would have to make for the doubtful privilege of drawing a card.

I managed to convince him that bluffing is a loser's strategy. That you should bluff rarely and only when you think you have a reasonable chance of winning a pot. And never try to bluff a poor player. A good player may read your moves as typical of holding a certain hand and, therefore, drop out. A poor player won't make the connection. Even if by some slight chance he does, a poor player will always call – he just can't resist paying money to see your cards.

After draw poker, we moved on to the differences for stud poker where one card (five card stud) or two (seven card stud) are dealt face down and the rest face up for all to see. Don't draw unless you can beat the exposed cards, and so on.

Then the effects that 'jokers wild' had on assessing your hand and the chances of improvement.

After poker we covered brag, nap and pontoon.

During each of our sessions I concentrated as hard as Arthur, making sure I expressed myself simply and patiently until the point I was trying to get across finally sank in.

When I felt his mind could no longer focus on the concepts

or the numbers, I let him get his own back. Allowed him, willingly, to take me into his territory – for I was hungry to learn. Without his knowledge how could I hope to stand alone against those to whom violence was second nature?

He kept it simple too, recognising my weaknesses as clearly as I had identified his own. Drilled me in the more straightforward ways of defending myself. Laughed as I tried to shift his bodyweight to throw him off-balance. Demonstrated crude, but effective, ways of disabling an attacker. Deftly handled my first bumbling attempts at placing a knee in his groin.

It was a painful process for each of us.

But we both learnt how to get by.

When I finally unleashed Arthur on the world, it wasn't ready for him.

He caught them off guard. Made all the right moves. Played tight. Let them make the mistakes. Steadily, unspectacularly, he cleaned them out. 'Like taking candy from a baby,' he laughed.

I felt a warm glow of pride. I could see how much his triumph meant to him.

CHAPTER FOUR

During what remained of that night Arlene and I talked, made love and slept in just about equal proportions. I soon discovered that beneath the confident, commanding exterior lay a lonely woman. Maybe we could do each other some good for a while.

The holiday had not been her idea. A few concerned friends had first cajoled and then browbeaten her until it was easier to give in than continue to resist. In the three months since Cy's death they had watched anxiously for signs that the grieving was abating. But Arlene continued to shrink both mentally and physically. She became unreliable at work, spent too much time on her own, drank more than was good for her: the only plus point in her opinion was the loss of fifteen pounds in weight – okay, she admitted, so she might never see size 12 again, but at least the days of squeezing into a 16 were past. The tour was supposed to be a complete break, a change of scenery, an opportunity to mend her tattered emotions. Armed with a new wardrobe and a fistful of traveller's cheques she had been despatched with strict instructions to take Europe by storm – be indulgent, savour every moment, use the present to erase the past.

Arlene had taken their advice literally. She was determined to spare no expense in her hedonistic conquest of the major capitals. Her suite alone must have cost a small fortune. But it was all part of the new lifestyle – if you're gonna do it, do it in style.

The trolley weighed down with our late breakfast was wheeled ceremonially to the table. I sat there feeling awkward and conspicuous in the towelling robe. In contrast, despite wearing only a skimpy translucent wrap, she signed the bill without a hint of embarrassment. The pale blue silk gave a touch of softness to round out the hard edges of her character: it was a big improvement on the severe black and white outfit she had worn the night before.

The top tier of the trolley bore a jug of fresh orange juice; heavy silver domed dishes containing scrambled eggs and bacon so crisply grilled that it crackled; a rack of brown toast, butter, conserves and a pot of coffee the size of a skyscraper. Below, along with the glasses, plates, cups and cutlery was a parcel. Arlene handed it to me with a smile. 'This doesn't make you a gigolo, okay. Just a bit more presentable.'

Inside I found a bone-handled razor, a pack of blades, shaving cream and the most expensive after-shave I had ever used. There was also a new shirt, socks and change of underwear – all bearing the Austin Reed label. As I had found out the night before, Arlene thought of everything.

Her appetite was voracious.

And not only for the food.

After breakfast I showered and shaved. Stepped out of the bathroom. 'And where do you think you're going?' she asked, an impish grin on her face.

She pushed me back inside the door. I showered again. This time with her. A mutual lathering, the climax of which only served to add fuel to the white hot fire of her desire. Damp and breathless, we returned to the crumpled sheets of the double bed. At this rate, if I lasted out that is, it wouldn't take long to catch up on all I had missed during seven years behind bars.

It was gone two o'clock before I arrived at the office, legs shaky and muscles aching from physical effort.

I would have to work fast.

There was a lot to do before Arlene and I would be ready to leave for the private gambling club.

The club I had been due to visit with John the previous evening.

*

Jameson Browns is one of the larger firms of chartered accountants in London. I owed my job there to tokenism and Timpkins. Probably in equal measure.

I was the token reformed criminal to complete a set of gays of both sexes, ethnic and religious minorities, and left-wing radicals. We were all pawns in a devious masterplan hatched to deflect criticism from the younger staff that the company was boringly conservative and in danger of losing ground to its more dynamic and forward-thinking competitors.

Timpkins was my cell-mate at Chelmsford. It was he who had persuaded me to harness my intuitive feel for numbers into an area where the rewards were high and the intellectual challenges fresh each day.

And Timpkins should know.

He was an embezzler.

Norman Timpkins – small, timid, insignificant – had risen through the ranks of a company which manufactured die-cast metal toys and models. Ten years after joining as a wages clerk he had reached his goal of Financial Controller. Ten years in which Norman had worked quietly and diligently. Never creating any waves. Never pressing for salary rises. Good old, steady Norman. Dull but reliable. And totally trustworthy.

After ten years and three months Norman had stripped the company bare.

Meticulously, he massaged every figure in the books. Money was siphoned off through dummy invoices into a dozen different mailbox companies he had set up years before. By the time the regular suppliers had come knocking at the door irately brandishing unpaid bills, Norman had the million pounds that had been his target.

He gave himself up.

Was willing to accept a short prison sentence.

After all, the money could not be traced. It was earning interest every day of his stretch. And he could show how clever he was. Laugh in the faces of those who had looked down on him all those years. A triumph for the little men of this world.

Norman had wanted his hour of fame – and the public degradation of others – almost as much as the money. Some criminals are like that.

For five years Norman helped me with the correspondence course that he pushed me into taking at Chelmsford. He nagged me to study at times when my motivation or morale was low. Explained the theory better than the text books. Took me through the practical examples. And then, for our joint amusement, demonstrated how he could divert funds and still come up with the same answer for the balance sheet and profit and loss account.

With Norman's help I achieved a distinction in the exams for The Chartered Association of Certified Accountants. And survived what otherwise would have been the spirit-breaking tedium of imprisonment.

In order to qualify for membership of ACCA – paradoxically, my offence of murder did not prohibit me from joining, whereas a conviction for the lesser offence of fraud would have done so – I needed three years of practical experience. Easier said than done! Out of all the firms to which I had written, only Jameson Browns, dragging itself kicking and screaming into the twentieth century, had been willing to give me that chance.

That Saturday afternoon was bright with a cool light breeze. The warm sun I had felt during yesterday's eventful walk now burnt off the few clouds that blew lazily across from the east. Looking up from the pavement I could see, not unexpectedly, a handful of lights burning in the office windows. In a profession where many of the people spend a large slice of the week on clients' premises it was common practice for some urgent report to be produced at the weekend.

Ted, the doorman-cum-security guard, jerked in his chair at

my knock and looked up from the portable television on which he was watching the final of the NatWest Bank Trophy.

In normal circumstances he would have told me the score, given me edited highlights of the morning's play, re-opened our ongoing debate on the merits of seam (dependable and boring – just like accountants – I would tell him) and spin (too bleeding risky, Mr Shannon, he would reply with a dismissive shake of his head and a knowing smile on his lips).

Today he wanted to pick my brains on other matters. He had heard the news.

His voice displayed exactly the right level of distress, but his animated state betrayed his true emotions – excitement and curiosity. He dogged my heels as I walked to the stairs, firing a series of questions I was either unable or disinclined to answer. I fobbed him off with a weary look and a muttered 'maybe later'.

I shared an office with John – all part of the traditional learning process known in the educational world as 'sitting with Nellie' – although, because of the itinerant nature of our work, we were rarely there at the same time. A brushed metal plate was screwed to the door. On it were etched the words 'Acquisitions and Mergers'. That was how the outside world knew us. Internally we were called 'DDT'. The 'Due Diligence Team'.

When one company agrees, in principle, to take over another, it needs hard facts to finalise the terms of the deal. There are two ways to approach this data collection exercise. The first – the disclosure method – saves time and money and places the burden of proof on the seller. The potential acquirer submits to the seller a list of questions (past performance, profit and cash flow forecasts for the future, details of salaries and contracts for staff, names and purchasing history of customers, pension commitments etc. – the list usually runs to several tightly typed pages). All the details of the agreement as far as the purchaser is concerned – including, most importantly, the price – are derived from the answers received. If, within a set time-scale (five years is the norm), any of the information is found to be inaccurate or incomplete then the buyer sues for recompense according to the tightly worded warranty or indemnity clauses in the contract.

The other method – due diligence – is where the accountants get involved (for a large fee, naturally).

If one of our clients was planning an acquisition (or taking the dominant role in a merger), John and I would be sent into the target company. The cupboards had to be laid bare before us. Our remit was to take every possible care (hence the term 'due diligence') to discover the truth, warts and all. To examine critically every aspect of the seller's business – including, of course, all the financial details. No stone must be left unturned – no matter what maggots might be lurking underneath.

After weeks, sometimes stretching to lucrative months, of assiduous work, checking the past and making predictions as to the future, we would recommend the price to be paid by our client.

The arrangement suited both sides in the deal. The clients making the acquisition were able to minimise the risk, calculate the real worth of their target (and try to get away with offering less); they could also hand an independent report to those who would be providing the finance. The sellers, on the other hand, could claim that absolutely nothing had been withheld – that 'caveat emptor' applied: there could be no comebacks if future performance proved to be a disappointment.

Although we were a team, the division of work between John and myself was by no means equal. As the lowly articled clerk, I would do all the donkey work – collecting, scrutinising and collating information into a standardised and easily understandable form. John, the recipient of my labours, would act as inquisitor of the management and then write the final report. Because of the number of clients we serviced, I rarely had the opportunity to see this finished product: John was a hard taskmaster. There would be time enough to learn more of that element of the job, he said whenever I pressed him: I would be despatched off to the next company, to tick away furiously at columns of figures, up against some new deadline.

I sat down at his desk and began to examine its contents.

Even though John was dead it still felt somehow wrong to be prying into his personal possessions and papers.

The small wide drawer in the middle of the desk contained only a collection of assorted stationery – pens, pencils, paper and the like. I pulled open the topmost of the two drawers on the right hand side. There, along with two packs of playing cards, was the plastic wallet I sought.

As an afterthought, I decided to look inside the lockable, deep lower drawer that housed the rack of working files. I searched in vain for the key. I need not have bothered. The drawer slid out when I pulled the handle. It should have slid smoothly in the runners: instead, it snagged momentarily and a small splinter of wood broke off.

On closer inspection I saw the scratchmarks on the face of the drawer.

The lock had been broken.

Someone had been here before me.

I felt my skin prickle; sweat form in the palm of my hands. Bending down to examine the contents of the drawer, I hoped – sensed even – that I was on the verge of an important discovery. Something would be missing. A second trail would open up. Another path to explore in the search for a reason for John's death.

I was disappointed.

The bubble of excitement deflated slowly rather than burst. I pulled out file after file. Mentally ticked each off against the checklist in my memory. Added, one by one, to the disheartening pile on the desk.

As far as I could tell, nothing had been removed.

All the files relating to the current projects were there, together with a few others, their covers dog-eared and faded with age, which I resolved to send to their rightful place in the archives on Monday morning when I set about the task of clearing up in earnest.

I knew that each file, at some stage, would have to be scrutinised in turn to check for any missing papers. That could wait too. I could summon little enthusiasm for what would be a laborious exercise. And, I was increasingly convinced, a fruitless one. I didn't expect a thorough examination to come up with anything. If a thief had been at work then it would be too revealing to take individual documents: surely it would be less conspicuous to steal a whole file – best of all, why not totally cloud the issue by walking off with the entire contents of the drawer.

The voice of reason told me to leave the files where they lay. Collins, it said wisely, will want to search the office. He can't help but notice the broken lock. Then you know where the questioning will lead. Walk away, Shannon – you've got what you came for.

But reason sometimes speaks too calmly, too softly for its own good. It can be hard to hear against the clamour of more powerful emotions. My curiosity shouted its impatient demand to be satisfied. My lack of faith in the police joined the lobby. What if Collins takes the files away before you have the chance to delve into them? He wouldn't be able to make head or tail of the papers – let alone spot if anything was missing. If you want the job done properly, Shannon, then do it yourself.

Against such determined opposition there could be only one winner.

I was loading everything into two carrier bags when the telephone on my desk rang.

I hadn't appreciated just how tense I was. I jumped at the noise, dropping one of the files with an involuntary butter-fingered start. A jumble of papers spilt onto the carpet, spreading out in an arc. My heart pounded within my chest. It was as if the telephone had sprung to life and was shouting accusations at my snooping.

Who knew I was here? I hadn't given Arlene the number. Christ, was I being followed?

I realised I was becoming paranoid. Shrugging with embarrassment at my flight of fancy, I picked up the receiver.

At first the caller was unrecognisable: the voice was abnormally high-pitched and shaky. And the words were totally incoherent.

In the pause between sobs, I urged calmness. Told the girl – for that was all I was sure of – to slow down and take deep breaths.

Another pause. I could almost feel the effort of will at the other end of the line.

'God, Nick, it was so awful.'

Suddenly it all made sense. The who, the where and the why. It was like some bizarre declaration in a game of Cluedo – Sofia, in the mortuary, with the handkerchief.

'I tried your home,' she said. 'The office was my last hope. Thank God I've found you. John,' – there was a sharp intake of breath as she mentioned his name – 'said you were the one to trust if I ever needed help. Don't let me down. Please.'

The brief interlude of self-control was over. Once more she was swept under by the turbulent waves of emotions.

From the stutter of barely intelligible phrases my mind pieced together a picture of the full horror she had experienced. To formally identify such a corpse: it did not bear thinking about. But, as much as I tried, I could not rid myself of the image of John lying on a slab. Had they warned her what to expect? Placed their hands firmly on the top of the white shroud to forbid its complete removal? Or did she feel compelled to see it all for herself? Seeing is believing, after all.

I made what soothing noises I could. Waited helplessly for the crying to abate. Juggled with my own feelings. Was it better to rush to her side? Try to comfort her in person rather than at the end of a telephone wire? Or should I hang on? Not let this opportunity for catharsis go to waste. Hope that her shock and sorrow would run its course if given a little more time.

A new voice, controlled and authoritative, solved the dilemma.

She identified herself as Sally, Sofia's flat-mate.

'I'll look after her,' she said protectively. I had the feeling she didn't want me involved but perhaps that was her natural caution of strangers. 'I'm taking her home now. She needs sleep more than anything else. I've got some pills that will do the trick. Ring me tomorrow. Maybe she'll be well enough to see you then.'

Before I could reply, Sally was reeling off their telephone number. I scribbled it down on the front of one of the files. Had no chance to read it back, commiserate, even say goodbye. The click of the receiver being replaced signalled the end of the one-way conversation. It seemed I had my orders.

*

I had only encountered Sofia three times in the past – if you discount a fleeting moment on the doorstep of her flat when acting as John's personal postman, delivering some urgent flight tickets into her hands. But each time had made a lasting impression on me. She had the same effect on everybody. Once seen, never forgotten.

My first sight of her was at the Christmas party (where I was forced to observe her from the other side of the room or over the shoulder of whoever had dragged me onto the dance floor). The next time was three months later at the celebration when John was made a partner (I was deemed worthy of a formal introduction by that time). Lastly, a few weeks ago, when they announced their engagement (and I had at last been able to study her up close during a conversation I selfishly prolonged until John arrived to whisk her away with a scowl on his face and a proprietorial hand on her arm).

John liked to keep her very much to himself. Only on those rare occasions when office protocol made it unavoidable would he bite back his jealousy and parade her before an appreciative audience.

Sofia Kalamboukis had the black hair and brown eyes of her Greek father; the height and grace of her English mother. The combination produced a harmonious synergy where the sum was infinitely greater than the constituent parts. She possessed the kind of beauty which, when first encountered, sends the brain into overload. A beauty so rare that the bedazzled observer is either rendered speechless or, worse still, reduced to the level of a gibbering idiot.

Her presence at these office gatherings invariably produced the same response. You couldn't blame the women for bitching. Or the men for staring lasciviously. But the respective sneers and leers were always followed by creased brows and thoughtful, puzzled expressions. One question unspoken on every pair of lips. What did this Greek goddess see in the man by her side?

Awkward, self-conscious girls of her height would have described themselves as five foot twelve. Sofia, even in the flat shoes she sensitively chose to wear, was a good eight inches taller than John. Her body was spare and lithe: he hid the beginnings of a self-indulgent, expense account paunch under the folds of a double-breasted jacket. John's suits, although tailor-made, never appeared quite right on his short, squat frame. Sofia, on the contrary, had no trouble finding exactly what suited her. The dresses she wore looked like they had been air-brushed directly onto her naked body by the luckiest artist in the world.

She could have been a model.

If it were not for the scar.

The thin, four-inch line of dark red tissue was barely visible – in my opinion at least – under her skilfully applied make-up. It ran diagonally from below the right eye to finish level with her ear lobe.

On a lesser beauty this flaw would have become the cruel and unavoidable focus of attention: with Sofia the mark hardly had a chance to register before your gaze was captured by the rest of her face. She had eyes like galactic black holes, deep mesmerising pools, drawing you intractably within. Her lips, full and red, carried the threat that one kiss and your tongue would explode with the taste of sweet Morello cherries.

I wondered how she looked today. Had she bothered with the camouflaging foundation and blusher? Had her tears, the result of the sadness and distress she seemed so anxious to share with me, unkindly washed the veil away?

I pushed the thoughts of Sofia aside – it sounded as if she was in capable hands. Having drawn a circle round the telephone number, I put the file with the others in the bags. Scooped up the papers at my feet. Stuffed those in too. Carried the burden with relief. I couldn't wait to escape from the emotionally charged atmosphere that now permeated throughout the office, to lose myself in the comforting normality of the shoppers on the crowded streets.

I took the stairs two at a time, shunning the lift with its frustrating slowness and claustrophobic reminders of solitary confinement. Approaching the last flight I heard the voices.

I lurched to a halt, working hard to keep my balance against the forward momentum of the heavy bags.

I slowed my breathing. Stood silent and immobile, straining my ears. The voice of Ted, the doorman, drifted up the staircase. 'Most irregular,' he said in a crusty voice. I heard him add a grudging and meaningless 'sir' as his footsteps retreated to the desk.

'You search Weston's desk,' Collins barked at Baxter. 'I'll take Shannon's.'

Well, that was a surprise!

The bell on the lift pinged and they stepped noisily inside.

The doors closed shut with a soft whoosh. I shot from my hiding place.

Ted spotted me. He shouted in my direction, grey Goochian moustache wagging up and down with each unheeded word.

I also ignored the semaphore waving of his arms as he tried once more to attract my attention.

It was a new world record for the sprint from stairs to door. I'd forgotten it would be locked.

If I'd been an angina sufferer then the events of the last twenty-four hours would have finished me off by now.

Ted was in no hurry. I was trapped, so what was the rush? He sauntered across, his military-style black boots squeaking with each slow measured step. He viewed his frustrated quarry with a half smile, and stared directly at the two carrier bags.

'Off now, are we sir?'

I nodded. Made an effort to look more foolish than guilty.

'Can you open up, Ted?' I asked. 'I'm in a bit of a hurry. Thought I might finish this lot at home.'

'You don't expect me to believe that, Mr Shannon?'

'What do you mean?'

'You'll have your feet up watching the box if I'm not mistaken. What with Sussex playing as well. Your old team set a record score, you know. Should romp it, the pundits reckon. But what do they know, eh? Take that Boycott, for instance.' He launched into what promised to be the first in a long series of character assassinations.

Not now, Ted, I thought. Give me a break. Open the bloody door.

This was no time to be subtle. I cast an exaggerated look at the clock behind him. 'Is that the time?' I said, sounding shocked. 'I didn't realise it was that late.'

He brushed my gambit aside with the contempt it deserved. Made no attempt to take the key from his pocket. Switched tack instead.

'Two gentlemen,' he said in a tone clearly indicating he thought they were nothing of the sort, 'are on their way up to your office. Police officers, Mr Shannon. I don't suppose they would want to see you, would they?'

I couldn't believe it. Was that a wink he had given me?

Whatever they had said or done they had somehow managed to get on the wrong side of Ted. Shown no interest in the score, perhaps? No, there was more to it than cutting Ted off in his commentating prime.

While in prison I had noticed with wry amusement the clash between opposing uniformed bureaucracies. From time to time the police would arrive demanding to question an inmate. The warders resented this intrusion into their domain; the disruption to the normal routine, the finding of a suitable room, the journey to a distant wing to fetch the prisoner. They were used to giving orders, not following them. Ted, steward of this small territory, was experiencing the same emotions. His puffed-up chest said it all. This was his patch. Invaded by outsiders. No proper authority. A search warrant was not the way things were done. They should have had a partner present.

He unlocked the door.

'Best be on your way, sir. You don't want to go wasting your time on the likes of them upstairs. After all, they didn't actually ask to see you. Mind you,' he added, the conspiratorial smile no longer concealed, 'I didn't tell them you were here.'

CHAPTER FIVE

Arlene, with all the panache and ruthlessness of a reincarnated Boadicea, carved a swathe through the Saturday afternoon crowds. I followed in her wake.

She had insisted on kitting me out for the evening ahead. I had tried ineffectively to persuade her that my old suit would be perfectly acceptable. She looked at it disapprovingly. Rolled her eyes. Tutted loudly.

Nothing but the best 'tuxedo' – and all the trimmings – would do.

Throughout the process she ignored my flagrant glances at my watch and sent me back repeatedly to the changing room.

Finally she was satisfied. Perfect fit: a pair of trousers long enough for my height of six foot three; a jacket with cuffs that stretched to my wrists without having to settle for a bell tent of excess material flapping over my forty-inch chest.

She was right to persevere. I was pleased with the overall effect as I stared at the unfamiliar person in the mirror. I could happily have dispensed with the 'No Dad' waistcoat, though. But who was I to argue? Arlene was paying. And, more importantly, I wanted her to be happy. It would help her to relax when we faced each other across the table. At my first mention of cards Arlene had boasted to me that she was a good bridge player: regularly finished in the top three at her local club; generally came out on the plus side during friendly games at people's houses. I would have to take her word for that. There wasn't much time for tutorials.

I was tired by the time we got back to the Savoy.

Too much tension. Not enough sleep.

She ordered a pot of coffee and an assortment of sandwiches. The caffeine revived me more than the food. We sat side by side at the table, cobbling together some sort of system.

Tonight we wouldn't just be playing bridge. It would be high stakes bridge – a whole lot different from anything Arlene had experienced. And, at some stage in the evening, we would cut to play against the strongest pair at the club. I didn't want us to finish up looking like two skinned rabbits. We needed to talk fast. The first priority was to agree on a basic style and approach that would see us through the evening.

Then, while she was getting ready, I intended to study the notes in the plastic wallet I had taken from the top drawer of John's desk.

There are two distinct elements to the game of bridge – the bidding and the play of the hand. It was the bidding that provided the biggest obstacle to our success.

The first stage of a hand of bridge is an auction. The object is to see who will play the hand, at what level (how many tricks must be made) and with which suit as trumps (or, if it seems best according to the cards you and your partner hold, with no suit acting as trumps). Accuracy in this auction is vital. Points awarded for achieving the contracted bid go towards game: winning a rubber (the best of three games) carries large bonuses, as does bidding and making a slam contract (a small slam being twelve tricks, a grand slam all thirteen): conversely, penalties are imposed for failing to make the required number of tricks.

The final contract is arrived at through an exchange of information between each pair. Each bid made conveys details such as the strength of a player's hand, the number of cards held in a suit or suits, the number of aces etc. With the aid of this knowledge, the pair hope to assess which suit they want as trumps and the number of tricks they can make. This coded exchange (the meaning of which, for fairness, must also be made available to the opposition) is known as the bidding system. Our problem was that the Americans use a different system to the British. If we couldn't find a common language it would be like speaking in Chinese whispers – the message received would bear little relation to that sent.

When the late Jeremy Flint, one of the best British players to represent his country at international level, paired up with the American Peter Pender they took *five days* to hammer out the initial blueprint for the system they would play – Arlene and I spent an hour. We arrived at a simplified amalgam of Standard American and ACOL (the English system) and, just in case they came in handy, added a few basics from the bewilderingly complex methods used by the Italians.

I hoped we could remember it all when the heat was on.

If we were lucky we should live to fight another day – after all, this was supposed to be a reconnaissance mission, a testing of hypotheses.

Arlene took her notes into the bathroom. Studied them while relaxing in a long hot bath. I rang down for more coffee and, as a postscript, added two large vodkas to the order.

I removed the contents of the wallet with a sense of exhilaration.

A mass of miscellaneous pieces of paper – whatever John had to hand at the time – now lay on the table in front of me. Each scrap was covered with untidy jottings and a scrawled diagram of the cards held by the four players during a particular bridge hand.

The older hands I did not recognise. The more recent ones, though, were familiar. These were all instances of deals we had played against Emsby and Morton, the star pair at the club.

Taken individually each example contained little of merit to an analyst of the game: a shrewd bid here, an inspired defence there, and so on. Exactly what one would have expected from an expert duo.

Taken as a whole, however, there was a pattern.

The suspicions aroused by John's cryptic note had been confirmed.

I didn't know how, but I was convinced the pair were conveying illicit information.

In everyday language, they were cheating.

Okay, so I'd used the odd bit of legerdemain in my youth when the situation was desperate. But they were old enough to know better. And some things in life have to be sacred!

*

At eight o'clock that evening Arlene and I cut left off Piccadilly to walk the last fifty yards to Latimers. Arlene looked dubiously at the shiny brass plate to the side of the door – no name, just a number.

'Don't worry,' I said. 'It's supposed to be a sign of class. A bit like shopping in Bond Street – if you have to ask the price, then you can't afford it. All new members here have to be brought along first as guests. Even the number's unnecessary – except for the postman, that is. Being anonymous helps to keep out the riffraff.'

'Doesn't always work it seems,' she replied.

'Make sure you hang on to that sense of humour,' I said. 'You may need it.'

I rang the bell. The door swung open, inch-thick solid steel rising up effortlessly on oiled hinges. We waited patiently in the lobby while the doorman scurried about his duty. There was no John to sign me in this time. Someone else would have to volunteer.

I didn't anticipate any problem. The dramatic death of a fellow member would be the only topic of conversation. They'd be slavering with hunger for gossip; falling over each other in the scramble to be the first to quiz me on my inside knowledge.

I identified Stapleton, the Duty Director, to Arlene as he walked enthusiastically towards us. He was the club's resident professional and arbiter of any disputes that might occur during the course of the evening's play. We were honoured, indeed.

My eyes flashed a quick message to her – charm him; get him on our side. She smiled back. Let me know she understood. Trust me, she mouthed silently.

She was even better than I could have hoped. Broadened her

accent to play the role of an awe-struck Southern belle. Told him how 'ther-rilled' she was to meet such a legend. That she was an avid devotee of his column which was syndicated in an American magazine. Then she switched her attention to the decor inside the Regency building, emitting 'oohs' and 'ahs' to accompany the expansive, thespian gestures of appreciation.

She continued to chatter, but now in respectful whispers, as we entered the bridge room. I cast my eyes around to register the other players present, mentally preparing short notes on their strengths and weaknesses for Arlene's benefit.

I had learnt bridge at school. Polished my skills – too devotedly, my tutors would perhaps have said – at university. During those years before prison I had played at a variety of venues across the country. The bridge room at Latimers put the rest to shame.

I could imagine what must have been going through Arlene's mind.

My first impression, I remember vividly, when walking through the vast double doors was the sheer size of the room. Forty feet by thirty. High ceilings stretching up, emphasising the classical proportions of the period. Walls lined with an embossed paper, deep blue and maroon stripes separated by wafer-thin columns of gold. Duck-egg blue paint on the ceiling and above the mahogany picture rail. Wall lights shedding a soft glow to the outer edges. Chandeliers casting direct light down onto the four tables – one in each quadrant of the room.

The tables themselves, veneered in walnut with a rich deep shine, were splendid examples of Victorian folly. Large, irregular octagons – four long sides where the players sat, four short corners from which flaps could be slid out to accommodate ashtrays, drinks and scorecards. There were heavily padded carvers for the participants and circles of smaller, only marginally less comfortable chairs for the kibitzers (as the spectators are termed).

The only difference between the four tables was the stakes played at each. I told Stapleton we wished to play at the top table. He looked at me with surprise and then a deep furrow formed to line his brow.

Although this was the table where John and I habitually played, we made no secret of the arrangement whereby he covered my losses and gave me ten per cent of the winnings. Stapleton had naturally assumed that, without John's backing, I would be forced to play at the lowest stake table. Arlene, none too discreetly (as we had planned), produced a wad of dollar traveller's cheques. Stapleton, relieved of any possible embarrassment, took the money to lodge later at the cashier's desk and led us to two spare ringside seats at our chosen table. From these we would observe the play while awaiting our turn to cut in.

The stakes here were one pound a point – each player that is, not per pair. At this table the play was slower paced, more studied and deliberate than elsewhere in the room. The kibitzers showed a higher degree of reverence, talking among themselves in hushed voices, making fewer comments to the players and, appreciating the pressure, being less critical of mistakes. Depending on the luck of the cards, and the skill with which they were played, a rubber might last as little as two deals or take ten or more hands if contracts were consistently failing. But, whatever transpired, an average rubber would be worth somewhere between a thousand and fifteen hundred points to each of the winners. If the run of the cards was against you, you could lose your shirt in a very short space of time indeed.

I attempted to compartmentalise my mind for the different tasks to hand.

Watch closely our target pair – Morton and Emsby.

Mark Arlene's card.

Reassure her of our competence.

Give her time to adjust to the new and overwhelming environment.

And, at the same time, cope with the unwanted interruptions. Utter brief thanks or show mild displeasure, accordingly, to those who either offered condolences or probed with indelicate and unwelcome questions.

All too soon our chance came.

The cards, in their whimsical way, had been kind to a pair I had never considered a real threat before. Morton and Emsby, losers of the 'best of three' rubbers, were now forced to sit out while we took their place.

Such twists of fate are generally met with equanimity by the experts – although I am sure it still hurts! They know that, in the long run, the odds are in their favour. The expert may have only a slight edge in rubber bridge, fifty-four per cent to forty-six per cent it has been estimated, but this is enough to produce a healthy income. Playing five nights a week, I had once calculated, this small percentage difference could add up to around two thousand pounds.

Nervously, we took our places. Exchanged pleasantries with our opponents. Enquired of their system. Explained our curious hybrid in turn. Suffered the mocking glances of all those within earshot.

Six deals and forty minutes later we were back among the spectators.

Three thousand points down.

Poorer by six grand.

*

We retreated to the bar to lick our wounds. Or, at least, take a little alcohol to anaesthetise the sting.

Arlene looked dejected. I could tell she shared my shame at the ease with which our opponents had beaten us. But she had the financial loss to worry about. And I, as its cause, was struggling to cope with the guilt.

The bar, thankfully, was quiet. A few couples – middle-aged businessmen and their youthful mistresses – sat close together enjoying pre-dinner whiskies and multi-coloured cocktails; a handful of younger men were taking a breather from the roulette and blackjack tables upstairs. The sounds of a third-rate pianist giving a poor impersonation of Alan Clare drifted through the open doors to the restaurant. He was murdering *Mood Indigo* with the aid of a wooden interpretation and clumsy fingers. It was the sort of performance that gave jazz a bad name.

I would have preferred to stay in the bridge room, keeping an eye on Emsby and Morton. But it was more important to re-establish morale. And, I hoped, the drink might help Arlene to settle down. Not that she had played badly – neither of us had. We had simply been overwhelmed by the high cards that gravitated to our opponents.

I had always found it fascinating the way the game of bridge acts like an injection of scopolamine – each player's true character rises uncontrollably to the surface. The kindly old lady who sits timidly during WI meetings becomes a man-eating tiger on picking up thirteen cards; the normally decisive businessman dithers for an age and then selects a bid that puts the onus squarely back on his partner; the politician who loses his temper and ends up saying exactly what he feels for once; the doting husband who mercilessly savages his wife if she fails to return his suit. (In Kansas City in 1931 John S. Bennett was shot dead by his wife whilst playing against another married couple. His wife was tried for murder. And acquitted! Mr Bennett – the expert witnesses testified – had misplayed the hand.)

Arlene showed herself to be a good solid player – if anything, a trifle overcautious. None of her usual bluff or bravado manifested itself at the table. She made a reliable partner – analytical, possessed with good judgement, trusting, sound in defence or attack. I would have chosen her in preference to John any day.

John was one of the best card players I had ever seen.

But he needed to be.

During the bidding he seemed impervious to risk. He was pushy to a point that fell the width of a razor blade short of aggression. Overconfident of his own ability. Forever propelling us into overambitious contracts which only stood a chance of making if you played like a demon.

He was at his best when attacking, possessing a killer instinct which was unleashed the moment he sensed the opponents were in trouble. He was hard to play against – and just as difficult to partner.

Since John would always overbid, I was forced to adopt an

opposite style: to underbid my hand in what was often a vain effort to compensate. Playing with John was never dull. It was fatal to let your concentration lapse, even for one moment. At the end of a three-hour session I would feel mentally drained.

Due to my mathematical training, I was more aware than most of the risks he took. John, most of the time, showed no respect for probabilities. He had an innate belief in his own ability and his power to induce mistakes in opponents – this, he was convinced, gave him that vital extra edge.

Arlene and I sat side by side in the deep armchairs, our backs to the heavy oak panelling and racing prints that lined the walls of the bar. We sipped our vodkas slowly, making them last – one drink was all we were allowing ourselves. I talked her through a few of the hands until she was satisfied that we had been unlucky, nothing more. I asked her to stick to her style – I was used to it now and could make the necessary adjustments in my own play. No heroics, please. Leave that to me – if it becomes necessary. Play straight down the middle.

And then a friendly word of advice – try not to look at your opponents during the bidding. It was considered bad form. More suited to poker where it is legitimate, vital even, to study a player's demeanour and draw assumptions from his expressions or body language. In bridge it laid you open to allegations of being 'sharp'.

'Sorry, Nick,' she said. 'It's the American way. In future I'll keep my eyes in my lap. Or yours,' she added with a smile.

As we walked arm-in-arm back to the card room, something started to jangle around in my mind. 'The American way' – where had I come across that phrase before? A long time ago, I was sure. Arlene had set a chord sounding – but, try as I might, I couldn't place the tune.

Forget about it for the moment, I told myself. I knew from experience it would pop into my brain if I didn't worry away at it.

By the time we took our seats Morton and Emsby were well on their way to a ritual crucifixion of their opponents.

Emsby had been nicknamed 'The Weasel' by John. He had a

long, thin body, grey hair, a sharp nose and round framed spectacles which emphasised pinpricks of eyes. He was quiet, nervous, a living catalogue of annoying little habits. With his constant fidgeting, he could easily break your concentration: fill your mind with irritation at his hyperactivity until you suddenly realised you weren't counting the cards anymore. He would pick up the hand, arrange the cards, study them briefly, close the hand again. And fan the cards with exasperating slowness each time he contemplated a bid.

Morton, in the animal kingdom of bridge, was the fox   if an overweight specimen. Like Emsby, he was in his late fifties but that was their only common characteristic. Morton was round, with a rich head of bushy, sandy-coloured hair and a drooping moustache stained yellow at the lips with the nicotine from his beloved cigars. He was crafty, full of guile; snappy, terse, often impolite, sometimes downright rude. Irritatingly, when making a killing defence he would flick the card down onto the table, knuckles producing a sharp knock from the hard wood.

John had always criticised them for being unimaginative – a little hard, I considered, on a pair that had been on the verge of selection for England several times over the last decade. But he seemed to have their measure. Money usually flowed in his direction when we played them.

My thoughts were interrupted. Morton had tabled his cards, claiming the rest of the tricks. I realised I had drifted. Kicked myself for the lapse of concentration. Resolved not to make such a stupid mistake when at the table.

The last rubber was over. Scores were agreed. Emsby and Morton plus four thousand three hundred pounds. Stapleton brought the chitties. The players signed: settlement would be made at the end of the evening.

We moved to the table and chose a card from the spread pack. Arlene won the cut. Out of superstition for the way the cards had been running we opted for the blue pack. Out of cussedness we chose the seats that Emsby and Morton currently occupied.

Amid the disgruntled scuffling, we took our places.

Arlene dealt. Opened the bidding.

I hogged the contract. Made sure I played the hand so as to give Arlene maximum time to relax. Squeezed home in a thin three no trumps. First blood to us.

Morton dealt and passed. I looked down at a vast collection of aces and kings. Arlene made encouraging noises to my bid, and then played carefully to make the final small slam contract of six hearts. First rubber in the bag and three and a half thousand pounds recouped.

I sensed we had them rattled. Now was the time to push.

Two deals followed with neither side making much. On the next hand Arlene dealt and passed. Morton passed too. I looked down at the sorry collection of cards in my hand. Normally I would have passed without a second thought. But I decided instead to take a risk – adopt John's tactics and force for an error. I jumped in with a 'psyche', a poker-style bluffing bid. I heard myself say 'One heart' in an unwavering voice, announcing in our system a hand with at least twelve points (four points for an ace, three for a king etc.) and a minimum of four cards in the heart suit.

It had the desired effect. Misjudging my strength, Morton passed his partner's overcall. They had missed a game.

That was the turning point.

They were rankled at being conned. Thereafter pressed too hard to make up for the loss of face and money. They failed in three consecutive game contracts that were never really on. Squandered the cards they had been dealt.

Two hands later, Arlene and I had wrapped it up. We sat back congratulating each other. Another three thousand pounds to the good. Definitely time to quit.

'Thank you, gentlemen,' I said. 'If you will excuse us, my partner has a plane to catch tomorrow.'

Morton would have needed a personality transplant to let us leave without him having the last word.

'You were lucky, Shannon,' he said with bad grace. 'The first time you've ever psyched and you get away with it. Taking a leaf out of your late partner's book, eh? Consider me forewarned.

Next time you won't have such an easy ride.'

I suppose it was the atmosphere of bad blood that acted as the trigger in my mind. I experienced a strange flashback to one of the many bridge books I had read all those years ago at school. Of course I would need to check with John's collection of hands – but I was already convinced that I knew exactly how they were cheating.

Arlene must have picked up my smile of self-satisfaction. Fed off the confidence it contained. The cards abandoned, she was a lioness again.

'You talk too much, mister.' She was looking Morton directly in the face: her expression made it obvious she did not like what she saw.

Stapleton frowned. Started to frame the words for a rebuke.

She was too fast for him. Morton was in her sights. Nothing would interrupt the stalking of her prey.

'Can that big mouth of yours manage to say five pounds a point?' she challenged.

Morton flushed with anger.

A moment's hesitation. Swift glance across at Emsby. A curt nod in reply.

'Agreed.'

'Then same time next week. Be here. I wouldn't want to be disappointed.'

Arlene turned to me with a broad grin.

'Let's cash up, partner. Time for us to celebrate . . . while these guys put in some practice!'

She rose majestically from the table.

Stapleton stopped her. There were formalities to complete before we could get her travellers' cheques back and claim the five hundred odd pounds we had won. Emsby and Morton signed quickly, Arlene next. When the sheet came to me I noticed that her signature was almost illegible. She was trembling as I led her from the room, shaking violently with temper by the time we stepped onto the pavement.

'Jesus! That self-opinionated, self-important, chauvinistic, puffed-up, arrogant son of a bitch.'

PAUL BENNETT

The sight of her standing there hurling abuse, right foot girlishly stamping at the ground in a metronomic punctuation of her flow of invective suddenly struck me as hilariously funny. I tried to fight back the laughter building up inside me. But it was impossible. The smile on my lips widened to a grin; the grin broke into a chuckle; the chuckle burst forth in an uncontrollable guffaw.

She flashed a look of fury at me.

Then, to my relief, saw the comical side as well.

'You bastard,' she said, squeezing my hand. 'I'm sorry, Nick. I hope I haven't made everything worse.' She paused to reflect on her impetuous action.

'Dammit,' she said with resignation. 'You wanted something on them, didn't you? If they don't cheat for five pounds a point then you're on the wrong track.'

I told her that it made sense. And for one hell of a needle match.

In the cab we talked practicalities: argued over how we would raise the stake money; what changes we needed to make in our hastily developed system to give us a better chance of winning; how best to rearrange her schedule so that she could return to London for the game.

Back in her room we forgot the problems. Arlene kissed me. The tension exploded. I pulled her tight against me.

She broke away. Gave a knowing laugh. Pointed to a bottle of champagne she'd had the foresight, or supreme confidence, to order earlier.

We took it to bed.

Tomorrow she would pack up and resume her travels. Tonight, the fire in her eyes said, must last us a week.

CHAPTER SIX

Brixton

Three months? Was that all it had been? In ten minutes Arthur would walk out of the door – a free man. I should be congratulating him, not lying here sullenly on the bunk while he cleared his things. In the hot-house of prison, Arthur had rapidly grown into the best friend I had ever had. I felt selfish and ashamed. I didn't want to see him go.

'Stand up, kid,' he said. 'Wish me luck. Shake my hand.'

I rose from the bunk, a lump forming in my throat. Extended my hand towards him.

He swung a right hook, swift and hard, at my head.

Jesus, what was going on?

I ducked low. Sprang back up immediately his fist had passed me. Punched him hard in his undefended abdomen. Watched in horror and confusion as he doubled up.

He took a pace backwards. Slowly stretched to his full height. Looked me straight in the eye. And laughed.

'There you are. Will you believe me now? You can do it. Just watch your back and you'll be all right.'

He held out his hand again. 'No tricks this time,' he said.

'Thanks, Arthur,' I said, feeling his powerful hand wrap gently around mine. 'I couldn't have got this far without your help.'

'Nothing to thank me for, kid. It was a trade, remember. And you'd have managed on your own. You may have been green but you were never yellow. Stand up to these blokes and they back down easy enough. You'd have sussed that for your-self.'

They might back down for you, Arthur, I thought, but I'm not sure they would do the same for me.

'Anyway,' he continued, 'you'll be out of here soon. The trial can't last much longer. Or maybe there'll be some room in the remand block soon.'

Neither of us really believed that. We both knew that once you were absorbed into the main prison you were as good as forgotten.

The bolts slid back. Arthur shrugged his shoulders.

'See you soon, son,' he said. 'On the outside.'

'You bet,' I said.

'No you don't. No more betting for you.' It was a final warn-ing to keep clear of the card school. I didn't need it. No sense looking for trouble – I had a feeling it would find me soon enough.

The door opened.

'One out. One in,' said the warder. 'Duggan, you come with me. Shannon, meet your new lodger.'

*

He didn't bother telling me his name. That was low on his list of priorities.

'Right,' he said as the door closed behind him. 'Who do I see in here to get hold of some tackle and the fit?'

From that moment I knew he was bad news.

Arthur had explained the jargon: 'tackle' is heroin, and 'the fit' is the equipment for injecting. He'd also told me the rumours: a whole landing where forty people had shared the same needle for three months; another case where ten men used one needle for a month, and so on. And if the addicts couldn't get needles then they were resourceful – and desperate – enough to cobble together a workable alternative from a Biro. Pass that round instead. Along with septicaemia, hepatitis B, AIDS. They must have had a death wish.

The drugs themselves enter via three main routes. The first is prison visits (transferred through a seemingly innocent cuddle and kiss, known as 'gob-grabbing'), the second is after a temporary release (anyone let out for a funeral or on other compassionate grounds was usually bribed or pressurised to smuggle something in). The third route, and by far the most common source of syringes and needles, is the staff: one corrupt officer can keep an entire wing supplied with all they desire – providing their friends on the outside can find the cash.

As far as I was concerned he could find out for himself.

'Tackle? Fit? What are you talking about?'

I'd commandeered the top bunk and sat there expressionless: inwardly, I winced. He was twenty-five and acted like he'd taken a postgraduate degree in 'street cred': he was constantly on the move – even when standing on one spot. His body swayed with a dizzying rhythm, transferring the weight of his small frame from one foot to the other, as if his flapping ears were picking up the latest techno-rave hits; his head nodded in counterpoint from side to side. His eyes darted about the cell: I expected him to cast a nervous glance over his shoulder any moment.

He stopped his punchdrunk ducking and weaving motions for long enough to roll his eyes and open his mouth – obviously didn't have the brain power to continue the movement and speak at the same time! 'You're a lot of bloody use, aren't you,' he said. His voice had the inbuilt bored tone of a lifelong Arsenal supporter.

I jumped down from the bunk, watched his momentary panic fade as I moved past him to the table. I copied Arthur's disinterested attitude: sat there and picked up the pack of cards.

'Darren,' he said. Christ, it gets worse, I thought. 'Five years. Possession and supply.'

I gave the cards a deft riffle shuffle, the two halves of the pack intertwining perfectly as I locked onto his shifty eyes. 'Shannon. Murder.' That shut him up.

During association I joined the couch potatoes around the television and watched Darren out of the corner of my eye as he cruised around like a hungry shark. It didn't take long before someone pointed him in the right direction. Then he became a leech, and firmly affixed himself to the side of Freddie Ronson.

Freddie had been in here a long time. And before Brixton he'd made the recidivists' grand tour of Her Majesty's lodging houses. He knew all the ropes and, as far as our wing was concerned, pulled all the strings. Freddie could get you anything from hard drugs down through tobacco or alcohol to more homely pleasures such as Mars bars. He would even give a little credit. But God help those who couldn't produce the cash when the time came.

But Darren didn't care about reputations. Nor was he put off by Freddie's grotesque appearance: Darren would have had sex with Quasimodo if it brought him a week's supply of heroin.

Over the next fortnight I became sickeningly accustomed to Darren's disappearances: a quick huddle with Freddie then back to the cell, only to emerge five minutes later to return the needle surreptitiously to its keeper. Then one evening he came back hugging his stomach and complaining bitterly. He put it down to 'dodgy dogs' and shuffled off for an early night. I could tell what everyone was thinking: it wasn't the sausages that were the problem – Darren had overdone the dose tonight, or, worse still, maybe it was a bad batch. Freddie took it seriously: he had his business to think about. He threw in his cards with a sigh of resignation and went off to investigate.

What little concern I had soon evaporated when I entered the cell: Darren was snoring like a pig with terminal sinus trouble. I prodded him sharply with my boot: he rolled further towards the wall, blankets wrapped tightly around his head. I undressed, climbed into bed and read a chapter of my book before the main lights flickered their five-minute warning and then snapped out.

Sleep came quickly.

So did waking.

It's amazing how fast the brain kicks into action when it feels a cold blade pressed against the throat.

'Climb down, real slow,' a voice whispered in my ear.

It wasn't Darren.

The snoring bundle I'd kicked had been Freddie. I felt sweat break out over my body.

'Nice and easy,' Freddie continued. 'Any sudden movement, any sound, and I'll stick you.'

I did as he ordered – what choice was there? In the dim glow of the night-light I could see the hand-made blade. It was a rough tool – a single length of sharpened metal, the top wound round with string to serve as a handle – but I had no illusions as to its effectiveness.

'Up against the wall.' The knife moved so that its point dug into my stomach. With little jabs he forced me back till I could go no further.

I thought of Arthur's words. Okay, my back is up against the wall – but what do I do now? I couldn't afford to look around for a weapon, had to keep Freddie in my sights: in any case it would have been a useless move, there was nothing here that could help me. I would have to improvise – better and quicker than any of the jazz pianists I admired.

'You stitched me up, Shannon. Did you think, after all this time, I'd forgotten? No one makes me look a prat and gets away with it.' His smile was a sadistic slash across his face like a three-year-old girl's uncoordinated attempt to put on lipstick.

'Don't worry,' he said, in a tone that was at odds with the words, 'I'm not going to kill you. That would be a waste. Eh, Mr Smart-arse?' He gave a deep, guttural chuckle that sent a chill running down my spine.

His left hand went to his trousers and fingered the top of his flies. Slowly, so he could relish to the full the look of abject fear that spread across my face, he started undoing the buttons.

'Turn round,' he leered. 'Drop your pants.'

It was now or never. I raised my hands in submission. Whimpered at him.

'You've got it all wrong, Freddie. It was fair and square.' I cringed in front of him. Brought my hands together as if in supplication. 'Look, I can get you money. How much do you want? Not this, Freddie. Please.'

He brought the knife close to my face: his hand was shaking wildly. 'You make me sick,' he said. The feeling's mutual, Freddie. 'Take it like a man,' he laughed.

I let my terrified gaze move down to the bulge in his trousers. His eyes followed mine. He swelled with pride.

My hands moved with the speed of a praying mantis. The left had only inches to travel before it chopped into his wrist, forcing him to drop the knife. With my right hand I plunged two fingers up his nostrils and hoicked him upwards with all my strength. As he reeled back in pain, I withdrew my hand and punched him hard in the stomach. He folded in the middle. I interlocked my fingers and hit him on the back of his neck. He dropped to the floor.

I stood, breathing hard and fast, rooted to the spot, my eyes fixed on the door and the knife which lay two feet to its left. Once at the door, I would bang and shout loud enough to raise the dead. A mere ten feet separated me from safety. But, to cover that short distance, I had to get past Ronson.

He was stronger, more resilient, quicker to recover than I had reckoned. He rose from the floor like a titan, an evil kraken about to tear apart some ancient city with his bare hands. There were no smiles or leers now. Only madness in his eyes.

I made a break for the knife.

But the table was in my way. Freddie was there before me. I skidded to a halt just in time to avoid the first slash. The second caught me unbalanced, ripped through the flesh of my upper arm. I jumped back as he thrust again. Took three steps back. I was against the wall again.

'Pax,' I shouted like a frightened schoolboy as he advanced. I held my left hand aloft in the peace sign.

He didn't even blink. Just ran toward me. And met, full force, my rigid fingers as they stabbed deep into the sockets of his eyes.

He let out a howl of pain. Dropped the knife. Clutched at his eyes. Staggered about the cell, wailing like a banshee. In his blindness he banged into the wall and fell to the floor.

The warders came running, following the sounds of the screams.

They found Freddie on his knees. And me in the corner emptying the contents of my stomach.

CHAPTER SEVEN

'Take that smile off your face,' Arlene said, her hands on her hips in exasperation.

She had been packing and eating a croissant at the same time. Except it didn't work out like that. She would take a bite of the croissant, carefully wrapped in a napkin to keep the buttery crumbs from her fingers, put it down somewhere while she folded a dress and then forget what she'd done with it. Already behind schedule, her attempt at two simultaneous tasks just made each take longer. I was watching with uncontrolled amusement through the open door to the bedroom.

'This is all your fault,' she continued.

'I didn't hear you complain at the time,' I replied. 'Come on, I'll give you a hand.'

'No thank you. I'll do it my way. Just let me get on.'

She turned her back to me: her head swivelled around the bedroom.

'Arlene,' I said.

'What now?'

'It's on the dressing table.'

She located the croissant, tossed it vengefully in the bin and closed the door.

I returned to my breakfast. It had been the same waiter this morning but a very different look. Gone was the superiority and the mild amusement at my embarrassment. Instead there was a nervous sideways glance, critical and questioning. He left the trolley a few feet from where I sat at the table and backed hurriedly from the room without even bothering about the formalities of a signature. I put it down to an overnight attack of morals or a bad case of insufficient tipping.

Still, the coffee was as good as yesterday: a thick, black, pungently aromatic liquid with a dose of caffeine large enough to wake up a corpse. I picked up the rain forest that had been transformed into *The Sunday Times* and, without unfolding it, studied the top half of the front page. I skimmed over the stock story on the effects of the recession. Read the first few paragraphs of a claimed exclusive about the prominent politician tipped to replace the Chancellor at the next Cabinet reshuffle. He was handsome, personable and, through his experience in business, financially astute – totally unsuitable, it seemed to me. When the article started to read like a press release I turned the paper over. Nearly choked on my coffee. There, across two columns, was a picture of me.

It was an old photograph, blown up to blotchy graininess and cropped to head and shoulders, which had been taken at the conclusion of the trial.

I'd forgotten the toll the months on remand had taken. Was this really how I had looked? Deep worry-lines etched around the eyes; a face painfully thin, almost emaciated; collar and tie hanging loosely about a scrawny neck. I shuddered. In the physiognomy of crime this snapshot had 'murderer' written all over it.

Somehow they had also managed to obtain a picture of John – the contrast between the two of us was like a poster for an amateur production of *Dr Jekyll and Mr Hyde*. Well-fed, well-groomed, well-dressed, he smiled at the camera. Even his contact lenses, having caught the light, seemed to add a twinkle to his eyes.

Less than half the piece was devoted to the murder. The lion's share replayed my own history. Opened up the rights and wrongs of my crime and the sentence meted out. I did not blame the writer for that – there was more scope in my story for developing an opinion, for taking a stance. More human interest too. Without my involvement, the journalist would have been reduced to padding out his report by printing an insubstantial biography of John.

The police, probably in the hope of shocking anyone with information into coming forward, had released a photograph of the murder weapon. A different journalist had been given a few column inches to debate the issue of whether such potentially dangerous articles should be on sale in this country. It included an injudicious account – it read more like an instruction manual – spelling out in fascinating detail how easy it is to remove the deliberate blunting produced at the factory and impart a razor-sharp edge to the sword.

I tossed the paper on the floor in disgust. Abandoned the breakfast. I had no heart for it any more.

I went into the bedroom, placed my hands lightly on Arlene's shoulders and turned her round to face me. She didn't resist the kiss. Her urgent, searching tongue told me she shared my misgivings: continuing the whistle-stop tour with short hops to Paris, Rome and Florence had seemed the right decision at the time. Now I realised I would miss her. The easy manner; the boundless confidence she had in me; her unwavering support. And, perhaps more selfishly, it would seem lonely at night without her warm body by my side.

*

There was an envelope pinned to the door of my bedsit. I stuck it in my pocket while juggling with my collection of carrier bags and jiggling my key in the cheap lock. I swung the door open on the room I had never got used to calling home.

I carried the bags inside. Placed them on the gate-leg table by the window. Opened the curtains. Looked out at the Sunday stillness of the shunting yard behind Liverpool Street Station: regimental lines of goods wagons and vast rectangular containers all ready to clank and clang at the stroke of five o'clock tomorrow morning.

Two nights at the Savoy had spoilt me. Softened me up so that the return to the room hit me hard.

I had done what little I could – salary and landlady permitting – to brighten it up and add a little colour to the drab nicotine-yellowed emulsion. A collection of holiday posters, donated by a short-lived ex-girlfriend who worked in a travel agency, was fixed to the walls by blobs of Blu-tack – Rule Number 5: The use of drawing pins and Sellotape is not permitted! From my single bed I could lie and dream of sandy Caribbean beaches, the crystal-clear waters of the Great Barrier Reef or the fjords of Norway with their mirror reflections of snow-capped mountains.

It didn't help much. The staccato rhythm of the buffers on a line of trucks always brought me back to reality.

The room was adequate for my basic needs, but otherwise reminded me of a larger version of the cell I had shared in Chelmsford. Perhaps that was why I had taken it – the comforting sense of the familiar. The few items of furniture were serviceable, even if they did resemble oddments cast out by a disenchanted collector of fifties memorabilia. The melamine shelves were strong enough to house my large collection of bridge books, paperback fiction and jazz cassettes. On the top of the Baby Belling I could cook an omelette; grill bacon or toast beneath. I had my radio for the morning news, the second-hand television or Walkman as alternatives for the long evenings. And, along the corridor, a shared bathroom complete with an ancient gas geyser that gurgled threateningly before spitting out a slow stream of tepid, rusty brown water.

It was all I could afford.

Some would say all I deserved.

But it was a start.

I made some coffee. Drank a little: let the rest get cold as I lost myself in John's evidential anthology of bridge hands. I broke off briefly to root out a half-full pack of stale cigarettes from its hiding place in the tallboy. Without realising, I chain-smoked half a dozen while making my own notes alongside John's.

I could have stopped after an hour – the pattern of the hands seemed so conclusive. But, due to my training, I carried on to the very last scrap of paper. Then selected one of the books from the shelves as a final check.

I set it all down in a long letter to Arlene.

It was mid-afternoon before I remembered Sofia.

Guiltily, I rushed down the stairs to the pay-phone. Apologised to a moody Sally. Ran out of the front door. Used five pounds of my winnings for the cab ride to their flat.

Sally let me in with a faraway air and a perfunctory wave of her hand in the general direction of the stairs. Her face was pale, save for a blotchy-red puffiness around the eyes.

She introduced herself, speaking in a quiet voice laced with the short 'pass-the-salt' vowels of a Yorkshire accent. Her hand thrust towards me in formal greeting. It felt small and cold within mine. She withdrew it quickly.

As Sally led me into their sitting room I wondered whether Sofia had chosen her flatmate deliberately. There was no chance of these two ever sharing each other's clothes.

Sally must have been about five foot three at the most, more like John's height than Sofia's. She was dressed in jeans and wooden-soled exercise sandals with a dark blue leather strap. Hair, the colour of straw, parted simply in the middle, hung straight down onto the shoulders of a black sweatshirt. She tossed her head, flicking a stray strand from in front of her eyes. Blue eyes. As pale as Sofia's were dark.

She was thin, waif-like; could have been an extra in a TV adaptation of *Oliver Twist*, wrapped in a black shawl selling flowers in a London square. Whereas Sofia aroused the carnal instincts in a man, Sally clawed at your heartstrings, silently crying out for protection.

'You might as well take a seat,' she said.

'I can come back another time. Just say the word.'

'I'm sorry,' she said, sounding anything but. 'I don't mean to be rude but . . . Well, it's a difficult time.' She played for time by scraping her hair behind one ear. 'This isn't my idea, you know. Sofia and I would be better on our own. It's too soon. We need more time to ourselves. I told her that. But she insisted you came. Personally . . .'

The ringing of the telephone brought a welcome interruption. Sally ran across the room and scooped up the receiver.

'Yes?' she said breathlessly.

A look of frustration spread across her face as she listened to the caller. 'She's sleeping,' she finally said, failing to keep the irritation from her voice. 'I'll tell her you called. Okay? Yes, thank you. Tomorrow, maybe.'

'Please sit down,' she sighed. 'I'll brew some tea. Sofia will want some when she wakes.'

She left me sitting ill-at-ease in the armchair. I looked around the room, seeing little touches of what I took to be Sally's homely influence on Sofia's flamboyant style. Lacy curtains and cushions softening the sharp lines of the arabian blue leather suite. Vases of carnations standing on the glass dining table and window sill. Copies of *Bella* and *Best* peeking out from under a pile of back issues of *Vogue* on the long, low coffee table.

A photograph album lay open on the settee, one of those upside-down nurse's watches marking the page. I rose from my chair to sneak a closer look. Absentmindedly stuck my hands in my pockets. My fingers found the envelope that had been pinned to my door.

I lost interest in the album. Glanced away from an old photograph of a teenage Sally and a boy grinning at the camera.

I walked to the window for the extra light and opened the letter. I read the words in disbelief. Felt the heat of temper rising within me. Angrily, I crushed the paper into a ball.

'Something wrong?'

I spun around.

Sofia had padded noiselessly into the room. Bare feet, toenails painted the colour of blackberries, peeped out beneath a red silk dressing gown that brushed against the carpet. No lipstick today, I noticed. Simply a little foundation hastily applied to her face.

'I've just been kicked out of my bedsit,' I answered bitterly. 'It seems my landlady doesn't like what she reads in the papers.

Or being woken in the middle of the night by some tabloid hack hammering on her door.'

I became aware that I was only adding to Sofia's burden. My troubles were small compared to hers.

'Still,' I said with a forced smile, 'at least she's given me till the end of the week. It really doesn't matter. I'll find somewhere else. What about you, Sofia? How are you coping?'

She floated across to me. Her eyes, unadorned by liner or shadow, were free to shout their sadness. Clinging to me for support or comfort, she pressed her cheek hard against mine. I felt the sticky wetness of her tears as they trickled down my face. The smell of her perfume drifted up. Strong, heady, saved from being overpowering by a merest hint of lemon cutting through the musk.

She didn't speak – either the words wouldn't come or she couldn't bear to say them. Even her crying was soundless. None of the deep sobs that had punctuated the telephone call to summon me here. I wanted to look into her eyes, read her emotions, respond to them, but I stood there passively, afraid to do anything that might break the tenuous control she exercised over her feelings.

Sally came back and instantly registered my awkwardness. She placed the tray on the table. Led Sofia firmly to the settee, sat her down and then positioned herself on the floor. She took hold of her flat-mate's shaking hands.

'It's okay,' she said soothingly. 'Let it out.'

I stared out of the window. Sally didn't need my help. Her voice was soft, gentle, calming. Gradually, osmotically, it seeped into Sofia's grief and dried up the tears.

'I'll be all right now,' she said firmly, giving us a half-hearted smile that only deepened our concern. 'You mustn't worry, both of you. The worst is over.'

She stroked Sally's hair. Seemed to draw strength and gain composure from the simple act. After a while she patted Sally on the head in a gesture of dismissal. With a brief nod of re-inforcement at the upturned face, Sofia pointed to the other chair: Sally obediently took her cue.

'Yesterday was a nightmare,' Sofia said. 'I don't ever want to live through anything like that again.' Her Greek accent had become heavier now, her manner of speech more stilted. 'I will tell you about it, Nick. Then I must forget. Shake it all off. Rebuild my life.'

She looked plaintively at me. 'You will help me, Nick?'

Whatever it was she was going to ask, I knew I wouldn't be able to refuse – no matter how much I wanted to.

She nestled back into the settee, tucking her long legs beneath her. I leaned forward attentively in the chair. Listened spellbound as she gave me a blow-by-blow account of the events of the previous day – stutteringly at first, then with increasing abstraction, deliberately consigning them to history, building an insulating wall to the past and a barrier to an uncertain future.

The police, she told me mechanically, had woken them early in the morning. A detective – Baxter I guessed from the description – and a woman constable. 'So young she was,' Sofia complained, 'what can she know of life – or death?'

They had found her details while searching John's house. Her name had been written as 'next of kin' on the top of a bundle of personal papers in John's desk.

Sofia described her first reaction as disbelief. Not shock at that stage – that came later, she said. Just a numbness, a stubborn refusal to take in the words. They drove her to John's house. Sally – here Sofia paused to give a smile of gratitude – came along too. 'They made her wait outside, Nick. Why would they do such a thing? Have they no feelings?'

I could not answer. Baxter must have had his reasons – or his orders.

They led her from room to room, made her check methodically to see what was missing. 'Such memories, Nick. Such pain.'

They left the living room till last.

The floor was covered with dirty white dustsheets to provide a measure of protection for her sensibilities.

She described with a wince the chalky feel of the fingerprint

71

powder on everything she touched. Now, even as she talked, she rubbed her hands subconsciously down her dressing gown as if traces still clung to her damp palms.

John kept some cash in the drawer of his desk. He always separated, she explained, his windfall gains from bridge from his other money. Saved it for their weekends away. Or special gifts for her.

The money was gone.

Nothing else, though.

His passport was still in the desk. Cheque-book and wallet in his jacket pocket.

She looked at me despairingly.

'Killed for a few hundred pounds,' she said, shaking her head in disbelief. 'Senseless. What a waste of a life.'

Sofia looked away from us. Swallowed hard, took a deep breath. She was gathering her courage, preparing to launch full-tilt into the most emotional part of the story.

'Then they took us to the mortuary.'

I shivered as she told us of the pervasive coldness of the room. The clinical cleanliness. The glimpse of shiny metal surfaces designed for ease of hosing down. The vinegary pickle-smell of chemicals in the air. The smooth roll of the castors as the body was slid out of the cabinet for identification. And the final sinking in of the truth as she recognised intimate details on the body.

I watched as her face turned white. It had all been too much for her.

She leapt from the settee. Ran to the bathroom.

I heard muffled retching sounds coming through the door. Sally and I, impotent to help, sat staring at each other.

'Best to leave her be,' Sally said. 'She's kept it bottled up till now. Wouldn't talk about it to me, you know.' She paused in contemplation.

'I'm sorry,' she said, this time with feeling. 'I was wrong. She needed a stranger.'

'You really know how to make a man feel welcome,' I said, only half in jest. 'Thanks for the apology, anyway.'

Sally blushed and shook her head. 'I didn't mean it to sound like that. Really, I didn't.'

I saw her face begin to crumple.

'Don't worry,' I said quickly. 'I understand. Okay?' I gave her a broad reassuring smile and hoped for the best.

Sofia – not a moment too soon – stepped back into the room. There were beads of perspiration glistening on her forehead. She walked unsteadily to the settee. Smiled bravely at Sally. Apologised, unnecessarily, to me.

'There is much to do, Nick.' A few minutes alone in the bathroom seemed to have given her a new determination. 'First I have to attend the inquest. I do not want to go alone. You will come with me, please?'

'Of course I'll come. Just let me know where and when. And if there's anything else I can do, you only have to ask.'

Sofia moved the photograph album to the floor, smiled at me, and patted the seat next to her.

I felt uncomfortable being that close to her. Wasn't sure if she wanted me to put my arm around her. My instincts told me I should keep a distance between us.

She leaned across. Took hold of my hands. Locked her eyes on mine.

'John made a new will six weeks ago. Left everything to me. Will you sort it all out for me, please. I never want to set foot inside that house again. I want none of his things. Too many memories.'

I nodded my agreement. She was beginning to look happier.

'You will move into the house for a while,' she continued. 'After all, you have nowhere else to go, now. Pack up his personal belongings for me. Send them to his parents. Make arrangements to sell everything else. Including the house.'

She squeezed my hands tightly. Chose her words carefully so as not to offend me with charity.

'Stay as long as you like. Keep an eye on the house for me – until it is sold. Please.'

I didn't know what to say. I was still searching for an answer when she hit me with the next bombshell.

'I'd like you to have the car, too. I'm sure it's what John would have wanted.'

I was lost for words. Confused. Felt I couldn't refuse her, even though my pride told me I should. Having a car again was tempting. And a roof over my head.

'Don't say anything,' she ordered, as if knowing the conflicting emotions going through my mind. 'Look on it all as a favour to me.'

Sally caught my eye. She gave an almost imperceptible nod. 'Do what she wants,' it said.

With reluctance, and a feeling of apprehension, I agreed.

Sofia released my hands.

'That's settled then,' she said, walking off to the kitchen. 'I'll get you the keys. And Mrs Simmons's number. She's the cleaner. You'll need her help, no doubt. John used to swear by her.'

I asked Sally politely for more tea. I wanted a moment alone. A pause to catch my breath and give me time to think.

Everything was happening much too fast. I felt like I was being swept along by the tide. The tide of Sofia's tears? I needed to feel in control again.

I dragged the heavy marble ashtray towards me. Lit a cigarette. Drew the smoke deep into my lungs. Made an effort to concentrate. Let my mind go back over everything she had said. And anything she might have left out. There was still the note to explain.

The two of them seemed to be gone a long time.

From the kitchen I could hear whispers but, frustratingly, couldn't make out any of the words.

They came back together. Sally filled my cup with fresh tea, Sofia sat down and toyed distractedly with the keys.

'Can I ask you a question?' I said to Sofia. 'Are you sure nothing else was missing? Just the money?'

'I think so,' she replied, 'but I can't be certain.' A puzzled expression spread across her face. 'I hadn't been to the house for weeks, you see.'

She seemed reluctant to continue.

'Go on,' I encouraged.

'John didn't want me there any more. He wouldn't give any reason. Just told me to stay away. We had an argument over it. A blazing row, really. He got very angry.'

Her face became serious.

'He'd changed, you know.'

I was curious. No, much more than that – intrigued. I couldn't let her throwaway remark go by without probing more deeply.

'In what way had he changed?' I asked.

'I don't know,' she said, her manner suggesting she was regretting ever mentioning the subject.

I had the impression she felt foolish. Afraid that I might think she was letting her imagination run away with her.

She hesitated over her next words. 'He seemed nervous. Always on edge. Couldn't relax when we went out.'

Then a long pause.

'I think he'd started taking drugs, too.'

I noticed a strange expression come over Sally's face. Pain? Guilt? I couldn't tell. She saw my interest and quickly buried her eyes in her lap.

I found it hard to believe my ears. It didn't sound like John. He didn't seem the type to mess with drugs.

'When did all this start to happen?'

'Immediately after the accident, I suppose.'

'What accident?' I shouted, making her jump. She looked reproachfully at me.

'I'm sorry,' I said, 'but John never mentioned anything to me about an accident.'

'It was nothing, really. It seemed worse at the time.' Her voice was shaky, her hands were trembling again.

Sally and I were pinned to our seats with the tension that radiated from Sofia's body.

'We'd been on holiday,' she said with the thinnest of wistful smiles on her lips. 'John wanted to get away for a while. He didn't like London in the summer; said it was suffocating, oppressive. We rented a little log cabin on the shores of Lake Geneva. Cool, clean breezes. So quiet, so peaceful.

'John said it could be an early honeymoon, something to celebrate our engagement.' She sighed. 'It was like a dream.'

Frowning now, she told us how the dream had become a nightmare the moment they had set out on their return journey.

The plane had fought against strong winds, the turbulence restricting them to their seats for the whole flight; it was raining at Heathrow; they'd had to wait an age for the courtesy coach to take them to the long-term car park; the M4 was treacherous, its surface wet and slippery. And the first time John had stamped on the accelerator, the cable had snapped.

'I didn't know what was happening at first. The engine seemed to roar and the car just shot forward.'

I could picture the scene. John swearing above the noise of the engine; the needle on the rev counter swinging into the red zone; the car accelerating unrestrained to its 120 mph limit.

'John was marvellous,' she said in admiration. 'I would have panicked. He couldn't use the gears. There were clouds of blue smoke coming from the brakes. But he was calm. He flicked on the hazard warning lights. Hit the horn and somehow cut a path through the traffic.

'He managed to get across to the hard shoulder. I saw him switch off the engine. Thought we were safe then. But the steering locked.' She shuddered at the memory. Stumbled over the rest of the story.

'We hit the embankment. Thank God the car didn't flip over – the wet earth absorbed the crash, I suppose. I don't remember the rest. John must have pulled me out of the car. The next thing I knew I was lying on the grass with John bending over me. We were lucky,' she concluded.

So lucky, I thought, that a few days later John had sat in a solicitor's office making his last will and testament.

'I think I'd like to go back to bed now,' Sofia said, all emotion now spent.

She looked pale. Unusually fragile.

In the short space of thirty-six hours, she had experienced so much. And, in the last sixty minutes, poured it all out until empty inside.

I took the keys and the slip of paper, placing them in my pocket. I put my hands over her quivering fingers. Kissed her lightly, like a brother, on the cheek. Watched pityingly as she walked in a trance from the room.

Sally led me down the stairs. When we reached the bottom she hung back from opening the door.

'Thank you,' she said warmly.

'What for?' I replied. 'The house? The car? It's the least I can do. And the arrangement suits me too, don't forget.'

'No. Not for that,' she said. 'For being here. For listening.'

'Any time,' I said, with an embarrassed shrug.

The faraway look with which she had first greeted me returned to her eyes. Her fingers played distractedly with a lock of hair, twirling it into an impromptu spiral.

'I . . .' she began, then stopped abruptly.

'Yes?'

Frustratingly, she shook her head and opened the door.

'Remember,' I said. 'Any time.'

'Let's wait and see,' she said

I walked, perplexed, down the street. 'Women!' I said to myself. Like Rubik's cube, it is possible to understand them. But only five men in the country actually do!

CHAPTER EIGHT

Sofia was right – John had changed. An hour spent reading through his report was proof enough of that. This wasn't the work of the John I knew.

Arriving back at the bedsit, there had been nothing better to do than open a bottle of red wine and begin working my way through the files. Bennington's was our latest project and the most urgent; it seemed a good place to start. And I was curious to see John's opinions of the company. It conformed to the 'benevolent dictator' style of management and – in my view – appeared to be struggling. Our client was very keen to buy: but what had John recommended?

The first surprise was that John had not sent the report. Granted it was only a few days late but, to my knowledge, he had never missed a deadline before.

In the file was a typed draft, and this a mess of inky amendments – not corrections as such (typos, transpositions of figures and so on) but whole paragraphs completely reworded. Yet, despite the checking and the changes, the report was still riddled with mistakes. A proliferation of slipshod errors that had an unfortunate snowballing effect on the conclusions he had reached.

His mind must have been elsewhere while he was writing. Preoccupied with larger issues or – could it be true? – under the influence of some drug or other.

Something here was out of character. He had always struck me as careful and thorough, meticulous to the point of being pernickety. These traits had been evident even at our very first meeting. That was a day I would never forget.

It was my second and, whatever the outcome, final interview for the job – Richard Goodwin had made that clear when he asked me to come back. 'Last hurdle, old boy,' Richard had said. I soon learnt that all Richard's sentences either ended in 'old boy' or with a slight pause where you were expected to mentally insert the words yourself, thus sparing him the need for constant repetition.

Richard Goodwin was Managing Partner of Jameson Browns – and to this day nobody was quite sure how he had contrived to land the top position. 'Tricky Dicky', that's how he was known behind his back – although I am sure he was aware of, and approved, the nickname.

He came down personally to collect me from Reception. Walking towards me, he caught sight of his reflection in the picture window and made a minute adjustment to the Windsor knot in his tie. Maybe it was just a mannerism, for it seemed to me as if he had marched straight from the parade ground. The jacket of his suit, pale grey with a thin pinstripe, was single breasted and unbuttoned to reveal the waistcoat beneath. The trousers were sharply creased and cut on the slant so that they rested on the laces of his shiny black Oxfords at the front and just touched the heels at the back. So fit did he look that it was hard to credit he was the wrong side of fifty. 'Distinguished' was what everybody said about Richard – what they said about 'Tricky Dicky' was another matter entirely.

He led me to the lift, a thin mist of spruce from his clean-shaven face wafting through the air as he walked. 'John Weston will interview you this time,' he said as he pressed his manicured finger on the button for the top floor. 'He's in charge of A&M – Acquisitions and Mergers, that is. You'll be working for John if you join us. You'll like John.' He tapped the side of his aquiline nose as if to add 'if you take my meaning, old boy'

We entered one of the smaller of the firm's conference rooms.

John was already seated at the oval table, my application form spread out in front of him. He rose to greet me. Craned his neck to look up into my eyes. I thought I saw a frown flash across his face but it disappeared before I could be sure of its existence.

Richard made the formal introductions and left us together. John motioned to the seat directly opposite him across the short side of the oval.

'Coffee?' he asked, reaching for the shiny insulated jug on the tray to his right.

'Please,' I answered. 'Black. Two sugars.'

While he poured I looked around the room. It was only about twelve feet by ten but large enough to accommodate the table and six swivel chairs which were the only items of furniture. There was a square double-glazed window behind John, its vertical blinds open so that the light shone directly behind him. A grey dial-telephone sat on the window ledge. It had a padlock in the first fingerhole.

John passed me the coffee: it was in a gold-rimmed, bone-china cup that struck a discordant note against the untrusting economy of the telephone. He took a cup for himself. Sipped, in the delicate and pensive manner of a *sommelier*, at the creamy liquid. He saw me look down at the black stubby Mont Blanc fountain pen and the pile of papers. With a sweep of his left hand he pushed them aside. 'I don't need any of this,' the gesture said. 'I know it – know you – by heart.'

At last he broke the silence.

'I don't intend to go into any of the technical points,' he said. 'Richard's been through that already – he seems happy enough on that score. And you passed with flying colours, so we could have taken that as read anyway. Let's find out a bit about you, shall we.' He ran his fingers through his dark hair. 'What was it like in prison?' he asked in the casual manner of someone eliciting information for an entry in a guidebook.

'The food isn't much to write home about. But the staff are very attentive.'

Prison was a subject to which he would return on many

future occasions. He seemed genuinely fascinated by my experience – he didn't do it just to make me feel small.

'Let's move on to hobbies, shall we? What do you do in your spare time? You must have had plenty of that?'

Afterwards he explained that the sole purpose of the interview was to see if we were *simpatico*; could we work together? At the time it was more like the Spanish Inquisition (and no one expects the Spanish Inquisition). His questions proved he'd read my c.v. He quizzed me ruthlessly on my favourite authors (early P.D. James, middle-period le Carré, almost all of Deighton, Patricia D. Cornwell for the forensics, Rendell but not Vine – too many 'sickies'), my taste in music (most jazz piano players – slight preference for the Tatum school over the hornlike playing of Powell and his followers) and then, when my defences were down, launched into a series of complex bridge problems. What would I bid on this, what would I lead on that? Finally produced a diagram, slid it across the table.

'Britain versus Canada,' he said. 'Imagine you're Boris Schapiro. You've opened two no trumps and Terence Reese, your partner, has raised you to three. How do you play the hand?'

West	East
S Q 9	S K 8 5 4
H K 10 6	H Q J 8 4
D A K Q 3	D 5 4
C A K 8 3	C J 9

'Interesting,' I observed.

'So what do you do?' he pressed.

'Start looking on the floor, I think. Looks like a case of "one card short of a deck" to me.'

John smiled. 'Reese had dropped the ace of hearts. Six hearts is cold. Even the best make mistakes sometimes.'

That was my first glimpse of his sense of humour.

I was to suffer many more examples during my baptism in the real world of Acquisitions and Mergers. They were all accountancy variants of the 'left-handed screwdriver' jokes played on engineering apprentices. Each became increasingly more convoluted and more tiresome than the last. It seemed like a long drawn-out – never-ending – initiation ceremony. Until one day I could stand no more. I exploded at him. Called him a stupid schoolboy. Told him what he could do with the job.

He burst out laughing.

To make amends, he bought me lunch. It was accompanied by an expensive bottle of claret and the first of his tutorials on 'the pleasures of the grape'. Then the biggest surprise – I was to partner him at Latimers that evening. I knew, without doubt, he considered me worthy. No more childish pranks. The period of testing was finally over.

To be honest, though, I don't think I ever came to like John.

Maybe it was simply all he had subjected me to in those first months.

Or was it more complex, I wondered? Could it be due in some part to an uneasy sensation that had the embarrassing knack of creeping over me in off-guard moments? Lost within myself I would stare involuntarily across the room at him until the spell was broken: 'A penny for them,' John would say on catching my blank gaze. Would he have considered it money well spent if I had told him what bothered me; come clean about the inexplicable tickle at the back of my mind? The one that kept telling me there was something about him that did not quite add up.

Or was I fooling myself? Perhaps, I admitted, it was just a doubt born out of envy of his lifestyle.

But, whatever my feelings or the reasons behind them, I felt I owed him a debt.

Without his nod of approval I wouldn't have got the job (or the chance to rebuild my life): without his teasing I wouldn't have put in the effort to become so good at it. And my ten per cent share of the bridge winnings provided me with a few luxuries from time to time.

I resolved to rewrite the Bennington's report before Richard had a chance to see the mess John had made of it. The least I could do was protect his reputation.

John had built up the department from scratch. Its success was his achievement, alone. It was his baby, and he clung to it protectively: others in his shoes would have moved on to the higher profile departments with their fast track to promotion.

There was never the need to go through the demeaning process of touting for business. Word-of-mouth recommendation kept us amply supplied with clients.

I liked the work. Didn't want to see it decline. I knew I would be moved on at some stage in order to broaden my experience but I wanted to postpone that time for as long as possible.

Setting aside the half-full bottle of wine, I substituted black coffee in its place – this was a job that demanded a clear head. I would need to go back to the very beginning, take my original working papers and build from there.

At ten o'clock I set to work.

Four hours later I put down my pen, rubbed my tired eyes and wondered what the hell to do next.

Finish the bottle seemed as good a starting point as any. There was little point in trying to get any sleep until my brain had stopped spinning like a catherine wheel, sparks flying in all directions.

The alcohol didn't work any magic trick. As I lay in bed staring up at the ceiling, I hoped it would all look better in the morning. Or at least different.

I was still awake when the knock came at the door.

Collins must have been outside in the street. Watching for the light to go out. Waiting another fifteen minutes to give me time to drift off to sleep. No rest for the wicked – that was evidently his philosophy.

He wanted to talk about files. Typical! It was the last subject I would have chosen.

I hoped he would confine himself to why I had taken them from the office and not delve too deeply into what they contained. Suspicion can be highly contagious.

CHAPTER NINE

What is it about Mondays that makes people behave like fully paid-up members of the Society for the Furtherance of Manic Depression? Some cyclical conjunction of the stars and planets maybe? The daunting prospect of all that must be done in the week ahead? A furry-tongued hangover from Sunday night? Over-exposure to *Songs of Praise*? I could blame red wine and Collins: what was everybody else's excuse?

Ted's smile looked out of place. The reception area was crowded with solemn staff unwilling to move towards their desks. Under the pretence of shaking the drizzle from their raincoats and umbrellas, small mutually exclusive cliques had formed. In the minority were those who had liked John – they stood around looking sad and being supportive of each other: those who hadn't cared much for him were feeling guilty – the consensus of opinion now seemed to be that 'he wasn't such a bad bloke, really'.

'Good morning, Mr Shannon,' Ted said in a loud voice. The effect was the same as if he had shouted 'Unexploded bomb'. There was a mad scurrying to clear the area. Suddenly we were alone.

'Cracker of a match,' he said enthusiastically.

Thank goodness for a note of normality. It would have been all the same to Ted if I had watched the game – once he got into his stride he was unstoppable. For the next ten minutes, I received an animated account of sweetly struck fours, tight bowling and sloppy fielding.

'What a turn-up, eh?' Ted said finally. 'Who'd have thought Sussex would lose? Last ball job, too. "It's never over till the end," they say.'

'Something like that, Ted,' I said with a wry grin. I turned towards the stairs.

'Oh. I nearly forgot, Mr Shannon,' he said. 'Mr Goodwin said to go straight to his office the moment you arrived.'

My grin broadened. 'Thanks a lot, Ted.'

Peggy, Richard Goodwin's secretary, greeted me with a glance at her watch and a click of her tongue. She was wearing a white blouse and a woollen skirt which hung three inches below the knee. In fact, she always wore a white blouse and woollen skirt which hung three inches below the knee: there must be whole production lines devoted solely to kitting her out. The only concession Peggy made to the change of seasons was to shed her cardigan in summer. Today her outfit was completed by a small china brooch in the shape of a miniature basket of primroses (she also had one of poppies and another of forget-me-nots), sensible flat-heeled shoes in soft leather and thick brown support-stockings. Her thick-rimmed reading glasses hung around her neck. She looked, and indeed was, the model of efficiency. What a wise choice, everyone agreed, Mrs Goodwin had made.

Peggy picked up the tray of coffee. I opened the connecting door to Richard's inner sanctum and followed as she bustled inside.

'Good to see you, old boy,' said Richard, welcoming me as if I had just returned from a round-the-world tour. He was wearing a charcoal suit – and a black tie. A casual wave of his hand invited me to sit down.

'I was just saying to Peggy what a bad business this is,' he said. She looked up from pouring the coffee and nodded. 'Bad business indeed, sir,' Peggy echoed. She was still tutting loudly as she left the room.

'Did that fellow Collins catch up with you?' Richard asked.

'Eventually,' I replied.

'Suspicious bugger, isn't he?' Richard said. 'Still, I suppose it's the number one requirement of the job. He was pretty cut up about the files being removed.' You don't have to tell me that, I said to myself. 'Imagined you were up to all sorts of skulduggery.' My bleary eyes were a testament to that fact. 'He seemed most disappointed when I told him that I'd been the one to break the lock.' Richard glanced at me to see my reactions. I raised an eyebrow to invite him to continue. It seemed as if he wanted to explain. I already knew the story – Collins had shown an unexpected talent at impersonation when relating it.

'I had to know exactly what was going on,' he said matter-of-factly. 'John didn't always keep me in the picture. Too damned fond of playing his cards close to his chest. There were plans to be made – life must go on, you know.'

He swivelled in the chair and stared out of the window. 'Lucky for you that I could tell Collins nothing was missing. Got you off the hook. I only had a quick look, of course.' He paused momentarily for thought before swinging back to face me. 'There was nothing unexpected, I suppose?'

'Everything seems to be there – as far as I can tell,' I said. 'I'll check more thoroughly in the next few days.'

He seemed satisfied with the answer. 'Down to business, then,' he said, closing the subject.

'I'm moving Metcalfe across to take over,' Richard said.

I tried not to show my surprise. It was not the choice I would have made. Metcalfe, the number two in the Audit Department, wasn't famous for his imagination. He was an old-fashioned, back room plodder rather than a front line man. It smelt like one of Richard's Machiavellian moves – another of his barons installed as Head of Department.

'You'll have to soldier on for a couple of weeks, I'm afraid. Audits to wrap up, clients to see.'

That suited me.

'The Bennington's report is the top priority. Should have gone last week, by rights. How much longer before it's finished? Can we say Wednesday?'

I played for time.

Told him about the inquest. My promise to Sofia.

He looked at me searchingly. Examining my motives, no doubt. I wondered if Richard had his sights on Sofia: although married with two teenage sons he had a reputation as an incorrigible philanderer. Did he see me as competition? As a threat to some scheme he was concocting?

Then he surprised me. Told me to take as much time off as I needed. Gave me till the end of the week on Bennington's. He would clear it with the client.

Richard collected my unfinished cup of coffee and placed it back on the tray. My audience was over.

I could get down to some work now. Well, not quite yet.

I spent thirty minutes guarding the fax machine as my letter to Arlene crawled its way along the line to her hotel in Paris. Then, back in my office, set about a long series of phone-calls.

Arranged insurance on the car.

Booked a slot with my bank manager.

Fixed to meet Mrs Simmons, John's cleaner, after work.

Spoke to Old Man Bennington himself – determinedly countered his excuses, stood impervious to his protestations, until he was forced to agree to an appointment on the Wednesday morning.

Eventually, I got down to some proper work.

Despite Richard's admission about breaking into the desk, I still wanted to go through all the files. Tidy up a little, prepare a progress report on all the projects for my new boss. Metcalfe had a lot to learn and I might as well start teaching him now.

I was only on the third file when Sofia rang.

She sounded more composed, if not exactly relaxed. Told me she had slept well, felt so much better; believed she could cope now – with my help, that is.

The inquest, she informed me, was set for 2.00 pm tomorrow. Would I pick her up at 12.30? Perhaps we could have some lunch first?

If that was the effect a good night's sleep had on her, then I wished I'd been granted one too.

*

My bank manager looked upon me as a personal challenge. He was one of the new thrusting breed raised on the sweet milk of the mother doctrine of cross-selling: to him, I was a 'prospect' rather than a customer. Never a month went by without my receiving some urgent, importuning word-processed communication extolling the virtues of a Tessa, PEP, pension plan, endowment policy or whatever other product was flavour of month. When the soft-sell brought no response, the campaign had escalated. I started getting phone-calls at work or invitations to see him at his office. He had only my interests at heart (how reassuring!) – I should make my capital work for me, not let it lie idle in a deposit account.

But I always refused to touch the money. Never gave any reasons. If he cared that much he could find out for himself. Why should I relive the painful memories just to fill in some field on his database? And, if I did tell him, where should I start and what should be included or omitted?

Susie was always Dad's favourite: he spoilt her rotten, especially as she grew older and I was away at university. It's only natural that there is a strong bond between father and daughter. So, I suppose, it was only natural that Dad should be hurt most by Susie's accident.

From that day, he was a broken man – never again the father I had known and loved. Each week brought a new depth to his depression and increased his autistic withdrawal from the world.

He lost his job – came close to losing our sympathy, as well. Too apathetic for anything else, he spent all his time sitting and staring into space. But that wasn't the worst of it all. Susie was his baby, his little darling: yet he never even spoke to her after that first night in the hospital.

I used to wish he would let his emotions spill out, even if it meant an explosion of anger. All I got was a grunt from time to time: Mum was ignored totally. The doctor tried his bedside manner and a variety of pills. A psychiatrist spent fruitless hours in an effort to break through. But nothing seemed to make any difference.

Until my act of murder. That merciful release provided the catalyst to bring him round.

My mother, on her only visit to Brixton, smiled for the first time in months when she told me he was making progress. A new drug he'd been prescribed seemed to be working wonders. This was the turning point, she said. Everything would be all right from now on. I knew just how wrong she was, but I couldn't bring myself to spoil her moment of happiness. I squeezed her hand tightly.

Three days later the police found them. The postman had noticed a strange smell wafting through the letter box.

Mum was upstairs in bed, a pillow over her face.

Dad had killed her. Then taken all the pills he'd been hoarding for such a purpose – how devious the mind of a madman.

He chose Susie's bed as his last resting place.

I suppose their death was another reason why I accepted prison so philosophically. Was I guilty of murder after all?

The money we were about to discuss was what remained after selling the house and settling the mortgage and other debts. My solicitor had handled the whole sorry business for me. He had even tried to persuade the insurance companies to pay out on the policies – but suicide and murder were not covered. I didn't give a damn. The money could rot for all I cared.

But now I had found a purpose for it.

'So you have finally decided to make use of the money?'

I could see cash registers ringing in his eyes.

'Yes,' I informed him with a straight face. 'I'm going to stake it all on a game of cards!'

That shut him up. He sighed and drew a mental line through my name on the mailing list.

He made a token effort to dissuade me, but I detected a hint of admiration in his manner for the sheer daring, if not foolhardiness of my plan – perhaps deep down he longed to break free of his banker's shackles and do something reckless himself. So, in the end, he agreed. What else could he do? It was my money to do with as I liked.

He prepared a Letter of Credit for me to present to Latimers. I was good, it said in convoluted legalistic jargon, for fifty thousand pounds – the bank would honour any debt up to that amount.

Arlene and I had our stake.

And if I lost it all in a good cause, then what the hell.

Good riddance to bad money.

*

I arrived in the mews at six o'clock.

Stood wavering outside John's house. Still in two minds at the thought of living there. Was this really the right thing to do? Even for Sofia, could I go through with it?

I told myself not to be stupid. It was only a house after all. If I believed in ghosts then there were enough in my past to haunt me without having to worry about one more.

I felt in my pocket for the key. Bright and shiny like a newly minted coin, it needed coaxing to open the door. I remember thinking I must change the lock as one of the first priorities. I had read that burglars had a habit of repeatedly robbing the same house. No sense in taking chances, no matter how unlikely it was that the killer would return.

I reached inside the hall and flicked on the light. Traces of carbon powder lined the surface of the white plastic switch. What I recognised as my own fingerprint – a series of complex whorls with three deltas which the arresting officer many years ago had described knowledgeably as 'accidentals' – stood out in sharp relief. I took out my handkerchief and started to wipe away the mark.

'Now, you just leave all that to me, Mr Shannon.'

I spun around to see Mrs Simmons standing in the open doorway.

She was short – and very round. Fourteen stone, I estimated. Mid-fifties. Dark hair set firmly into closely spaced, rippling waves that clung tenaciously around her chubby face as she shook her head at me.

'Why don't I show you around,' she said, 'and you can let me know if there's anything special you want done.'

'Could we start upstairs?' I said, hoping to leave the sitting room until I was mentally better prepared to cope with the memories of my previous visit.

She led the way, flicking on lights as she went. Up the steep stairs and into the bedroom at the front of the house.

'This is . . . was . . . Mr Weston's room.'

She marched across and drew back the heavy curtains to give more light. The room was a shambles (as were all the others, we would later discover). It had been searched thoroughly – and with a heavy hand. Bedclothes lay on the floor, the mattress bare and askew where it had been thrown back after the divan had been examined. The wardrobe doors were open, revealing clothes lying in heaps at the bottom. All the drawers from the bedside cabinet had been removed, their contents tipped into one pile.

Mrs Simmons shook her head in frustration. 'I wish I'd been here,' she said. 'I wouldn't have let them get away with this. I'd have given them a good kick up the arse – pardon my French – and then kept them here until they'd put everything back exactly where they'd found it.'

I wish I'd been here to watch, I thought. It would have been an interesting battle of wills: I knew which side my money was on.

'Don't you worry, Mr Shannon,' she reassured me. 'I'll have all this as right as rain by the time you move in.'

I followed her along the corridor to the second bedroom which John had evidently used as a study. It was just big enough to accommodate a single bed along one wall and a large reproduction desk under the window. A jumble of papers lay strewn over the inlaid leather top. I took three paces across the little room and looked out through the glass at the postage stamp of long, thick grass below. The garden was enclosed for privacy at ground level by a high brick wall along the three sides. A strong wooden gate, set into the far wall, provided access to the narrow alleyway beyond.

'I won't touch the papers, if you don't mind,' she said firmly. 'Mr Weston was most particular about that.'

Next on the guided tour was the bathroom. White powder had been puffed onto the mirrors of the open bathroom cabinet and the surfaces of the dark blue suite. Mrs Simmons scooped up the towels and threw them outside, ready for the first of many loads of washing in the morning.

Downstairs she showed me the galley-style kitchen and the adjoining dining area which extended back under the angle of the stairs. Unwashed mugs of coffee littered every worktop, evidence of how long the scene-of-crime officers had spent going over the house.

Finally we entered the sitting room.

Mrs Simmons gave a sharp intake of breath.

The shelves were bare. Books, CDs, ornaments had been scattered about the floor in random unsteady mounds. An electronic keyboard hovered precariously on its stand by the window. The adjacent wall bore a streak of red, evidence of the path the bloody sword had followed after slicing through its target.

Thankfully, the dustsheets were still on the carpet.

Knowing what she would find underneath, Mrs Simmons did not flinch. She marched purposefully across and pulled back the edges of the cover.

'I'll do the best I can,' she said with resignation. 'Lots of cold salty water is the best thing. But the stain will still show, you know.'

She saw the appalled look in my face. Gave me a big motherly smile.

'I'll make us both a nice cup of tea. Don't you fret, Mr Shannon. It will look a lot better once I've given it a good going over. Come on. This way.'

I sat at the black oak dining table. Watched her don a pair of rubber gloves and run a sinkful of hot water while waiting for the kettle to boil. By the time she joined me, the kitchen was a long way towards meeting her exacting standards – worktops shiny; fridge examined and offending contents emptied into a black sack; everything gradually returning to its proper place.

I asked her what John paid her. It didn't sound much,

especially given the nature of the extra work involved in putting the place to rights. I proposed a higher figure. 'Let's see how we get on, shall we,' she replied, to my surprise. 'Give it a couple of weeks and see how you feel then.'

'How often do you come in?' I asked as I drank some of John's Earl Grey tea and she downed a steaming cup of Tetley.

'I used to come in on Monday and Thursday mornings.'

'What do you mean "used to"?'

'I thought you knew. You working with Mr Weston and all. He gave me the sack a couple of weeks ago.'

The least Sofia could have done was warn me.

'Mrs Simmons . . .' I started uncertainly.

'Call me Rita, dear,' she interrupted.

'Rita,' I began again, 'why exactly did he . . .' I searched unsuccessfully for a euphemism that didn't sound trite or archaic, and then settled lamely on repeating her word . . . 'give you the sack?'

'A bolt out of the blue, it was,' she said. I made myself comfortable. She would tell me in her own time and way, it seemed.

'He phoned during *Coronation Street*,' she said in a tone that made it sound like a crime that should carry the death penalty. 'I didn't really take it in at first. There was this big row going on, you see – that bleeding Irishman on his high horse again.' She blushed briefly before racing on with the story. 'I had to ask Mr Weston to repeat what he'd said. That just made him more angry.

'He was screaming fit to burst,' she said. 'Accused me of going through his papers. Called me a nosey old bag, he did.'

She looked at me for some sort of reaction. I shook my head in disapproval, reserving my options on disbelief.

'I told him straight. I'd never touched his precious papers. But he was like a madman. Wouldn't listen. He said I could whistle for my money. And if I didn't give him back the keys, he'd set the police on me. Bloody cheek. I told him where to stick his lousy few quid.'

She picked up her cup, her hand shaking with temper, and finished off what little remained.

'Let's have another cup, Rita,' I said. 'This time I'll make it.'

She looked at me uncertainly, decided I could probably manage the important task of tea-making and nodded her assent.

Her fury at John seemed genuine enough. And he had obviously trusted her enough to leave large sums of money lying around. Why kick up such a fuss? From what little I knew of her, and my new-found knowledge of John, I was inclined to take her side. The episode sounded very much like a replay of the argument with Sofia. All emotion and no logic. Classic symptoms of paranoia.

There was another possibility, of course: both Rita *and* John believed they were telling the truth.

CHAPTER TEN

Two hours later, and none the wiser, I shut the door and stepped out into the mews. A kitten, invisible but for its bright yellow eyes, made me jump as it miaowed loudly and then skittered nervously out of my way.

It was a black, moonless night. The harsh cones of sodium from the widely spaced streetlights were tiny islands in a sea of darkness. A soft glow leaked through the thick curtains of the windows opposite, casting pockets of thin, misty light into the air. Half a mile away at Victoria Station the streets would be alive with the hustle and bustle of London night-life: here, the mews was empty and noiseless.

Rita had given me directions to the row of lock-up garages where the residents kept their cars. The cottages in the mews fronted directly onto the narrow, cobbled street. I had to pick my way slowly and carefully to avoid stumbling on the uneven surface. My footsteps were light and measured.

The ones behind me were quick and heavy: they made dull thumping sounds on the stones.

I turned right towards the garages and glanced back over my shoulder.

There were three of them. None over the age of twenty. Clone-like, they all wore jeans, black leather bomber jackets and Doc Martens. They looked like a deputation from the radical wing of the Millwall Supporters Club, except for the absence of scarves tied to wrists.

I could see the row of garages ahead of me. No more than fifty yards. It might just as well have been fifty miles.

'Here you!' one of them shouted.

I turned to face them. I could tell instantly that it would be a waste of breath to reply. This wasn't three lads out for an evening constitutional around the backstreets of London. They were looking for a fight. And I was the convenient victim.

They split up and took positions as if this were a well practised set-piece – a corner followed by a free kick, probably.

The ringleader stood in the middle of the narrow cul-de-sac. I couldn't see his face because the light from the lamp-post was shining directly behind him. He cast a long, dark shadow. He looked as big as a mountain – and just as immovable. His two sidekicks, only small by comparison, took up positions on either side, close to the walls.

My retreat was blocked.

And, in front of me, nowhere to run. I'd never reach the garage and get it unlocked in time.

There were no preliminaries. No taunts; no jibes; no 'What have we got here, then?' They needed nothing from me to stir them. Their minds were already made up. A simple nod of the head and movement of the hand from the one in charge and they were running towards me.

I backed against the wall. Limit the attack to one direction – that's what Arthur had counselled.

What else had he drummed into me?

When threatened by a group – go for the leader (or the biggest if you're not sure who is giving the orders). If you make the mistake of taking on – and managing to beat – one of the minions, then the leader will still fancy his chances. You're no better off. But if you can eliminate the main threat, the rest will think twice and most likely turn tail and run.

And, Arthur was prone to counsel, try to do something unexpected. Throw your attacker a curve: cast doubt in his mind.

Above all else, think quick – or you're dead.

It seemed a lot to put into practice.

I took out the set of keys. Held the ring in the palm of my right hand. Pushed each of the three keys into the spaces between my fingers. Clenched my fist.

A simple, but effective, knuckleduster. How's that for improvisation, Arthur?

They must have thought it would be easy. Hadn't anticipated any resistance. Expected me to roll over like a lamb to the slaughter. They hesitated now, the sight of the three pieces of metal gleaming in the yellow light from the lamp causing them to reassess their plan.

'Man Mountain' reacted first. He charged like a lumbering bull, legs kicking out wildly as he came within reach of his target. I could see the deep-patterned heavy sole of his right boot as it travelled in an arc. Straight for my stomach.

If it connected, I would finish up on the ground and my head would be next on the hit list.

God, he was big. But he lacked agility.

I sidestepped quickly to the left.

Saw his boot miss me by inches. Heard a dull thud and a curse as he kicked a cloud of red dust from the brick wall.

I hit him in the back of the neck with my elbow. All my strength focused in that blow. His head rocketed forward and crashed against the brickwork.

He turned around, a dazed look on his face, blood running down from his temple.

I hit him full force on the right cheek. At least that had been my intention.

He had bobbed his head to the left.

The keys scraped across the stubble on his chin. Three thin, shallow lines of blood. That was all.

He came straight at me.

I was facing the wall now, my back open to attack from the others. They advanced on me.

Three against one. My heart sank. The outcome was inevitable.

With wildly swinging fists and kicking legs more usually employed as a last resort by prey in a school playground I kept them at bay. But only for a minute or two. That was as long as it took for them to grab my arms and pin them behind my back.

Defenceless, I braced myself. For the blow that would surely come. From the man who wasn't too pleased about the scuffs on his shoe and the blood on his face.

His fist drew back. His face grinned, then froze in the glare of the headlights.

A car raced down the street, its engine revving fit to burst. As it screeched to a halt, the door was already being flung open.

Out jumped DCI Collins.

'Police. Don't move.'

They shot past him like scared rabbits fleeing from a baying hound, and disappeared into the darkness from which they had come.

I don't think Collins was too bothered about their escape. He probably reckoned there were better causes than mine for which to get into a fight.

'In the car,' he said, jerking his thumb in the general direction of the passenger seat.

As I walked out of the light, I saw him reach down and scoop up something from the road.

'You owe me, Shannon,' he said. The thought seemed to please him. 'I think you and me ought to have another of our little chats,' he said.

It was an order – not an invitation.

*

We returned to the house. I found some whisky for Collins – an Islay malt, duty-free litre size – which he sipped respectfully like a true connoisseur. I poured myself a small slug of armagnac and downed it in one gulp to calm my nerves.

'It's a good job I've been keeping an eye on you.'

He motioned towards the dining room table and sat himself

directly opposite me in a deliberate move to replicate the environment of the interview room.

He took off his jacket and dropped it on the floor. Nicotine-stained fingers yanked at his tie and undid the top button of a shirt that looked like it had been slept in – and not just for one night either. He leaned back in the chair rocking it on two legs until he found a precarious point of balance that was supposed to demonstrate relaxed control. I thought he'd kick his shoes off next!

He pinned me to my seat with his eyes. They were blood-shot – serves him right for waking up innocent people in the middle of the night – and might have been a colour stylist's recommendation to co-ordinate with the light brown pupils and ginger eyebrows. His mouth, even with the constant snarl, was thick-lipped and boyish.

'Time to repay your debt, Shannon,' he said sternly. 'Tell me about John Weston. Everything you know. I don't care how small or insignificant the detail might seem. I want to understand the man.'

Me too, I thought.

During my monologue he nodded at regular intervals to encourage me to continue. Stopped me from time to time to clarify a point or probe in greater detail. Where fact became supposition, he questioned my reasoning. Throughout he was alert to every word and studied attentively the expressions on my face.

His eyes never left mine – not even when he was refilling his glass. Which he frequently did.

'This job of yours,' he said, changing the subject, 'does it involve handling money?'

'Not as such,' I said.

'What the hell does that mean?'

I explained briefly the nature of our work. That it involved large sums of money certainly, but that we never saw any of it, all transactions taking place by CHAPS (Clearing House Automatic Payment System) – an electronic transfer from the bank account of the buyer to the seller.

'No cash, no cheques even?'

'All we do is recommend a price: the lawyers handle the final details and prepare all the documents including the transfer authorisation.'

He seemed to be trying to frame a supplementary question when the idea came to me. It must have been lurking in my mind since the Saturday afternoon at the office and then begun to rise slowly to the surface during the inspection of the house.

I asked Collins to wait a moment.

I went to every room in turn. Searched them carefully this time. Looked inside cupboards. Even checked under the beds.

'Well?' Collins asked on my return.

'His briefcase is missing. It wasn't at the office. And there's no sign of it here.'

'What does it look like?' he asked.

'Very big. Black. Pilot's case. A lot of accountants use them. Stacks of room inside for all the clutter we carry around.'

'I think,' he said, after a little deliberation, 'we can now be sure what happened to the head.'

'Yes,' I said thoughtfully. 'But what puzzles me is why?' I had a strange sinking feeling that I already knew the answer to my question.

'Do I really have to spell it out for you?' He was testing me again, reading my face with an eye for the smallest trace of confirmation of his pet theory – he never gave up. Collins sighed wearily. 'How many people do you know, Shannon, who are capable of murder – let alone chopping off a man's head?'

He didn't wait for my reply. The first hint of my pause proved his point.

'Exactly,' he said. 'But it takes a whole lot less guts to hire someone to commit a murder for you. And what better proof that the killer has carried out his part of the bargain?'

Collins reached down for his jacket and fumbled around in the pockets. 'That's one mystery solved,' he said, 'in part, at least. Now for the next one.'

He unfolded a scrap of paper and passed it to me. It was my picture, torn from a newspaper.

'I found that in the road where you were attacked,' he said. 'You weren't the victim of a random mugging – somebody targeted you. Now, why should they do that, I ask myself?'

'Believe me, I have no idea. If I knew, then I'd tell you. I don't want to be forever looking over my shoulder, do I?' The expression on his face told me he was unconvinced.

'Do you frighten easily, Shannon?'

'No,' I said, resenting the question. 'If you're suggesting they were trying to scare me into doing something – or not doing something, for that matter – then it wouldn't work. I don't quit. Threatening me doesn't work.' I hoped he understood what I was saying.

'For once I believe you. I always had you marked down as a stubborn bastard.' I took it as a compliment – I thought I might as well, it was likely to be the nearest I would ever get to hearing one from Collins.

'Still,' he continued, 'they may not know that. Which leaves me with my two original alternatives. Either they were hoping to frighten you into silence or they were going to silence you for good. Like John Weston.'

Collins gave me a smile so brittle with insincerity that it seemed like it would crack into a thousand pieces with the next movement of his lips. 'Whatever, it makes no odds to me. I'm still left with the big question. "Why?"'

He picked up his coat and slipped it on, preparing to make his exit. In the doorway he paused for his passing shot.

'It doesn't look very good for you, does it Shannon? I wonder,' he reflected. 'Who will get you first? Them – whoever they are? Or me?'

*

It was the first time I had driven in eight years.

I looked around the dashboard. Familiarised myself with the minor controls; indicators, lights, heating and so on. Repositioned the mirrors. Set off – apprehensively at first – back to my bedsit.

On the way back my confidence grew. So much so that I had to fight a burning desire to head for the nearest fast stretch of road and test the limits of the car's power and handling characteristics. But I wanted to start packing. It would take at least three trips in this car to transport my few possessions to John's house.

Even so, I postponed the packing for a while. I stood at my window like a child at Christmas, gazing lovingly at my new acquisition below.

It was a conspicuous, idiosyncratic, car – rarely seen on the roads nowadays. John had bought it secondhand as a present to himself when he was confirmed in his position as head of Acquisitions and Mergers. It was one of the post-1981 relaunch versions of the Lancia Monte Carlo, the previous model having been withdrawn after a serious problem with the braking system (any problem with the braking system on this car was serious!).

A two-seater, mid-engined sports car; this one in gleaming silver. Designed by Pininfarina (better known for the flowing curves on Ferraris). Tiny, totally impractical boot at the front. Two litre engine mounted behind the driver's seat giving it the benefit of leech-like road holding with the weight bearing down on the wide rear wheels. And the disadvantage, at anything above three thousand revs, of producing a noise level worthy of a badly serviced jumbo jet.

Immaculate. Still in showroom condition, it appeared. John had twice had it stripped back to the bare metal, the rust (the main reason why so few of the limited production run have survived) scraped away, and resprayed.

Like a child with a new toy, I dragged myself reluctantly from the window. I clipped the Walkman to my belt, turned the volume up on Earl Hines and began stacking books in the cardboard boxes.

It was a therapeutic, mechanical task which without the music would have had my mind wandering down avenues I didn't want to explore. Like tomorrow's inquest, for instance. And the fact that I'd felt it necessary to wedge a chair under the handle of the door to the bedsit.

CHAPTER ELEVEN

Brixton

My new cell was an oversized coffin with amenities. Into a space no more than eight feet by six had been crammed a small table, a chair, and the three b's – bed, basin and bog. In the official terminology I was now a Rule 43 prisoner – under solitary confinement for my own protection. To the other inmates I was 'down among the nonces'. The jargon wasn't strictly correct: there were a few bent coppers along this corridor as well as the rapists, child molesters and other assorted perverts. The common denominator was that none of us would have lasted five minutes anywhere else in the prison.

Ronson had kept his mouth tightly shut, the prisoners' code unbreakable even in his pain and blindness. And the last thing he wanted was for the authorities to take any action against me. That was not the way things were done. The score would be settled his way. Some time, some place, when I least expected it.

Solitary wasn't that bad. I was allowed books and tapes and was able to pass much of each day in these lonely pursuits. And, now that the trial had begun, I had the added diversion of attending court. But there was still too much time for thinking, too many opportunities for drifting unconsciously into the troubled inner reaches of the brain. The last week had provided an aching gut-full of food for thought – and all of it poisoned.

Initially the trial had been a breath of fresh air. My barrister, whose name misleadingly was Ernest, was a tonic to my ailing spirits. He had come highly recommended – which was just as well since his appearance and manner belied his talents. At our first meeting he had arrived breathless in a bright blue track suit, having run the five miles from his home as part of his training for the Berlin marathon. He had acted like an over-grown schoolboy, cracking old jokes, making terrible puns, drawing from a bottomless well of rambling anecdotes and reciting limericks about a young lawyer called Rex. But in court he was a different animal. Serious, concise and sharply aware of the importance of each word spoken or left unsaid.

The schedule of the trial was erratic, being dictated largely by the availability of the expert witnesses. On our side we would be calling on several specialists to give evidence on the medical and psychological problems of paraplegia – both as far as the victim and the relatives were concerned. Our second line of attack was a polemic on euthanasia: among those helping us here were representatives from the Netherlands where this so-called crime was legalised in 1983. The prosecution, for its part, would assemble an equally erudite cast to further its cause and to counter each of our arguments.

I was prepared for the moral and ethical debate, upsetting though it would be on a personal level: before this stage, how-ever, we had to go through the motions of hearing the routine evidence relating to Susie's death.

Doctor Winstanley, the pathologist, made an immediate impact. With his long, uncontrollable grey hair and half-frame spectacles he reminded me of an absent-minded professor. He was in his mid-fifties (a good age for an expert witness, Ernest told me: old enough to leave no doubt about depth of knowl-edge or experience but not too advanced in years so as to appear out of touch or on the borders of senility). He spoke in the detached, almost bored, tone of a man for whom the world held no surprises.

There seemed little point in his testimony: just a confirma-tion of what was already known and admitted. After Winstanley had informed the jury of the cause of death and Susie's medical condition, Ernest prepared himself to rise for the brief utterance of 'No questions'. But the prosecution had not finished.

'Doctor Winstanley,' the Prosecuting Counsel stated, 'you said earlier that your examination was comprehensive in every aspect. Would you be so kind as to tell the jury your findings regarding Miss Shannon's maturity.'

It sounded a bloody funny question to me. Where was it leading? I began to wonder if Winstanley was for some reason going to claim that Susie was incapable of making an adult decision. It was part of our defence that she had knowingly submitted to the injection.

'Although, due to her extremely low bodyweight,' Winstanley began in reply, 'Miss Shannon had ceased to menstruate, she was in all other respects a normal adult female. Indeed I stress the word adult. I found that she was not what is termed "virgo intacta" .' He turned to the jury and, with a condescending smile, said, 'That means she was not a virgin.'

We objected on the grounds of relevance: the prosecution claimed the relevance would be made clear by later witnesses. The judge, true to form, overruled.

I failed to understand what was going on. It made no sense.

Ernest answered my whispered question. 'They've just got themselves another motive,' he said gravely.

'And what the hell might that be?' I asked, still puzzled.

'I hope, for your sake, they stick at jealousy.'

'You're not suggesting . . .' My stomach churned as the implication sank in. 'It's not true. Jesus, only a sickie could believe something like that.'

I hoped to God I was right. Over the course of the next few days I had been unable to restrain myself from jumping to my feet and shouting angrily as I was forced to listen to a series of neighbours and 'friends' make mountains of out molehills. Susie and I were 'very close', they claimed. What did they expect – we were brother and sister, weren't we?

Ernest cross-examined skilfully and scornfully. He exposed the prosecution's stratagem as just that – it was bricks without straw, hypothesis without any solid basis of fact. But the mud (or worse) had been thrown and their hope was that some of it would stick.

I don't think the jury bought any of it for one minute.

Only one person was taken in.

Dad.

I looked again at the letter. The warder had given it to me that morning. It had been opened, of course, and read by the Peeping Tom whose duty it was to act as official censor. (Privacy doesn't exist in prison: that's why you guard with your life what is going on inside your head – it's the only place they can't reach.)

The words were barely legible, the sentences lacked any signs of rationality: bile and rage had driven the pen.

I tore the paper into shreds. Flushed it down into the sewers where it belonged. Then I cried. I cried for Susie. For Mum. For the father who was a stranger to me. And, last of all, I cried for myself.

'I wish they still hanged murderers,' was his final sentence.

That makes two of us.

I should have told Mum about the letter. Warned her that the madness hadn't abated – it had merely changed. And become more dangerous with the new disguise. But my courage failed me: when it came to telling the truth I had been found wanting.

I'd been granted one chance – and fluffed it.

CHAPTER TWELVE

The court was modern, light and garish. It didn't seem right for such an occasion. Traditional, dark and solemn would have been more fitting. The walls were vast landscapes of those rusty-red bricks more usually found on housing estates in Enterprise Zones: in patches, the surfaces were disfigured by the white salts of efflorescence. The roof, absurdly high, was a dome-like construction of huge sheets of glass: the room would be bitterly cold in winter and insufferably hot in summer. Each piece of furniture had been fashioned from the same pale-blonde pine: it had been insufficiently seasoned so that dribbles of shiny, sticky resin stood out like beads of perspiration. The architect must have been either high on some mind-bending drug or have borne a deep personal grudge against the coroner.

A morning spent in ceaseless activity – some of it purposeful, the rest purely displacement – had failed to stop me worrying about how Sofia might react to the inquest. I made four trips to transfer my belongings; sifted diligently, but fruitlessly, through two more files; toured the office drinking coffee and chatting to secretaries; finally resorted to clearing John's desk ready for the next occupant. While spinning out the last task I came across his precious fountain pen. Placing it carefully in an envelope, I wrote Sofia's name on the front and tucked it away in my top drawer. It was too soon now, but maybe she would like it at some future time.

I had arrived at Sofia's flat expecting to see her swathed dramatically from head to toe in black like some Hellenic version of the Scottish Widow. Instead she had dressed as if attending an important business meeting. Grey pinstripe suit, skirt two inches above the knee, navy blue blouse. And high heels. They made her legs look even longer. Was she wearing them for my benefit? Or was it part of a concerted effort to break with the past?

Over lunch, an awkward meal where she had picked at the food and spoken only infrequently, I had confessed my intention to move into John's house that evening. To me it felt like an unduly precipitate leap into 'dead man's shoes'. But the thought didn't seem to cross her mind. Or, if it did, she was untroubled by it.

Sofia and I sat in the front row of the banked seats. A group of journalists perched like carrion crows on the top tier: from this vantage point they could look down on everybody and chatter among themselves without fear of being overheard. Collins, in the central bear pit built to accommodate the various legal professionals and learned experts, turned his head in our direction. To me, he gave another of his porcelain smiles in acknowledgement: to Sofia, an overlong stare. Maybe the combination of short skirt and front row seat hadn't been a wise choice. Or was there more to the look than that? Was he secretly sizing her up to see if she fitted his accomplice theory?

The jury – silent, serious, apprehensive – peered down from a raised platform on our left: the coroner was partly hidden behind a large elevated desk on our right. He looked solid and immovable as if he had been a prop forward in his youth, although too many deskbound days had transmuted the muscle of yesteryear into today's flab.

Most coroners, I learnt later, are part-time and drawn from the ranks of solicitors, barristers or medical practitioners. As this was a busy City Court it warranted a full-time coroner with training in both medicine and the law. Our man spoke in a clear, loud voice that projected up into the far reaches of the room. I noticed a faint Scottish burr to his vowels (trained at St

Andrews?) as he outlined to the attentive jury the purpose of the inquest and their duties.

Under the guidelines issued by the Medical Protection Society there are fourteen individual circumstances whereby a death must be reported to the coroner. In the current case, the pathologist had cause to notify a death under Category Five, 'result of crime or suspected crime'. It was the duty of this inquest to ascertain three issues: the identity of the deceased; how, when and where death occurred; and particulars required by the Registration Acts concerning the death.

DCI Collins was called first. His evidence was brief and to the point. He made reference to the 999 call, read my statement as to the time of my arrival at the house and then gave the bald details of the report from the two officers who attended the incident. Even without any embellishment his description of the body and the scene of the crime was sufficiently graphic to cause the more imaginative members of the jury to shudder.

Sofia's statement formally identifying the body was then read out to the court, relieving her of the ordeal of giving her evidence in person.

The pathologist was last to mount the stairs to the witness box. As he passed in front of me, my nose wrinkled at the smell of formalin which clung to his clothes in an invisible mist. He betrayed no sign of recognising me. But I could never forget – or forgive – him.

Doctor Winstanley had aged badly. Maybe there was some justice in the world, after all. His promotion, secured by dint of the publicity from my trial, from the sticks to the big city had brought problems as well as rewards. What little hair he had left was as white as the aluminium powder he used for lifting fingerprints. He looked tired and care-worn as if retirement could not come soon enough to free him from the unsocial hours and nights of broken sleep. He walked slowly under the excess weight he carried. His breathing was laboured as he prepared to speak.

Much of his evidence, given in the matter-of-fact monotone of boredom rather than detachment, on the conclusions he had drawn from the post-mortem examination was corroborative in nature. A mere formality, it appeared, in the light of what we had already been told.

Time of death he put as certainly less than an hour, and possibly as little as thirty minutes, from his first examination at the scene of the crime – this would coincide almost exactly, he declared with self-satisfaction, with the timing of the 999 call.

He had based his estimate, he explained in a professorial manner for the jury's benefit, on three separate observations.

Firstly, rigor mortis (an unreliable method in isolation of ascertaining time of death) was not present – the body, therefore, had been dead less than six hours (when signs of rigor are detectable) or more than forty-eight (when the stiffening of the body wears off).

Secondly, the body temperature – a cooling of one degree had been recorded: this indicated an elapsed time of approximately forty minutes since death.

Thirdly, the absence of any signs of hypostasis or postmortem lividity (a patchy, bluish-pink discoloration of the skin caused by the cessation of the circulation of the blood): this normally becomes evident between thirty minutes and one hour after death.

Turning to the matter of identification, Winstanley regretted the absence of the head (so did John, I thought): the skull and teeth, he sighed, provide a wealth of information especially in terms of age (the teeth show a remarkably consistent pattern of development up to the age of twenty-five; the sutures of the skull vault begin to close at a fairly standard rate above the age of forty). His findings, nevertheless, did coincide with the description supplied of John Weston – adult Caucasian male; uncircumcised; height (from measurements of the femur and tibia) five feet four inches, plus or minus one inch; blood group O; fingerprints of the victim corresponded to those on all personal items in the house; contact lens found on the carpet matched the prescription on record at Mr Weston's opticians; no scars, tattoos or other peculiarities.

Analysis of the blood showed the absence of alcohol.

However, he concluded as he shuffled his notes together,

internal organs did show the presence of a significant – but non-lethal – amount of cocaine.

Sofia gave me a 'told-you-so' look then shook her head sorrowfully.

The jury trooped out. And returned after a matter of minutes. There was nothing for them to discuss. No need for debate. The coroner had directed them as to their only verdict.

John Weston, the foreman announced, had been killed by 'person or persons unknown'.

It seemed all over. Only the jury to be thanked for their time and then we could leave. The coroner turned to Collins.

'I have received requests from the parents of the deceased, and from Miss Kalamboukis, for the body to be released so that the appropriate arrangements may be made for the funeral. Do the police have any objections?'

Collins consulted Winstanley.

He chose his words carefully.

'Although we understand the wishes of those concerned, we regret that we are unable to comply with these requests. I am sure the court will appreciate that we have to guard against the possibility that when an arrest has been made, and the culprit subsequently brought to trial, defence counsel at that time may wish to commission an independent post-mortem analysis. I would like to express my sympathy to the relatives and to emphasise that this is common practice. Not merely a whim on our part.'

His last remark was aimed solely at the reporters. A preemptive attack in case any of them were thinking of painting him, or the authorities he represented, as callous and unfeeling.

In spite of appreciating the reasons for the refusal to release John's body, I felt sad for those who needed the finality of a funeral to lay his memory to rest.

At my side, Sofia's expression said it all – disappointment, disillusionment at the system and, above all, despair.

She was as much in limbo as John.

*

I took Sofia back to her flat. Politely, she refused my offer to stay until Sally arrived back from work. She wanted to speak to John's parents, break the news of the court's decision before they heard it on the radio or read about it in the papers. Then decide what next to do.

There seemed little point in going back to the office, even if I had felt in the mood. I set off for my new home, collecting a few groceries and stopping off at a butcher's en route.

Mrs Simmons had done a marvellous job. The house bore little resemblance to the distressing sight we had witnessed the previous evening. Order had been restored. Just a damp, slightly stained carpet and a conspicuously clean stripe on the wall remained as evidence of what had occurred.

For the next couple of hours I pottered around. Unpacked my boxes and bags. Began to clear the wardrobe and drawers in the bedroom. I wanted at least one room in the house that was mine – not John's.

I filled four black sacks with his clothes. Dumped them out of mind's eye in the study.

I was in the kitchen making coffee when the doorbell rang.

My first thought was that it must be the maternal Mrs Simmons coming to check on me.

Instead it was Sally.

Same jeans and sandals. Same 'little girl lost' look. The only difference in her appearance was that her long straight hair had ridges of tiny creases at the sides where it had been pinned up all day.

She thrust a bottle of wine into my hand. 'Peace offering,' she said. 'Sorry for being such a selfish pig. I was so wrapped up in my own thoughts that I forgot my manners.'

'You apologised before,' I said with an understanding smile. 'Even that wasn't necessary. You said yourself it was an awkward time. I appreciated that.'

'Anyway,' she continued, 'I thought you might be in need of some company tonight. May I come in?'

'On one condition,' I replied.

She frowned, unsure of what I would say next.

'That you join me for dinner. How good are you in the kitchen?'

She gave me a weak smile as I ushered her in. I could tell the evening was going to be hard work.

For such a simple meal it took a long time to prepare. With neither of us knowing where anything was kept we made a pretty inefficient team. And my mind was still preoccupied with trying to work out what was troubling her. Give her time, I decided. She'll tell me when she's ready.

The kitchen seemed to have shrunk in size as we both bustled about getting in each other's way. She brushed against me once. Became flustered. Backed off quickly.

I poured the red wine. Suggested she set the table. Left to my own devices, I quickly finished off making the salad, mixed some olive oil, garlic vinegar and mustard for the dressing and flash-fried the fillet of lamb. With the French bread it would stretch for two of us – I doubted if either of us had that much appetite, in any case.

She had placed the cutlery so that we were seated opposite each other. Napkins, unearthed from some hiding place, rested underneath the knives. The lights had been dimmed by a notch or two. Their glow was soft and warm – I wished that a little of those qualities would rub off on Sally.

In an effort to break the ice I asked her about Sofia.

'She's all right,' Sally said. 'Almost back to her old self by the time I left. She'd talked to John's parents. They've decided to hold a memorial service for him. I think Sofia feels that will be the end of it. She can pay her last respects. Then start a new life. She's even talking of going away for a holiday.'

'Maybe the worst is over,' I said.

'Yes.' Her reply lacked conviction. She opened her mouth as if about to continue but thought better of it. Her attention turned towards the food. Cutting a small experimental slice of lamb, she popped it gingerly between her lips.

'This is good,' she said, sounding surprised but genuinely enthusiastic. At last, I thought. The barrier's coming down.

'It just goes to show,' I said with a grin, 'that not all men are absolutely helpless.'

The knife and fork fell from her hands and clattered onto the plate. Tears formed in her eyes and then streamed uncontrollably down her cheeks. She clutched at the napkin and hid behind it.

I moved around the table to squat beside her. Put my arm on her shoulder and drew her towards me, cuddling and comforting her tiny body.

We stayed in that position for so long that the muscles in my legs began to ache. At last the tears dried and the shaking stopped. Then she let me coax the story from her.

Afterwards, alone with my thoughts, I didn't feel I had been much help. Apart from listening, that is. Despite my own misgivings, I had advised her to go to the police. Collins and Baxter would be sympathetic to someone like her. And they were the professionals, after all. They would know what action to take – if, indeed, any was needed.

But it was not what she wanted to hear.

The suggestion filled her with horror.

It would be like an act of betrayal, she had said.

CHAPTER THIRTEEN

The following morning I stood, knees bent, in front of the mirror on the bathroom cabinet. Shaving. Very awkwardly. If I was going to stay in this house for any length of time then raising the height of the cabinet would have to be my second priority after changing the locks.

I took out the after-shave which Arlene had provided. Used a liberal, wince-inducing palmful to staunch the cuts. Replaced the bottle in the near empty cabinet once packed to bursting point with John's lotions and potions.

It was a little past seven when I tossed my briefcase onto the front seat of the car. By ten to eight I was free of the traffic and approaching the Eastway. A few more miles and I would be on the motorway and the car could have its first real test. I settled back in the black leather racing seat, felt its contours hug my body. Scrabbled around in the door pocket where John kept his cassettes. The boxes were all unlabelled so my choice, if that is what you could call it, was made at random. I slipped the tape in the machine. Cut off some rural cleric – apart from Rabbi Lionel Blue they all sounded indistinguishable to me – in mid-parable during *Thought for the Day*.

I actually jolted in the seat with surprise. The steering wheel twitched in my hands. The car zigzagged momentarily along the road until I regained control.

I had expected John's taste in music to be pretty much

middle-of-the-road (Phil Collins, maybe, Fleetwood Mac, that sort of thing – easy to listen to, aural wallpaper).

Out of the four loudspeakers boomed the unmistakable sound of New Orleans. Jelly Roll Morton, the self-styled 'inventor of jazz', was honky-tonkying his way across the keyboard playing his own composition *Mr Jelly Lord*.

Every day brought some new surprise about John.

I was beginning to wonder if I knew him at all.

*

I stopped for breakfast and to give my ears a break from the thunder of the engine. In my haste to put the car through its paces, I'd set off ridiculously early. I lingered, against the better judgement of my stomach, over the inexpertly cooked, unappetising plate of greasy food and the thin, weak coffee that accompanied it. At least an article in *The Times* brought a smile, albeit a cynical one, to my lips. It was an interview with David Yates, whose constituency lay in my home territory over to the east, in which he uttered unconvincing protestations denying any interest in the Chancellor's job ('but if, in the Prime Minister's wisdom, he were to . . .'). He had all the confidence of a self-made millionaire – and about as much charm. He handled the media well – courted publicity and knew how to use it to his best advantage. Hardly surprising, I thought, since the report said he had spent his early business life in advertising.

John would have cut ten minutes off my travelling time to Cambridge. But he liked to see if he could scare me at a hundred and ten or more miles per hour. I was happy cruising along at eighty (with the odd burst of a hundred on the clear stretch north of Bishops Stortford – but only when I was sure there were no police cars around). I throttled back in alarm at one point when a white Sierra hung tenaciously a couple of hundred yards behind me for a good five miles before eventually turning off at Duxford.

When I arrived, Old Man Bennington treated me with typical contempt: he made me wait in reception until twenty minutes after the time of our appointment. If I was right, he was playing it cool.

Bennington's had built their name by manufacturing (if that was not too vulgar a word to use) luxury hand-made travel goods in leather and canvas. The design of their suitcases had been largely unchanged since the days of the Raj: classic lines, solid construction, thick straps and buckles, steel reinforcement to the sides which produced a gross weight that only those buyers with a retinue of servants could contemplate. A Bennington suitcase had been the acme of fashion, a visual demonstration of style and status. In the early eighties it had experienced a revival, gaining a new following: pop stars, TV personalities, international footballers carried them – or paid someone else to do so.

Charles Bennington – called 'Old Man' by his workers to distinguish him from 'Young Mister', his son who worked in Marketing – was the third generation of his family to preside over the company. His grandfather had founded the business during the last years of the Victorian era when the Empire was at its height and 'gentlemen' travelled its length and breadth administrating – or just plain adventuring. His father had taken the company through the lean years of the Second World War by winning government contracts to supply the Army with cheap cardboard suitcases. Through his efforts the company survived, if not actually prospered, until peace returned. During the fifties and sixties he added extensions to the range – handbags, purses, briefcases and the like – and Bennington's flourished once more.

Charles, not the brightest of the clan, had done his limited best when the reins eventually passed into his hands.

But he was hampered on two fronts. A desire to break new ground for its own sake – to be seen to be doing something different from his forebears; to prove himself as an individual. And a complete lack of any strategy to accomplish that aim.

His management style could only be described as schizophrenic. He was forever in two minds as to where the company should be heading – small quantities of high margin goods (safe

117

but unoriginal) or high volume, mass market, 'value for money' products (a risky new horizon).

So he tried to have the best of both worlds.

And suffered the inevitable consequences.

While continuing with the traditional items against increasing competition from designers such as Louis Vuitton and the new wave labels, he also dabbled in products like 'bum belts' and went into the hitherto uncharted territory of mail order – such moves only serving to cheapen the respected name.

In recent times Bennington's had seen its profits decline year after year. With no suitable successor – Charles had placed his son in Marketing because he felt that was where the boy could do least harm – there was only one alternative left.

Sell the company.

Get what he could for it while there was still the chance of attracting a buyer. That was where John and I came into the picture (a Hieronymus Bosch seemed most fitting).

Our client was an upmarket travel company (expensive cruises up the Nile, tented safaris, exotic secluded destinations, cultural tours of China and the like – not quite 'across the Andes by yak', but almost). They saw a benefit in the Bennington name. Recognised that its connotations of quality and nostalgia could add value to its own image. It would be a logical acquisition. At the right price, that is. They planned to strip the company back to its roots. Invest in the brand. Sell off the unwanted parts of the business (a swift kick up the bum bag, John had joked), together with their freehold properties.

From the figures I had pored over for three weeks in some cupboard unworthy of being called an office, the company was not worth much. Especially when compared to what it could have fetched ten years ago.

It is a relatively simple matter to calculate the worth of a company, once its profitability has been determined (and that is the hard part). The base value of the company follows a formula whereby the post-tax profits for the last year (or, where recent events have affected the performance significantly, the forecast profits for the coming year) is multiplied by a factor –

the Price Earnings Ratio – that reflects the element of risk in the business and the market in which it operates. Safe blue-chip companies (banks, insurance companies and the like) can command factors of twelve or more; risky ventures may have a factor as low as five. To this valuation an adjustment is then made for the assets of the company – the properties it owns, the reserves it has put by in the past, for instance. But the biggest determinant of price is the level of profits, since this figure is multiplied up by the PE Ratio (and in many companies the assets may be very small if the company has no property, or has always distributed its profits as dividends rather than building up reserves). Hence the importance of our calculations of profit, since a small error may be multiplied ten fold – overestimate the profit by £100,000 and you finish up by overvaluing the company by a million pounds.

As far as Bennington's was concerned, even if we recommended paying seven or eight times the post-tax profits (and that seemed a trifle generous on recent performance), plus a little extra for the fixed assets, then two million pounds would be a reasonable offer.

The valuation in John's draft report had been nearer to three.

*

Old Man Bennington at least paid me the courtesy of rising from his desk when I entered his office. He was in his late fifties. Almost bald. Short. And extremely fat. He reminded me of an aged Billy Bunter. With the same impish mind too, I suspected.

I suppose he was hoping for a series of routine technical questions. Ones for which he had already prepared answers. He seemed calm enough.

'I want in,' I said, looking him straight in the eye. It wasn't a particularly subtle opening gambit I admit, but I didn't think subtlety was Charlie's long suit.

He went red in the face. His blood pressure, normally high under the best of circumstances, rose to dam-busting proportions. In the silence of the room I could almost hear his heartbeat. And his mind ticking away as his tiny porcine eyes looked at me in confusion.

After a pause that made Arthur seem like a member of MENSA, Charlie said, 'I don't know what you mean.'

I didn't think it sounded very convincing – even to himself.

'The deal you had with John. I want a slice of the action.'

'I'm sorry to disillusion you,' he said, trying to sound affronted, 'but you must have made some mistake. If that's all you have come here to say, then I'm afraid this meeting is at an end.'

He rose unsteadily from the desk.

I sat where I was.

'Come on, Charlie,' I said, following my hunch with mounting confidence. 'Don't play the financial virgin with me. It doesn't suit you.'

I took out a cigarette. Lit it despite his appalled look. Calmly blew the smoke across the desk.

'Whose idea was it?' I asked. 'John's or yours?'

His hand hovered over the telephone. Was he going to call my bluff? Have me ejected from the building? Forcibly, if necessary?

He couldn't make up his mind.

Time for a different approach. Increase the pressure.

'Did you get cold feet, Charlie? Did you think he'd keep coming back for more? Is that why you had John killed?'

Panic set in. He had been prepared to defend a minor crime but this was a different league.

I saw the desperation in his face.

'Believe me,' he begged, 'I had nothing to do with Weston's death – although I wasn't sorry to read about it. I thought he was a little shit, if you must know.'

His new-found honesty didn't change my opinion of him. Pathetic!

'It was all his idea,' he said excusingly. 'He made it sound so simple. Said he'd done it before. No chance of getting caught.

'Where was the harm in it?' He looked at me for confirmation. Saw my look of contempt. 'After all, it's just petty cash to your client.'

'No-one likes being conned out of a million pounds, Charlie. It's a dangerous game at those stakes. Did John pay for it with his life?'

'Look, I've told you. I didn't kill him. I had no reason. Weston was safe from me. He said he would have to smooth out the first audit. Cover our tracks. I needed him till then.'

And what about after, I wondered?

'So it was all his doing, was it?' I asked. 'John suggested fiddling the work-in-progress, did he? What did you do? Bribe a few hard-up buyers so that you could invoice them for goods they hadn't received?'

'If I were that clever do you think I would need to sell the company? Weston knew all the tricks. He explained that a few grand laid out in backhanders would allow us to move revenue into the sales ledger – increase the profits at a stroke. It wasn't as if we were never going to deliver the goods. What difference does a few weeks make?'

There are strict guidelines – defined under SSAP 9 (Statements of Standard Accounting Practice) – laid down for the treatment of work-in-progress. For the very simple reason that it is often a cloudy and judgemental issue – therefore, very easy to fiddle. It was one of the areas where we spent a lot of time verifying the company's calculations. If a company has produced goods but not sold them then it is not permitted to take the profit on those products. In accounting terms, a company may only value work-in-progress according to the cost of manufacture of those goods, not their sales value. Move an item from work-in-progress into sales and the value increases dramatically – and the profits rise commensurately.

'And upping the value of your stock of hides? Was that John's doing?'

Bennington nodded.

'Who engaged the surveyor to revalue the property?'

'That was John too. They were old friends. He'd used him before – lots of times, he said.'

'And what was John's cut from all this?

'Just five per cent of the increase in value,' he said. It must have seemed a real bargain to Bennington.

'I had to pay upfront,' he continued. 'He insisted on that. Said someone had tried to renege on a deal in the past.'

I could see Bennington making calculations in his head. The look of fear left his eyes. The glint of greed replaced it.

'What if I offer you the same deal?' he said. 'Fifty thousand pounds. Just think what you could do with that.'

I had what I had come for. Confirmation of my suspicions. I didn't need to think about the offer.

'I've spent enough time in prison. I don't intend to go back. Ever.'

Bennington saw the determination on my face. He slumped in the chair, finally accepting defeat. From his mouth came a loud groan. The thought of a term in prison must have filled him with dread. The disgrace. The loss of liberty. The food!

'How much is your freedom worth, Charlie?'

I could see him ready to clutch at the straw I was offering.

'I'd be willing to turn a blind eye,' I said, 'on one condition.'

A spark of hope lit up his face.

'Anything,' he said.

'I'll recommend a price of one million,' I said. 'You better take it. Sauce for the goose, Charlie.'

CHAPTER FOURTEEN

What did it matter that Charles Bennington was an entrepreneurial palooka. That he would never win a 'Mr Nice Guy' award. Despite my feelings about the man, I couldn't help but believe him. There was the ring of truth in his story. It didn't seem possible that he had been behind John's death. For one thing, the concept of murder would have been too much for his mind to grapple with. It was simply too big a decision for him ever to make.

But there might be others who were more strong-minded. Single-minded even, when it came to dealing with blackmailers.

From what Bennington had said I had the sneaky feeling that John would not have been satisfied with just one payment. When it came round to the time of the audit, he would have come back for more.

And would it have stopped there?

If Charlie was telling the truth, this was not the first time that John had pulled this stunt. For all I knew there could be dozens of similar examples in the past. There was only one way to find out. Wade through the papers on every job since John had started in the department.

I found the prospect daunting – but exciting.

The chirpy voice of Timpkins floated into my mind. As if he were there at my side. Like in the old days. Encouraging me. 'You can do it,' he seemed to say. 'You're beginning to know his mind. Concentrate on the scams he would most like to brag about if he were alive, safe on some desert island, lying in the sun, dusky-skinned bimbo by his side. The dodges, the deceptions, where he would have derived the biggest sense of achievement. Those that would have been stunningly obvious to someone with an equal brain and an ounce of insight.'

All this occurred to me on the drive back, my system floating high on a tidal flood of bitterness and anger. I was bitter at John; felt wounded by him. But I was angry at myself.

I had been listening to another tape. This one had turned out to be Oscar Peterson. I came to the demoralising conclusion that John must have assiduously assembled a complete collection of the type of music I had listed on my application form. That, even before I had joined the firm, he had tried to get inside my brain.

I resolved to pay him back in kind.

He had been a false friend. Used me. Found my faults. Exposed them – if only to himself, and now to me. I felt ashamed. Embarrassed at myself. Like the Emperor in his new clothes.

It was all a game with him. I had only been selected because John felt I posed no threat. He must have been laughing behind my back all the time.

Nick Shannon – too stupid, too trusting to ever suspect. And I, in my vanity, had considered myself to be so clever. A natural. Without equal.

I gunned the engine. Felt the surge as the needle on the speedometer swung to a hundred, a hundred and ten, a hundred and . . .

I realised I was being stupid.

John had made me careless.

That would get me nowhere – except into trouble.

I braked hard. Feathered the throttle. Slowed down to seventy.

Due diligence.

Let that be my maxim from now on.

*

It took me two hours to finish redrafting the Bennington's report. In the typing pool I wheedled my way to the top of the waiting list by a touch of flattery and an almost genuine look of helplessness.

Louise, a pretty brunette, who because she was only eighteen always drew the short straw, was glad of an excuse to put aside Metcalfe's tedious audit report. She examined the changes, sucking air between her lips like a plumber or car mechanic about to say the word 'tricky'. Seeing my look of disappointment, she stopped her teasing. Smiling confidently, she assured me it would be on my desk first thing the following morning. Then, with a flirtatious twinkle in her eye, she said it would cost me a lunch. Tomorrow would suit her fine!

Sometimes it can be pleasant to be blackmailed.

I rang my client, promising delivery of the report by lunchtime. After giving him the gist of the recommendations, I suggested forcefully he ring Bennington straight away – get his verbal agreement to a million, rush a contract over to him.

'I'll give it a shot,' he said dubiously. He was humouring me. No doubt John had already primed him for the much higher figure. Why should he trust my judgement over the proven record of my late boss? I kicked myself, cursing my naivety. In my quest for justice over Bennington I had failed to think the matter through. I hoped that my client's sudden good fortune over the reduction of the purchase price would prevent him examining events too deeply. If he started to hear alarm bells then I guessed it would be me who would be deafened by them.

I made two further phone-calls (one to Arthur, who I had not seen since Brixton, and one to Sally) rather than the three I had originally planned. After the unsettling conversation with my client I had decided not to call Collins and hand him Charlie Bennington's head on a plate. Granted it might have bought me a place in the suspicious inspector's good books but the risks of being thought to have an ulterior motive seemed too great. Anyway, I didn't have the heart to be the one responsible for sending Charlie to prison.

I worked till six, managing to check three more files. I felt distinctly pleased with myself.

I'd found another example of John's creative handiwork. It was one of the reports I'd pressed John to take me through as part of my training. No wonder he had been so committed to packing me off to the next client: I bet his shirt needed a double dose of biological detergent that day.

Even with such early success I tried not to delude myself – this was the easiest part of the exercise. For the recent projects, all the relevant papers were together in one place: everything in the older files was now inconveniently on space-saving microfiche, the working papers long since shredded and the master copies of the reports safely locked away in fire-proof cabinets. More importantly, though, the files checked to date were jobs with which I had been personally involved. Ahead of me lay unknown territory. The further back I went, the more difficult it would become.

Still, I remained determined. I would uncover every trick John had pulled. And expose those involved.

Better not tell Richard for the moment, I reasoned. He would only see the downside. The publicity. The possibility of negligence claims. He might even try to hush it all up. I wasn't going to let that happen.

By the time I left I was starting to consider another possible consequence of my action. Another downside. The 'shoot the messenger' syndrome. I would probably finish up out of a job.

*

Arthur was stomping up and down the mews when I arrived. A curtain twitched in the house opposite. What were the neighbours making of him? Probably thought it was time to move elsewhere if this was the type of person now frequenting the area.

It wasn't that Arthur looked disreputable as such – well perhaps a little, I had to admit – he simply couldn't help but look threatening.

That was why I needed his assistance.

He hadn't changed much over the years. His hair was a little longer, his nose seemed to have acquired another kink. He was wearing a dark blue donkey jacket, collar turned up against the wind, that made him look even wider than ever.

I shook his giant's hand. Placed my arm behind his broad right shoulder. Gave him a hug which produced a gruff 'Geroff' of embarrassment. Led him inside the house.

'It's been a long time,' I said tritely, emotion robbing me of a more original opening line. 'Still playing cards?'

'Yeah. Too old to change. I do all right, thanks to you. Win some, lose some. How about you? Still can't keep out of trouble?'

He stripped off his jacket, hung it on the stand in the narrow hall. He was wearing his uniform – dinner suit and clip-on bow tie ('you can't get throttled by a clip-on,' he had once explained). I took him into the sitting room – had to start using the room at some time!

'Drink, Arthur?' I enquired. 'For old times' sake.'

'Just a beer. I'm working later. You need a clear head in my game. It's not like the old days anymore. Some of the kids come tooled up, now. Spoiling for a fight, they are. Knives, mostly. Though I've come across the odd gun too.' He shook his head. 'I'm getting too old for this lark, you know.'

He settled himself in one of the Chesterfields and critically inspected the room. The stark Japanese theme with the black table and Bonsai trees obviously impressed him.

'A bit poncey for you, isn't it?' he said.

'Thank you, Loyd Grossman,' I replied.

I could only find some Mexican lager at the back of the fridge. He regarded the bottle suspiciously. Took an exploratory sip.

'I'll bring us a six-pack next time,' he said with a smile.

While we were waiting for Sally we talked nostalgically of old times. Then swopped stories to bring each other up to date.

'I hear Freddie Ronson's out,' he said as if the subject couldn't be avoided any longer.

'And what else do you hear?' I asked.

'A lot of jokes – bank clerks being handed demand notes in Braille, heat-seeking sawn-off shotguns, that sort of thing – but not much else. Nobody seems to know his whereabouts. Or intentions.'

I guessed that Arthur had been trawling the dark waters of the underworld for information – still looking after my safety.

'Let me know if you come up with anything. And, Arthur,' I said sternly, 'I don't want you flying solo. Is that clear?'

He looked at me innocently. 'Who me?' he said.

Sally arrived in the middle of my sigh of exasperation.

'Is he here?' she asked, hope written large on her face.

She was dressed for an appointment with the Chief Constable rather than a meeting with Arthur. Smart grey skirt, knee length, short waisted jacket. Prim white blouse, buttoned to the collar. Matching grey shoes and handbag. Blonde hair swept back and held in place by two dark brown tortoiseshell combs.

I looked at her admiringly.

It was the first time I had seen her legs without the protective covering of denim jeans. I realised she wasn't actually thin – just petite. Not my type, I thought, but very pretty. There was an aura of complete innocence about Sally. She was the type who could not have spotted a lie even if you wrote it down and double-underlined the words in red ink.

I introduced her to Arthur. She studied him in much the same way he had examined the room. Her face took on a dubious, disappointed expression. I smiled to reassure her.

'I said I couldn't make any promises. It's a long shot, we both know that. But Arthur might just be able to help. I'd trust Arthur with my life. I suggest you do the same. Tell him your story. From the beginning, please.'

Arthur still had a way to go before developing a perfect poker face. His eyes betrayed his thoughts – what are you getting me into, Nick? And how deep are you prepared to go?

*

Sally sat upright on the settee, legs crossed demurely at the ankles, eyes firmly fixed on Arthur – and away from the carpet. She seemed uncomfortable: so did he. My long-bodied friend wriggled about in his seat – the low back providing him with little support. Nevertheless, he listened intently, leaning forward, hands clenched on his knees, straining to hear the quietly spoken words. There was none of the authority in her voice that she had displayed when first we spoke on the telephone. Her confidence was linked to her profession – in unfamiliar circumstances she was shy and uncertain.

I left Sally to tell her story. Maybe a smaller audience would help her relax. Anyway I had heard it all before. And it was important that she forged a bond with Arthur – I was just the intermediary.

I walked through to the kitchen to get more drinks: white wine for Sally and myself, 'something decent this time' (a very small scotch) for Arthur. After handing them their glasses I retreated and sat on the floor outside the room, my back propped against the wall, listening through the open door.

She spoke slowly, sensing perhaps that Arthur needed time for the facts to sink in. As a narrator, she lacked her flatmate's natural ability to dramatise and capture one's imagination. But, to be fair, her tale had less inherent drama.

She was hesitant at first, breaking off at frequent intervals to take small distracted sips from her glass while searching for the right words.

At the age of sixteen, independent, determined to become a nurse, she had left Huddersfield for London. Studied hard, worked long hours at Guy's during her training and for a further two years after qualifying. Then frustration had set in. Exasperated by low pay, the increasing demands on her time and diminishing returns in terms of job satisfaction, she had left the National Health Service for the private sector. For the past year she'd worked as an agency nurse undertaking temporary assignments at the private hospitals and clinics in and around London. Found enjoyment in her work again. Better environment, better remuneration.

With the change of employment came a necessary move from the nurse's home. But she was earning enough to make her dream affordable. To get somewhere to live, even if shared, which felt like a home rather than just a place to rest her weary head after a long day. It was then that she moved in with Sofia.

All this was a prologue to the real story. An easy way for her to begin. An oft-repeated background. She was using familiar territory as a springboard to more personal admissions.

I heard the crinkle of the plastic carrier bag at her feet as she reached inside. She took out the photograph album I had briefly peeked at in the flat. Flicked through the pages. Found the picture she had shown me when we last met. Passed the book to Arthur.

A family group.

Christmas time. Directly behind them, a heavily decorated artificial tree, snowy white and slightly tilted, with twinkling multi-coloured lights frozen into stars by the camera. In the far background, an electric fire set in a small grate; the cheap tiled mantelpiece above overflowing with garish holiday souvenirs made out of painted seashells.

Mother dressed in her Sunday best. An older version of Sally – pear-shaped, heavier around the breasts, hips and thighs, two chins rather than one, but the same shining gold hair and palest of blue eyes.

Father self-conscious in a new beige, toggle-buttoned cardigan. A few inches taller than Sally. Brown hair thinning at the temples, streaks of grey at the sides. His face bore the hardened appearance of one of life's battlers. Nothing had come easy for this man. He had worked hard for everything – what little – he possessed.

Sally like Alice in Wonderland. Pretty blue dress, white trimmings at the neck and cuffs. Carefree. Laughing, head thrown back, bright teeth sparkling at the lens.

Her brother wore a strained, unnatural, dry-lipped smile. The brooding eyes were gloomy – resentment and aggression, barely hidden beneath the surface, straining to escape.

Like his father, he was short. Deceptively young because of

that. Brown hair shiny, slicked back with grease or gel. Small gold ring glinting in his right ear. He looked like a lot of other kids you see milling about on street corners. Perhaps that was why he had seemed somehow familiar – I didn't think I'd ever met him.

Sam.

The cause of all the trouble, all the worry.

He was a born loser, she told Arthur in a cracked voice.

I heard the catching of breath and the scrabbling noise of her hand as it searched for a tissue in the depths of her bag: she could contain the tears no longer. I went back into the room to lend moral support.

She paused to dab at her eyes and blow her nose; gave a little giggle of embarrassment, then continued.

Sam. Picked on at school because of his size: forced to steal money from his mother's purse to appease the playground bullies. Poor at sports, worse academically. He became withdrawn, sullen in class: even the teachers, frustrated at not being able to get through to the boy, turned him into the butt of their jokes.

He left school on his sixteenth birthday. Went from one low paid job to another, each more shortlived than the last. It wasn't long before he was unemployable – no skills, no references. No reason for anybody to give him a chance. He took what handouts were going. And hung around with a bad crowd – misfits and malcontents like himself.

Nor was there to be any relief at home. Father and son – maybe too similar? – argued incessantly. About money (which Sam was always trying to borrow), commitment (none), attitude (bad), the earring (what did he look like? Gypsy? Queer?).

Sam moved into a squat for a while but couldn't cope when left to his own devices. Soon came scurrying back. Said it was for the sake of his mother – more likely missed the creature comforts of home.

He kept out of his father's way as much as possible. Spent the days in bed or watching television: went out each evening. Became a small cog in a gang which roamed the streets breaking into cars, stealing radios and vandalising vehicles out of spite and envy.

It was a natural progression to houses. They got drunk on whatever booze was handy. Sprayed angry slogans on the walls. Took what they could carry – videos, stereos, portable TVs, jewellery – items for which there was a ready market in the pubs and clubs or which, for a smaller profit, could be fenced.

A few weeks ago he had learnt his lesson. Come within a truncheon's length of being caught. He had outrun a burly, flat-footed policeman. His accomplice had not been so lucky.

Sam had known it wouldn't be long before the police had his name. He packed his bags and left home for good. Deciding to head for 'bright lights, big city', he had rung his little sister and begged to crash out on her floor – just for a few days, till he found a job and a place to live.

That was the last Sally had heard of him.

'Help me find him, Arthur. Please.'

He found her as irresistible as I did.

Arthur knew it would be like looking for a needle in a haystack: every day in London a hundred hopeful – or hope-less – people disappear without trace.

But he couldn't turn her down.

'I'll do what I can,' he said. The accompanying smile was reassuring. It almost had me fooled.

Sally looked relieved.

I had spelt it out previously. If she wouldn't go to the police then there was only one way to find Sam. Someone would have to schlepp around the likely haunts and question those who frequented them – petty criminals, junkies, rent-boys and the like. Sally – although she wouldn't have admitted it – had known that all along. That's why she had come to me. An assumption that prison somehow equipped me for the task. Arthur, I told her, was a better choice for the job. Because of the fear his physical presence could engender, he would get straighter answers than I. And no one was going to mistake Arthur for a cop.

He listed the places he intended to visit: Piccadilly; the Embankment; charity-run night shelters; all the main-line stations, especially King's Cross – the addicts' Mecca – if there was any chance he was on drugs. Sally shook her head – she didn't think he would be that stupid.

Arthur removed the photograph from the album. He shook Sally's hand.

'I'll let Nick know how I get on,' he said. 'Try not to worry, miss. Leave it all to me.' He gave her a broad grin and a wave.

In the hall I asked him in a loud voice for the name of a trustworthy mechanic to service the Monte Carlo. Then, having established our cover, we stood talking in whispers by the door.

'It's a waste of time. You know that, don't you, Nick?'

I nodded grimly.

'Do the best you can,' I said. 'Who knows, he might show up of his own accord. He knows where she lives, after all. Sounds the type who could turn up there one day with his tail between his legs.'

'Maybe,' Arthur said. 'More likely the police will collar him for something – sooner or later. May already be banged up, for all we know. Might be just what he needs by the sound of it. Short, sharp shock and all that.'

I shrugged. I knew what he meant. If it had been anyone else but Sally then neither of us would have given a second thought to getting involved.

I wished him luck.

'Yeah,' he said, reading my mind.

On my return to the room, Sally showed no signs of wanting to leave. She was tinkering with the keyboard. Her right hand played the slow, mournful melody of *Amazing Grace*, her left hand picked out the accompanying long, sustained chords using the one-finger option: she stopped abruptly when she saw my involuntary frown.

I poured us some more wine. Went to investigate the freezer. Wished I'd thought of buying something fresh on the way home. There was a pile of convenience meals – and little else. I stuck a couple of the least offensive packs in the microwave and prepared my apologies.

Looking through the CDs that Rita Simmons had stacked back on the shelf, I found the originals from which John must have recorded the tapes for the car. His collection wasn't a duplicate of mine, it was better. I eyed it enviously. I decided to make Sofia an offer for it – when the time was right.

Sally looked tired, washed out by the spilling of emotion. Neither of us seemed in the mood to talk much so I chose a *Best of Basie* compilation. Heaved a sigh as the first notes drifted across the room. The master of economy. Style derived from Fats Waller – a young Fats had taught an equally young William Basie (they shared the same birthday) to play the organ – but stripped bare so that only the cornerstones of the original structure of the song remained. The incomparable suspense between the widely spaced single notes. Each empty space as important for creating a mood of tension or relaxation as any note he played.

One bottle of wine led to another. One thing led to another.

Or could so easily have done.

I realised in time that I didn't need any more complications in my life. That if she stayed, we would finish up in John's bed going through the motions of making unsatisfying love for, and because of, all the wrong reasons. I knew why she lingered and cuddled up against me on the settee. It wasn't because she found me overpoweringly attractive – her type was the clean-cut, dextrous surgeon or gentle-handed consultant. It was her misguided, ingenuous way of paying in advance for services about to be rendered.

Not a very flattering end to the day.

CHAPTER FIFTEEN

The distant noise of a car horn blaring in anger woke me with a start. I rubbed the sleep from my eyes, looked at my watch and gave an audible groan. Without the cacophonous morning alarm call of the shunting yard I had overslept.

It was a poor start to an inconclusive couple of days. A time when the words 'cheat, liar, swindler' were never far from my thoughts. But the words were like an incomplete series of simultaneous equations: whichever way I looked at the problem there was always a missing element – exasperatingly, the identity of the unknown refused to reveal itself.

Throughout Thursday and Friday I spent almost all my time examining the reports in the files (and dodging phone-calls from my bank manager who must have been hoping to dissuade me from using the letter of credit). The result of my labours was a lot of suspicions – but no hard proof.

With Bennington's the original undoctored figures were fresh in my mind: John's sleight of hand had been easy to spot. When I studied the earlier projects it was like watching the well rehearsed act of an adept conjuror – there had to be a trick involved somewhere but I couldn't say for certain what it was.

There were some instances where the same surveyor had been used but too much time had elapsed to be able to tell whether these had been fair valuations or not. In other cases the figures just did not smell right – Jesus, I was beginning to sound like Collins – but I could not prove that any manipulation had actually taken place.

By Friday afternoon I had compiled a shortlist (!) of fifteen possible frauds – and, if I was right, fifteen potential blackmail victims. For thirteen of those companies I had nothing that would stand up in a court of law. I realised that I had to find something more concrete when I waded through the microfiche records in the basement. On current evidence, I doubted whether I could overcome Richard's self-interested scepticism and convince him of the scale of John's duplicity.

But I trusted my nose. And the pattern which seemed to run through all the examples I had discovered.

Each company was medium-sized, unquoted on the Stock Exchange, privately owned by one individual who was unanswerable to other shareholders and sufficiently powerful to be untroubled by any embarrassing questions from his fellow directors.

Only one acquisition had attracted any publicity – and that purely because of the personality involved.

For the third time in less than a week I had come across the name of David Yates.

As I read the report, my imagination went into overdrive.

Yates, a voluble back-bencher eight years ago, had sold his advertising and public relations concern in order to concentrate his energies and talents on his boundless political ambitions. His holding company, Adcom, following the recommendations in the report, had been acquired by John's client in a multi-million-pound deal. The individual operating companies – frustratingly – had then been merged, subsumed within the acquirer's diverse communications empire. They had ceased to exist as separate, identifiable trading entities: from the published accounts of the new parent it was impossible to tell how Yates's companies had performed after the sale. But I did establish one fact – this was the last time the department had been commissioned to carry out a study for that client.

Yates, over the intervening years, had built up a reputation as a shrewd operator and a surefooted politician. I would have to tread carefully. If the merest hint leaked out that I suspected him of underhand dealings then I would be in the libel courts quicker than the Monte Carlo could cover 0–60 miles per hour.

The only bright spot in those two days at work (apart from an all-too-brief but pleasurable interlude of lunch with Louise, the flirtatious typist) was a clipped conversation in the corridor with Richard. Even that was a double-edged sword. He relayed a message of appreciation from our client on the Bennington's acquisition (signed and sealed for one million pounds) whilst tempering it with a rebuke for not having shown him the report before it went out. He put me firmly in my place by reminding me that, despite my years, I was still a junior – and must abide by the rules without question. I looked forward to the time when I could jolt him with the story behind Bennington's: but till then it had to be 'Yes, sir. No, sir. Three bags full, sir.'

My spirits were low when I left the office. For all my high expectations I seemed to have achieved so little.

And there were more clouds gathering on the horizon.

Any pleasure I felt at the thought of seeing Arlene that evening was mitigated by the prospect of the bridge game. The encounter with Emsby and Morton had once seemed the focal point of the mystery: the needle match, because of my recent discoveries, had shrunk in importance since then. I now had a bewildering multiplicity of contenders for the roles of cheats and swindlers – even John wasn't as squeaky clean as I had once thought. Was the game now an unnecessary gamble?

I was back in the house packing my clothes for the weekend when the idea first struck me. Maybe I was approaching the problem from the wrong direction.

John must have amassed a small fortune over the years. Where had it all gone?

His lifestyle, admittedly, was a little ostentatious – but it couldn't be termed extravagant by any stretch of the imagination. That would have given the game away. What had he done with the money? Somewhere there must be a record of the payments he had received – a bank statement, share certificates, maybe. If I could only find that, then there was a chance the individuals could be identified by matching dates or amounts (working on an assumption of a five per cent cut, à la Bennington's).

In the small back-bedroom I sat at his desk and sifted through the litter of papers. Okay, so the police had already been through everything – but they hadn't known what to look for.

I found only the normal clutter of everyday domestic life: credit card statements (no tell-tale repetition of a travel agent's name which might have led me to investigate destinations); bank statements (no large payments into his current or deposit accounts, alas); a few insurance policies (all for relatively insignificant amounts); telephone bills and the like. Nothing at all to suggest he was anything but an average accountant whose sole income had been a regular monthly salary.

He wouldn't have been so stupid to keep the money in cash – far too risky. And, in any case, there would have been too much to hide inconspicuously. No, it had to be in a bank account or other form of investment someplace. Probably a foreign bank (Liechtenstein or Switzerland seemed the best bet – those countries asked the least questions) or some off-shore fund, otherwise there was a chance the Inland Revenue might get to hear about it.

I wondered ironically if, after all the time and effort involved, the money might be lost forever.

Or would Sofia, as his sole beneficiary, be receiving an unexpected, and extremely large, windfall?

*

'How was Paris?' I asked Arlene.

'Full of the French being full of themselves. Arrogant, intolerant, constantly refusing to understand my accent.'

'And Rome?'

'Bottom-pinching Italians.'

'Florence?'

'Just one dusty old art treasure after another. God, how I've missed you, Nick. Come here.'

I dropped the bag at my feet. Wrapped her tight in my arms. Her lips trembled against mine, tongue urgently exploring my mouth: her hands locked on my shoulders, pulling me hard against her.

She broke off for breath.

'We've got an hour till dinner. Let's work up an appetite!'

*

We sat at a table in a quiet, unfavourable corner of the Grill Room where we did not need to whisper for fear of being overheard. She had treated herself to a new dress in that mellow, buttery colour the Italian women wear so well. Her 'pasta present', she called it: not exactly a size up but cunningly cut so that it hung loosely below the high waist. Over drinks – frosted glasses of Polish vodka on the rocks – I began to relate the long and complex story of the events which had transpired since she had departed on her travels.

Her insight into John's character was acute – if not laudatory.

'What a shit!' she said with feeling. 'Are you sure you want to go through with this match? Is it really worth taking the risk for that son of a bitch?'

I shrugged my shoulders indecisively.

'Maybe you're right,' I replied. 'I don't owe him anything now.'

Not for the first time in my life (and probably, I thought, not for the last time either) I let my heart rule my head.

'All I know is I won't be satisfied until I find out who killed John. I'm not a quitter, Arlene. Anyway, I'm in too deep to pull out now – that would only condone John's crimes. There's a chance – slim, I admit, bearing in mind there are so many other candidates – that Emsby and Morton were behind his death. And, even if they are in the clear for the murder, I don't see why they should be allowed to get away with cheating people.'

'Christ, you're one hell of a stubborn bastard when you set

your mind to it.' An anxious look swept across her face. 'I only hope I don't let you down.'

She decided to make one last effort to get me to change my mind. Took my left hand. Looked straight into my eyes. 'You deserve that money, Nick, after all you've been through. Use it for a new start in life – don't throw it all away on some personal crusade. You, more than anyone, should appreciate that we don't always get justice in this world. Wake up, Nick. This is real life.'

'Life's not Hollywood, it's Cricklewood, eh?' I said.

She nodded, understanding the meaning even if the exact geographical reference eluded her.

'Listen to me, Arlene. We are not going to lose. We are going to beat them at their own game. You have to believe that – or there's no point even trying.' It was my turn to squeeze her hand. 'Trust me,' I said.

I went through it all again for her. Although I had written the bare bones in my letter, she deserved the full picture. And to hear the confident ring of my voice.

To cheat at bridge, I reminded her, is remarkably easy: getting away with it over a prolonged period is much more difficult. The hands talk. They show patterns which can only lead to one conclusion.

The simplest method would be some small gesture that told partner whether one was strong, medium or weak for the bid one had just made. But, if consistently used, that degree of pinpoint accuracy in the bidding would soon be noticed. The same problem arises for a signal that would tell partner which suit to lead when defending. Too much inspiration would look suspicious. Emsby and Morton needed a way of improving the odds to a small degree. A few per cent would be enough to net them plenty of money over the long term – and would be virtually undetectable.

Arlene had been the catalyst in cracking the code: the discussion about bridge etiquette in the bar at Latimers had given me the clue. At the time I could not place where I had come across the phrase that had bothered me.

'The American way.'

Then my brain had linked it with John's criticism of the pair as being unimaginative.

The innocent phrase brought back memories of a book I'd read a long time ago: the inside story of the biggest scandal in the history of bridge. It had taken place at the World Championship played for the Bermuda Bowl in Buenos Aires in 1965. Terence Reese and Boris Schapiro – the best players Britain has ever produced – were accused by the Americans of using illicit finger signals.

B.J. Becker of the North American team – a man who fixed his opponents with an unwavering hawk-like gaze during the bidding of a hand (the American way) – claimed to have noticed that Reese and Schapiro were holding their cards in a peculiar manner. Convinced that signals were being exchanged, he secretly arranged for the pair to be watched at subsequent sessions.

There was little love lost between the British and American teams. The Americans, undisputed holders of the world title for so many years, had come to regard it as theirs by right. To their annoyance, first the British, then the Italians had wrested the Championship from their vice-like grip. Perhaps an element of sour grapes affected what the observers saw – or thought they saw.

On the final night, with Britain in with a chance – albeit small – of winning, the Executive Committee of the World Bridge Federation issued a short statement concerning 'certain irregularities'. The British Captain dropped Reese and Schapiro for the remaining sessions. And, to make matters worse, conceded the earlier matches against America and Argentina. The implication was clear as crystal.

Back on British soil, the two accused took the only course of action open to them if they were to salvage their reputations. Pressure was applied to the British Bridge League until an independent inquiry was convened. After more than a year of hearing evidence and examining the hands, the Inquiry finally exonerated Reese and Schapiro from the charges, casting a shadow of doubt, it might be said, on the motives of some of the accusers.

The alleged method of exchanging information was that finger signals were used to show the length of the heart suit in a player's hand. Emsby and Morton had taken a leaf from this book. They had just enough imagination to make one small change. Emsby's fidgeting, Morton's bluff manner were intentional distractions. They were changing the number and position of their fingers as they held the cards in order to indicate how many spades they had. My analysis of the hands that John had assiduously collected proved the mode of cheating beyond doubt – the killing leads, the deft bidding, had all been related to the spade suit.

'All you have to remember,' I instructed Arlene, 'is that when you see just the thumb, it means a void in spades: one finger means a singleton: two, three or four fingers held tightly together indicates that number of spades: if the fingers are widely spaced apart then two shows five, three shows six etc.

'Their information,' I concluded, 'is now our information. If we watch them carefully, we too will know the number of spades each of them holds. And, because each of us can count up to thirteen, you can work out how many spades I hold, and vice versa. Armed with that knowledge it should be child's play to modify our bidding, and to find the best defence or play of the hand.'

'If you say so, honey,' she replied.

I didn't have to be a mind-reader to know what was going on in her head. Even the best of plans could founder on the rocks of a bad run of cards.

'Don't worry,' I said, trying to send waves of confidence across the table. 'Tomorrow their luck runs out.'

CHAPTER SIXTEEN

It was as if a film director had strode onto a set and shouted 'Action'.

Our clapperboard entrance produced an instantaneous reaction. As we stepped through the double doors of the card room, the hubbub of excited conversations died at a stroke; hastily abandoned sentences left words hanging on the static of the electrically-charged air. The cast of extras, a flock of scavenging magpies in their black dinner jackets and white shirts, turned hungry faces in our direction. The stage was set. The stars had arrived on cue.

Arlene froze. Her fingers, rigid with fear, clamped tightly onto my hand. She stared blankly into the distance, blinded by the unexpected transformation since the previous week.

There must have been more than a hundred people present, two or three times the number she had anticipated. Where there had been four tables, tonight there was only one. It dominated the exact centre of the room. And, since the table was in the null point of the light from the four chandeliers, spotlights had been set up at each corner. They glared down, bleaching the green baize with their harsh beams. Parallel rectangles of seats surrounded the table. The outer ranks were cheap foldaway chairs, specially imported for this one evening: they looked strangely out of place among the rich splendour of the antique furniture. Arlene had mentally prepared for a bridge match: instead she had stepped into a scene more suited to a contest between prize-fighters.

My stomach turned. If anything was going on in her reeling mind then it was second thoughts. At any moment she might spin around on her high heels and walk straight out. Hurriedly, before the panic became unstoppable, I pressed my lips against her ear.

'Smile for your fans, baby,' I whispered. 'Knock 'em dead.'

I never knew whether it was the words themselves or merely the effect of my hot breath against the cold, blood-drained ear: but the spell broke. The pincer grip on my hand relaxed, little by little. She inhaled deeply, let the breath out in a long sigh. Flashing a broad smile to anyone and everyone, she began to walk forwards, outwardly calm and confident.

Like the Red Sea, the crowd parted as we walked slowly and steadily to the table: Arlene was Moses, I was simply her staff of support. Every eye was focused on her. Those already seated rose politely as she passed, creating the impression of an impromptu Mexican wave.

She had chosen her dress with deliberate premeditation: the iridescent shade of blue-green stabbed at one's eyes as the silken material shimmered and changed colour with the slightest movement of her body. Straps, the width of dental floss, struggled to hold a neckline which plunged like Niagara Falls in the rainy season. By some miracle of structural engineering, her breasts – one of them sporting an eyebrow-pencilled beauty spot! – defied logic and gravity: her every breath promised – threatened – a mammary fallout of nuclear proportions.

She was wearing the complete 'mugger's paradise' set of jewellery from our first meeting. Plus one extra item, purchased during her morning's shopping trip to Oxford Street. Alongside the rings and bracelet there was now a cheap chain hung with thinly plated gold 'charms': it played a discordant Stockhausen symphony of sound each time she moved her wrist.

Twirling in front of the hotel mirror as we made our final preparations to leave, she had brushed aside my stunned, open-mouthed gape. Wasn't it worth looking like a tart if it caused Morton or Emsby to play one wrong card during the match? Whatever the effect on our opponents, I dare not look at her, that was for sure.

Stapleton, the Director, spread the cards deftly across the green baize. Four hands dipped into the neat line to make their selection.

I cut the Ace of Spades – the motif on John's cufflinks and ring. I would have preferred any other card.

All serious card players are superstitious: they each follow elaborate – and laughable – personal rituals in appeasement of the goddess of chance (often wearing strange or inappropriate items of clothing with some spurious correlation to good luck in the past; taking a particular position at the table; walking three times anti-clockwise around their chair to change a bad run). They are, also, ever on the look-out for signs as to their fate. This card was an ambiguous omen. How should it be read? It was long held to be the card of death. Yet, in bridge, it is the highest card in the pack – unbeatable.

Ever the optimist, I smiled broadly at Arlene. Waved my hand to offer her the choice of seat. Morton moved to her right, sitting down immediately; Emsby, on her left, at least had the manners to wait till she was seated.

Arlene settled herself, wriggling her body provocatively in the chair, her breasts swinging from side to side like a heavy pendulum. She extended the pull-out flap to its limit. Set down her matching evening bag. Removed a plain gold cigarette case and lighter. Positioned these by her right hand. Fiddled with the ashtray as if unsure of where was the best place to site it. Moved her score-pad. Repeatedly clicked the button on the top of her ball point pen.

I thought she was overdoing the nervous activity. So did Morton.

He shot her a glance worthy of a character in the *Beano* – an invisible wave of daggers streamed in her direction.

Arlene, unchastened, returned the compliment – Medusa would have been proud of the look she gave him.

'When you're ready, Mr Morgon,' she said deliberately. 'May we begin, please? Your cut to my partner I believe.'

The Director made a short statement to the audience. First, he stated the stakes: five pounds a point per player, ten pounds per pair. It was an unnecessary reminder – why else would the room be so crowded? This was certain to be the biggest game the kibitzers would ever witness. A tale to upstage the fortunate few old-timers who still dined on stories of 1969 when Arturo Franco, at the impetuous age of twenty-three had needled world champions Belladonna and Garozzo into a match of one hundred rubbers at three dollars a point. (He lost by the way – 10,000 points down at the end of the first day, he was never able to make an impression on the lead.)

Stapleton completed his preliminaries. 'In the case of appeals,' he said firmly, 'my decision is final and binding. In accordance with Club rules, I have here a letter of credit for fifty thousand pounds on behalf of Mr Shannon: the same amount had been deposited with the cashiers by Mr Emsby and Mr Morton.'

He sensed the crowd was growing restless – the mention of the money had set them buzzing. Signalling for me to deal, he took his front-row seat, bisecting Morton and Arlene.

I wiped sweating palms on my trousers and picked up the cards. They felt heavy, a solid gold ingot in my left hand. As I dealt, the spectators leant forward like bloodthirsty observers at a contest between pit-bull terriers. The Committee, present to a man, had exercised their right of privilege and commandeered the comfortable ringside seats close to the action.

After all the build-up, I suppose it was inevitable that the first hand would be an anti-climax. I opened the bidding with One No Trump and everybody passed. Both Emsby and Morton had shown four spades by their finger signals. Emsby led the two of spades against my contract: since, conventionally, they led the fourth highest of a suit then the play of the two confirmed his finger signal – he had exactly four cards in spades. It was an encouraging sign.

Though they defended well, I scraped the seven tricks needed for the contract and scored forty points. First blood to us, if only from a scratch. Four hundred pounds to the good and, more importantly, a step towards the hundred points required for game.

On the next hand we bid to two spades – worth sixty points if we made the contract, and taking us in sight of a seven hundred point bonus if we won the rubber in two straight games, or five hundred if it went to the third. Morton, however, was not prepared to let the bidding rest there: he had no intention of giving us an easy ride. His sacrificial bid of three hearts became the final contract. Falling one trick short, the penalty was fifty points. A cheap save as far as he was concerned – I would have done the same in his position.

Red deck. Blue deck. Both were stone cold.

It happens sometimes like that. High cards divided almost equally between the players. No spectacular hands. No big gains or losses in either direction. One low-level contract followed another. For any other stakes it would have been boring.

It took nine deals and a full hour before we finally emerged as winners of an evenly matched first rubber. Eleven hundred points to the good – not much perhaps, but a small cushion if the luck swung for a while towards our opponents.

We took a short break. Stretched our legs. Ordered some drinks – the one vodka and tonic we had again agreed should be our ration while playing. Emsby, as daring as ever, sipped daintily from a glass of mineral water. Morton swirled the contents of a brandy balloon in his hand, sniffing loudly at the rim as the heat from his stubby fingers sent the fumes rising in the glass. He lit an evil-smelling cigar. And placed it in his ashtray where the acrid smoke snaked upwards in a foul blue-grey stream towards Arlene.

She was having none of it.

Her left hand snatched the cigar and ground it angrily into the bottom of the crystal ashtray.

I saw a smile pass fleetingly across Morton's face. He had achieved his objective. She was rattled. Her concentration broken.

Play resumed, the tension in the crowd moving up a gear.

Arlene played in a contract of four spades, game if she made it. Her bracelet jangled like a badly rung carillon of churchbells as she selected one card from her hand, hesitated, replaced it, chose another. Morton smirked as he registered her indecision. He grew in confidence with the slowing of the tempo, taking heart from Arlene's obvious problems. Then, as he leaned forward like a vulture preparing to swoop onto a corpse, she tabled her cards and claimed eleven tricks – one more than required.

Arlene had been stringing him along. Building up his hopes so as to dash them down from the greatest possible height.

The blackness of Morton's expression told me he'd reached the same conclusion. I could see his temper rising. He opened his mouth, some cutting remark or thinly veiled insult about to issue forth.

'Well played, partner,' I interjected.

I pushed the red deck towards Emsby.

'Your deal, I believe.'

He dealt quickly, sharing my desire to silence his partner.

The heat at the table transferred itself to the cards.

We arrived at a contract of six spades, Arlene showing by cue bids of clubs and diamonds that she held these aces. I needed to make twelve of the thirteen tricks: even though I knew we were missing the ace of hearts, the small slam seemed a fair bet. If successful the contract carried a bonus of seven hundred and fifty points. We would win the rubber by nearly eighteen hundred points.

A total of eighteen thousand pounds rested on how I played the hand.

Emsby led the ace of hearts. Arlene laid down her cards. We were short of the queen of spades.

Which opponent held the critical card? Find the lady. Make or break.

After Emsby had cashed his ace, I needed to take the rest.

I won his next lead of a low heart in my hand and took stock of the situation. If the signals were to be believed then Morton had one spade and Emsby four. Arlene's spades were king, ten, nine, six. Mine were ace, jack, eight, seven.

I entered Arlene's hand and selected a small spade. Morton played low.

Emsby must have the queen.

I played my ace. On the next trick I led the seven of spades and, when Emsby dropped a low card, played the nine from the table. I held my breath.

The nine won the trick: Morton – no trumps left – discarded a heart.

After that it was a simple process to return to my hand and play another spade trapping Emsby's queen. Contract made. Wide grin from Arlene. Wall-to-wall scowl from Morton. And from Lady Luck too.

For the next hour we picked up the worst collection of cards I had ever experienced.

Emsby and Morton notched up game after game. Rubber after rubber. With depressing – and expensive – regularity.

I could feel the crowd's sympathy growing with each new deal. This was no contest – it was ritual slaughter. They had come to watch a gladiatorial spectacle not the devouring of helpless Christians by the lions.

I could only admire Arlene's *sangfroid*.

She showed no hint of panic nor loss of judgement, resisting the temptation to overbid in a foolhardy effort to turn the tide. Her concentration, for what it was worth, was maintained. She approached each new hand with an air of calm optimism.

Until we could continue no longer.

Stapleton rose from his chair. He called a halt to the proceedings: stopped the fight.

There was nothing left of our stake money.

Every penny of the fifty thousand pounds was gone.

*

Stapleton led the procession to his office. The time of settlement had come.

149

As Arlene and I walked in silence from the room the kibitzers shook their heads. They muttered embarrassed commiserations and slapped our backs as if we were the true victors.

Emsby's face showed no trace of triumph. The size and manner of their victory had robbed him of any satisfaction. I truly felt he was ashamed.

Morton gloated. Loudly. Insensitively. A deep, throaty cackle of a laugh that brought disapproving scowls from the members – and the urge from me to lay him flat. I resisted. What was the point?

From the reaction of the crowd, I reckoned his chances of finding opponents in the future were close to zero. If it had been America, then I suspect someone would have called for a lynch mob. In this Club they would content themselves with sending him to Coventry.

Arlene and I strode hand in hand, our dignity, at least, intact.

Defiantly, she stopped a passing waiter. 'Champagne,' she announced loudly.

What a woman! I was proud of her.

We trooped into the Director's room, sat silently around the mahogany table. Arlene showed no interest in the surroundings – the highly polished cups and ribboned medals, the framed photographs of Stapleton rubbing shoulders with one immortal or another – here a handsome Zia, there a dapper Jeremy, everywhere a smoking Omar.

Morton, flamboyantly, lit another cigar. Even Emsby looked at him in disgust.

The champagne arrived while we were awaiting the appearance of the cashier. I poured a glass for everybody. We could show them how to behave.

Arlene and I raised our glasses.

Our eyes met.

We toasted each other.

'To you,' we said simultaneously, unable to suppress a shared laugh that bordered dangerously on the hysterical.

Stapleton raised his glass too. And pressed a button on his desk.

The cashier responded promptly to the signal.

A line of black jackets followed him into the room. Arlene ignored the funereal gathering of the Committee. Nonchalantly, she continued to sip at the champagne.

Stapleton produced a pen. And a single sheet of paper, tightly typed. He set it carefully on the table in front of Emsby and Morton.

'What the hell is this?' shouted Morton, reading the first few lines.

'Exactly what it appears to be,' replied the Director. 'Sign against your names, please. Both of you.'

'You must be mad,' said Morton angrily. 'I want my money.'

'Let me explain, gentlemen,' Stapleton said calmly. 'So there can be no misunderstanding. '

Stapleton spoke with all the gravity and authority of a high court judge – and one who, mentally at least, had donned the black cap. 'Members of this Committee,' he said, 'have observed you both most carefully during the course of the evening. There is no shred of doubt in our minds,' – the bystanders nodded supportively – 'that you have been using illicit signals to indicate the length of the spade suit. In these lamentable circumstances I have no option but to declare tonight's game null and void. If the pair of you – I cannot bring myself to use the term 'gentlemen' – wish this scandalous affair to remain private, then I urge you to sign the document we have prepared.'

Emsby looked around the room with horror. He saw the unswerving resolution written on Stapleton's face, felt the hostility and contempt of the Committee. Any trace of hope left him. His fingers trembled as he reached for the document and signed his name. A beaten man, he slumped back in his chair shaking his head at his own folly.

There was nothing Morton could do now. His partner's signature was as good as a joint confession. He grabbed the pen with characteristic bad grace. Scrawled his name. Stared across at me with hatred in his eyes. Could he hate enough to kill, I wondered?

The Director signed his own name in turn.

'If you would be so kind as to endorse the document,' he said, passing the sheet of paper to Arlene and myself.

We read the conditions the Committee had laid down in return for their silence on the matter of cheating.

Number one. Morton and Emsby were to resign from the club.

Two. They were never to partner each other, anywhere, under any circumstances, in the future.

Three. They were to pay Mrs Arlene Tucker and Mr Nicholas Shannon the sum of five thousand pounds each as compensation for their time and trouble in bringing the matter to light.

We took great pleasure in signing our names!

The cashier unlocked his box. He withdrew ten bundles of crisp new fifty pound notes – the money our opponents had deposited prior to the game – and laid them out on the table in front of Stapleton. One beautiful bundle was handed to Arlene, another to myself: the remainder divided between Emsby and Morton.

They stuffed the money into their pockets and rose from their seats, Emsby somewhat unsteadily, Morton defiantly.

'Before you leave, gentlemen,' Stapleton said, 'allow me to introduce you to Detective Chief Inspector Collins of the Metropolitan Police. I believe he wishes to question you in connection with the murder of John Weston.'

Theatrically, Collins stepped out of the shadows at the back of the room.

A pair of handcuffs – purely for effect – glinted as he moved into the light.

It was all too much for Emsby. His body crumpled like a suddenly stringless marionette, arms waving floppily, legs buckling at every joint. He fell in an untidy heap to the floor.

Morton's face lost the purple of rage and changed to ghostly white. He stumbled across to Collins, wrists compliantly pointing at the handcuffs.

*

The night was cloudless, crystal clear, a thousand stars sharply defined against the backdrop of the ebony sky. The temperature seemed to have dropped ten degrees since our arrival at the club. Hugging each other for warmth, we walked along the quiet street towards Piccadilly where we could hail a passing cab.

Despite the closeness of our bodies, Arlene's manner was distant. There was fire in her eyes as she looked up at me. 'Why didn't you tell me you had Collins standing by?'

'Believe me,' I said in self-defence, 'it wasn't that I didn't trust you. I simply wanted you to play normally. It had to look real – as if we were playing for our lives. The slightest suspicion from Emsby or Morton of a set-up and they wouldn't have risked cheating. I couldn't afford for that to happen — Stapleton had taken a lot of convincing, even with the evidence from the hands John had collected. He was giving me one chance to prove a theory. I didn't know what sort of actress you would make. Another time, and maybe I'll play it differently.'

She wasn't to be appeased that easily. I turned her face toward me, brushed a loose strand of hair from her eyes. And let my fingertips linger on her cheek.

'I'm sorry I kept you in the dark,' I said, bending down and kissing her gently. My tongue fluttered teasingly over her mouth. Breaking off, I transferred my attention to her ear, nibbling at first, then whispering. 'Wasn't it generous of Stapleton to let us have the money?'

I turned her face towards me, showed her the grin I could no longer suppress. 'It was you who suggested the amount, I presume?'

She smiled coquettishly.

'You weren't the only one to take out insurance. I paid Stapleton a visit this morning.'

A taxi, responding to my signal, drew up at the kerb.

As we climbed inside she took off the charm bracelet – source of distraction, excuse for her absence. She dropped it in the gutter. It had served its purpose.

*

It was dawn before Arlene finally fell asleep. Her breathing was deep and regular: in the shaft of light from the half-closed curtains I could see her pupils darting to and fro beneath her eyelids as she dreamed of I know not what. She was still sprawled across me. Gently lifting her head and shoulder, I slid carefully from under her body.

Arriving back at the hotel we had been like a pair of eagles, soaring effortlessly upwards on the rising thermals of our triumph. Everything was perfect. The champagne. The money we threw in the air like confetti. The flood of adrenalin from the moral victory. All combined to make us lightheaded.

Our first coupling was loving and unhurried. At times we ceased all movement and simply gazed incredulously into each other's eyes. Neither of us, it surely seemed, could believe that life could be this good.

But it did not – could not – last. The sense of elation was all-too-brief. As the night wore on it faded into a dark cloud of doubt.

I couldn't tell what was going through Arlene's mind but, for my part, I was confused. Within me was admiration for the way she had taken everything so calmly; gratitude for her support; pride at the loyalty and faith she had shown in me. I liked her sense of fun; respected her determination; desired her ample body. I knew I cared for Arlene. Cared a lot. But would that be enough for her?

The sand in our personal hour glass trickled grain by grain from the top to the bottom. Our love-making became more urgent. More frenzied. More selfish. Each trying to grab as much as was humanly possible from a relationship with a short past and an uncertain future. Tomorrow – no, today now – she would fly back to America.

Silently, like a thief in the night, I collected my belongings. Took them and my bag into the sitting room.

Once dressed I wrote her a letter.

I hoped she would understand. It was the only way I could think of to give her a pressure-free exit route. Even your average ex-con carries with him a staggering weight of emotional baggage: I needed a pantechnicon. Before she arrived at any decision I wanted her to appreciate fully the load she would be sharing.

Goodbye or au revoir. It had to be her choice.

CHAPTER SEVENTEEN

Back at the house I took the phone off the hook. This wasn't
the time for unwelcome callers. My system was drained, its batteries desperately in need of recharging. Sleep was the first
priority, if only to clear my mind and approach the rest of the
day afresh. And when I woke up Arlene would be winging her
way across the Atlantic.

In the bedroom I stripped off my clothes and threw them
onto a chair. Jumping into bed, I pulled the duvet tight around
my shoulders. It was a cold room. The monochrome theme of
the sitting room had been continued here giving an air of stark-
ness to what might otherwise have been cosy and comfortable.
There was a surfeit of hard lines to the furnishings and fittings:
geometric patterned curtains and bedclothes, more sharp angles
picked out in white on the black doors of the wardrobes. And
the whole impersonal effect then doubled in size by the reflection in the floor-to-ceiling mirrors along one wall.

I was too tired, too emotional, too tense for sleep to come.
My mind refused to switch off. After half an hour of tossing
and turning, I dragged myself moodily from the bed and went
along the corridor to the study. On the floor was a box filled
with the bottles I had cleared from the bathroom cabinet. Inside
was John's bottle of sleeping pills. With a sense of revulsion I
saw the contours of his fingerprint plainly etched in white powder on the dark brown surface of the glass.

I made my mind up there and then. I must leave this house. Get away from the macabre memories and the constant reminder of John's duplicity. Start looking for somewhere else the next day. Do what I could to sort the place out. Get hold of an estate agent. Keep as much of my promise to Sofia as would seem reasonable. Then clear out. Never come back.

I tipped two of the pills into the palm of my hand. Swallowed them with water from the bathroom tap. Crawled back into bed. Prayed for sleep.

I got my wish.

The land of Morpheus can be a cruel place. Even in my dreams there was no respite, no escape from John's haunting presence.

It was a surrealistic nightmare: stark images forced themselves on the captive audience of my pupils like scenes from Bunuel's *Le Chien Andalou*. With that lack of apparent reason one experiences in dreams, I was sitting, John's stubby fountain pen in hand, diligently writing labels on a mountain of cassettes. The floor was a snowdrift of white powder. Three feet deep, it reached to my knees. Its weight held me prisoner in my seat.

I stared down. From out of the quicksand of heavy cloying dust, in tormentingly slow motion, pale white fingers began to emerge. One by one. Until they formed a claw.

The bony hand darted out. The fingernails were long and pointed: they scraped across my skin before snatching the pen from my grasp and disappearing back into the whiteness. I waited helplessly. It would not end here – the conclusion was inevitable. I tried to scream but no sound came from my open mouth.

Like some ghoulish Aphrodite breaking through the waves, the corpse rose up.

John's corpse.

There was a sneer across the bloodied face. Red light shone from the eyes. The arms, stiff with rigor, moved like a badly lubricated robot. Then came to rest, palms clamped against the sides of his head. The hands thrust upwards and tore the head from the neck, leaving a jagged edge and a snake pit of quivering nerves and squirming muscles.

The disembodied head looked down upon me. But only for long enough for the threat to register.

Like some diabolical basketball it was thrown towards me, traversing a slow smooth parabola, lips cackling with demonic laughter, into my waiting arms.

The scream came to my rescue. It sprang from the very depths of my body in a high-pitched elongated wail that jarred me into wakefulness.

Jerking upright, I sat staring into the darkness. An uncontrollable seismic shaking had taken hold of me. I felt icy cold, yet there were rivers of sweat running down my body.

The sound of knocking waded unsteadily through the thick treacle of my drugged mind.

I stumbled out of bed. Pulled on a pair of jeans. Came close to tripping, in my haste, down the steep flight of stairs.

The banging grew louder. Increased in frequency and agitation.

I threw the door open.

Sofia took one look at me. Her expression shamed me. From the mirror of her face I saw what a pathetic sight was standing before her.

*

She led me by the arm along the hallway. Sat me down at the dining room table. Watching me with a look of puzzled concern, she brewed a pot of coffee. Poured a large measure of armagnac into my mug.

My hands trembled as I drank.

She opened her red lips.

'Just give me a moment,' I said quickly. 'Please.'

She left me alone. I heard the door of the sitting room creak as she satisfied a morbid curiosity to view the scene of the crime. Then, a few minutes later, the scrape of her stilettos mounting the stairs and entering the bedroom.

On her return she handed me a shirt, socks and shoes. She remained silent while I dressed, then could restrain herself no longer.

'Where have you been?' she said. 'I've been trying to get hold of you since Friday evening. I was worried. What on earth's been going on? I could hear you screaming from the street.'

The coffee and brandy started to work. I shuddered as I took another gulp of the thick brown liquid, its raisin sweetness and alcohol sting thumping at the back of my throat. My system reeled as if it had been kick-started by a twenty-stone Hell's Angel wearing leaden boots.

I felt foolish now. I wasn't looking forward to admitting that I had been reduced to this state by a mere nightmare. I played for time. Parried her question with one of my own.

'Why were you trying to contact me?' I asked. 'Is something wrong?'

'No. Nothing's wrong,' she replied. 'Just urgent, that's all. John's parents have arranged the memorial service for tomorrow. I wanted you to know. They asked if you would come.' She put on that wheedling voice that she had used so successfully before. 'Please say you will. It seemed very important to them.'

'Of course I'll go,' I replied. I was secretly relishing the opportunity of meeting the notorious Jack Weston. 'Would you like me to drive you?'

I should have guessed her reaction.

'I'd rather take the train, if you don't mind.' It came out more curtly than she intended. In an attempt to compensate she spoke the next sentence more softly. 'You do understand, I hope, Nick.'

I understood only too well. She still couldn't face sitting in the Monte Carlo. The car was too evocative of John. And there was the bad association with the 'accident' too, I supposed.

Her curiosity was not going to be stalled for long by talk of trains and cars. 'Nick,' she said with a determined look on her face, 'you're holding out on me, aren't you? What is it? What are you afraid to tell me?'

She sat herself down opposite me, crossing her legs so that

the pointed toe of one shoe was tucked behind a trim ankle. With both hands she pulled ineffectually at the hem of her red dress.

'Well?' she said, locking her eyes onto mine.

'It was just a nightmare,' I confessed. 'A silly nightmare.'

Sofia took a pack of cigarettes from her leather handbag. Lit one delicately with a gold lighter. Seeing my hungry expression she slid the pack across the table. I fiddled with the plain white box with its red designer logo, turning it over in my hand before taking one of the long thin cigarettes. The pack had no health warning. The almost complete absence of taste in my mouth as I inhaled made me wonder if one was necessary.

I sensed a growing impatience in Sofia. The scar beneath her eye give a barely perceptible twitch.

'Nothing else?' she asked.

I launched into the story about Emsby and Morton.

Perhaps I'd been hoping that she would get bored by the bridge talk, make some excuse and leave me in peace. But she listened attentively as I recounted how I had discovered they had been cheating. Her mood brightened when I came to the part about their exposure and the subsequent humiliation in front of the Committee. And when she heard the punishment imposed, a satisfied smile spread across her lips.

'John would have been pleased with you,' she said. 'He hated the pair of them. Always wanted to see them taken down a peg.'

'You're missing the point, Sofia,' I said. 'John knew they were cheating. He was blackmailing them, I'm sure.'

I paused. Waited for some reaction. Some clue as to how much she already knew. A look of bewilderment was all that came back in my direction. No words. Just a tilting of the head to one side. 'Go on,' she seemed to say. The ball was hit squarely back in my court.

'I think Emsby and Morton let us win when we played them. It was John's way of extracting the blackmail money from them.' I refrained from voicing my conviction that it also served to feed the sadistic streak lurking beneath John's cool exterior.

Emsby and Morton were forced to eat humble pie: at the same time John's stature was enhanced in the eyes of the kibitzers.

'He never said anything to me about blackmail,' she stated definitively. She knocked the ash from her cigarette with three sharp taps from her long fingernail.

'Even if it's true,' Sofia continued, watching me closely, 'didn't they deserve it? Was it so wrong of John?'

I shrugged my shoulders. This wasn't the time for some complicated Jesuitical discussion of whether the ends can ever justify the means. Perhaps it was too close to home – if put to the test, which side would I support?

I decided not to tell her of my other suspicions – that Emsby and Morton were only the tip of an iceberg of extortion.

Instead, I broke it to her that I was planning to leave.

What had I expected?

Disappointment at a broken promise? Uncertainty as to how she would sort out the affairs on her own? Frustration? Anger, even? Any of those emotions I could have coped with.

But I was unprepared for what followed.

Sofia broke down in front of me. A look of absolute hopelessness. A steady trickle of tears. A slow dissolving of her face before it was buried out of sight in her hands.

I sat helpless, knowing that if I walked round the table to comfort her then my resistance – already weakening – would crumble to nothing.

She scrabbled in her bag for a handkerchief. Dabbed at her eyes. Looked dolefully at me.

'I'm sorry,' she sniffed. 'I thought I was getting over it. I'd even arranged to go away on holiday. I hoped you might have everything sorted out by the time I returned. I suppose I'll have to cancel now. It would have done me so much good.'

If I felt a louse then, her next words made me feel ten times worse.

'Please say you'll change your mind. Don't make me beg, Nick.' There was despair in the deep pools of her brown eyes. 'If you only knew how much I was counting on you. Don't let me down, please. There's no one else I can ask.' She reached across and grabbed my hand. 'It's at times like this,' she said, 'that I regret being an only child. I feel so alone. I wish I had a big brother I could turn to.'

She had found my weak spot. After that it was just a case of negotiation. We settled on three weeks – four at the absolute most!

She stood up to go, all smiles now. Thanked me 'from the bottom of her heart'. Kissed me on the cheek. Hugged me. More tightly than I had expected.

I felt the firmness of her breasts as she pressed against me. Placing my hands on her tear-stained cheeks, I pulled her warm body even closer. Drew her lips towards mine.

The bell rang.

Our bodies went rigid.

We broke apart with the urgent haste of teenagers caught behind the bike sheds. She was flustered. Her hands ran down the front of her dress, smoothing away imaginary creases.

'I must go,' she said, avoiding my gaze.

We were nearly at the door when she stopped abruptly.

'Come for dinner. Thursday. Eight o'clock,' she said. 'Sally's on nights this week.'

She opened the door before I had a chance to reply.

Arthur stood there blocking her exit. He hesitated before moving only slightly to one side. Sofia brushed past him, avoiding his searching look as best she could. His eyes lingered on her swaying hips as she disappeared down the street.

'We need to talk,' he said, stepping inside.

*

Arthur walked silently through to the sitting room, his mind working away at some problem that I assumed would soon become mine. His huge hand was wrapped around a six-pack. He set it down on the coffee table and shook his head as I started to go to the kitchen to get some glasses. Ripping off the ring pull, he took a deep draught from the can.

'Who was that?' he asked, tossing a beer in my direction.

I only got as far as uttering Sofia's name and reminding him she was Sally's flatmate when the bell went again.

With a sense of annoyance I went to answer the door. Arthur rose from his seat, beer in hand, and scanned the contents of the bookcase in an effort to occupy himself during my absence.

'All finished, Mr Shannon.'

Jimmy, the mechanic recommended by Arthur, stood proudly alongside the Monte Carlo patting the bonnet. His navy-blue boiler suit was lost against the background of darkness, giving the unsettling impression of a blonde-haired head floating six foot above the ground. As he stepped into the light from the hallway I could see his narrow face: it was smeared with grease – worn like an official badge of his trade – where he had at some time distractedly rubbed his forehead with the back of his oily hands.

'What a bugger,' he said as he walked inside. He didn't have to squeeze past me – he was thin and wiry as if his body had evolved specifically to fit underneath the chassis of a car.

'What a bugger,' he repeated, in case I had missed the import the first time. I resigned myself to listening to the well prepared, long drawn out monologue about the impossibility of servicing the Lancia.

'Hallo, Arthur. One of those beers going spare?'

Without waiting for an answer he swooped up a can and stretched out on the Chesterfield. He gave the impression that at any moment he might plant his size 12 boots on the coffee table. Maybe even ask me to switch on the television or get some crisps to go with the beer.

He ignored me and spoke directly to Arthur.

'I was telling Mr Shannon it was a real bugger.' Jimmy worked on his own and obviously didn't get much practice at conversation. 'You know I had to crawl inside the engine compartment to reach the guts. Played havoc with my back, it did.' He paused for sympathy. Not a flicker from Arthur. 'What a state it was in too. Still, all fixed now. Good as new.'

Jimmy turned towards me. 'Nice little motor,' he said, taking a grubby piece of paper from the pocket of his overalls.

He handed me the bill. Saw my shock as I read the all-important total at the bottom. Three hundred pounds was a lot more than I was expecting for what was supposed to be a quick service.

'I did it trade, Mr Shannon,' he countered. 'But parts are bleeding expensive on this model. I was bloody lucky to get them in time.'

The writing was almost indecipherable – not that it would have made any more sense to me even if written in neat copperplate. My knowledge of the internal workings of cars was limited, to say the least – to be perfectly honest, they were a complete mystery to me. I scanned the long list. The first line, decoded, seemed to be 'plugs and points' – I'd heard about those; there was a squiggle which resembled a capital A and C, which I took to be something to do with the battery; 'oil' was understandable, although there seemed to be a bewildering variety of items with this word appended.

Arthur took the bill from me. He examined it carefully and knowledgeably before placing it on the table like the prime exhibit at Jimmy's trial. He scowled across the room.

'I know what you're thinking,' Jimmy said quickly in his own defence. 'But it ain't like that.'

He turned away from the threatening glower coming from Arthur and looked pleadingly in my direction.

'I wouldn't con you, Mr Shannon. You being a mate of Arthur's and all. It's all legit, I swear. If you don't believe me, look in the boot. I put all the parts I replaced in there so that you could see it's straight.'

Arthur seemed satisfied. Nodded at me.

I went upstairs. Extracted six fifty-pound notes from the unbroken bundle in my jacket.

Jimmy was relaxed again when I returned. The crisp notes disappeared into one of the cavernous pockets of his overalls. He finished his beer and reached unselfconsciously for another. Arthur raised his hand and shot a warning glance.

'Time I was off then,' Jimmy said.

Arthur nodded.

Jimmy moved fleetfootedly towards the door. 'Any time you need me, give me a bell, Mr Shannon. The number's on the bill.' He flashed me a cheeky smile. 'No job too large,' he said.

'Jimmy's alright,' Arthur said when we were alone again. 'I trust him. But only because I scare the shit out of him.' He gave me a broad grin and broke into a series of short guttural chuckles that sounded as if they had come from a bear with hiccups.

'I've had a bit of luck,' he said, when he had recovered from the effects of his laughter. 'At least I think I have,' he added, so as not to build my hopes too high.

He talked of how he had toured the bleak haunts of the junkies, drop-outs and runaways: completed two circuits of the mainline stations; stood, bored as hell, in amusement arcades; hung around Piccadilly Circus; spoken to the pimps in Soho. The photograph had been flashed so often it had become battered and torn. And with each exposure the same negative result.

'Nobody recognised him,' he said. 'But what did we expect? There's too many runty kids running around London. Why should one stand out from the crowd?'

A gleam came into his eye.

'Then I had a brainwave.' He paused to wait for some sarcastic remark but I was too curious to interrupt. 'I tried Victoria coach station. Thought that if he was strapped for cash he might have taken the cheapest way to London.'

Arthur leaned forward in his chair. 'I spoke to a girl,' he said proudly. 'She's got a pitch there. Professional beggar, you know? Borrows a neighbour's baby. Ponces off the passers-by. Makes a good living out of it. The picture rang a bell with her. Wasn't a hundred per cent sure, she said. But thinks she might have seen him just a couple of days ago.'

I couldn't wait to tell Sally the news. To see her face when she learnt her brother was safe.

Arthur killed my feeling of exuberance. He must have known what I was thinking. Frowning at me, he shook his giant's head in warning.

165

'Don't get carried away,' he said. 'It's nothing definite. I want to see her again. Can you get hold of some more photographs of Sam? Come and talk to her yourself. See what you think of her. She might just be trying it on – stringing me along in the hope of making some easy money.'

We arranged to meet on Tuesday. I would need to talk to Sally to borrow more pictures of her brother: somehow make it sound innocent, keep any hint of optimism from my voice.

I opened another can of beer. Sipped it thoughtfully. Something was bothering me.

I didn't get the chance to dwell on it. There were three sharp bangs on the door. Christ, this was beginning to resemble a scene from a Whitehall farce, people darting in and out like a fiddler's elbow.

When I opened the door there was no one there. Whoever it was must have run off down the street. But not before leaving a message.

A six-inch nail had been hammered into the wood of the door. The nail passed through the kitten's throat. Its neck had been broken: the tiny head lolled at right-angles to the dangling body. The poor creature's fur shone red where it caught the light. The blood had run like crimson tears from the eyes.

Or, more accurately, from the sockets.

The eyes themselves had been gouged out.

If it was meant to shock me then it didn't work. I was too sad and much too angry for there to be room for any other reaction.

'Bastard,' I shouted into the darkness. 'Bloody bastard.'

Behind me, Arthur swore too. 'What the hell is that,' he said.

'It's a warning, Arthur,' I replied, pushing past him.

I found a big square biscuit tin in the kitchen. Eased the limp body off the nail, cuddled it briefly, then curled it inside as best I could.

Arthur watched me as I worked the rage from my system by digging a shallow grave in the garden by the light from the kitchen window. The shadow of his head moved to and fro, shaking with bewilderment, as I worked. I had to use a metal serving spoon. It was all I could find.

'Drink this,' Arthur said, pressing a large brandy into my muddy hands.

'No thanks, Arthur. I need to think. This has got to be sorted out. Once and for all.'

'Then we'll need this,' he said, handing me a slip of paper. 'It's Ronson's address. I'll come with you.'

'No,' I said abruptly. It came out sounding ungrateful: that hadn't been my intention. 'Look, I'm sorry, Arthur, but I can handle this on my own. There's no need for you to get involved. This is my fight.'

'You haven't changed, have you?' he said. 'Always got something to prove, haven't you? When you land in trouble, I only hope you have the sense to call on your friends for help – if you can remember who they are, that is!'

He stormed out of the house in a temper, leaving me feeling stupid and ashamed.

I found Sofia's cigarettes and lighter on the dining room table. I tore the tip from one and lit the jagged edge, drawing deeply on the annoyingly still-thin smoke. 'Think, Shannon,' I told myself.

Back in the sitting room, I put a disc in the player. Sat broodily listening to Art Tatum and staring at the walls for inspiration.

How did Tatum do it? Blind in one eye, he was still technically the best. Swift, effortless, virtuoso movements along the keys of his concert piano: each tune he played possessed such variation as to encapsulate the entire history of jazz. He could play more notes in the opening four bars than Basie did throughout the whole number. Sometimes he wandered a dangerous path between interpretation and overcomplication but he was always far too accomplished to let himself get carried away.

John's photograph album caught my eye. It was jutting out from Mrs Simmons's neat arrangement on the top shelf of the bookcase. I took it down and leafed through the pages.

I did not recognise all the places. One deserted beach can look pretty much like another when a palm tree and deep blue sea is all you have to go by. Or if one is distracted from the scenery by the sight of Sofia's darkly tanned body encased in flowing white cotton, black hair specially fashioned in the beaded Caribbean style, wet lips pressed against John's in a loving kiss.

There were cities I did recall from travel programmes – the tilting houses of the Alfama in Lisbon, the Blue Mosque of Istanbul, Gaudi's unfinished cathedral in Barcelona. But it was the recurring theme of Switzerland that captured my attention and drew my interest.

Not because of the mountains.

Nor the lakes.

But the thought of all those banks.

With their strict code of secrecy.

And because, in the last few pages of the album where the pictures of the latest holiday had been neatly arranged, there was a blank sheet – four black corner mounts still attached. Where once a photograph had been.

CHAPTER EIGHTEEN

Brixton

This was to be my last night in solitary. The trial was over, the sentence passed. Tomorrow morning I would be escorted from Brixton to the relative comfort of Chelmsford.

I lay on the hard bed taking a long, last look round the cell and committing it to memory in case I was ever stupid enough to consider doing anything that might land me back here. Mark it well, Shannon. The thick, crisscross pattern of the bars on the window that cast an elongated chess board shadow on the cement floor each afternoon. The scatless loo with its flushing button – no chain or handle, too dangerous – and its cistern boxed away out of the reach of vandalising hands. The walls, so thinly whitewashed that the outlines of each individual brick were clearly visible. The graffiti scrawled by the illiterate hand of some pervert who wanted to do obscene things to 'littal girls'. Christ, I couldn't wait to be free – what a joke – of this place. Chelmsford was supposed to be even more overcrowded than Brixton, but at least it housed a better class of criminal.

This was the lowest I'd felt since my arrest. I knew the worst now – and the best. Provided I kept my nose clean I would be released on licence ('lifers' are not paroled like ordinary criminals) in a little under seven years, given the time already served. But in seven years the world would have changed. I would be like a time traveller setting foot on the surface of a strange land, locked in a past time. Seven lost years.

And seven years in which the trail for Susie's destroyer would grow icy cold. What a hopeless, pointless future.

I cried myself to sleep.

The morning brought a fresh dawn. Having hit rock bottom, there was only one thing to do – claw my way back up. I made a concerted effort to pull myself together. Hadn't I always known the likely repercussions of my action. 'Think positively,' I told myself. There was always the appeal: okay, so the prospects of success weren't that great but there was still a chance, wasn't there? And anyway, if that failed, well at least the music I liked was out of date already: seven years wouldn't make any difference to that – I could listen to Fats and pick out some of his tunes on any spare piano I might come across.

The two warders were as punctual as ever. It was six o'clock precisely, an hour yet before the rest of the corridor would welcome the day. Their faces showed no emotion: even the sight of my red-rimmed eyes failed to move them. Throughout my three months in solitary they had never allowed themselves to relax or show their feelings, not even for the briefest moment. This final duty was bound to be as cold and businesslike as everything else they had done.

They were hard, pitiless men – but I suppose that comes with the uniform. From their external appearance they seemed as if they would have been more at home locked inside a cell rather than being members of the privileged class who held the keys. McKellen, the taller of the two by an inch, stood six foot three in his shiny black boots. His nose had been broken so often that it was squashed sideways and made him look like he was already wearing the stocking mask of a bank robber. Sneed, the other half of this unsavoury pairing, had an unblemished boyish face: his complexion was greasy, however, and gave him the slippery demeanour of the ducking-and-diving species of villain – car thief and wheelman, perhaps. There but for fortune, I thought with all the philosophy that comes with too much time to think.

'Get up, Shannon,' Sneed said from his position by the door.

McKellen unclipped a pair of handcuffs from a loop on his belt. 'It's bracelet time,' he said. 'Come on, let's have your wrists.'

'Is this really necessary?' I asked. 'What do you think I'm going to do? Overpower both of you and then pick every lock in the place?'

McKellen's face twitched with the unaccustomed beginnings of a smile.

'Just do as you're told,' Sneed shouted impatiently. He moved closer, whistle in hand. 'Now, be a good boy and stick out your wrists.'

With a wearisome shake of my head I held out my hands, fists clenched to expand the muscles so that the cuffs wouldn't rub when I relaxed.

McKellen grabbed my hands roughly.

Sneed blew his whistle. I looked at him in disbelief.

'What the hell's going on,' I said. 'I'm not going to give you any trouble.'

'Oh yes you are,' McKellen said. 'You're trying to escape. Isn't that right, Tony?'

The whistle blew again. Long and shrill. Sounding a warning; demanding action.

McKellen started to drag me towards the door. Sneed came over, whistle clamped between his teeth, and took hold of my right arm. I kicked out at him in panic, landing a sharp blow on his shins. He swore loudly at me. But his grip didn't falter.

McKellen responded with one quick sweep of his foot, knocking the legs from under me. They held on tight as I fell, catching my body and supporting its full weight.

Perhaps, given some warning, I would have been able to put up more of a fight. But the element of surprise was against me – too much of a disadvantage to overcome. I was no match for the pair of them. Relentlessly, they manhandled me forward.

Sneed, with his free right hand, swung the door back on its hinges.

'Think yourself lucky, Shannon,' McKellen said breathlessly.

'Ronson asked for your eyes. But that would have been too difficult to explain to the Governor.'

With one last tug he pushed my left hand into the jamb of the door. Folded back two fingers. Pressed down with all his strength on the outstretched index and middle fingers. Satisfied, he gave a nod to Sneed.

The door – metal edged like a guillotine – slammed shut.

The pain was an atomic bomb exploding in my brain.

I dropped to the floor.

It took only a second before I lost consciousness. But that was long enough to register the sight of the blood pumping from my hand. And to work out how it was possible to be lying here on the floor – when the door was still tightly shut.

CHAPTER NINETEEN

'Mrs Ronson?'

'Who wants to know?' she snapped back at me.

It had taken an hour and a half to weave my way through the traffic and eventually locate this satellite-dished enclave of houses north of Romford. Ahead of me lay the unpleasant prospect of a meeting with a highly insistent bank manager followed by a frantic dash to Bristol for the memorial service. I had neither the time nor the inclination to be messed about. Anyway, if she wasn't Ronson's wife she would have said so.

'I need to talk to Freddie,' I said. 'Now, are you going to invite me inside or do I have to push you out of the way?'

'Just try it.' The warning came not from Mrs Ronson but from a shadowy figure at the end of the narrow hallway.

It had been a long time since I last heard that voice.

'What are you doing here?' I said.

'I might ask the same of you, Shannon,' Armed Robbery replied.

'So you're Shannon, are you,' the woman said. 'Piss off.'

She crossed her arms in front of her chest and stared defiantly into my eyes. George Turner walked to her side and placed his arm protectively around her shoulder.

They made an odd pair.

She was pushing fifty – but dressed like an eighteen-year-old hairdresser on a Sunday morning. Grey sweatshirt, matching leggings tucked into black slouch socks. Brilliant-white designer trainers with glittery pink laces and thick ankle straps. Bleached blonde hair, scraped back from her forehead and up from the neck, held in place by a wide elasticated gold band so that it stuck up like a badger-bristle shaving brush. Her face was heavily made up. A thick coat of foundation to cover the lines; blusher, mascara, pale blue eyeshadow, lipstick, all to divert attention from the stretchmarks around her neck. Her build was what is often described as 'athletic' – over-exercised and underfed.

George was at the opposite end of a series of semantic scales. Life on the outside had made him soft and flabby. He sported a vest – and red braces that struggled to hold up trousers hanging perilously below a beer belly. His face was bloated and the skin around his nose was flecked red with a rash of vessels broken by alcohol-induced high blood pressure.

He ran his fingers through dark, greasy hair in a movement that might have served some purpose a few years ago: there was too little remaining now for him to have to worry about it obscuring his vision.

'You heard her, Shannon,' he said gruffly. 'What are you waiting for?'

'I came to see Freddie,' I said. 'I'm not leaving till one of you tells me where he is.'

She looked at her watch and cast an impatient glance at George. In response he thrust a fat hand lazily at my chest in an economical attempt to knock me aside. I caught hold of his wrist and yanked him out of the doorway. His slippered foot missed the step and he stumbled past me, landing ignominiously on his knees on the gravel drive. Before he had time to react, I grabbed his arm and twisted it high behind his back so that his hand touched the base of his flabby neck.

'Now, can we go inside and talk,' I said, pulling him to his feet. 'Or do I have to break your arm.'

'All right,' she said resentfully. 'You've made your point. Let him go.'

I could see why they didn't want me in the house. The large, modern sitting room screamed at me: too much money – and too little taste. It had been decorated according to the whims of a chromatically insensitive interior designer who'd taken a few hours off from refurbishing chain hotels: three shades of pink with contrasting – conflicting – colours that drew their inspiration from a greengrocer's display of assorted apples. A job lot of sofas had been arranged in purposeful groups on the shag pile carpet – three in an open square in front of the fireplace, two curving around a television so colossal it could have been used in the local Odeon, four in a rectangle surrounding an oblong mahogany and brass coffee table – all covered in a satin print of rambling roses. There was enough electronic gadgetry to give a technophile an instant orgasm – three different satellite decoders, two videos, a camcorder nonchalantly posed on the mantelpiece, and a stereo with four speakers big enough to pump sound into the far reaches of the Albert Hall.

George waded through the thick carpet, painfully rubbing his arm. Shakily, he poured himself a large whisky from the cut glass decanter on the wood and ironwork bar.

'Christ, George,' she barked, sitting herself down near the fire, 'it's only half-past eight. Put that down and go and make some tea. And ring Debbie. Tell her to open up for me.'

George mooched sulkily from the room. 'Bloody hopeless,' she said, rolling her eyes. 'You know, there was a time when I thought you had done me a favour. Now I'm not so bleeding sure.'

'Where's Freddie?' I said.

She looked down at her nails. They were long and sharply pointed, reminding me disturbingly of the claws of a cat: her eyes had the same predatory feline look about them.

'How should I know?' she said. 'And why should I care? I've been Mrs Turner for the last five years. For better or worse.'

'You haven't answered my question,' I said, my temper rising.

'Why should I?' she replied without emotion.

I sprang up and grabbed her by the shoulders, shaking her roughly.

'Tell me where he is,' I shouted.

'Or what?' she sneered. 'You don't frighten me. After twenty years with Freddie, nothing scares me anymore.'

This was getting me nowhere.

'Okay,' I said calmly, 'I'll pay you for the information.'

She waved her hand, pointing around the room.

'What do I want with your money?' she said.

George came back bearing a tray of tea. He smiled, sensing the impasse from our moody silence. She looked long and hard at her husband; seemed to notice the singlet for the first time – the way it stretched so tightly across his stomach that the weave showed the colour of the flesh underneath, the black hair sprouting from out of the armholes, the wet, dark brown stain that smelt of cooking brandy as he set the tray on the table in front of us.

'Get dressed, for Christ's sake, George. Then lose yourself for a while. A long while. This is personal.'

He glared at her. But she just stared back until his nerve deserted him and he broke the eye contact. Five minutes later, we heard the front door slam behind him.

'Right,' she said. 'Let's get down to business. You mentioned payment, I believe.'

*

Brenda Ronson had learnt everything there was to know about Freddie. George had made sure of that.

For two years she had visited her first husband, making the long monthly trip to Broadmoor by a combination of slow trains and special coaches crowded with dutiful wives. By rights, Freddie shouldn't have been there: but where else could they put him? He couldn't have managed in an ordinary prison. In Broadmoor, at least they knew how to cope with difficult cases.

At first she had felt pity for Freddie – and vengeful anger at me. He had told her a sanitised version of the truth where I was the villain and he was the unfortunate victim. George set her straight – made sure her lasting emotions would be bitterness and revulsion.

George had always fancied her, she had said. But he didn't have the guts to do anything about it until Freddie posed no threat.

Brown paper parcel under his arm, George came directly from Brixton to see her. Had to tell her in person, he'd said sadly: it was only right she should know.

Brenda had been stunned by the news of her husband's drug addiction: the thought of needles always made her feel queasy, she admitted. If only that had been the end of it. She'd been spared none of the details of her husband's homosexuality – had run to the bathroom and knelt on the floor with her head down the toilet. She hadn't known what to do or where to turn. A good job George was there to comfort her, wasn't it? He had been clever – she realised that now.

She'd divorced Freddie – Christ, didn't she have grounds enough? – and remarried as soon as the decree absolute dropped through the letterbox. George had filled the vacuum in her life – given her everything she'd asked for: a new home, money to spend, even set her up in business running a ladies health and beauty club. Okay, so it was a bit like going from the frying pan to the fire: but at least George was 'straight' and legitimate now – well almost.

I didn't need to know all this.

But Brenda was taking great delight in spinning out the story, releasing pockets of information in dribs and drabs while I was made to sweat. When I reached my limit, she gave me an address.

She was laughing as I drove away.

The pressure from the back of the seat made me wince. I could feel the blood seeping stickily into my shirt where her nails had scratched deep furrows from my shoulder blades right down to the bottom of my spine.

CHAPTER TWENTY

If the cobbler's child is the least well shod and psychiatrists have the highest suicide rate, then accountants are among the worst people at looking after their own finances.

When I finally answered my bank manager's telephone call his tone was not the spreading oil-slick of the salesman but the 'see-me-in-my-study' of the headmaster: I must have slipped into the red on my current account and sent him into an advanced state of apoplexy. With the cushion of the money in the deposit account having disappeared in the letter of credit, it was 'naughty-boy' time – a large helping of humble pie, a rap over the knuckles and then despatched with a flea in my ear.

Naylor, the manager, held court in a soulless office, its walls lined solely with a progression of framed certificates bearing the impressive logo of the Institute of Bankers. Nothing betrayed any interest outside the bank. What about the family portrait that most executives place in a prominent position on the desk (a characteristic that John regarded caustically as particularly 'suburban')? Didn't he have a wife? Kids at school? He was probably quite a good sort underneath the dull suits, crisp white shirts and clipped haircut. If that was the case, I was unlikely to find out today.

I could tell immediately that this was going to be a heavy session: Naylor had summoned reinforcements. A thin, silver-haired man sat in Naylor's usual chair. He was studying my file.

Naylor coughed nervously and pointed to one of the hard chairs on the opposite side of his desk.

'This is Mr Battersby from our Head Office,' he said, nodding a deferential head at the man who now peered searchingly at me over the top of his half-frame spectacles.

I had expected a carpeting but this was more like they were going to nail my head to the floor.

'Here's the letter of credit,' I said proudly. 'I didn't need it after all.'

'Yes, thank you.' Naylor said inconsequentially.

He passed the letter to his superior who scored a diagonal line across it with the sharp point of a fountain pen and wrote 'cancelled' in a slow, painstakingly neat script.

'May I, Mr Naylor?' he asked.

'Please do, Mr Battersby,' Naylor replied, sounding distinctly relieved.

I stifled a giggle, expecting them to break into the song and dance routine of a music hall act.

'Three days ago, Mr Shannon,' Battersby said solemnly, 'you deposited a large sum of money in cash in your account. We would like an explanation, please.'

'Hang on,' I started to say, before the Head Office hatchet man cut me off.

'I can understand that you consider this an intrusion on our part,' (you're bloody right I do, I thought with mounting anger and total bewilderment) 'but let me explain our – the Bank's – predicament.' Battersby interlocked his fingers in the manner of a clergyman about to give a sermon.

'Under the terms of The Banking Act 1987, the Bank as a whole, and each employee personally I may add, is liable – and I use the term in the strict legal sense – to inform the police of any unusually large cash deposits. We are placed in the unenviable position of being cast as a watchdog over our customers' accounts – a "grass" as you might say.' He gave me a small, smug smile, evidently pleased with himself for his ability to use the vernacular. What an effort he was making to communicate with me! Even Naylor blushed with embarrassment.

'Bearing in mind,' he continued, 'the size and nature of an individual customer's pattern of deposits, we are obliged to bring to the notice of said authorities any transaction that might – and I stress 'might' – be related to money laundering or the proceeds of the criminal trade in drugs. Now, in your case . . .'

'What the hell are you talking about?'

'I thought I had explained perfectly well.' Battersby took off his glasses and placed them carefully on the desk. He addressed me as one might a subnormal child with hearing difficulties. 'Over the time you have had your account with this bank, the only deposits that have been made clearly relate to your monthly salary. This recent cash deposit, as well as being conspicuously large, is significantly divergent from your normal pattern. We are duty-bound to report the matter. Failure to do so would mean prosecution for the Bank and the staff involved.'

He turned from me to Naylor, piercing him with cold eyes.

'I should add, for the record, that I believe we should have taken such action when the alleged offence was first discovered. Mr Naylor here has urged caution. He has pointed out your background, and spoken up on your behalf of your efforts at "going straight". He believes you should have the opportunity to defend yourself.'

Good for Naylor. At least someone was reserving judgement in the case.

I realised the weakness of my position. The Banking Act, as I knew only too well from my studies, is purely concerned with identifying laundered drug money – if a cash deposit represents the proceeds from an armed robbery then the reporting is purely discretionary! In order to get off the hook I had to establish a provenance for the cash. Without this evidence the thought processes of the police – and anyone (presumably including Battersby) who read the newspapers – would follow the logical path: John's body contained a large dose of cocaine; Shannon's bank account swells via a large injection of cash; *ergo* Shannon is dealing in drugs.

Unfortunately, it's a little tricky to establish a provenance for money you know nothing about! Still, I wasn't going to take this lying down.

'Listen to me for a moment, Battersby. In spite of your predilection for arcane English and your long-winded way of expressing yourself, I understand exactly what you are saying. About your responsibilities, that is. And what I might term the necessity to "cover your arse".' I returned his earlier smug smile with interest. 'The point at issue, the nub of the argument, the native inhabitant in the woodpile, is that I have not made any cash deposit, large or otherwise. I'm afraid you have made a very serious mistake.'

He gave me a 'nice-try' look and handed me one of five white deposit slips that lay on the top of the desk.

'This is your name I take it? And your account number? There is no mistake, Mr Shannon. Not on our part, that is.'

'Yes, it's my name. Yes, it's my number. But I did not pay in any money. Someone else must have done. If you had a Boy's Own fingerprint kit you'd discover in a minute that any prints present on the slips are not mine.'

'We have a fairy godmother, do we, Mr Shannon? In any case,' Battersby replied obstinately, 'the money was paid into *your* account. Who exactly paid it in is of no relevance.'

'Excuse me, but it's highly relevant as far as I'm concerned.'

'The problem – your problem – still exists, Mr Shannon.'

I spoke directly to Naylor. At least he seemed to have some sympathy for me. Perhaps I could get through to him.

'Someone,' I said, as calmly and reasonably as I could manage under the circumstances, 'is trying and succeeding, it seems – to cause trouble for me. To stitch me up. I don't know why. I don't know who bears me so much malice as to do such a thing. Help me find out who it is. Believe me, I know nothing about any money. I don't even know how much you're talking about.'

Naylor consulted his notes. 'The total amount was twenty-five thousand pounds.' A gasp escaped from my lips. Naylor paused, registering my surprise, before giving me the full details.

'Five thousand in fifty pound denominations in each of five envelopes placed in our rapid deposit facility.'

So, no cashier involved. No face to be remembered. And, with this new knowledge, I was willing to bet that whoever had filled in the slips had worn gloves. I could feel a net closing in around me.

'Is there nothing you can do to help me?' I asked. 'Can't you trace the money. Find out where it came from? Maybe that would give me a clue.'

'It is impossible to trace used notes,' Battersby said pragmatically. 'And these were all used notes.'

'All but three, sir,' Naylor said to his superior's surprise.

'What?' Battersby asked. 'Why didn't you tell me this earlier?'

'We only discovered the fact this morning. We rechecked the money just before you arrived. Three of the notes were new. It's nobody's fault: they were almost impossible to spot among so many.'

Christ, there was some hope after all.

'So can you trace those three notes?' I said.

'That might be done,' Battersby said, pondering the matter. 'Yes. If the notes are truly new – they could appear unused but still have passed through several hands, you know. But why should we go to the trouble? This seems like a police matter to me.'

Naylor came to my rescue. 'Surely the police would want to know where the money came from. We could ask the Bank of England to trace the notes and *then* take a decision. After all, we would look a little foolish if we found the money did in fact come from some well-wisher. If that were the case, Mr Shannon might have some sort of action against us. Defamation?' He looked enquiringly in my direction.

'I would hate to have to involve the courts,' I said, 'but . . .'

'Very well,' Battersby reflected. 'But only on condition that all Mr Shannon's accounts are frozen until we are fully satisfied.'

I nodded my agreement. 'Can you tell me one thing? How might someone get hold of my account number?'

'The bank would never release such details, Mr Shannon,' Battersby said defensively.

Naylor was more informative. 'Account details are printed on receipts from cash machines. That's why we provide boxes for unwanted receipts.'

'Any other way?'

'If you have direct debits or standing orders, those companies would have your bank details. And, of course, there's always your employer. Your salary is paid directly into your account.'

'Thank you for your help,' I said, rising to go.

'I hope you appreciate the risk Mr Naylor is taking on your behalf,' Battersby said. He had his scapegoat all staked out in case I skipped the country. 'You will come to see us again in three days' time, Mr Shannon. Shall we say eleven o'clock?' He wrote the time in his diary without waiting for my reply. 'Then we must resolve the matter. One way or the other.'

Three days.

It didn't give me much time.

I hoped I could find all the answers by then.

If not, Battersby would follow the procedures to the letter of the law. He would report the matter to the National Criminal Intelligence Service. Via this postbox service the information would be circulated to the appropriate area. That meant Collins would get to hear about it.

And then Shannon tartare would be the dish of the day.

CHAPTER TWENTY-ONE

Richard was snappy and irritable when I phoned, as if he had been harbouring some grudge all weekend and I had provided the first opportunity for him to vent his spleen. He left me with the distinct impression that he was regretting his magnanimous offer of taking as much time off as necessary.

Perhaps, I rationalised, he was simply a victim of the Monday morning malaise: more likely, though, the relationship with his wife was not going smoothly.

Arabella Goodwin came from a family with 'old' money. She was used to handling servants – treated Richard like one on occasions, it was rumoured. I wondered if he endured this treatment as a Catholic does the confessional – a penance that wipes the slate clean for the chalking up of future sins. She organised their busy social calendar with a ruthless efficiency that ate, purposefully, into Richard's philandering time. And carefully selected their circle of friends with a special eye on the women. Maybe he had spent the last two days locked in their country house with a bunch of hooray Henrys and their horsy wives.

Whatever his problem, there was nothing I could do about it. I was phoning from the wind-battered kiosk in the desolate landscape of a service area east of Swindon: too close to my destination to make turning back worthwhile even if he had ordered it. Probably the *fait accompli* had not helped Richard's mood.

After the phone-call I bought a map of Bristol. I had hoped to find one in the Monte Carlo but all my first investigation of the glovebox revealed was the manual for the car and another unmarked cassette. I placed the latter on the passenger seat for playing later, hoarding it like a treasure-trove in the hope that it might turn out to be Fats Waller. Among the aristocracy of jazz (Duke Ellington, Count Basie, Earl Hines, Nat 'King' Cole), Fats was the clown prince. The unparalleled master of humour, and of surprise. Every time he recorded a song, whether on piano or organ – you couldn't even guarantee which with Fats – the treatment was different. Sometimes he would play as if it was an exercise in self-parody, the accompanying throaty chuckle being the giveaway clue; at other times he would demolish the ego of any one of his contemporaries, be it a jazz or classical pianist, by executing an extravagant pastiche of their style. Yes, Fats would be the perfect antidote to the memorial service.

I examined the boot but that was mapless too. Empty, in fact, except for the discarded parts Jimmy had saved as insurance against distrust. For all I knew they could have been the essential ingredients for building a nuclear reactor or a giant food processor.

Jimmy, I acknowledged with respect, had done a brilliant job. The car responded immediately to every command: accelerated smoothly, braked in a short, arrow-straight line. Even the engine sounded quieter, purring contentedly rather than roaring like a hungry lion.

The final forty miles of the journey along the M4 to Bristol took less than half an hour. The sun, unhampered by clouds, shone warmly down on the car, the tinted windows inefficient reflectors of its strength. I regretted not dumping the contents of the boot into one of the bins at the service area: I could then have removed the roof panel and stowed it away. Perhaps on the way back – if the weather held.

My thoughts centred on Sofia. And the uneasy feeling she gave me. Was she as innocent as she seemed at first sight? Or playing a waiting game – biding her time till the will was finalised? Then hop aboard the next plane to Zurich. Collect a small fortune from the impregnable vaults of an anonymous bank. Vanish out of sight. Start a new life on the distant shore of a country with no extradition treaty with Britain. Was her forthcoming holiday some sort of reconnaissance mission?

I gave her the benefit of the doubt – for the moment at least. John had comprehensively fooled me; might he have hidden his darker – and richer – side from her? Afraid, maybe, that she might only have been after his money?

My troubled mind leapt from one problem to another, reminding me now of the missing photograph. Had she slipped it out of the album while I had been sitting pathetically sipping her brandy-laced coffee?

I was forced abruptly to abandon my conjecture. On leaving the motorway I was plunged into the unfamiliar complex of roads that led to the heart of the city. With the aid of quick sideways glances at the map, I managed to negotiate the network of roundabouts and find the right route for Redland.

The church was impossible to miss. A towering Victorian folly built by some wealthy merchant (sherry? corn?) in the Gothic basilica style: huge flying butt.....s, piers and half arches, forming two naves distinctl.....wer than the central tower. The local stone, once crea....lad discoloured with the passing of time and the relentle....larch of pollution: the external face now had a dark and....bidding appearance.

In contrast to the size....the church, the car park was tiny. Three cars stood in....leat row: a maroon Sierra, a white Cavalier and a dark-blue Escort, six or seven years old from the prefix on the battered registration plate.

A taxi scrunched to a halt on the pea shingle.

Out stepped Sofia.

Dressed in the customary black of widow's weeds – from pillbox hat down to patent high heels.

I walked across to greet her. Kissed her lightly on the cheek. A brief premeditated peck designed to keep a distance between us; avoid awkward memories of our hasty parting the last time we had met. My lips were still brushing her skin when I heard the click of a shutter and the whirr of a camera's motor-drive.

As we turned in the direction of the sounds they were repeated again and again, the occupant of the Sierra snapping away with all the unhurried speed of a true professional. Before we had time to react, the engine of the car was turning over and it was speeding past us. I hoped it was only a local rag that would carry the photographs, not one of the more imaginative nationals which might weave an interesting – but embarrass-ingly inaccurate – story from the picture of this innocuous kiss.

Sofia was furious. As we passed under the central arch and through the outer doors of the church she was ranting on ven-omously about invasion of privacy and an unwarranted intrusion into a moment of personal grief. I mused cynically on her sanctimonious attitude. Despite her collection of *Vogue*s, she worked in the advertising department of one of the mass-market women's monthlies – the sort that is half-full of telephoto pictures of the Royal family, the remainder padded out with features which were poorly disguised rewrites of press releases issued by manufacturers of cosmetics or slimming aids. She owed her living to the snooping of the paparazzi: why make such a fuss?

Once inside the church, her tirade suddenly ceased. There was an atmosphere of complete calm, heavily laden with that deep serenity that comes only from the silence: it pressed down from the high curved cciling, defying any sacrilegious breaking of the peace within. It stilled – chilled – one's very spirit.

The vicar, his white-robed back turned to us, knelt in medi-tation in the flickering twilight of the candle-lit altar.

Only four people were seated in the pews: their heads were bowed reflectively, private thoughts as hidden as the downcast faces.

I took Sofia's arm as we walked up the aisle. Heads turned at the rhythmic clacking of her heels on the stone. Two men of about my age let their eyes enjoy a slow wandering journey over Sofia's body. An elderly couple – white-haired lady and balding man – I took, in the absence of other likely contenders, to be John's parents. They acknowledged my presence with economical nods. The woman gestured for Sofia and I to sit in the empty pew behind them. In reverential whispers they introduced themselves to me as Alice and Jack.

I suppose it was a necessary ritual. An act that had to be performed to satisfy some sense of rightness and assuage a moral duty to give a little dignity to John's departure from this world. A way of saying goodbye in the inconvenient interregnum before there was a body to cremate and ashes to seal away in an urn along with the memories.

The vicar's booming voice echoed in the void, drowning out the self-conscious mumblings as the six of us sang the hymns and obediently gave the required responses to the litany of prayers.

I felt like a hypocrite as I listened to the false tribute to John's rectitude.

The only saving grace was that this ghastly pantomime did not arouse in me any painful reminders of past funerals. To me, the service was a mockery of the real thing – too far removed from my own experiences to evoke true sadness.

When at last the ordeal had ended, we filed back down the aisle without a word being spoken. Sofia climbed with studied grace into the back of the Westons' Escort: John's two schoolfriends prepared to follow in the Cavalier.

I brought up the rear, grateful for a few minutes alone to prepare myself for the wake.

*

The house was part of a gloomy late nineteenth-century terrace. It sat perched high on a steep hill. The street was narrow and acted as a corridor down which the wind could whistle unchecked. The tall buildings on either side must have blotted out the rays of the sun for all but an hour or so either side of noon. The only difference between the Westons' property and its neighbours was that they were slightly better maintained – and that wasn't paying them any compliments. The paint was faded and so badly cracked and peeling that the frames on the sash windows looked like they had a bad case of eczema. A section of the metal guttering, ragged-edged with rust, hung precariously where it had slipped from out of its supporting bracket. Some of the slates on the roof were split and badly in need of replacing. The chimney listed to one side crying out for repointing, if not rebuilding. The house was an accident waiting to happen. Whatever John had done with his money, I reflected dismally, he had lavished little of it on his parents.

Although the inside of the house was in need of a coat of paint, it was clean and tidy. The lavender scent of furniture polish floated in the air. The six of us stood in an awkward group in the small rectangle formed by the boundaries of the television and the three-piece suite that surrounded it. A miscellaneous collection of glasses had been filled with sweet Cyprus sherry: each sip clung tenaciously to the roof of the mouth like hot treacle tart. What little conversation there was flowed as freely as hard liquor at a meeting of Alcoholics Anonymous.

Alice went off to the kitchen to make sandwiches which nobody wanted. Her husband's lined face wore a sour expression. 'Don't blame me,' it seemed to say, 'it wasn't my idea. Give me a quiet life any day.' I tagged along after her, looking for any excuse to postpone talking to the dwarfish man for as long as politeness would permit.

The kitchen was long and narrow, the original scullery wall having been knocked down at some stage in the declining fortunes of the house. The work surfaces and cupboards were white melamine trimmed with that malicious sort of cheap metal edging that cuts your fingers if extreme care is not exercised. A stock-pot bubbled on the gas cooker, the greasy steam from a chicken carcass escaping like smoke signals from the ill-fitting lid.

'We haven't always lived like this, you know.'

It was the start of an explanation, not an excuse. I could tell that, although used to better surroundings, she was not ashamed of the inside of the house. It, and everything contained within, may have been old but it was spotless. She had made the most of what little money they had. And, I thought with a deepening respect, judging by the thinness of her frame, she had provided for her husband's nutritional needs at the expense of her own.

Alice washed her hands and dried them on a blue and white striped towel that hung limply from a wooden roller. She put the loop of a floral pinafore over her home-permed hair to protect the charcoal-grey woollen dress. After tying a neat bow at the back, she began to cut straight, uniform slices from a fresh crusty loaf with the close-toothed serrated edge of a long breadknife.

'We once lived in Washington,' she said to my surprise. I had expected the tale of Jack Weston to be a bigger taboo than the works of Enid Blyton in the public library of a labour controlled council. For some unaccountable reason it seemed like I was going to be privileged with her inner secrets.

'It was a lovely apartment,' Alice said in a soft West country accent. 'Huge rooms. Tall ceilings. Big picture windows, glorious views over the city. And all the mod cons a woman could wish for – we even had a dishwasher.' She smiled wistfully to herself. Allowed herself a moment's reflection on happier times.

'Jack was working in those days, of course,' she continued, sighing deeply. 'Civil servant. Foreign Office. John was born while we were there.'

A tear formed at the corner of her eye. She dabbed it away quickly with a handkerchief retrieved from the sleeve of her dress, lest its presence became an invitation for others to join it.

'Thank you for coming today. It wasn't much of a turn-out, was it?' She shrugged her bony shoulders. 'Only to be expected, I suppose. John never had many friends. – I didn't really think anyone from his school would bother to come – I bet they drew straws!'

She stared at the white tiles on the wall, immersed in thoughts of long ago. I took the bread from the board. Picked up a knife, its bone handle yellowed with age. Spread butter, frugally, over the slices.

She turned her sad face toward me.

'John didn't come to see us very often. Once every couple of months was enough for him. I think the house brought back too many memories. John lived for the present and the future: we only served to remind him of the past.' Alice looked at me thoughtfully. 'When you first went to work for John he used to talk of you a lot. About how you were his protégé – his sorceror's apprentice, he called you. He played tricks on you, I suppose? Was that why you fell out?'

She noticed my puzzled expression.

'That's why I wanted you here today. I hoped you might make your peace with him. Forgive and forget. Bury your differences.'

'There wasn't anything to forget, Alice.'

'Something must have happened between you? Something made him turn against you. There came a point where he wouldn't even have your name spoken.'

'Somehow you've got the wrong end of the stick,' I said shaking my head. 'I've never done anything to hurt John. Even if I had, then surely he would have given me some sign. John didn't say a word to me about any rift between us. Neither has Sofia for that matter.'

She paused as if weighing up in her mind whether it was better to stop now or continue until a reason was found. 'Maybe it was just because of your height: John would have been jealous of that. He so hated being small. He would have given anything to have been as tall as you.'

'No, that can't be it. He wouldn't have given me the job in the first place if that were the case.' There may have been some truth in what she said, but somehow I couldn't admit to her that John had selected me solely because I posed no threat.

Alice looked at me pensively. 'When you were friends,' she said, 'did he ever tell you about his schooldays?'

'He never talked about himself much at all. Or encouraged any questions.'

'He had a terrible time, you know. Best years of your life, they say. Not for someone as tiny as John, they weren't. The other kids poked fun at him – no, worse than that. They bullied him. Mercilessly, if the truth be told. It started in America. We thought it might be different in England, but it was worse.'

She fought back the tears, shaking her head helplessly.

'We didn't make a very good job of John, did we?'

Alice continued without waiting for a denial.

'I was far too soft with him – made him a real Mummy's boy. But then, what could I do? Jack left me no option – he was always so strict with John. He said it was for John's own good. He made him hard inside – told me it would help to protect John against the taunts. Hide your true feelings, he told the boy. Don't give the bullies any satisfaction – and eventually they will leave you alone. I don't think it worked in practice. Or if it did, too much damage was done in the meantime.'

I waited for her to tell me more about her son. Instead she shot me a question from out of the blue.

'Prison didn't change you, did it?' she asked.

'In more ways than you can imagine,' I answered.

She blushed, her eyes registering my buttering of the bread.

'I'm sorry,' she said. 'I meant . . .'

'It's okay,' I replied. 'You're right. Prison might have forced me to grow up but deep down inside I suppose I'm still the same person as first walked through the gates. I adapted to the life, if that's what you could call it. It was being there in the first place that I found hard to take. It wasn't all bad. I made some good friends. And learnt what was really important in life.'

'It changed Jack,' she said. 'Destroyed him.'

I wondered whether she had been bottling this up for years. Did my spell in jail make me the ideal listener – or would any outsider have done? Or was it simply the moment that was important? This wasn't just Jack's story: it was John's too. Jack Weston, inadequate and misguided father when he was around – and a liability when he wasn't.

It had all happened a long time ago, just a boyhood memory to me now.

Jack Weston, minor clerk in the British Embassy. Jack Weston, traitor. Five years for selling state secrets to the Russians.

It was not a glamorous case. Jack Weston had not been seduced by a beautiful Russian spy or galvanised by any burning political fervour –he had committed treason purely and simply for the love of money.

There were few embarrassing ramifications for national security. They had caught him before he had risen to a rank which would have given him access to material of any real significance. Much of what Jack Weston told the Russians they had known already – the small acts of treachery were simply bait on a barbed hook left dangling in the water for the bigger haul that would come with promotion.

John, if my memory was correct, would have been about eleven or twelve at the time – that impressionable pubescent time of life when one fluorescent pink spot at the end of your nose can make you feel suicidal. Like me, the boys at his school would have been greedily devouring the diet of spy stories served up at that time by the television and cinema. We probably paid more attention to the publicity than our parents, enthralled as we were by the world of espionage with its black and white morality and easily understood cast of heroes and villains. Jack Weston, in those days of Napoleon Solo, James Bond and Harry Palmer, would have slotted easily into the pigeon-hole marked 'rogue and scoundrel'. And his son categorised likewise. Untrustworthy. Unforgivable.

The sins of the father!

'It couldn't have been easy for any of you,' I said somewhat lamely.

But she was not seeking sympathy. Just catharsis. John was being laid to rest right here in the kitchen.

'We sold the house in Cheltenham. Moved here. The money kept us going for a while. That and my job. Of course that meant I wasn't around much for John. By the time I realised what John had become, it was too late.'

She was being unfair on herself. Need not have shouldered any of the burden. But, I appreciated with admiration for her courage, it was her way of coming to terms with the situation. To put all the blame on her husband would have ended the marriage – left her with nothing to show for her life.

'Somehow,' she continued bravely, 'John managed to get

through school. A test of survival, I suppose. He became single-minded – more determined than ever not to be a loser like his father. Win at all costs. That was what mattered to him.' She turned her head away in shame at her son's philosophy.

'By the time he went to university his father's crime had been long forgotten. I'm glad, in the end, John found success. He wanted it so badly.'

She added sprigs of parsley and wedges of tomato to the two plates of sandwiches. Gazed down unhappily. Not for the reason that she was dissatisfied with the result. But because the task was finished.

'We best get back,' she sighed. 'Thank you for listening to an old fool.'

I took her in my arms and hugged her tight. 'You're no fool, Alice. There are worse sins than spoiling a child. Don't blame yourself.'

We trooped in together, trying not to look conspiratorial. Jack Weston went off to fetch the sherry bottle. Sofia seized the opportunity to pounce.

'What the hell took you so long?' she whispered angrily. 'One more minute with that man and I would have gone mad.'

I wondered if she had bitten the bullet and told him about the will. No, she must have steered clear of the subject. After all, I hadn't heard any shouts of abuse coming through the kitchen door!

She nibbled circumspectly at a ham sandwich. Consulted the jewelled face of her gold wristwatch. Effected an expression of surprise. Declared with insincere regret that she had a train to catch. Phoned for a cab with indecent haste.

'See you Thursday,' she reminded me as she made her escape.

Pausing briefly at the front door, she promised the Westons faithfully that she would keep in touch.

None of us believed her.

Or, for that matter, cared much that it was such an obvious lie.

*

I lasted only another half an hour after Sofia's departure.

The scene at this dreary wake reminded me depressingly of the time I had tried to impress an intellectual girlfriend by taking her to a performance of Mahler. I remembered sitting down at 7.30 in the evening, listening to three hours of wonderful music, looking at my watch and discovering it was still only a quarter to eight.

Each minute in that cramped living room passed as slowly as in the concert hall.

Jack Weston drained the sherry bottle. And became more voluble with each sip. He was an expert on every subject. Especially the state of the world and what should be done to put it to rights. For every ill, he knew exactly where the blame should lie – on somebody else's shoulders. Throughout our conversation, his diatribe, I looked down on him – in both senses.

On leaving, I gave Alice my sympathy. I'm sure she understood that it was intended as much in regard to her living husband as her dead son.

Outside, at last, I breathed in the fresh air and perversely lit a cigarette. I stood by the car taking a final look at the bleak house and waiting for John's two schoolfriends to make their escape. I was grinding the butt beneath my shoe when they emerged.

Steve, a six-foot West Indian with prematurely grey hair that made his black skin shine like the darkest ebony, walked across and ran his hand lovingly over the front wing of the car.

'Thank God that's over,' he said with a lisp so heavy that I had to strain to understand the words. He smiled at me. There was a thin sliver of ham stuck between two of his teeth.

Loosening his tie, he took a pack of Camels from his suit pocket and flashed it in the general direction of myself and his friend, Terry, as if hoping that neither of us would take up the offer. We disappointed him, and stepped into the cover of the privet hedge to light up.

'It must be twelve, thirteen years since we last saw John,' Terry said with a faraway look in his eyes. He was a thin, serious man with the pallor of a librarian and the thick-lensed spectacles to match. 'The papers say he'd made quite a success of his life. Sounded like a bit of a whizz kid. You worked with him, didn't you?'

If he'd read the papers then he knew the answer already.

I nodded though, to keep him talking.

'How did he turn out?' Terry asked.

'The consensus of opinion seems to be that he was a little shit,' I said, ignoring the advice of the proverb about not speaking ill of the dead. It was controversial enough to engender some response.

'That makes sense,' Steve replied. 'Easier for a leopard to change his spots.'

'But you were friends of his, weren't you?' I asked.

'No way.' Steve spat the words into the air.

'Then why did you come?'

'We had our reasons,' Terry answered.

'And what were they?' I gestured to the house. 'Don't worry, they can't hear you – although I doubt if anything you say would be a surprise to them – and you won't be offending me. He was no friend of mine, it seems.'

Terry looked enquiringly at Steve. A shrug of the shoulders came back in answer.

'It was all such a long time ago,' Terry said.

'But some things can't be forgotten,' Steve added quickly.

'It was our fault, Steve. I thought we'd agreed that. Anyway, once a shit always a shit. Isn't that right?'

If you tell me what happened,' I said, 'it might help me to give you a straight answer.'

'You tell him,' Steve said, walking away. 'I'll wait in the car.'

So Terry told me the story. His hand shook as he smoked the cigarette.

There had been five of them in the gang at school. More a group than a gang, Terry explained. Until John came along. 'Okay, so it was wrong to pick on John. We know that now.' But back then John was just a little kid who couldn't take the jokes about his father. The more he snivelled at their gibes, the more they teased him.

Steve had been the one to move it on a phase. Or so Terry said. Because he was black, Steve was used to being on the wrong end of the bullies. It was good to be hunter rather than hunted.

But there came a time when extorting John's pocket money and beating him up to keep him from informing didn't seem to provide the same degree of pleasure. They decided to play a trick on him.

They'd had a change of heart, they told him. We can all be friends, they had said with smiles.

John could join the gang. Be one of them.

If he underwent the initiation ceremony.

Of course they'd never had any intention of keeping their side of the bargain but that hadn't crossed John's mind. To him the answer to all his problems was simple. All he had to do to be accepted was pass the test.

Over the fence into the adjoining girls' school. Steal one of the pink gingham dresses and a straw hat. And back the way he'd come.

Wearing the dress and hat, naturally.

John was given a time limit of ten minutes. Steve had borrowed a stopwatch and pressed the button as John set off from the quadrangle. He somehow scrambled himself up and over the five-foot iron railings and ran full-pelt towards the games pavilion where, he had reasoned, he would find least difficulty in snatching the clothes.

As soon as he was out of sight the crowd gathered, a flood of uncontrollable giggling coursing through them at the thought of the sight of John when he made his triumphal (!) return.

He had looked just as silly as they'd imagined. The pretty pink dress flapping around his ankles as he ran, one hand clasped to his head to keep the hat from blowing away in the wind.

If he had chosen a smaller dress, he might have made it.

Conscious of the stopwatch ticking away, he launched himself at the railings in a flying leap and by sheer willpower climbed to the top. As he prepared to jump to the ground his feet became entangled in the hem of the dress. He lost his balance. Swayed. Toppled. And fell.

Not forwards. Or backwards.

But straight down. On the iron spikes.

'He was off school for a long while,' Terry said, ashen-faced. 'We tried to make friends with him then. Bury the hatchet. I even shared a cubicle with him when our class went swimming. The doctors had patched him up pretty well. You could hardly tell they'd only managed to save one of his balls.'

My stomach was churning inside. I even began to feel a little sympathy for John.

I thought with anger of Winstanley and his shoddy autopsy. The bastard was more interested in the internal workings of an innocent girl than the external appearance of a grown man. The sooner they retired him the better.

'John got his own back,' Terry said, interrupting my reliving of old grudges.

'To show there were no hard feelings – what a joke! – John gave us a bag of doughnuts. Steve was the first to take a bite. There was a razor blade inside. Steve cut his mouth to pieces.'

From the look on his face I could tell it was a vision that had haunted him all this time. In spite of this, Terry had come along to make his peace with John. I didn't speculate on Steve's motives.

*

I stopped at the first service area on the motorway. Drank two cups of coffee to clear the sickly-sweet taste of the sherry that lingered in my mouth and to give my brain the shot of caffeine it needed for the drive home.

I phoned Sally. I was so anxious to call her when Sofia would not be around that it slipped my mind that Sally was on nights. Her voice was distant and dreamy – until I mentioned her brother. When asking for the extra photographs I stressed she should not build her hopes too high. But she clutched at the straw, sounding genuinely cheerful for the very first time.

The drive back was tedious. The novelty of the car was beginning to wear off. Embankments swallowed the scenery whenever there was the prospect of it becoming remotely interesting. A succession of old men in hats drove at seventy miles an hour, morally guarding the outer lane and refusing to let me pass. Each mile closer to London brought an increase in traffic, demanding more concentration for diminishing returns in speed.

The final chord on the tape filled the car. I replaced the cassette with the one from the glovebox, clinging to the hope that it might be Fats. Maybe Fats would be successful in diverting my mind away from gruesome mental images of iron railings and doughnuts.

No, it wasn't Thomas Wright Waller. Something even more surprising.

Stupidly – since I was alone in the car – I felt my face flush.

I wanted to turn off the sounds.

But felt a compulsion to listen.

A nauseating rhythm.

Building to a clamorous crescendo.

Richard's voice deafening me with obscene climactic shouts.

And Sofia urging him on to orgasm.

CHAPTER TWENTY-TWO

The tape was the turning point.

Before its discovery it had been like trying to complete a complicated jigsaw without being able to look at the picture on the lid of the box. Up until then I had only managed a partial solution to the puzzle. The corners and edges may have been settling nicely into place but they were featureless, providing me with a basic outline but showing no pattern. What I had lacked were any reference points from which to guess the hidden image of the finished product.

As I lay in bed that night, going over all that had happened, examining every scrap of evidence with a fresh eye, the first dawn of realisation broke. There were still many pieces of the puzzle to fit into their proper positions. But it was just a matter of time now. The picture was clear. At last I understood.

*

The following morning found me in no great rush to get to the office. There were only two things I needed to do at work. One of those was to talk to Richard. And that would be whenever it suited me – not him.

I got up late. Had a painful shower, the jets of water stinging the deep fingernail cuts on my back. Shaving wasn't much better. I walked to the little parade of shops around the corner to stock up on food. Then scoured the shelves of the chemists for a styptic pencil for the nicks on my face and a few other essential items. The last stop was the off-licence: I went in for some special wine, weakened and came out with two packs of cigarettes as well.

After a leisurely breakfast I made a copy of the cassette on John's double tape deck and spent the next couple of hours adding large amounts to the profits of British Telecom.

Towards the end of the second call I needed something to write on. Jimmy's bill still lay on the coffee table. After scribbling down the details, I idly turned the piece of paper over. My eyes drifted down the long list of work carried out, the parts that had been replaced.

I finished the call hurriedly.

Sat back in the chair staring at an item half-way down the bill.

'AC.' It wasn't anything to do with the battery. Schoolboy physics should have told me that. Batteries are direct current – DC. AC was Jimmy's shorthand for accelerator cable.

Only one thought crossed my mind.

Who did I trust more?

Jimmy or Sofia?

Jimmy won hands down.

There had been no accident, I realised, on the motorway. No attempt on John's life. According to Sofia's story the accelerator cable had snapped – a new one would have had to be fitted to make the car drivable. There was no chance a replacement could have worn out so quickly.

Sofia had lied.

This time it was the sin of commission. Rather than omission, as in the case of Richard and the tape.

Another piece of the jigsaw fell into place.

*

I had left the call to Arlene till last, aware of the anti-social circumstances of the time difference and the unsatisfactory way we had parted. She must have been deeply asleep when the phone rang: the high-pitched tone beeped away for nearly a minute. Her speech was slow and hazy with more than a touch of irritation from the effects of the rude awakening. I spoke quickly. Told her to make herself some coffee. Said I would call back in fifteen minutes: it was very important. Then put the receiver down before she had a chance to go through the 'do you know what time it is?' or the 'you bastard!' routine.

By the time I called back it sounded like she had forgiven me – she mentioned neither the hour nor my letter.

It was good to talk it through with someone. Although she listened to the story without interruption, I could visualise the encouraging nods of agreement and the expression of tacit approval coming from the other end of the phone.

We left our personal thoughts to the very end. Her words of caution continued to echo in my ears as I closed the front door and set off to work.

Richard looked like a guard's officer in mufti. His blazer, complete with shiny gold buttons, was being treated to a final outing of the year before the chill of autumn set in with a vengeance. The striped tie could have been from any of a number of good public schools or regiments, but was more probably chosen by Arabella from 'Daddy's' tailors in Savile Row. The knot was a double Windsor (never trust a man with a Windsor knot, they used to say – did a double make him twice as untrustworthy?).

His mood was even worse than when we had talked on the telephone. And a far cry from the last time I had sat in his office. No offer of tea or coffee this time. No pleasantries. No polite enquiries about the memorial service for John. No 'old boy' either – more 'my man'. I was still settling myself in the chair when he embarked upon an abrasive lecture about my commitment (or lack of it) of late. He reminded me curtly of my joint responsibilities to the firm and to Metcalfe whose misfortune it would shortly be to pick up the pieces and sort out the mess which, Richard assumed, would be the poor man's inheritance.

I listened without reaction or emotion. Gave him none of the humility he expected as of right, and that would have been taken as encouragement to continue the harangue.

My silence neither confirmed nor denied his accusations about my performance. It only served to make him more angry.

He went apoplectic when he saw me take the Walkman from my pocket. His disbelieving face turned red with temper. I could see veins pulsing in his forehead.

His expression turned to surprise as I passed the machine across the desk to him. Then he must have realised what was coming. The angry red turned to a shocked white.

'I think you ought to listen to this,' I said with all the authority that comes with newly-discovered power. 'It won't take more than a moment or two – after all, you've heard it before. Just enough to refresh your memory. Then we can talk some more about responsibility.'

He hesitated. Picked up the headphones. Gripped them tightly in an effort to disguise his trembling fingers. Thought long and hard about what to do next. Tried to read my face. Was I bluffing? Did I simply suspect what had gone on but lacked the proof? Would agreeing to listen to a tape be, in itself, an admission of guilt?

But he was a coward at heart. Had to know for sure.

He slipped the headphones on. Pressed the play button. Closed his eyes in despair when the sounds he had dreaded hearing for so long reverberated in his ears with the rhythm of a manic metronome.

'It's what you were looking for, isn't it?' I asked. 'When you broke into John's desk.'

He gave a weary nod in answer.

'It was a stupid thing to do,' he said.

I wondered to which of his two ill-considered acts he was referring. Breaking into the desk? Or succumbing to the temptation of Sofia?

'I panicked when I learnt of John's death. The police were bound to search his office. If the tape was there, I had to find it first. Destroy the damned thing before they had a chance to listen to it. I knew how incriminating it would sound. An obvious motive for killing John.'

He looked at me anxiously. 'What are you going to do with it? Give it to the police? My wife?'

'I haven't decided yet,' I replied, leaving the threat of exposure hanging over him like the proverbial sword of Damocles. I wanted him to have time to think – let his mind play on the repercussions, magnify them until talking to me seemed like the least of all evils.

'It depends how honest you are with me,' I said. 'I want the whole story. Then I'll let you know.'

Wisely, he spared me none of the details – there was nothing to be gained any more by lying.

He did not look at me once throughout the sad soliloquy: just sat pathetically with downcast eyes, elbows resting on the desk, hands on cheeks, his little fingers pressed against the sides of his mouth so that I had to lean forward in the chair to hear the confession.

It had happened three years ago.

At that time the working relationship between the two men was strained. Richard was trying to persuade John to move departments. It was the firm's policy to broaden the experience of the younger members by switching them around every few years. But Richard had another, more delicate, reason: he had received vague complaints from a couple of dissatisfied clients – acquisitions where the profits had fallen disappointingly short of expectations. Nothing could be proved, of course. No formal accusation of negligence or malpractice had been made. But, to Richard's eye, the mud was beginning to stick to John's tailor-made suit.

John baulked at any move from A&M. He threatened petulantly to reconsider his whole future at the firm. Then asked for a week's holiday to think it all over. Richard, sensing a weakening in his opponent's stance, readily agreed to the request. It was an easy get-out, he admitted to me: after a few days off, John might come to his senses and the final confrontation be avoided.

Sofia had phoned the next day, sounding distraught. There were little pauses in her sentences: Richard imagined she was wiping away tears!

I sympathised briefly with him at this point – I knew how good she was at playing the damsel in distress. How all too easy it was to be taken in by her, even when bent on resistance.

John was so unhappy, she had said dolefully, that he had gone away without her. He'd never done that before. She wanted so much to help him. Could she talk to Richard? Maybe together they might be able to work something out. If not a compromise, then perhaps some way of sugaring the pill and making the move more palatable for John.

And then the sting had come.

She appreciated how busy Richard must be. Couldn't possibly disrupt his working day. Maybe they could talk over dinner?

The invitation – as she and John had always known – was far too tempting for Richard to resist.

They met at an Italian restaurant in the Strand. The Paradiso e Inferno. They went downstairs, prophetically perhaps for Richard, where the lighting was dim and the tables discreetly sectioned off from each other by the high backed wooden pew seats. She sat opposite him, dressed, as he later realised, with only one purpose in mind. Plain white dress. Very short. Material stretched tight over her breasts. Halter neck. Arms bare but for a plain gold bracelet. Tanned shoulders crying out to be caressed.

According to Richard, she had made the first move. At the time he had put it down to a combination of too much wine and, conceitedly, his own much-practised expertise in the art of seduction.

Sofia's hand strayed from the glass and settled upon his. She let her long nails play distractedly over his fingers. Above the table he stroked her arm, feeling the soft down of the sun-bleached hair. Below, her leg began to rub against his calves until the heat inside him rose and he could stand it no longer.

She was giggling as they left the restaurant. Pressed her body against him as if to gain support for her unsteady legs. Nestled in his arms in the taxi back to her flat. Put her hand inside his shirt. Teasingly scratched at his chest.

The rest he left unsaid. Knew I'd heard it first-hand already.

'When did John put the squeeze on you?' I asked.

'He didn't waste any time. Walked right in here the very next day. From the look on his face I knew immediately what had happened. He hadn't been away at all. It had all been a set-up. My only doubt was the price of his silence.'

I imagined the look on Richard's face as the tape was produced. I wondered if John even had to voice the threat. Then thought that he would have milked the situation for all it was worth. Sadistically droned on about Richard's rich wife and her startled reaction when she opened the envelope, read the anonymous note, played the tape. The disgust, the fury, the divorce that would inevitably follow.

'He didn't ask much,' Richard continued. 'Just to be allowed to carry on in A&M. And to run his own show – with no interference from me, he made that clear. It seemed a very small price to pay.'

'Was the partnership part of the deal?'

'No. John didn't care about that,' he explained. 'It was something I had to do to cover myself. As time went by with no signs of John being moved, the other partners would have started to ask embarrassing questions. Giving John a partnership was a way of convincing them that I believed he was doing such a good job he should be rewarded and left where he was.'

'One more question,' I said. 'How much did you know of what John was up to? The backhanders he was taking for inflating profits.'

'Like I said, there was never any real evidence of any malpractice. A few suspicions, that was all. It seemed best to turn a blind eye. Anyway, I thought he was too clever ever to get caught.' Richard saw the look in my eyes and rounded on me. 'What else could I do under the circumstances? What would you have done in my shoes? Justice doesn't get a look-in where self-preservation is concerned. Don't try to tell me you would have reacted any differently.'

The moment of defiance passed. 'You must believe me,' he pleaded. 'I've told you everything. The tape might seem like a motive for murder but I swear to you I didn't kill John.'

'I know that,' I said.

He looked at me strangely. A mixture of annoyance at talking so freely when it had been unnecessary, and hope that I would explain my statement and satisfy his curiosity as to the true culprit.

I kept my silence.

His mind turned inwards to ponder his fate. 'What are you going to do? Don't tell Arabella, please. She mustn't hear that tape.' His expression changed. A smile crept over his lips. A new thought had crossed his mind.

'I can make life very awkward for you, old boy. You understand what I'm saying? It's only your word against mine that you weren't a party to what John was doing. The police might find it hard to believe you didn't know what he was up to.'

'Don't make the mistake of threatening me, Richard. Better people than you have tried – and failed. If you know what's good for you, old boy, you'll keep your mouth shut and listen to what I want.'

Ten minutes later he was a relieved man. Much of his normal swagger had returned by the time he pressed the button on his phone to summon Peggy, his secretary. She stood erect, pad in hand, as he dictated the arrangements he wanted her to make. A barely perceptible twitch of her eyebrows was the only indication of her surprise.

Richard had probably feared that I was going to ask for money – an amount so large that it would have looked suspicious on his bank statement (joint account, I suspected). Or a promotion that would have been impossible to justify to the other partners.

But all I asked of him was a week off.

And for Norman Timpkins to be allowed to sit in the bowels

of the building with a microfiche reader and unlimited access to the records.

*

I met Arthur at a bustling café on the northside approach to Westminster Bridge. We sat at a table by the window with a clear view of the Houses of Parliament, munching on hot salt beef sandwiches with lashings of eye-watering mustard and drinking mugs of freshly brewed tea strong enough to melt the plastic spoons. For once, my appetite seemed better than his.

He was edgy. Anxious to leave. I was quite content to have another mug of tea and take in the view. Across the road, with Parliament in recess, there was a sense of emptiness and inactivity like a boarding school during the long summer holidays. A lone official car drew up and waited for the policeman on duty to scrutinise the faces inside, checking them against the mental picture gallery of his phenomenal memory. Satisfied, the policeman swung back the tall, heavily barred gates and waved the black Rover through.

It started to drizzle as we left the café. My plan had been to walk, but Arthur would hear none of it. He wanted to keep dry. And get our rendezvous over and done with as quickly as possible.

The taxi driver was terse and sullen, reluctant to take us on such a short journey when the weather was providing an abundance of more lucrative trade. But he lacked the courage to refuse my burly friend. We got our own back, childishly, for his surly behaviour by paying with a fifty pound note, forcing him to tramp inside the terminal for change while we sat laughing in the dry.

Victoria Coach Station was a depressing sight. Full of unsmiling, impatient faces. Littered with the plastic cups and hamburger boxes discarded wantonly by the restless queues. Clouds of diesel fumes puffed stutteringly from the exhausts of coaches waiting testily for passengers to board. The pavements were coated with a thin black sludge produced by the onset of the light rain. As we walked it spattered on the toes of our shoes and kicked up on the backs of our trousers.

Arthur pointed her out to me. She wore an ankle-length, gypsy-style dress in reds and browns with a khaki army-surplus jacket, tightly zipped against the elements. On her feet were those industrial boots that had for some inexplicable reason become fashionable among the young: on her they looked purely functional. Her frizzy black hair was long and unbrushed, stray strands sticking damply in rat tails to her forehead. The baby in her arms – a year old, maybe, to my untrained eyes – was well wrapped inside a thick tracksuit and dirty anorak.

I watched her target one of the groups of people: as she neared them, they turned their backs in a variant of the loony-on-the-bus syndrome, hoping to avoid embarrassment. But she knew the soft touches. Picked out the old ladies and middle-aged men. Took their coins and moved on round her continuous circuit of the constantly changing crowd.

We took her to the snack bar. Bought her tea and a hot dog; a small packets of biscuits and a glass of milk for the child. Arthur introduced me vaguely as someone to be trusted – and the man with the money.

I handed him the pictures of Sam that had arrived from Sally: it was his show. He laid them out on the high counter in front of her and waited till she had taken a good long look at them.

'Tell him what you told me,' he said softly. 'About seeing this man.'

'Last Friday, it was,' she said, staring up at the ceiling as if trying to picture the incident. 'He was just hanging around, you know? Didn't seem to be waiting for a coach. Wasn't in any queue, like. Didn't watch any of the passengers getting off either.'

'Are you sure it was him?' Arthur pointed to the clearest of the photographs.

'I think so,' she said slowly. Then the doubt left her mind. 'Yeah. Little guy. Jeans and windcheater, like in this picture.

209

Collar turned up. Woollen hat over his head. Couldn't see much of his face. But he was creepy looking. Shifty. Like he didn't want to stay around too long.'

'Where did he go?' I asked.

'I didn't see. I'm sorry,' she said in a worried tone, obviously wondering whether the unhelpful answer meant that she wouldn't get her money.

'That's all right,' I said. 'You did well to remember him.' I took a fifty pound note from my wallet and placed it on the counter. Arthur covered it quickly with his hand.

'And the rest,' he ordered the woman.

She looked longingly at the money. Kept glancing from me back to it as she spoke.

'Well,' she said, addressing me. 'As I told your friend, I wouldn't have paid much attention if it hadn't been for the girl.'

Arthur studied my face carefully.

'She was a real looker. Legs up to her armpits. Clothes must have cost a fortune.'

Arthur reached into his jacket. Took out another photograph. Showed it to the woman.

'Take a good look,' he said. 'Is this her?'

'Yeah. Gorgeous, ain't she? Course, you can't see the scar in this picture.'

*

'Sorry to spring it on you, Nick,' Arthur said as we walked the short distance to the house. 'But as soon as I saw Sofia, I recognised the description. I didn't know how deep you were with her. It seemed best you heard it for yourself – straight from the horse's mouth, like. I took the picture from the album so there wouldn't be any doubt in your mind.'

'You did well, Arthur.' I didn't tell him I had already guessed as much – it would save repeating myself later. Instead, I explained that the problem was what to do next.

I wanted Sofia followed. But she had seen Arthur. And he was unforgettable, even to someone as self-centred as Sofia.

'Do you know anyone who could tail her?' I asked. 'It needs to be a woman – less conspicuous, and fewer problems if Sofia disappears inside a toilet in some public place.'

We were indoors by the time he came up with an answer. He had walked silently as if considering the candidates and weighing them up in terms of how they might cope with any likely danger.

'There are a couple of girls at the club who might do,' he said, sounding less than convinced.

'Let me talk to them,' I said, determined to take the ultimate responsibility.

We agreed on a time and place and I handed him a hundred pounds: fifty pounds each as an added incentive – as if Arthur wasn't enough! – for the girls to show up. Brushing aside his protests, I insisted he took five hundred for his own trouble to date and as a downpayment for future services.

Arthur stood in the kitchen watching me as I took the steaks from the fridge and laid them on the grill rack. He turned up his nose when he saw me chop two cloves of garlic into tiny pieces. Then smiled as I sprinkled them on only two of the three thick slices of sirloin.

I opened the two bottles of Rioja I'd bought to make Norman feel at home. Poured us both a couple of inches in John's biggest goblets. Swirled the glass. Let the aroma of oak and vanilla drift into my nose. Took an appreciative sip. It tasted good already. Would be even better as it breathed.

We took our drinks, and the bottle, through to the sitting room. Sprawled out on the sofas waiting for our guest. And for our council of war.

I thought about what I should tell Sally.

Nothing, I decided. Not yet. She might jump the gun and spoil my plans for Sofia.

To be honest, I held out little hope that having Sofia followed would yield anything. It seemed unlikely they would make the same mistake again. But it was worth a shot. Due diligence, after all.

Anyway, our amateur surveillance might pay off in a few

days when, as I was convinced they would, they made a run for it. Unless I could stop them.

I thought of Sam. Had he been seduced by love or money? A bit of both, I suspected. Whatever the reason, Sally, I was sure, had seen the last of her brother.

CHAPTER TWENTY-THREE

Chelmsford

The first thing that struck me about Chelmsford was the open doors. Then I noticed the casual manner in which the inmates drifted from cell to cell. The whole mood was vastly different to that in Brixton: above all, the air lacked the electric charge produced by the omnipresent threat of violence. Don't get me wrong, I was under no illusions about this being some kind of holiday camp but it seemed the sort of place where I might have the best opportunity to heal the scars.

Norman jumped to his feet as I entered. He read my expression as my eyes took in the surroundings.

'You were expecting the Ritz?' he said with a smile. 'I'll get straight on to Complaints in the morning. Bloody Public Relations department. It's always the same.'

The cell was a disappointing duplicate of the one I had shared with Arthur.

'You're lucky,' Norman explained. 'This place has got seventy per cent overcrowding. By rights there should be three of us in here, but the Governor has decided to give you the kid-glove treatment. Anyway, welcome to the university.' He extended his hand. On his arm was the red band of a 'trusty'.

'Why the university?' I asked, as he knew I would.

'Because in here you can learn any subject you like. You won't find a better collection of talent anywhere in the country – including the redbricks.' He winked at me. 'Lawyers, stockbrokers, top-flight entrepreneurs, you name it, and we've got 'em. All bent of course, but that's what makes them so good. I've already planned your curriculum. Mustn't stagnate, you know. Wouldn't want you wasting your time on card games, would we?'

'I'm a bit limited in the shuffling department at the moment,' I said, waving the thick bandage at him.

'Thank goodness for that,' he grinned. 'I like to get a good night's sleep.'

There was a soft knock on the door, followed by a polite clearing of a throat. I turned to see a well-rounded man in his early sixties. His red face beamed at me.

'Hallo, Norman,' he said in a thick Lancashire accent. 'And you must be Nick. Pleased to meet you.' He was carrying a white chef's hat. He pumped my hand vigorously as if he were drawing water from an underground spring. His palm was hot and sweaty.

'You missed supper,' he said. 'So I brought you this.'

He dug into the folds of the hat and pulled out a greaseproof paper parcel.

'You do like sirloin steak, I hope?'

'Yes, wonderful, but how . . .?'

'Toddy works in the kitchen,' Norman explained. 'He's the best cook in the whole of Her Majesty's Prisons. Even if he does say so himself.'

'Not just in prison,' Toddy reprimanded Norman. 'Better than most of those so-called chefs in fancy restaurants too,' he said proudly. 'You can always tell what you're eating with my food. Not like the messed-about foreign muck you get served everywhere nowadays.'

'Yes, but sirloin steak?' I persisted, unwrapping the warm sandwich. The aroma of grilled meat and English mustard wafted up into my nostrils. My mouth began to water uncontrollably. I took a bite. It was heaven encased in two slices of crusty bread. A trickle of juice ran down my chin. I wiped it off on my sleeve.

'Sorry,' said Toddy, 'I must remember the napkin next time.'

'You see, Nick, Toddy has two great skills. Cooking is one. Forgery is the other. For special occasions like this, Toddy adds a line to the daily order that the kitchen warder writes out. I'd defy even a trained eye to tell the difference in handwriting.'

'But,' I said again, 'surely someone notices when the bills come in?'

'Not when I'm doing the accounts for the Governor they don't,' Norman said with a cheeky grin.

*

Norman told me all about himself during the course of the evening. I didn't have to reciprocate much. He'd read my file already.

It was the best time I'd had since the days with Arthur. In hospital there hadn't been much to smile about. I was able to talk with the other patients through the open door of my private room, a guard permanently on duty outside; but there were too many lost causes to make laughing a worthwhile pursuit.

As the evening wore on and lock-up approached, Norman sensed my tension and made sure I had little time to think. He talked the hind legs off a donkey and then moved on to the rest of the unfortunate victim's stablemates.

'Let me tell you about the criminal mind,' he said, without a pause to mark the end of the previous subject – whatever that had been.

He brushed aside my broody disinterest. 'Now, your criminal mind is a strange animal. It is unpredictable by any normal criteria. Take Toddy, for instance. Brilliant forger. Made the best plates you'll ever find. Undetectable twenty-pound notes. Better than the original, he says! He's going along quite nicely, making a good living, thank you very much. Then one day he gets fed up with the anonymity of his craftsmanship. Yearns for kudos. A deserved recognition for his labours. So he decides, out of pure vanity, to sign his name on the next set of plates. Very

215

small, you understand. Nothing flashy. Just enough to satisfy his pride. The rest is history.'

I nodded distractedly at him.

'And then there's my story,' he continued, taking a quick breath.

A bell rang in the corridor. There was a shuffling of feet and an exchange of ribald banter as prisoners returned to their own cells for the night. The sweat started to break out on my forehead. I couldn't stop it. I was trying, I swear.

I looked at Norman helplessly.

'Don't let them close the door,' I begged.

It banged shut as he was framing his answer. Panic swept through me.

'It's all right,' he said. 'I'm here. It's just a door, nothing else. You'll be okay.'

He'd seen the file. Read the doctor's notes – and the psychiatrist's analysis. He knew the problem. It wasn't just a door to me. It was a source of past blinding pain. And a permanent projector of mental images that my mind was fighting a losing battle to blot out.

One night in Brixton had turned me into the world's worst claustrophobic. Being in a confined space with a closed door, or even a door that threatened to close, was intolerable.

Norman was shouting at me. I didn't hear what he was saying. I was too busy hanging on the door handle, pulling on it with all the strength I could muster in my one good hand.

'What's one and one?' Norman yelled at me.

'I don't know,' I screamed back.

'What's one and one?' he said again.

'I don't care,' I screamed louder.

He grabbed me by the shoulders and dragged me away from the door. He slapped me round the face so hard that my cheek stung.

I balled my hand into a fist and took aim. I didn't know what I was doing anymore.

He slapped me again.

'What's one and one?'

216

Thank God I didn't snap. Something deep inside stopped me from hitting him.

'Two,' I said, gaining an extremely tenuous hold on my emotions. 'Wrong,' he said, a look of relief spreading across his face. I cast a glimpse at the door and shuddered. I looked away quickly. Think, Shannon, I ordered myself. Get a grip on yourself. You can do it.

'Three, then,' I said, concentrating hard. 'You're talking about synergy. The sum can be greater than the parts.'

'Wrong,' he said again. He was smiling now. He knew he had me hooked.

'Okay. I give in. What's one and one?'

'Whatever you want it to be,' he laughed.

And so began my first lesson in creative accounting. And my deep friendship with Norman. I never fully overcame my irrational fear, but that crafty old bastard helped me to control it.

CHAPTER TWENTY-FOUR

Norman had changed so much from the Chelmsford days that I hardly recognised him at first: I stood speechless on the doorstep caught in a double-take.

'Excuse me,' he said shivering, 'but when you've finished your impression of a tit-in-a-trance, do you think I might come inside?'

No wonder he looked so cold: he was wearing a lightweight jacket and trousers more suited to a stroll around the tapas bars of his adopted country than the chill of this late September evening. Prison clothes have the effect (fully intended, one would imagine) of robbing the wearer of a large part of his individuality. They focus attention on the face for clues to personality and mood. Norman's new style of dress might have emphasised the easy-going and untroubled side of his new life but a closer examination of the person underneath told a different story.

I had expected to see him at least a couple of stones heavier than the days after Toddy's release when our staple diet reverted to standard prison fodder – uninviting, and unidentifiable, daily stews accompanied by vegetables boiled to the point where all taste and texture disappeared. But he had somehow contrived to lose weight. A lot of weight. Despite the calorific Spanish food, the skin on his face and neck now hung in loose folds and his sharp aquiline nose seemed to stand out like Concorde emerging from its hangar. His clothes, though appearing to be recent acquisitions, floated more freely about his frame than was ever intended for the style. The crocodile belt bore two flat notches where it had been progressively tightened since first worn.

His face, tanned and weather-beaten, had the same leathery texture and mottled appearance as the Moroccan hide of his loafers. I had the feeling that without the cosmetic effect of the sun the skin underneath would have been pallid and wan. There were lines under his bloodshot eyes, as if he had been having trouble sleeping.

But he was in good spirits, if not health. He gave me a firm handshake and a broad smile. Moved his head slowly up and up by degrees, in mock astonishment, as he acknowledged Arthur. Then quickly flashed his speciality cheeky grin to make sure the gesture was understood as a joke.

'When did you acquire your other bodyguard?' Norman said as we filed through to the sitting room. He walked across and drew back one of the curtains.

'That's Collins,' I said with a sigh of exasperation. 'The typical British bulldog – never lets go. Smells not dissimilar too. I'll fill you in later. Don't let him spoil the reunion.'

Standing there together, Norman and Arthur looked like the sort of pairing only seen in comedy double acts. Each emphasised the other's deviation from the norm of build and intellect. Opposite ends of a Darwinian spectrum showing the branching off of evolutionary trees. But they had something in common. A bond that brought them naturally together. Nick Shannon.

They had a great time – at my expense.

Throughout the meal, much to their delight and my obvious discomfort, they swapped apocryphal stories of my innocence and naivety before their education had worked its transformation. I let them get on with their good-humoured jibes, even found myself joining in the laughter at the embarrassing punchlines. Each was a good friend. I wanted them to be friends, too.

They both ate heartily – Arthur like a true trencherman,

Norman with the air of the resigned enjoyment of a condemned man.

I was regretting only buying two bottles of the Vina Real. Arthur, against all my expectations that he would turn his nose up at the wine and insist on sticking to his usual tipple of beer, was draining his goblet in huge bacchanalian gulps that kept me constantly busy on refill duty. For someone unused to the pleasures of good red wine he was making up for lost time like there was no tomorrow. Giving them free rein to embroider their stories further I went to investigate John's wine rack: almost full on my arrival, it now had more holes than bottles. I settled on the powerful Chilean Cabernet Sauvignon. What a mistake that was!

I opened three bottles and put them in the middle of the dining room table.

Calling the pair of jokers to order, I told them that if we were going to talk business, then we had better do it now. It was a shame to break up the party but in another hour, I suspected, none of us would be sufficiently coherent for discussion – or capable of remembering in the soberingly cold light of morning what we had said.

'So you're in trouble, Nick,' Norman said. 'I hesitate to say again but . . .'

'Too right,' Arthur grinned. 'You'll love this one, Norman. So far we've got a murder, a missing person, Freddie Ronson in homicide mode, fraud, blackmail and a frame-up. All we need is for Saddam Hussein to walk through the door with an IRA bomb under his arm and we've got the full set.'

'It's not quite as black as Arthur paints it,' I countered.

Arthur rolled his eyes.

'Okay,' I said grudgingly. 'It is.'

'You didn't say much over the phone – just enough to get me interested. Why not sod originality and start at the beginning. So your boss got his head chopped off. Correct?'

I paused for a moment, considering the complexities of the story to come. Who would struggle most – me as narrator, or Arthur and Norman as listeners.

'No,' I said, still thinking. 'It wasn't like that.'

'Come on,' said Arthur. 'That's how it started.'

I came to the conclusion there was no easy way to acclimatise them to the enormity of what was to come. So I bowled the bouncer full pace.

'It wasn't John,' I blurted out.

They both looked at me as if I had completely taken leave of my senses.

'It's a bit complicated,' I said apologetically. 'That's why I didn't try to explain to either of you earlier.'

'Humour him,' Norman said to Arthur. 'If it wasn't John, then who the bleeding hell was responsible for the do-it-yourself dye job on the rug?'

'Sam.'

'Okay,' Norman said with a sigh, 'I'll play straight man. Who is Sam?'

'Sam is our missing person,' I explained. 'Except he isn't. John is the one we need to find.'

'What have you been putting in this red wine – LSD? Can Arthur and I have a recap, please.'

So I told him about Sam. And Sally. And Sofia. How, presumably, Sam had phoned his sister and Sofia had answered. Instead of offering to give a message to Sally, Sofia had invited Sam round. Used her charms to make him feel secure – desired too, no doubt. Sofia must have seen the photographs of Sally and her family – and known then that Sam would fit the bill.

'Sofia persuaded Sam that he could hide out here in John's house. And before Sam moved in I think that John spent a whole lot of time diligently wiping away every fingerprint he had ever placed in the house. When Sam was murdered they had to be sure that only *his* prints would be found. Then the natural assumption would be that the corpse was the person living here. Sofia then identifies the body as John's and the perfect switch is complete.'

'So John killed Sam?' Norman asked.

'I think so, yes. I can't see Sofia swinging a Samurai sword.

And they would want her, as a possible suspect, to have an alibi. I imagine Sofia let Sam have some cocaine, something to help relieve the boredom – and make it easier for John to surprise him.'

'You're sure about all this, Nick?' Norman said.

'Pretty much so. It all fits. Even down to getting rid of the cleaner. Plus I did a little forensic work myself. Bought some talcum powder and took a fingerprint from John's pen at work. It doesn't match the ones on all the junk I cleared out of the bathroom cabinet.'

Arthur was struggling by this stage. 'But why?' he said.

'That's where we come to the fraud and blackmail,' I said.

Arthur groaned. 'Christ, I'm still having problems with the murder bit!'

'John has been running this racket at work for years – I'll give you all the details later, Norman – defrauding the clients by overinflating the purchase price of acquisitions and taking a cut of the difference. Probably also blackmailing the sellers afterwards. But he knew he couldn't get away with it forever. Questions were being asked. Sooner, rather than later, he would have been found out. John, naturally, wanted to skip the country and retire on the proverbial ill-gotten gains: what he didn't want was to be forever looking over his shoulder for the Fraud Squad. No one searches for a dead man.'

'A question,' Norman said.

'Fire away.'

'How's he going to get out of the country? You said his passport was still in the desk. Forged passport?'

'Doesn't need it,' I said. 'John was born in America. He's got dual nationality. With all the benefits – including an American passport. Arlene's checking it out for me so we can be absolutely sure, but I don't have much doubt about it.'

'What I don't understand,' Arthur said, 'apart from most of it, that is, is this note he sent you.'

'Norman can explain that to you. He gives a good lecture on the criminal mind.'

'This John is a real sickie, right, Arthur?' Norman said.

A long drawn out 'Yes' came in reply.

'Well, lying in the sun sipping rum punches and bonking this Sofia – not necessarily all at the same time – is not satisfying enough for him. He needs to show the world just how clever he is. How he's outwitted everyone all these years. And he likes to make trouble too, I would say. "Not enough to succeed, others must be seen to fail." Isn't that what I once told you, Nick? The note worked out just as John had intended. It stirred Mr Justice here into poking his nose in. Nick was John's tin-opener for the can of worms. Or do you prefer muckraker, Nick?'

'I know my faults, Norman. You don't have to rub it in. Yes. I'm ashamed to say I did exactly as John predicted. Mind you he did try to motivate me with the mugging.'

'I thought that was Ronson,' Arthur said, his brow becoming more furrowed by the minute.

'No, John set it up. His thugs were supposed to work me over. Tell me to mind my own business. John knew what my reaction would be: a stubborn bastard like me would become even more determined. Besides,' I said, 'Ronson's dead.'

'Who says?' Arthur asked. 'I never heard anything.'

'I've got the scars to prove it, Arthur. All down my back. I was given – no, make that was made to pay for – his address yesterday. He now resides at South Essex Crematorium. Hush-hush funeral to save embarrassment. Ronson died of AIDS two months ago.'

'I suppose then that the dead cat was John's handiwork too?' Arthur said with a wince.

'It was certainly his idea. I doubt that he did it personally – far too risky. Meant to have the same effect as the mugging. Another warning he knew would only serve to drive me on. Except Ronson was an added ingredient that had us confused for a while.'

'Okay,' said Norman with uncharacteristic seriousness, 'I get the picture now. But why are we sitting here? Why aren't we spilling it all out to the boys in blue?'

'First of all I'm due to have dinner with Sofia on Thursday.'

'We wouldn't want to interfere with your social calendar,' Norman interrupted.

'Sofia,' I said patiently, 'has been pulling my strings all along. All this bullshit about an accident to make me suspicious of John. "Have the house, Nick. Have the car. It's what John would have wanted." Just so it's easy for them to spoon-feed the clues and keep an eye on me at the same time. Check that I'm following the right trail. They haven't finished yet. Still got something up their sleeves. I want to find out what that is.

'Second. We don't know where John is hiding. If we tell the police, then they interview Sofia. She denies it all. Says it was a genuine mistake when she identified the body. Distraught with shock and all that.' I shook my head in frustration. 'You haven't heard this girl lie, Norman. She treats being economical with the truth as if it were an Olympic event and only the gold medal will do. And what happens when she walks out of the police station? John vanishes, that's what. Where's the justice in that?'

'I don't expect your low opinion of the police has anything to do with it, Nick?'

'They couldn't catch the bastard who ran over my sister. John's too clever for Mr Plod. He makes Moriarty look like Simple Simon.'

'What the hell have the Goons got to do with anything?' Arthur asked.

'One particular goon is our next problem. Collins. He's convinced I'm in this up to my neck. I think his current theory is that Sofia and I cooked it up together. The house and the car haven't helped there either. It makes it seem like I've taken over everything John once had – and that would include Sofia.'

'But if you can prove that the body isn't John's, then doesn't that get you off the hook?' Norman asked reasonably.

They were old friends. It should have been easy to admit to them the added problem of the money paid into my bank account. The time bomb that was ticking away, threatening to land me up to my neck in the raw material of the sewage farm (or however else Norman would express it). It should have been easy – but it wasn't. I'd heard too many anecdotes over dinner about my naivety and how I was a human flypaper for any trouble that was looking for a place to land. Confession may be good for the soul, but it's not usually the best way to massage a bruised ego.

'Can you imagine Collins's reaction to the news?' I said. 'That Nick Shannon with the aid of some talcum powder and a pastry brush can outsmart a fully trained SOCO team and a forensic scientist of thirty years' experience? I'm not exactly going to win the Popularity category in the Murder-Suspect-of-the-Month awards. Collins will find some way of twisting the facts to his advantage, you can be sure of that.'

'So what do we do?' Arthur asked.

'Find John,' Norman and I replied. 'Somehow get a confession from him.'

'Well, if that's all,' Arthur said, 'I think I'll have another glass of plonk.'

'That sounds like a good idea, Arthur,' Norman said as he stretched across the table for the bottle. 'Might I ask exactly how we're going to find John?'

'I have a sort of plan,' I said.

'Somehow, Baldrick,' Norman said, 'that does not exactly fill me with confidence. Elucidate, please.'

'Basically,' I said, 'we wait till Thursday. See what Sofia is up to. Meanwhile, we carry on as normal. Just as if we suspect nothing. John's still in the country, I'd stake my life on that. There's some vital part of his scheme to come. That's what is keeping him here.'

I turned to Norman. 'Will you dig into the files for me? Assemble all the evidence on the frauds? Maybe something new will turn up. And if the worst happens, it may win me some brownie points with Collins.'

'What can I do, Nick?' Arthur asked.

'Let's get the tail on Sofia sorted out. Then you stand by in case the going gets rough.'

'Here's to the three bleeding musketeers,' Norman said, draining his glass.

By one o'clock we were all suffering. The deep, dark Chilean red was taking its toll. The bonhomie was rapidly degenerating into slow repetitive statements and circular arguments that bore only a slight resemblance to conversation and indicated, if we'd had the presence of mind to appreciate the fact, just how little concentration we all possessed.

Norman looked drained. Despite his efforts at polite concealment, his yawns of exhaustion were coming with increasing frequency and lasting longer on each occasion.

For my part, the heavy boots of a hangover were already marching past the broken defences of my brain. I knew from bitter experience I was going to feel like a zombie in the morning.

Arthur, hot and flushed, rose unsteadily from the table. We heard his leaden feet as they plodded, a step at a time, up the steep flight of stairs to the bathroom.

The loud crash snapped Norman and me out of our drunken stupor. The sound reverberated through the ceiling. The hanging lamp in the middle of the dining-room table swung backwards and forwards above our heads.

I raced up the stairs, fully expecting to see Arthur comatose on the floor. Instead he was standing at the bathroom door looking dazed and strangely sheepish. Behind him I could see the cabinet lying broken on the cork tiles. One of the doors had come off its hinges. Its contents lay scattered in all directions. The cardboard cylinder of talcum powder had split under the weight of Arthur's foot. French chalk covered one of his shoes and ran up his trouser leg in a dusty white crescent.

Through the slur of Arthur's voice we pieced together what had happened. He had been leaning over the sink to splash his face with cold water in an attempt to clear the alcoholic fog swirling round inside his head. Eyes shut, body still bent, he had felt around till he found a towel. In his blindness he had straightened up too quickly and banged his thick skull into the bottom of the cabinet. Hoicked it off the mounting. Sent it crashing to the floor.

He cast his eyes downwards. Looked mystified at the impossibility of the sheer amount of the mess at his feet.

'Sorry,' he said for the third time.

'What the hell,' I said casually. 'I'd been meaning to move that cabinet, anyway. You've done half the job for me.'

I led him awkwardly down the narrow staircase. Eased him onto the settee, where he lay back painfully rubbing the back of his head. Leaving Norman to act as nursemaid, I went to the kitchen to find a dustpan and brush. Then trudged wearily back up the stairs to sort out the shambles in the bathroom.

How had I not seen it earlier?

Too much attention to the chaos on the floor? Too concerned for Arthur?

There was no missing it now.

I stared in disbelief at the wall.

At the gap where the cabinet had been.

In the middle of the twelve by eighteen inch rectangle of unfaded paint there was a nine inch long hole formed by the removal of two bricks.

I stepped tentatively among the toiletries on the floor. Removed the sheaf of paper from its hiding place. My fingers touched the cold, hard metal beneath.

With a deliberate caution borne out of fear and loathing for such objects, I carried the gun gingerly downstairs.

Norman, well used to fending for himself, had brewed three mugs of very strong, black instant coffee and filled a jug with iced water. I found him sitting beside Arthur, forcing the groggy giant to drink glass after glass of water before finally handing over the coffee.

They looked at me wide-eyed. The sight of the gun hanging limply like a dead rat between my fingers sobered Arthur up more rapidly than either of Norman's beverages.

'Arthur?' I said with an uncontrollable grin on my face. 'I don't suppose you've ever heard the word "serendipity"?'

He stared at me blankly.

'Just take it from me that it means you're a bloody marvel.'

I explained about my discovery. Set the papers on the coffee table for Norman and myself to examine. Slid the gun, muzzle pointing towards the wall, across to Arthur for his opinion.

Circumspectly, he snapped the chamber free. Tipped the six bullets into the palm of his hand. Let the tension flow from his body. He inspected the bullets first, then the gun itself.

'Hammerless revolver,' he said expertly, astonishing his attentive audience. 'Smith and Wesson .38 calibre. Maybe ex-Army – I've seen some like it during my National Service. The bullets are definitely military issue.' He tossed one to me. 'Full-metal jacket – not usual for this type of gun. And take a look at the head stamp?'

I squinted at the row of tiny letters, symbols and numbers on the base of the cartridge case.

'The numbers indicate the maker and calibre,' he explained. 'The last two digits are the year of manufacture. Only military issue bear that code.'

I bowed to his experience, not that the knowledge seemed to help us much.

The papers, on the other hand, were a veritable gold mine. The information they contained would make Norman's task a whole lot easier. In chronological order they constituted a detailed list of individuals and their companies, together with every transaction that had taken place over the last eight years. Norman now knew exactly where to look for the supporting evidence.

Two things struck me as Norman and I delved more deeply into the names and figures.

Firstly, the total amount of money extracted by John (excluding Emsby and Morton who warranted a separate sheet to themselves) added up to close on two million pounds.

Secondly, showing at least some restraint, he had never gone for more than two payments from any of his victims.

With the exception of one.

The very first on the list.

Then cropping up time and again with monotonous regularity.

Last payment – just five weeks ago.

It was that name again.

David Yates.

CHAPTER TWENTY-FIVE

The adrenalin surge produced by the excitement of the discovery revived our tired brains. Our animated self-congratulations, further fuelled by the caffeine from two more cups of strong black coffee, kept us going for another hour. Then the conversation regressed to the slow and circular. We were back to functioning on automatic pilot. It was time to call it a day.

Arthur phoned for a cab and returned to his empty flat. Norman, seeming ready to drop, dragged himself up the stairs. He flopped out, still fully clothed, on the spare bed in the study. I spent fifteen minutes in a token effort at making the place look a little less like the epicentre of an earthquake, then crawled into bed feeling as if I could sleep for a millennium.

Five hours later the alarm beeped its annoyingly chirpy reveille. I knocked on Norman's door to wake him: inside my head it seemed like a heavy metal band was playing a gig for an aurally challenged audience. Downstairs, the house smelt of garlic, cigarettes and the vinegary dregs of red wine. I flung the kitchen window wide open and stood gulping down lungfuls of chemically-rich London air.

'You look as bad as I feel,' said Norman when I turned around.

'As long as I don't feel as bad as you look,' I replied.

With little appetite, we shared a breakfast of grapefruit juice, tea and toast. Norman smiled weakly at me as he washed down a cocktail of pills with the mouth-puckering, acidic juice.

We munched broodily on the toast, both clearly troubled by unspoken thoughts.

Norman pushed his plate emphatically aside in order to attract my attention.

'I didn't like to mention this last night,' he said, his brows solemnly knitted together, 'but Yates is a new dimension. He won't roll over and put his hands up like Bennington: he's got too much to lose to go down without a fight. I don't like it, Nick. Money and power made him the perfect victim for blackmail – but they also make him a very dangerous man to cross.'

'Are you getting cold feet, Norman?' I didn't like the sound of this. Yates had him spooked. 'If you want out, you better say so now.'

'No, I don't want out,' he said, sounding offended.

'Then what are you suggesting? We dig the dirt on the others on the list and leave Yates alone? One law for the rich and powerful, another for the rest? It's all or nothing in my book. Understand?'

'It's you who has to understand, Nick.' The old fire was back in Norman's belly. 'If we go after Yates then our case has to be completely watertight. That's all I'm saying.'

He dropped the level of his voice by a degree and spoke like a lecturing parent. 'Just think about it for a minute. On one side, three ex-cons. On the other, Yates and the best lawyers in the land. They'll run rings around us. And what if Yates decides it should never come to court and uses his pull to rope in Special Branch, or whichever freewheeling arm of the secret service looks after the likes of him: we'll need more than Arthur to protect us. Unless we're a hundred and ten per cent sure our evidence would convince his own mother, we let Yates alone.'

'Then we'd better get started,' I said.

'There's one other thing that's troubling me,' he said.

'Spit it out.'

'I've been thinking about serendipity.'

'Me too,' I admitted.

'And did you reach the same conclusion? Do you get the uneasy feeling we're following a path that John has carefully mapped out?'

'Yes. It's all too easy. I think I was supposed to find the list. That's why Sofia was so keen to keep me in this house. They knew, sooner or later, I would have had to move the cabinet. The list was left on purpose. Is that what you reckon?'

Norman nodded. 'John's way of speeding up the search process. And an insurance policy in case you overlooked any of the people he wanted exposed.'

'Agreed,' I said. 'But that isn't really the problem, is it? If the list was meant to be discovered, then so was the gun. Why the gun? That's the big question. If you know the answer just ring this number: calls charged at 48p per minute.'

Norman frowned. 'Don't joke, Nick. Give me the gun. Now.'

'Don't you trust me, old friend?'

'I don't know what's going on in that warped mind of his. Neither do you. But if John wants you to have a gun then that's reason enough why you shouldn't. Hand it over, Nick.'

When Uncle Norman gets a bee in his bonnet there's not much point in trying to refuse. He sent me off to get the car while he hid the gun somewhere he hoped I wouldn't find it.

During the short drive I explained to Norman the record-keeping system at Jameson Browns. All important paperwork, including in the case of A&M a master copy of each report, was kept locked away in fireproof filing cabinets. The easiest way for Norman to conduct his search was to ignore the cabinets and base himself at the microfiche reader: there were reductions of the reports on microfiche together with all the working papers for each project.

When we arrived at work Ted carried out the customary security check on Norman's briefcase and we headed down the stairs to the basement. The whistle-stop tour of the archives was followed by five minutes running through the rudimentary push-me-pull-you operations of the antiquated and cumbersome machine. Then I left Norman alone to get on with the leg-work while I killed some time at the nearby library before meeting Arthur.

The *Who's Who* entry for David Yates gave a lot of detail, but none of it threw much light on the man himself – his personality, what made him tick. In the tiny, eye-straining print I read a dreary record of dates and facts that failed to kindle any interest in me. Full name – David Montgomery Yates (poor sod, I thought, to be saddled with a middle name like that – father presumably a Desert Rat, or some sort of sadist). Forty-eight years old. Made a Privy Counsellor two years ago – sounded young for such an honour, I thought, without any real knowledge of whether that was true. Degree (BSc. Econ.). MP. Details of father (Peter); wife (Margaret); school (never heard of it); university (LSE). Then a long curriculum vitae detailing first his private business interests (Chairman of Adcom until its sale, then several non-executive directorships including a TV station and a PR company), his membership of various all-party delegations to banana republics and war-torn African states, and an impressive list of committees he had chaired. Address – House of Commons, SW1 (very useful!).

I passed a further hour over a copy of *The Times*, sitting in the reading-room in the company of the pensioners huddled there for warmth. Then took a long, slow walk to the pub where I was due to meet Arthur.

It was still only twelve o'clock!

The place was almost empty – it deserved to be. It was a free house in the spit-and-sawdust style: lights with 40 watt bulbs to hide the smoke-stained ceiling and the grubby floor; uncomfortably low wooden tables and stools, the latter covered in red velveteen and cigarette burns. Save for myself there were only three customers, two labourers making their selections from the racing pages of the *Mirror* and a bored youth who was unsuccessfully trying to beat the Trivia machine.

I ordered a thirst-slaking cold Pils as a hair-of-the-dog and the 'special of the day' – lamb curry and rice. The girl behind the bar turned down the corners of her mouth, leaned closer to me and whispered 'last night's leftovers'. She recommended the cottage pie instead. I took her advice and watched her hungrily as she poured the beer and walked across to fill a plate with the piping hot food.

She wasn't your usual London pub barmaid. Not Australian for a start. And didn't look like she'd come straight from an all-night session at the nearest disco. She was tall, pretty and young – rather than tall and pretty young. I put her at twenty, twenty-one at the most. Her face was a perfect canvas for the minimal brushstrokes of the soft browns of her eye make-up and the deep russet of the lipstick. The long, chestnut hair was scrunched into a carefree style. Her clothes were inexpensive, an eclectic collection of individual garments which is termed 'grunge' by those who must attach labels to fashion. Black, wide-bottomed trousers floating over low heeled, multi-laced granny boots. Loose-fitting, red and white checked man's shirt worn outside the trousers. Long, flowing, light-grey cardigan that stretched past her knees. Voluminous black woollen scarf worn like a shawl as the outermost layer. Rows of beads around her slim neck. Wooden bangles on her wrists. Shiny costume jewellery rings on her elongated pianist's fingers. The first impression was that the constituents of the outfit had been selected completely at random – then I realised she had probably taken a lot of time and trouble to put it all together.

She brought back my food and went off to serve a group of three spotty-faced office workers who had arrived for an early lunch break. I carried my plate and glass over to a corner table and prepared to wait for Arthur and the first of the two candidates to show up. The pie, against all the omens, was surprisingly good: it tasted home-made by a cook who hadn't packed it out with vegetables in order to save on the meat. The barmaid deserved a drink later, when our business was concluded.

I was thoroughly bored by the time Arthur arrived. The only diversion had been watching the three youths down pints and play darts, and that had begun to pall as they grew more raucous.

'This is Tracey,' Arthur said to the accompaniment of my

inward groan. The name was about as promising as her appearance.

She sat down opposite me, flashing thighs and teeth, and limply extended a delicate hand as if expecting me to kiss it. 'Pleased to meet you,' she said in a high pitched nasal whine which set my teeth on edge. The barmaid looked across and gaped open-mouthed.

Arthur returned with a pint for himself and a Medori and grapefruit for Miss Tottenham 1993. I scowled at him as he took his seat.

It took twenty embarrassing minutes to get rid of her. In that period she giggled at every question I asked, and gained time for thought – always insufficient, it seemed by her answers – by crossing and uncrossing her long legs.

'Thank you,' I finally said, trying to keep the relief from my voice. 'Arthur will let you know.'

She trip-trapped to the door, drawing wolf-whistles from the darts players.

'Christ,' I said to Arthur, 'I hope the next one is better than that.'

The look on his face banished any remaining hope I might have held.

'I could only think of these two girls from the club,' he said apologetically. 'The best two, mind,' he added.

If that was the case I dreaded to think what the rest were like!

'Arthur,' came a shrill shriek from the open door.

That was it. I'd had enough.

'They both look like tarts, Arthur.'

'Only part-time,' he said.

'Get rid of her,' I said wearily. 'Let's not waste any more time.'

'What are we going to do,' he asked after he had finished bundling Tracey's clone out of the pub.

'Have another beer and pray for inspiration,' I said.

We sat quietly drinking and racking our brains. I thought of Louise, the typist at work, then scratched her name off the list as too much of a security risk.

'Come on,' I said to Arthur. 'Finish your pint and let's go. Some place where we can think in peace. Those louts are beginning to get on my nerves.'

The youngest of the three acne sufferers had been dispatched to get another round of drinks while his friends cleaned the blackboard with a torn piece of dishcloth.

'What do you mean I've had enough already,' he barked at the barmaid.

I had watched him trying to chat her up earlier. She'd rebuffed him brusquely then: this second refusal added insult to injury. A loud argument ensued between the pair of them. The only man – correction, male – behind the bar registered what was happening and went down to the cellar to check the pipes. Arthur looked enquiringly at me. I nodded and we both stood up.

By this time, all three lads were shouting at the girl. One of them screamed the biggest insult his tiny mind could produce on the spur of the moment – not that another three hours would have made much difference.

'Bloody dyke,' he yelled.

It was one of the sweetest right hooks I'd ever seen. The mouthy lad never knew what hit him. He knocked over two of the tall barstools, ricocheted off his mates like they were the flippers in a pinball machine and crashed to the floor. Arthur and I ignored the semi-conscious body for the time being and grabbed a yob apiece: one look at Arthur and they were as meek as lambs. We turfed them out onto the pavement and told them to wait. But they didn't hang around. They were gone by the time Arthur had carried their friend outside and dumped him on the pavement.

The cowardly barman slunk back from his hideaway, only to walk into a hail of abuse from the girl.

'You can't talk to me like that,' he said, backing away from her. 'You're fired.'

'I quit,' she shouted, picking up her handbag and marching from the room.

'Quick, Arthur,' I said. 'Don't let her get away. We've just found our girl.'

We had to run to catch up with her, so fast was she stomping down the street. 'Thank you,' she said as we trotted alongside, 'but I didn't need your help.'

'Can we buy you a drink?' I asked. 'Somewhere quiet so we can talk. We've got a proposition to put to you.'

'I bet you have,' she said, thinking of the *tête-à-tête* with Tracey.

'No,' I said quickly, 'its not what you think. I promise.'

'Oh, what the hell,' she said with a sigh. 'I'll give you ten minutes. And if I don't like what I hear I'll . . .'

'Yes. We know,' I laughed, putting my hands defensively in front of my face.

It was a risk, I suppose. But what other choice did we have? As I told her the story in the utilitarian upper floor of a wine bar, I realised how crazy it must all have seemed. Perhaps it was because it sounded so far-fetched that she believed me. After all, what sort of idiot would make up such a tale?

I could tell she was interested even before I mentioned the money: for a hundred pounds a day she became very interested.

Her name was Tina. A student in her last year at the University of East Anglia, reading for a BA in European Studies. She'd taken the job at the pub to help stretch her grant through the coming term. There was only a week left of the long vacation – but that would almost certainly be enough for our purposes. She told us proudly that she was a good driver (but I've never met anyone who admitted otherwise); had taken a short course in Self Defence; could keep her eyes open – and her mouth shut.

'Good enough?' she asked challengingly.

'Almost,' I replied. I gave her the picture of Sofia, the addresses for the flat and where she worked, a list of contact telephone numbers and money for the first two days as a show of good faith. I then handed over a further hundred pounds.

'What's this for?' she asked.

'As I explained,' I said, hoping that it would not come out sounding patronising, 'your job is to follow Sofia. Stick to her like glue. Without being noticed. No offence, Tina, but the money is to buy some different clothes. Something a lot less conspicuous.'

She looked at me with tight lips. 'Sounds like you're talking Etam rather than Oxfam. And if you're really serious about not being noticed then I'll need at least one change of clothes. A hundred pounds won't stretch to the sort of outfit you seem to have in mind.' She smiled broadly at me. 'No offence,' she said, 'but what hole have you been living in for the past few years?'

*

At ten minutes to five Tina was ready for duty. Arthur and I returned her parting wave as she loped off long-leggedly to take up position outside Sofia's office. She can handle herself, we told each other in an attempt to nullify our concern for her safety.

She was a smart kid too. That was evident from her choice of camouflage for the job in hand. Grey skirt, white blouse and navy blue jumper. Hair scraped back and twisted into a bun. The flat walking shoes and round-shouldered stoop of someone who spent eight hours a day hunched over a word processor made her look like a casting director's vision of a legal secretary. Despite her height, there was little chance she would stand out in a crowd. In her left hand she carried a reversible raincoat: in her right, a copy of the *Evening Standard*.

She was smiling when she left us – confident of her own ability and of the veracity of our story. We had the *Standard* to thank for the latter. The front page carried news of the scandal of Emsby and Morton and, less prominently, their release from custody after helping the police with their murder enquiries.

I didn't need more than two guesses on who had leaked the story.

CHAPTER TWENTY-SIX

I returned from my clandestine visit to the bank on Thursday to find Norman's bulging suitcase in the hall. It didn't take a genius to deduce something was wrong.

Norman had made good progress the previous day. But not that good.

He had traced back through four of the companies on John's list and found the emergence of a pattern. Each of the takeover targets had something more than just profit to attract a potential bidder. A strong brand name in one case. Another, otherwise ailing, was solidly established as leader in what should have been a lucrative niche market but which it had failed to exploit to any significant degree. A third had developed a new product that needed an injection of capital to launch it onto the market: because of the company's rocky financial position, it could generate no interest from external backers. A fourth had a prime site in the heart of the City. In each company there was a gold nugget to encourage the buyer to take an optimistic view of the figures. John had gilded the lily to the point where the price still seemed reasonable when all the intangibles were taken into account.

At his current rate, Norman had estimated he needed another three days to complete the task. He couldn't have finished already.

I found him in the kitchen drinking tea with Rita Simmons. She was standing at the sink washing up a frying pan. Drying her hands, she placed them around the teapot and, satisfied with its temperature, poured me a cup.

'I'll be off now, Mr Shannon,' she said, pulling her coat over the top of the pinafore. 'Now, you be sure to look after Norman. He needs building up, poor soul. I cooked him some eggs and bacon. Knew you wouldn't mind.'

She picked up her bag. 'Goodbye, my dears,' she said, with a special smile for Norman. He winked. She blushed.

'You dirty old man,' I said.

'You're only as old as you feel,' she grinned.

'You're only as old as the woman you feel,' Norman corrected, borrowing from the philosophy of the Rolling Stones.

*

'What are you doing here?' I asked when his paramour had departed. 'Why aren't you at the office?'

We had taken our tea into the sitting room. I sipped from the cup and felt my mouth pucker: if a billiard ball had a chest then it would have sprouted hair after tasting this brew.

'It's time to pack a bag, Nick,' he said grim-faced. 'You're in big trouble.'

'How did you find out?' I said. 'Did the bank phone? Have they made a decision?'

The look on his face told me that my mouth had been faster than my brain.

'Why do I have a strange feeling that you haven't told me everything?' Norman asked.

'Perhaps because I haven't told you everything,' I said sheepishly.

'Terrific,' he said. There was an unaccustomed anger to his voice. 'After the morning I've had, that's just what I wanted to hear! Suddenly become a believer in the mushroom theory of people management, have you? Keep us in the dark and shovel on the . . .'

240

'Okay,' I interrupted. 'I was stupid. It was just hard to admit the other evening.'

'Look,' he said. 'Take my word for this. We don't have the time to pussyfoot about. For Christ's sake tell me what's going on.'

'I'm being framed,' I confessed at last. 'John has paid twenty-five thousand pounds in cash into my bank account.'

I told him the full story of bank slips, automatic deposit machines and Battersby's inbuilt self-defence mechanism: and the lecture, delivered to a backbeat of weary shakes of his head, on the need to follow the letter of the law.

'I've been trying to persuade them not to report me. If Collins hears about it, you know what will happen? If he can't make a murder charge stick then he'll make sure I went down for fraud. Nothing would convince him I didn't know what John was up to. He'd see the money as my cut from some deal – or hush money, maybe. I don't know. Whichever way you look at it, I'm well and truly snookered.'

Norman nodded wisely. 'You're an ex-con. Who's going to believe you, eh? And having shared a cell with me won't help your case. This guy Collins will think you've been following in the master's footsteps.'

'Snap,' I said. 'My conclusion exactly.'

'So how were your powers of persuasion? What happened at the bank?'

'I left Battersby and Naylor arguing over my fate. Naylor's all for giving me the benefit of the doubt: Battersby wants me imprisoned in the Tower.'

'What about the money? Did they manage to trace it?'

'Yes. For all the good it did they might not have bothered.' I shook my head dejectedly. 'The three notes, when new, were part of a consignment from the Bank of England to the Banque Credit de St Gallen. Naylor's theory is that a sloppy clerk ran out of used notes when making up the customer's order. Dipped into the new batch to make up the difference.'

'And St Gallen wouldn't happen to be in Switzerland, by any chance?'

'Buzzers sound. Lights flash. You've won tonight's star prize.

The town of St Gallen is in north-east Switzerland, close to the borders of Germany and Liechtenstein. The bank's main branch is in Zurich.'

'So what is Battersby's problem?' Norman asked. 'It's not as if the notes were inscribed "if lost please return to the Heroin Distribution Company".'

'Put simply, his view is: English banks good, Swiss banks evil. If the money came from a Swiss bank then it must have a doubtful provenance.'

'Better go and pack that bag,' he said.

'And run off to Spain with you? What will that solve?'

'We're not going to Spain. Today's revelations merely up the pressure to find John. We're moving in with Arthur. I'm afraid there's more bad news.'

'I'd guessed that much.'

'I took a break about half-ten. Needed to photocopy something. Ted collared me on my way back down the stairs and invited me over for a coffee and a chat. I was sitting with him on reception when they arrived. Fraud Squad. Four guys waving a warrant under Ted's nose.' Norman looked at me helplessly. 'There was nothing we could do. Ted called Tricky Dicky – what a merchant banker he is. Talk about a brown trouser job. They just brushed him aside. One went up to your office, the rest down to the basement. They've confiscated all the records from A&M.'

I swore loudly. Not at the Fraud Squad or Richard. But at myself.

'It's my fault,' I said. 'That old blind spot again. But poetic justice, this time. I shouldn't have pressed Charlie Bennington so hard. One million was a bloody stupid figure – must have stood out like silicone breasts on an anorexic.'

I could picture what had happened. Alarm bells ringing in my client's ears. Sign the deal, then start asking questions. Ring around some of our other clients. The smell of rat wafting through telephone lines. Next stop, Fraud Squad. Net result – client squeaky clean and laughing all the way to the bank.

'How much time do you reckon I've got, Norman?'

242

'On the downside,' he said, his mouth sucking in air in contemplation, 'the Fraud Squad have the advantage of resources. I think we can assume the same policeman who came to the office will be working full-time on the records.'

I didn't disagree. He had experience in his favour.

'On the upside,' Norman continued with a grin, 'they're not as good as I am. They'll be regular police officers transferred from CID and given a quick two-week crash course in fraud. They're not trained professionals. And they don't have the benefit of John's list – they can't target individual companies. That will slow them up.' He shrugged and waved his spread hands vaguely in front of him. 'Four days, five if we're lucky.'

I tried to take an optimistic view. 'It might still work out. Battersby could decide not to stick his oar in. That gives some leeway before the police discover what's been going on, and get round to checking my bank account. Even then, it's still only circumstantial evidence.'

Norman shook his head.

'Not any more it isn't. There's one last piece of bad news.'

I groaned. It seemed we were not at home to Mr Optimism, after all.

'One of the reports,' Norman continued, 'had been microfiched badly. It was so blurred I couldn't read it. I had to work from the original.' He reached inside his jacket and passed me two pieces of paper. 'These are the photocopies I took this morning.'

They were copies of the balance sheet and profit and loss account for one of the recent acquisitions. John's initials, as required for authentication purposes, were at the bottom of each page. So were mine.

'He's stitched you up real good, Nick. I didn't have time to check any other reports, but I'll lay ten pounds to an urn of urine your initials are plastered all over them. John knew you'd use the microfiche – it was the logical way to work, everything in one place. You discover the frauds and report them just as he wanted – and all without realising that you're implicating yourself. Bloody clever.'

'But why me? Why did he hate me so much? Why go to all this trouble? I can understand him wanting to expose the cheats, the liars, the swindlers. But why go to all the extra trouble to frame me? What have I ever done to him?'

'There's only one way to get your answer. Back to Plan A. Find John.' Norman looked at me more seriously than I had ever seen him be before. 'Be careful, Nick. Whatever reason he has, you can be sure of one thing – it's going to be pretty sick. And a sick mind is an unpredictable mind.'

Norman stood up. 'Come on,' he said. 'Get packed. And let's go. No sense making life easy for Mr Plod.'

As we were leaving the room, Norman paused. He turned to the window and pointed to the keyboard.

'I bet the bastard couldn't play a note,' he said. 'Even with the full complement of fingers. You're right. He really does hate you.'

CHAPTER TWENTY-SEVEN

I stood hesitating at the door of Sofia's flat, my index finger poised inches from the bell. This would be the last time I saw Sofia. Of that I was convinced. The pleasure of my company or my sparkling wit was not the reason for inviting me to dinner. Her brief, without a shadow of doubt, was to set in motion the last element of John's plan. Once that was achieved there would be nothing to keep her in England.

Something, though, was important enough for John to be still hanging around. He would have left weeks ago otherwise. What was the final twist? The ace up his sleeve? If I could work that out – and seemingly go along with the plan – then I had a chance to find John.

My success would depend on two factors.

The ability to conceal my knowledge that John was not in fact dead.

And the infinitely more difficult matter of distinguishing truth from lie every time Sofia opened her mouth. The scar hadn't prevented her from becoming a model – it had stopped her being an actress. That was the profession which best befitted her talents. She was a gifted – and very dangerous – amateur.

I pushed the bell. Made some final resolutions. Stay sober. Keep my wits about me. Listen attentively for tell-tale slips of the tongue. Watch her reactions with the hawk-like eyes of a batsman trying to pick out the googly which might be bowled at any time by this crafty spinner of webs of deceit.

As she opened the door, I realised that one more resolution was needed.

She was dressed to kill.

Her dark hair was wild and free, caressing shoulders bare but for the two whisker-thin straps of the camisole top. Ivory white silk with pearl buttons. Loose and floating where it hung outside her skirt. Tight where it touched the swell of her breasts. So sheer I could see the deep brown circles that surrounded her hard, excited nipples. They were unmissable, my attention unfailingly drawn down by the arrowhead formed by the line of the necklace. The delicate chain was a weave of three different colours of gold – pastel blue, pink and matt yellow. It matched the bracelet on her watch and the band of the engagement ring.

She led the way – deliberately, I was sure – up the stairs, providing me with a panoramic view of tanned legs and trim curves which pressed tantalisingly against the tightness of the short black skirt. A thin line of fake diamonds ran down the back of her shoes and the four tapering inches of the stiletto heels.

It was not difficult to guess the part she had cast for herself. The room was her stage and had been propped accordingly.

The wall lights, turned down to their dimmest setting, gave a soft amber glow to the edges of the room – but penetrated no further. My eyes moved naturally to the intended focal point. The table. A red candle flickered, producing rainbows of reflections on the tall Swedish glasses. Somewhere in the darkness at the corners of the room the loudspeakers of the stereo were whispering a melody being played lovingly on the Spanish guitar – John Williams, Julian Bream? Concierto de Aranjuez. Obligatory background music in travelogues with heart-stopping scenery or television commercials with so little to say they had to fall back on filming cheap starlets through Vaseline smeared lenses.

I fought back a laugh. Managed to restrict it to a small smile touching only the corners of my mouth.

Christ, this was so corny!

I half-expected her to suggest we played chess so that she could sit running her fingers over the raised edge of a bishop while gazing meaningfully into my eyes.

She mistook the smile as a sign of approval for the pains she had taken. Placed her hands on my shoulders. Kissed me lightly on each cheek. The musky aroma of her perfume drifted up from her neck.

Stepping back, she noticed for the first time that I was carrying a bunch of flowers. She relieved me of them with an expression of gratitude so gushing it was embarrassing.

'Perhaps, Nick, you would pour the wine,' she said, disappearing into the kitchen with a sway of her hips. 'I'll pop these in water.'

I took the bottle from the cooler. Carefully measured out two glasses – more in hers than mine. Examined my glass by holding it near the flame of the candle. Saw the honey tones of the Meursault appear magically as it caught the light. If it was as good as it looked, it would be wonderful. Dry and mellow. And, unlike Sofia, subtle.

I raised the glass to my lips. Then put it back hastily on the table. Best to wait for Sofia to drink first. No sense in taking unnecessary risks.

All her preparation time had been concentrated on the room and herself. She had taken no trouble with the food – except, perhaps, to buy it. The first course was a small plate consisting of five giant 'Mediterranean' prawns arranged in a fan around a rose-coloured circle poured from a bottle of Thousand Island dressing. The prawns had been frozen at some stage in their factory-farmed history. They were limp to the touch, watery and needed the dressing to impart any flavour at all. Unfortunately, the mass-produced sauce left a fatty, insipid taste in the mouth – and, an even worse crime, killed the delicacy of the wine.

Sofia did not seem to notice anything wrong. She picked up each prawn by the small section of shell that had been deliberately left on its tail, dipped it into the sauce, toyed with it playfully between her red lips before finally biting.

I tried to ignore the oral foreplay. Disposed quickly of the prawns without resorting to holding my nose. Chewed on a brown roll (still icy cold from the fridge) to cleanse my palate. Savoured the wine.

The conversation was light; intended simply as an inconsequential prelude. She asked me about work and my future. I answered with genuine doubt – but cited a new boss as the reason. In my turn I enquired politely about her holiday (back to Jamaica, she told me wistfully).

She looked at her watch. Lit a cigarette from the candle, leaning forward so I could see down the front of the camisole. With less drama, I used my lighter. We sparred some more, tentative feints to test each other's defences, before a bell pinged in the kitchen. End of Round One.

Refusing my offer of help, she refilled my glass and cleared the plates.

The only good point about the main course was the Pomerol – John's favourite, I noticed – which was served with it. The grey, overdone, lamb steaks in a brackish-green herb and garlic marinade had made a swift and uneventful journey from chill pack to table via the microwave. The accompanying salad was ruined by sunflower oil and cheap vinegar.

I poured the claret carefully. Toasted her with a wave of my glass and sipped appreciatively.

She ate in a pretentious Americanised style, cutting the meat and salad into bite-size portions and then, with fork in right hand, transferring a little at a time to her mouth. It gave her the advantage of freeing her left hand. Distractedly – but that was surely the impression she was hoping to give – she drew small circles on the tablecloth with the long red nail of her index finger.

I was growing tired of the play-acting.

I placed my knife and fork in the middle of the unfinished food on the plate. Looked across the table at her. Spoke impatiently.

'Stop playing games, Sofia. What do you want from me?'

'Don't be angry with me, Nick.' She picked up her glass, the pack of cigarettes and a flashy box of matches embossed in gold with the words 'Hotel Flohof, Zurich'. Rising dramatically from the table, she switched off the music and sat down challengingly on the settee.

'Come,' she said in the voice of a siren.

I positioned myself at the opposite end of the settee. She slid across. Curled up against me. Kicked off her shoes. Drew her body into a protective ball.

'Put your arm round me. Please.'

I could feel the sensual warmth radiating through the gossamer thin layer of silk.

I did as she asked. Found myself running my fingers along the soft skin of her bare arms. Just as Richard had done years before.

She buried her head in my shoulder so I could not see her face.

'Tell me what you know,' she said quietly. 'Then I'll answer your questions.'

In the silence of the darkened room I told her first about the fraud and blackmail I had uncovered at work. She listened without interruption. Not with words, that is. But her left hand was on my chest, nails gently teasing with a slow, soothing rhythm.

Her body tensed when I came to the part about the discovery of the list and the gun. She tried to cover up her instinctive reaction by unbuttoning my shirt and sliding her hand inside.

My mind, with difficulty, ignored her – but my body stirred.

When I came to the part about Richard I felt the dampness of tears falling on my shirt.

She was good, I thought.

Very good.

Could even cry to order.

I placed my hand on her exposed thigh. Toyed with her for a change. Demonstrated how clever I was. The power I held over her. Delivered the rest of the pre-prepared script. The accelerator cable. The sighting with Sam – how easily the lie slipped from my lips – at Victoria Coach Station. Her involvement in setting up the murder.

'Now it's your turn. Fill in the gaps,' I said. 'And try,' I added wearily, 'just for once, to tell the truth.'

Sofia sat up. Peered into the gloom in an effort to read my intentions from the look on my face. Saw only determination written large.

She drank some of the wine. Stared at it reflectively as if only now appreciating how good it tasted. Delayed further by lighting another cigarette, striking the match away from her as only women do. Gave a long drawn out sigh. Finally dropped all pretence at innocence.

She confirmed all I had told her. Took great pride in doing so. Showed no remorse. Even boasted that the money was safely stashed in a bank in Zurich (although her frankness didn't include giving away which bank). Explained that she and John had made regular trips to deposit the proceeds of their crimes – all tickets paid for in cash by the money extracted from Emsby and Morton.

The admissions rolled off her tongue.

She laughed when she told me about Sam. How he had telephoned while Sally had been out at work. Swallowed the reassuring tones of her voice. Come to the flat. She sneered at how easily she had seduced him. And preened herself when she said that the money was no more than a secondary incentive to bend him to her will.

Her complete lack of conscience made me feel sick.

I got up from the settee. 'If there's nothing else, Sofia,' I said, striding purposefully towards the telephone.

It was time for the big bluff.

I dialled 999.

'I wouldn't do that if I were you,' she said.

I turned to face her, expecting to see a gun aimed at my head.

But she stood there unarmed and seemingly defenceless. Smug, though. Any moment now the twist would come.

'Don't waste your breath, Sofia,' I said angrily. 'There's nothing you can say or do. Save your next performance for the jury.'

The phone was ringing as she spoke.

'If you turn me in,' she said, 'then you'll never be able to live with yourself. You'll never know who was driving the car.'

She smiled confidently. 'Don't you want the name of the man who maimed your sister?'

I replaced the phone back in its cradle.

*

She had been working at the time in her father's taverna: a large portion, no-frills eating house in a little market town straddling the Essex/Suffolk borders close to my own home. Just sixteen. The same age as Susie. But not sweet sixteen like my sister.

Sofia had no idea what she wanted from life. But she knew precisely what she didn't want. Whatever the future held, she was adamant it would be something a whole lot better than waitressing in a Greek restaurant stuck miles out in the sticks.

Her father, still clinging to the traditional ways of the old country, was repressive. But his religion fought a constant battle with his greed. He adopted a convenient dual morality when it came to keeping his customers happy. Though he hated seeing his daughter flirting with the men, the businessman in him realised that she was much more of an attraction than the standard fare of taramasalata and souvlakia they dished up.

His convenient expediency, she told me with a wince of remembered pain, did not stop him from slapping her around from time to time.

She admitted to being precocious. Promiscuous even. To using her job as a means of honing her skills at manipulating men. She was biding her time. Waiting for the right moment to come along.

And come along it did.

In the shape of John and his companion. The one with the wallet full of money.

John was a new face to her. The man had been there before. It was a convenient stopping point on his journey to or from London. He always ate too much, drank too much, watched her with piercing eyes which seemed to strip the clothes from her body and feast on the delights revealed.

That night was no exception.

They had gorged themselves on a *meze*. Washed it down with two bottles of Othello. Accepted the offer of seven star Metaxa that came with the bill.

John, she said conceitedly, had stared longingly at her throughout the meal. While they drank the brandy the two men began to argue. As she watched them, she felt sure that she was the cause.

The man ordered more Metaxa. Asked her, in a tone which brooked no refusal, to join them. Paid the bill in cash. Took five hundred pounds from his wallet. Placed the money on the table. Put the proposition to her.

If the offer had been to go with the man with X-ray vision then, she confessed, she probably would have thought for longer. But there was something about John. He had some hold over his companion. Had won the argument. His eyes showed a desperation to possess her. She was sure she could handle him. She recognised a golden opportunity.

It was a snap decision. One which would change her life.

She accepted the money – and all it might entail. Went upstairs to pack a bag and write a vitriolic note to her father.

She left the restaurant for good – if that is what it could be called.

When she saw the car she was convinced she had made the right choice. If the little man had power over the driver of the Rolls Royce then he could be very useful to her.

She flung her bag into the back of the car without further thought. Climbed in next to John. Let him put his arm round her.

The driver turned on the stereo. Repositioned his mirror to watch the expected antics of his passengers. Steered erratically out of the car park. Drove slowly through the outskirts of town. Onto the quiet country road which would lead to the motorway. And a new life for her in London.

It was the days, she reminded me, before seat belts were

compulsory for the backs of cars. She and John were free to romp along the full width of the leather seat. But she knew what she was doing. She let him go so far – but not an inch further. Teased him with her hands and body. Made it clear that the rest would only be delivered when they were alone in his bed.

At first, she claimed, she was unaware of the increasing speed of the car. Until the moment she was thrown away from John as they rounded a tight corner on the unlit road. She looked up to see the driver leering in the rear-view mirror.

They entered the next bend more quickly than the heavy car could handle. The Rolls began to slide sideways. It seemed an age before the man's eyes returned to the road or his hands took any corrective action on the wheel.

By then it was too late.

She was thrown violently forward as the driver stamped on the brakes. Found herself travelling through the air towards the back of the driver's seat. Felt a cold wet trickle on her face. Heard the dull thumps from the twin collisions following rapidly one after another.

That was the last she remembered.

Until she woke up in John's bed. With a deep cut under her eye that would turn into a scar.

A scar on her face.

A worse scar on her mind, I thought.

John had looked after her. Told her they shouldn't – couldn't – go to the police. Explained his hold over the man. And how they could exploit the situation for their mutual benefit: wring more money out of the stupid man who feared bad publicity above all else.

She left the name of the driver to last.

David Yates.

*

The final discordant note in John's symphony had sounded.

It all became depressingly clear now.

The reason for the gun.

Swept along by a quest for blind justice, I was supposed to swallow Sofia's cock-and-bull story. Hook, line and sinker.

I was meant to kill Yates. An innocent man.

My pride was hurt. Very badly.

At a pinch, I could stomach Collins believing me capable of murder – he was simply a suspicious bastard. But John was a different matter. What sort of fool did he take me for? Just how stupid did he think I was?

I controlled the mounting anger. Then realised quickly that control was the last reaction Sofia would expect to see. I had to show emotion. Convince her I had taken the bait.

I let the anger flow from me like lava from a volcano.

And lava destroys everything in its path.

I was going to enjoy this.

This was my chance to hurt Sofia; exact a little vengeance for using my dead sister to make me stay in the house.

She saw the hatred in my face. Interpreted it, I hoped, as stemming from her involvement in Susie's death.

But she didn't back away – Sofia never doubted her power over men.

She approached me, if a little warily. Tried to put her arms round me, to use her body to still the fire raging inside me.

I grabbed her hair and pulled it towards me. Kissed her violently. Released my grip for long enough to put my hands on the camisole top. I tore it from her body, the buttons flying into the air. With all my strength, I pushed her against the wall. Felt some satisfaction as I saw the look of alarm in her eyes. The fear of the monster she assumed she had created.

'Don't hurt me,' she screamed in my face. 'You can have me.'

She looked towards the door to the bedroom. Her shaking hands fumbled to undo her zip. The velvet skirt was so tight she had trouble pushing it down over her hips. It fell silently to the floor. She stepped out of its folds. I stared at the tiny, black triangle of lace that was the last barrier between us.

She edged towards the bedroom, hands pushed out protectively in front of her. The door was slightly ajar. She kicked it open with such force that the heel of her shoe broke away.

'No,' she pleaded, as she limped into the room. She threw herself backwards onto the bed and whimpered that one word, over and over again. 'No. No. No.'

I followed her inside, unsure as to whether I was being driven by the need to keep up a pretence or by the excitement welling up inside.

The blow struck me on the back of the skull. Very hard.

I fell forward. Landed, poleaxed, on top of the suitcases by the side of the bed.

A black haze began to creep into my brain. I tried to move. It felt like I was immersed in a bath of treacle.

The second blow landed across the side of my neck. The force sent me deeper into the pile of leather luggage.

I had enough presence of mind not to turn round. If I couldn't overpower John – and I had no illusions on that count at the moment then it was best not to see him. After all, he wasn't going to kill me. There was still Yates waiting in the wings. He wanted me alive for his little denouement.

I summoned up my last resources of strength. Raised myself onto my hands.

I watched Sofia as she got up from the bed and walked deliberately towards me.

My vision was blurred by now.

But I could still make out the smile on her face as she stood imperiously over me.

The last thing I saw, before lapsing into unconsciousness, was the blood-red of her painted toenails.

The last thing I felt was the merciless kick of her foot as it connected with my mouth.

CHAPTER TWENTY-EIGHT

Hands grabbed my shoulders. Someone rolled me over onto my back, and simultaneously plunged red hot pokers into my body. I heard the wail of a wounded animal and took an age before making the obvious connection with my own lips.

Water splashed in my face. A bright light burned through my eyelids and scorched my retina.

I forced my eyes open. Two black shapes were silhouetted against the brightness. I groaned. Shut my eyes again.

From a far-off planet, alien beings spoke in a strange tongue. My name was the only word I recognised.

Awareness began to filter slowly back into my senses: it only made me feel worse. There was a pile-driver thudding away remorselessly inside my head. I could taste warm salty blood as it trickled into my mouth. I swallowed. Christ, even that small act hurt like hell.

More water. This time smeared lightly over my lips. A hand tenderly supporting my aching head.

There was my name again, but more clearly now. I forced my eyes into slits and gradually widened them so my pupils could acclimatise to the light. The shapes drifted into view. Swam about like formless blobs of seaweed bobbing on a rolling tide. Then coalesced. Into Arthur and Norman.

Arthur propped me up against the side of the bed. Norman – for some reason I could not fathom – fed me water from a teaspoon. He laid an ice cold flannel across the burning heat of my forehead.

I raised my hand to my mouth in an instinctive reaction to wipe away the blood. There was a balloon where my lips should have been. The light touch of my fingers detonated an explosion of seering fire. An agonised cry somehow escaped through the narrow gap between my lips.

'Come on, Nick,' Norman said. 'We're going to try to move you. We've got to get you out of here.'

I shook my head. Instantly regretted it.

My brain clutched onto the pain and used it as a focus for action: slowly, it fought its way back to consciousness.

My voice came in a barely intelligible drawl, like a patient who has been subjected to a dozen injections at the dentist.

'Not yet,' I slurred. 'Got to clear up. Sally mustn't know.'

Norman tutted and shook his head in irritation, then understood the problem. If Sally found out what had happened, she would want to go to the police. And that would put an end to any chance of my catching John.

'Explain everything later,' I mumbled to Arthur. 'Clean up. Leave no signs.'

They carried me to the settee where I could watch and direct their operations. The two of them set about the task with all the grace and skill of untrained school leavers on the first day of a YOP's course. Still, to give them their due, they transformed the room from an antechamber to her bedroom back to a lounge. Everything might not have been exactly in the right place, but it did at least have the semblance of normality. Good enough to stop Sally asking any awkward questions at any rate.

I heard them talking in low grave voices while they scraped food off plates and then washed up. They looked determined when they emerged from the kitchen.

'Right. Come on. Let's go,' Norman said.

I raised my hand. Wasn't going to repeat the mistake of shaking my head.

'Tidy bedroom,' I said to Norman. 'Paper. Pen,' I commanded Arthur.

Norman opened his mouth to tell me, I was sure, just what he thought of my requests. His face glowed the bright red of boiling temper.

'Important,' I managed to say.

Arthur said something to Norman and they went off huffily to complete their respective duties.

I wrote a note to Sally, concentrating hard to make my writing legible. Told her that Sofia had gone on holiday. Last minute change of plans. I had given her a lift to the airport. Added a postscript saying I would contact her soon about her brother. Lied when I said she must not worry.

Arthur helped me to the car. Virtually carried me, in fact. I passed out on the back seat, my head on Norman's shoulder.

*

I awoke in Arthur's spare bed. The sun was streaming through a gap in the curtains. My watch said twelve-thirty. I wondered what day it was.

I tried to get up. It was a stupid thing to do. My legs buckled as soon as they touched the floor: I went down like Arsenal's goalie, setting off a minefield of minor aches and major pains that ran the length and breadth of my body. My head felt heavy, like an axe had been buried deep inside. I touched it tentatively with my fingers. My hair was heavily caked with dried blood. Somewhere below the red matting was a long furrow caused by whatever weapon John had used on me.

Arthur appeared dutifully at the door. He picked me up with a sigh, wrapped an arm round his shoulder and supported me on the necessary journey to the bathroom.

'Wait outside, Arthur,' I drawled. 'This isn't Brixton. I'll be all right.'

Back in bed, Arthur propped me up against two pillows and sat down beside me. There were bags round his eyes because, I imagined, he and Norman had stayed up most of the night worrying or taking turns to keep an eye on me. He hadn't shaved. The stubble on his chin was as dark as the look on his face.

Norman arrived with a tray. 'How are you feeling?' he asked. 'Like I've just abseiled down Everest without a rope.' He managed the merest hint of a grin and handed me three paracetamol tablets and a glass of water. His head shook pitifully as I made pathetic attempts at finding the opening between my swollen lips.

He disappeared downstairs. Came back with a straw. I sucked up sufficient water to help the tablets slide down. Then used the straw to drink the tea. It tasted strong, sweet and, to my parched throat, very good.

I felt stupid.

And not just because I was drinking tea through a straw.

Arthur must have read my mind.

'Didn't exactly go to plan then?' he asked with a smile.

I didn't feel up to answering questions yet. Not till the tea and analgesics had a chance to work. The pain in my head made thinking a major exercise. My neck was stiff and resisted the slightest movement. There was also an intermittent stabbing from my chest that suggested a cracked rib or two – Sofia's foot again, I presumed.

'How did you come to be there?' I asked him.

He had decided to treat Norman to a meal. Thankfully, had the foresight to give the number of the Chinese restaurant to Tina. They'd been burning their tongues on toffee bananas when the call came through.

Tina had already been at her post for two hours when I arrived. She had assumed from Sofia's appearance when greeting me at the door that I was there for the night. Settling down for a quiet evening, she turned on the car radio and sipped coffee from a flask. At one point, she'd admitted to Arthur, she had wondered whether it was worth hanging around any longer.

John had appeared first. Struggled into the street with the heavy suitcases. Manhandled them into the boot of the car. Sofia emerged next, looking shaken. Her lightweight raincoat, buttons unfastened, belt untied, flapped about as if it had been put on in a hurry. Tina noticed she had changed her clothes, and the high heels had been replaced by a pair of more practical shoes. When the pair got in the car, Tina was in two minds as to what to do for the best. Her job was to follow Sofia – but her every instinct screamed that something was wrong.

She set off after the car, banking on them not going far, hoping she could get to a phone soon so as to share her anxiety with Arthur.

When they headed west, her heart sank. Their destination was sure to be Heathrow.

She phoned Arthur while the pair stood in line at the check-in desk. My friends had shot round to Sofia's flat. Norman had worked his way past the insubstantial lock with a credit card (Access?). They'd found me on the floor, and taken me for dead at first.

'Where did they go?' I asked Arthur.

'Sofia caught a flight to New York. John kissed her goodbye and then drove straight back to London. Tina followed him to the underground car park at Trafalgar Square. That's where she lost him. Can't blame the girl for that. Too many exits for one person to watch.'

'That's the bad news,' Norman chipped in. 'The good news is that the car is still there. Arthur and I have been taking turns watching it all night. Tina's back on duty now.'

'I don't want her involved anymore,' I said forcefully. 'Her job was tailing Sofia – not John. It's too dangerous now. We can't expose her to any more risks. Arthur, can you go and take over? I'll be along as soon as I can.'

'You're in no fit state to go anywhere, my lad,' Norman said. 'Christ, you can't even get out of bed without falling flat on your face.'

'This is something only I can do. Give me a couple of hours and I'll be on my feet again.'

Norman rolled his eyes in exasperation.

Arthur looked at me questioningly. 'What the hell's going on, Nick?' he asked. 'Why didn't they both make a run for it? What's he hanging around for?'

'Unfinished business,' I said. 'That's what last night was all about. I'm supposed to kill Yates. And John wants to be there at the death.'

I sucked up the last of the tea then launched into the full story, articulating the words as best I could.

'So,' I said in conclusion, 'I take the gun, walk up to Yates in some public place where there are witnesses by the score, and shoot him in cold blood. Go directly to jail. Do not pass Go. Do not collect £200. What a low opinion he must have of me.'

'Or a high opinion,' Norman responded. 'He may have underestimated – marginally, in my opinion – your intelligence and overestimated – ditto – your credibility but he was right on the button as far as your old-fashioned morality goes. Justice before self. Think about it for a moment. Be honest with yourself. If you hadn't worked out that John was still alive, what would you have done? Walked away from the chance to avenge your sister?'

'Huh,' I said.

'I rest my case,' he said.

'Back to your corners, please,' Arthur interjected. 'I want to know what happens now. What are you planning, Nick?'

'I'm going to meet John.'

'*Mano a mano*,' Norman said, shaking his head

'I have to make him admit everything. Get it all down on tape. That way I'm in the clear.'

'And just how are you going to extract this confession?' asked Norman. 'Thumbscrews? The rack? Say "pretty please"?'

'By letting him crow, that's how.' I paused, trying to improvise a plan on the spot.

'I'll go alone,' I said. 'I know John. Providing he's convinced he's in no danger, he'll strut and swagger. As long as he thinks he has the upper hand, he'll talk.'

'And what if he *does* have the upper hand?' Norman said. 'We found a gun, remember? He could just as easily have bought two, you know.'

'Don't worry,' I said. 'I'll think of something.'

'Very reassuring, I don't think,' said Norman.

'Well,' I said testily, 'it's the best I can come up with at the moment. Just give me a couple of hours, that's all. Now, Arthur.

Will you go relieve Tina, please? I'll be along soon.'

'No,' he said defiantly. 'Norman's right. You're in no state to handle this alone. Either I'm there with you – or you don't leave this room. Which is it going to be?'

Only an idiot gets involved in a Mexican stand-off with Arthur.

'It doesn't seem as if I have much choice. But stay out of sight. John has to think he's under no threat. Otherwise he won't talk.'

'Agreed,' said Arthur, happy now. 'I'll be off then. We'll all be a lot happier when Tina's safely out of the picture. What time will you be along, Nick?'

'I'll come at seven, although I don't expect John will turn up till much later. Yates is speaking tonight at some dinner at the Institute of Directors. The press say he's going to make his big play for the job of Chancellor. If I were going to kill him, like John expects, then tonight would be a golden opportunity. I think John will be hanging around somewhere when Yates arrives, in case I make a move then. When nothing happens, I'm hoping John will reach the conclusion that I've settled on a more private hit. Decided to follow Yates on his drive home and shoot him when he gets out of his car. So, if we're lucky, John will come to collect his car just before midnight. And we'll be waiting.'

'See you later, then,' he said, walking to the door.

'Arthur,' I said.

'What now?'

'Thanks.'

'Save the thanks till it's all over. Just watch your back. Right?'

'You bet,' I said as he left the room.

'And what is *my* role in this masterplan?' Norman asked.

'If I give you a list, will you go the shops?'

'Sure, bwana,' said Norman. 'Anyting for de great white hunter.'

*

262

Norman finished winding the bandage around my chest and stepped back to examine his handiwork.

'That's the best I can do,' he said. 'You need a doctor not an embezzler.' He looked at me sadly. 'But I'm wasting my breath, aren't I? It doesn't matter what I say, you'll do it your way.'

I smiled and tucked the black shirt into the black jeans. Norman sighed and fixed a Walkman onto my belt.

'You remember how to use this?' he said.

'Yes, Norman. Don't fuss. We've been through it three times already. Not again, please. You've already set it up for me. All I have to do is release the pause button and it starts to record. I think I can manage that.'

He gave me a pained look and watched as I took the tiny microphone in my left hand and slipped my arms into the sleeves of the black leather jacket. Despite the tightness of the bandage, my ribs found sufficient freedom of movement to send a sharp stabbing pain into my right side. I bit my lip, determined not to wince.

Norman clipped the microphone onto my sleeve. 'You'll do,' he said. 'Off you go.'

'Aren't you forgetting something?' I said.

'Don't think so,' he said innocently.

'Give me the gun, Norman.'

He sucked in air and ran his fingers pensively over his lips.

'I don't like it, Nick. You don't know the first thing about guns. Probably shoot yourself in the foot.'

'Give me the gun, Norman,' I repeated.

He walked with exaggerated slowness to the drawer of Arthur's sideboard and gingerly took out the gun.

'It's only for show,' I said, trying to reassure him. 'I won't use it, I promise.'

I snapped open the chamber and checked the gun – I wouldn't have put it past Norman to remove the bullets. Satisfied, I stuck it into the right-hand pocket of my jacket.

'Well, I better be on my way.'

He placed his hands on my shoulders and stared long and

hard at me. I got the uncomfortable feeling he didn't expect to see me again.

'Be lucky,' he said.

*

I sat in Arthur's rusty Dormobile van on the bottom floor of the car park. Outside, every thirty yards or thereabouts a wire-meshed light glowed so dimly you needed a guidedog to help you find your car. Through the open window came the musty smell of damp from the concrete walls. It was cold. I had given up hugging myself for warmth – it wasn't worth the resultant complaints from my ribs.

During the course of my vigil I had seen plenty of vehicles go, and very few arrive. The cars remaining now would almost certainly be here for the rest of the night. I had re-parked the van an hour ago so that it was directly opposite John's white Sierra. From this position there was an unobstructed view of the nearer two sets of stairs and of the lift. Arthur – out of sight, as ordered – had earlier taken up a position at the far end where he could watch the other two sets of stairs.

I checked my watch for the millionth time.

It was still only ten o'clock. I was beginning to appreciate just what a good job Tina had done. I wondered how she'd coped with the boredom without losing concentration. I wanted a cigarette but daren't risk it.

I yawned.

Five past ten.

Nearly two hours to go.

CHAPTER TWENTY-NINE

I had never seen John with a beard before. Nor, of much more immediate concern, with a gun.

Neither suited him.

The beard was dark, untrimmed and patchy, needing at least two or three more weeks of growth before all the skin beneath would be hidden from sight. It was an attempt at a naval style, but on such a small face the proportions were all wrong. It merely served to accentuate the area around his pale eyes, as if he were wearing a pair of white goggles.

The gun was large, far too heavy for his small hand. As he pointed it through the window of the van, it seemed he had to make a conscious effort to keep the barrel from tilting downwards.

'Fallen asleep on the job, Shannon,' he laughed. 'Too many late nights that's your trouble. Fancy meeting you here. I'd expected to see you out on the street keeping watch for Yates.'

My watch told me I'd slept for just over an hour – and that John was early.

'Get out,' he said, moving to the side of the door.

I climbed out, flicking the switch on the back-up Walkman hidden under the dashboard of the Dormobile: the black microphone was clipped inconspicuously to one of the wiper blades.

As John stood covering me, I saw how the mighty had fallen.

There were large bags under his eyes from lack of sleep – had he experienced nightmares too, or was it just the discomfort of a sagging bed in some cheap hotel where they asked no questions?

He had lost weight over the past few weeks – a result, no doubt, of a series of lonely snatched meals while in hiding. The pounds he had shed only diminished his already slight physical presence.

And I was used to seeing him dressed in suits. It was clear now just how much they had contributed to his customary air of authority. These clothes made him seem weak and vulnerable. On anyone else the jeans, open necked shirt and windcheater would have looked casual and comfortable to wear: John merely appeared awkward and ill at ease. Even the trainers looked unnatural on him, like seeing the Queen in a shell-suit. They added an extra inch to his height. He noticed me glance down at them and seemed embarrassed.

'Turn round,' he said, reinforcing the order with a sideways flick of the gun. 'Up against the van. Spread your arms and legs.'

I felt the cold muzzle of his gun press into the soft skin at the back of my neck. His free hand moved deftly down my left side.

'Naughty,' he said, feeling the bump of the Walkman on my belt. He ripped it free and examined the machine.

'Didn't even have a chance to switch it on, Shannon. You really are slipping.'

I heard the Walkman clatter to the ground and saw the toe of his trainer kick it casually under the van.

There was a momentary change in pressure on my neck: he was swapping hands to complete his search. Under different circumstances that would have been the signal to make my play.

'And what have we here, then?' He eased the gun from my pocket. 'This really isn't your lucky day, is it?'

'Some you win, some you lose,' I said.

'You'll never get anywhere if you think like that.'

'If you've finally done, do you think I might turn around now.'

'Oh yes,' he said. 'Show me that pretty-boy face of yours. I want to see the look on it – in the moment before I kill you.'

'I don't suppose you got that satisfaction with Sam, did you? That's the drawback with taking someone by surprise. Too quick for there to have been much pleasure in it, I expect.'

'Don't worry, Shannon. Killing you will give me enough pleasure to last a lifetime.'

He had a gun in each hand now. I could tell it made him feel good. The initial stiffness in his shoulders had loosened with the easing of tension. The smile on his lips no longer looked as if it had come straight out of the deep-freeze. He swaggered before me like a man with two extra sets of genitals – rather than one who'd been shortchanged in the testicle department.

My contempt must have shown. His left hand sliced lightning-quick through the air. The barrel of the gun smashed into the bruise on my mouth. I screamed and fell to the floor, stomach threatening to go into overload.

'Get up off your knees,' he said.

I rose shakily, my head still reverberating from the force of the blow and the resulting pain.

John tucked one gun into the waistband of his trousers: the butt sat proud of his jacket, ready for instant withdrawal if the need arose. He stared imperiously at me. He was the boss again, his control over me established as absolute.

'You were expecting me, then?' he asked.

'No,' I said, through the fresh blood. 'I'm on an Open University speleology course – you have to do the first year in underground car parks before you're allowed to graduate to caves and potholes.'

'Spare me the sarcasm,' he sneered. 'You'll live longer. Not much but . . .' He shrugged his shoulders in an unmistakable gesture of indifference – now, a few minutes' time, what does it matter to me when I kill you?

'Tell me,' he said, 'how did you know I was still alive?'

'The tape was the key to the puzzle,' I said, wondering if Arthur was already inching his way from the far stairs. 'It made me change my thinking. Up until then I'd been too busy congratulating myself on how well I had done. I'd uncovered the cheating; spotted the fraud; worked out your use of black-mail as a further source of income. It seemed all that was left was to figure out which of your many victims had finally had enough – and decided to get rid of you for good.'

I returned his sneer with interest – although mine must have looked pretty lopsided by now.

'The tape was too neat. It struck me I was being too lucky. Improbably so.'

It was hard to explain what had started as a hunch.

'If you're playing poker and someone deals himself four aces time after time, well, it doesn't take too long to cotton on to what is happening. But when someone repeatedly deals *you* the winning hand, it's all to easy to take it at face value. A lucky streak, surely? Why should you suspect cheating? What possible reason could there be?

'With Emsby and Morton the hands told the story – showed without doubt what they were doing. The hands you dealt me told a story too.'

He frowned. And tightened his grip on the gun.

'The tape made me think about the odds,' I continued. 'The timing of the conveniently cryptic note you sent – 'cheat, liar, swindler'. Certain to arouse my suspicions. And make me cast the net wide.

'Then finding the file of bridge hands, your conclusions plain to see with only the most casual of analysis. The Bennington report, still in draft – although it should have been sent out days before. The files which had no reason to be in your desk, so old they should have been out of sight – out of mind – in the archives. It started to smell like a deliberate plan rather than a series of fortuitous finds and shrewd deductions.'

I moved my right hand towards the pocket of the leather jacket. The gun twitched. 'I need a cigarette,' I said. 'Okay?'

'The condemned man's last request, eh? How can I refuse? But no tricks, Shannon. I won't hesitate to shoot. Is that clear?'

'Crystal.'

I lit the cigarette with deliberate slowness, using any excuse to give Arthur time to get into position. In the flare of light I studied John's face. His eyes were so cold they sent a shiver down my spine.

'Go on,' he said impatiently.

'When I understood the improbability – the impossibility – of it all, I could see your hallmark written large all over it. A classic case of overbidding.'

'Don't push me too far, Shannon,' he said, clutching the gun more tightly.

'And when you overbid, John,' I said, ignoring the warning, 'it means that you have to play like a Grand Master. You, on the contrary, made stupid mistakes.'

His mood was worsening rapidly. The self-satisfaction was being eroded by every word I uttered. Anger was rising to the surface. But I didn't care. Anger clouds thought – and breeds carelessness.

'It was very sloppy to meet Sofia in public. And just round the corner, too – didn't want to stop spying on me for too long, I presume? Being seen with Sofia was the first *real* bit of luck I had.'

'But you told Sofia she'd been seen with Sam.' He sounded hurt, like a schoolboy who has tossed his penny at the wall and then been told it's the one *farthest away* that wins. I almost expected him to stamp his feet and say it wasn't fair.

'Pardon me for lying, John,' I said. 'But would you be here right now if you had thought I knew the truth?'

Sullen silence.

'If you had only kept it simple,' I said with a critical shake of my head, 'then I might never have suspected – although the missing head always bothered me. Why should the murderer go to the trouble of taking it? He wasn't going to hang it on the wall as a trophy, that was for sure. I never really bought Collins's theory about it being irrefutable proof for a hired killer to claim his blood money – surely the news coverage would have been proof enough. And as for involving Yates . . . that was just an insult to my intelligence.'

'I haven't noticed any signs of intelligence tonight,' he responded. 'Far from it, I'd say.'

'Christ, John,' I said, raising my voice. 'Don't you understand. You overdid everything. You served me a meal that was too rich to swallow.'

'So I made the odd mistake. I still outsmarted you. Don't doubt that for one moment. You did exactly as I planned. Exposed Emsby and Morton; Bennington; Richard; all the others. You didn't kill Yates, granted – but that was the icing on the cake. Shame, though. I was looking forward to seeing you go back to prison. Murder, plain and simple. And not an ounce of sympathy this time.'

Against the dim glow of the cigarette his eyes shone with the enamel glaze of madness. The seeds of insanity sown in his youth had grown like weeds: in the garden of his mind, there was no room for anything else to survive.

I realised there wasn't much time left. He was dangerously close to the edge. I hoped Arthur was ready. The cigarette was our signal. When I threw it away, Arthur was supposed to move in.

'Spare me the gloating,' I said. 'Satisfy my curiosity instead. Answer me some questions, will you?'

'You mean to say you don't know it all? What is the great Nick Shannon coming to? You're not just trying to keep me talking, are you?' His face leered up at me. 'I hope you're not banking on the cavalry showing up to save the day.'

'It's just you and me, John.'

'It is now,' he said. 'I cracked your pet gorilla over the head before I woke you up.' He pointed into the darkness. 'I left him propped up against the wall. Looks for all the world like some drunken wino. If anyone comes, they'll step round him – this is London, after all.'

So it was back to the original plan – *mano a mano*. Nice try, Arthur. Hold on, my friend. I'll think of something. I promise.

'You had some questions,' John said. 'Ask away. But make it quick. My patience has almost run out.'

'First of all, where did you get the guns?'

'I checked you out most thoroughly. That much must have been obvious. I wanted to talk to Ronson, find out from him if

270

you had any weak spots I might have missed. I traced him through his ex-wife. Or, to be more precise, through a man called Turner. He was only too pleased to help – for a price, of course. Turner sold me the guns. The cocaine too.'

'And did you have to bribe anyone in the Audit Department to cover up the frauds?'

'No. You know Metcalfe, he's such a wimp he'll believe anything if you shout loudly enough. Still, it was a convenient little lie when I went back for a second bite of the cherry. How could they refuse? Couldn't take the risk of exposure.'

'And when did you first get the idea for your over-elaborate scheme?'

'The moment Richard showed me your application form. I'd had a good run. But I knew it couldn't last forever. I'd resigned myself to giving it just another few months. Quietly disappear. Then you came along. You were my inspiration.'

He paused to smile proudly at me.

'You had all the right qualifications. Clever enough – given a prod from me – to spot where I'd falsified the accounts. Pathologically' – Christ, I thought, that was rich coming from him – 'distrusting of the police. Stubborn as a mule. I didn't doubt for a moment you'd go it alone until you'd gathered all the evidence; assembled the case for the prosecution. Once I'd had the idea it was just a matter of waiting to find a suitable lookalike – or at least someone of roughly the same height and build.'

'And then Sam walked onto the scene,' I said. 'You must have thought Christmas had come early when he arrived. He probably felt the same, I suppose. Handed everything on a plate. A cosy little hideaway. Sofia strutting her stuff. A little cocaine to keep him passive. I bet he thought he'd died and gone to heaven. Poor sod.'

John glanced at his watch.

'Time for one more cigarette?' I asked.

'You've got a nerve,' he said.

I lit one nevertheless.

'Why frame me, John? I said. 'Why go to all the bother of

271

implicating me in the frauds? And why set me up to kill Yates?'

'You know what's always pissed me off about you, Shannon? Your ability to fall in the shit and come up smelling of roses.'

His voice had taken on a high, unnatural pitch.

'You lose two fingers. Does that put women off? No. Not for Nick Shannon, it doesn't. You kill your sister – everyone thinks you're a hero. It's the system that's at fault, they say. Not fine, upstanding Nick Shannon.'

He was trembling now, the gun bobbing about wildly in his hand.

'People look up to you, Shannon. I wanted to see you fall from grace. From the greatest possible height.'

I saw tears in his eyes. Knew I must make my move soon. His control – and my life – was hanging by a gossamer thread.

'Let's go, Shannon.'

He backed away from me, the barrel of the gun pointing shakily at my head. Wobble or not, I wouldn't have laid good money on him missing at that range.

'Get in front of me. Start walking.'

Reluctantly, I moved from the comparative shelter of the van into the wide open space of the car park. John motioned with the gun in the direction of the stairs. I walked ahead of him, listening all the time for the tell-tale last-chance click of the trigger being cocked.

Twenty yards on, he shouted.

'Stop there. Turn around and face me.'

I was maybe ten feet from the staircase. He circled me, watching for the slightest movement.

I drew deeply on the cigarette, using it to prime my system for the charge that couldn't be left much longer.

He pressed the button on the lift. Then stood back.

'You're a sham, Shannon.' He spat the words at me.

The lift door opened. He took the other gun from his trousers. Tossed it, frisbee style. It clattered along the concrete floor. And came to rest against the wall inside the lift.

'There you are, Shannon. Go get it.' He raised the gun. 'I'll give a count of three. Not that you'd go in there if I counted to a thousand. I know you for what you really are. Everything about you is a fraud. You're a coward, Shannon.'

He put both hands on the gun to steady the barrel.

'One,' he shouted.

I didn't move.

'What's the matter?' he crowed. 'Don't you trust me? Afraid I might press the button and shut you inside? Now, would *I* do a thing like that?'

I looked at the lift, and back at John.

'Go on. I won't even shoot to kill. Not with the first bullet that is. I'm taking special aim with that one. I want to see your balls explode.

One and one makes two, I said to myself.

'You're sick,' I said to John.

'And you're even sicker. Christ, I trusted you, Shannon. I thought you were my friend. I send you round to Sofia's with some tickets. And what do you do? You bastard! You raped my Sofia.'

I stared in total disbelief as he prepared to finish the countdown.

'I never touched her,' I said. 'Jesus, you know Sofia. She's a compulsive liar. At least with her you can always tell when she's lying. If she's got her mouth open, she's lying.'

'Shut *your* mouth, Shannon. Why would she lie to me? You're just trying to save your pathetic skin.'

'She's a born troublemaker, John. I bet she really enjoyed dumping Richard in the shit. She's done the same for me.'

'Save your breath, Shannon. Last chance.' He pointed again at the lift, and laughed.

'Three.'

It all happened very fast.

The gun moved down towards my groin.

His finger squeezed the trigger.

And I sprang forwards, simultaneously flicking the butt of the cigarette into his face.

John fired through the shower of sparks.

I felt the bullet hit my ribs as I dived.

I was sliding, rugby tackle fashion, into the lift when the second shot rang out. My leg jerked from the impact. I couldn't help but look down: two inches above the kneecap there was blood spurting from an artery.

My head hit the lift wall with a crunch. It had taken a lot of punishment in the last twenty-four hours. This was one blow too many. A galaxy of stars went into supernova in my brain. My subconscious took over. Began to run through its checklist to shut down all systems.

By pure instinct I reached out and grasped the gun. Rolled over. And fired.

I hit John in the elbow. It was a lucky shot: I was aiming for his heart!

He let out an ear-piercing scream and dropped the gun.

I fired again.

Not so fortunate this time.

The bullet hit the ceiling with a dull thud and careered off into the darkness.

The lift was beginning to revolve about me. I looked towards John as he used his left hand to pick up his gun. I was losing my vision from left to right.

I saw the flash from the muzzle of his gun.

Heard a sharp metallic ding as his shot ricocheted off the closing door.

Then I blacked out.

CHAPTER THIRTY

I awoke with a start, the index finger of my right hand pumping away at the trigger of a non-existent gun.

'Steady,' a voice said.

I felt a hand close on mine, stilling the involuntary spasms.

'It's all right. Everything's all right.'

'Norman?' I said, opening my eyes with difficulty.

He smiled down at me.

'Where am I?'

'Let me see,' he said. 'Unless the drips and the economy-size bottle of Lucozade are total red herrings, I'd say hospital was a pretty good guess.'

He straightened my bedclothes. 'By the way, Arthur sends his regards.'

The memory began to filter back.

'He's alive?' I said with relief.

'It takes more than a crack on the head from John to put Arthur out of commission for long. You'd need a sledge-hammer to penetrate that thick skull of his. He was pretty concussed, mind. They kept him in overnight for observation. He'll be along later, if I know him.'

I pushed down on the bed in an effort to sit up. I rose two inches then flopped back exhausted.

'Christ, what have they done to me? Given me a muscle transplant – with a gerbil as donor?'

'It's the anaesthetic. You spent a long while in the operating theatre. They removed one bullet from your leg and another from under your ribcage pretty close to a lung, so the nurses say.'

'I've got to get out of here,' I told him urgently.

'You're supposed to rest,' he fussed. 'Anyway, what's the rush?'

'I have to see Sally. Need to explain why I lied to her about Sam.'

'It will keep,' he said.

I shook my head, part disagreement, part sadness.

'You don't understand, Nick. You've lost a whole day. It's Sunday. Collins saw Sally yesterday.'

I groaned.

'Don't worry so much. She's in good hands. Tina's staying with her till her Mum and Dad arrive.'

'Okay,' I said weakly. 'Help me sit up, will you? I need some tea.'

'Is that wise?'

'I'll risk it. My mouth tastes like the inside of a horsebox.'

He grinned and pressed a red button above the bed.

'What happened?' I asked, a little later, sipping warily from a blue pyrex cup. There were enough pillows behind my back for pole vaulters to land on. I still felt uncomfortable. My chest felt tight and sore, twingeing at the slightest movement: shafts of only partly-dulled pain came at irregular intervals from my leg. A network of tubes resembling a map of the London Underground snaked in and out of my body. 'The last thing I remember is lying on the floor of the lift.'

'Well,' he said, stretching the word out. 'You didn't expect me to stay at home like Cinderella while you two went to the ball?'

'Yes,' I said. 'That's exactly what I did expect. But the self-satisfied smile on your face tells me you found yourself a fairy godmother.'

'More like a godfather, I suppose,' he said enigmatically.

'Come on, you crafty old bugger. What did you do?'

'Well,' he said again. 'You were so certain that John would

turn up. Stroke of midnight – to continue the analogy. Well . . .'

'Norman!'

'I went to see Collins.'

I slapped the heel of my palm against my forehead.

'Ouch.'

'Serves you right,' he laughed. 'Just look at it from my position. I couldn't sit back and do nothing. I'd have had a heart attack worrying about the pair of you. So I thought, "What is there to lose?". I'll go and tell the whole story to Collins. If he doesn't believe me – then I don't let him know where you are. If he does, then it seemed like some help from the police might come in handy. After all, that's what we pay our taxes for.'

'You don't pay any taxes, Norman.'

'Figuratively speaking, I mean.'

'So I take it Collins bought the story?'

'Yeah. It took a long time, mind you. Nearly a bit too long, as it happened. But Collins isn't such a bad guy when you get to know him. He sort of grows on you.'

'If he sort of grew on me,' I snorted, 'I'd sort of chop him off.'

'He saved your life, Nick. I might have played my own small part,' he blew on his fingernails and rubbed them on his collar, 'but Collins was the one to push the lift button. *And* he threw himself at John – without a second thought for the gun.'

Norman gave me a rare serious look.

'Forget the past, Nick. Bury the hatchet as far as Collins is concerned. You owe him.'

Why was I getting a strange feeling down the back of my spine?

'Anything else I should know, Norman?'

'No, I don't think so,' he said, hesitating. 'Except – maybe – that Arlene's on her way.'

He looked at me triumphantly.

'I thought that would bring a smile to your lips – sorry, balloon.'

*

It was five more days before they let me leave hospital. Five long days where Sally was uppermost in my mind. I felt unable to relax until I had seen her – only then could the curtain come down on this whole sorry business. So I let no opportunity pass: I badgered every nurse, every doctor, the physiotherapist too, with the same question – when can I go? I didn't win any nominations for Patient of the Year, but the strategy worked.

Arthur, Norman, Arlene and Tina had come to visit every day. Collins even put in an appearance – in an official capacity, of course. There was a statement to take, and a grunted apology to make.

When Arlene arrived on Wednesday afternoon, I had been sitting fully dressed in a chair for three hours, beating out a nervous rhythm on the floor with my walking stick.

They wanted to see me off the premises in a wheelchair but I, stubborn as ever, refused. Walking was how it had all started, and that was how it was going to finish.

Arlene took my arm and we followed the Ariadne-inspired colour-coded strips on the walls along the five-mile route march to the waiting taxi.

Back at the Savoy, I was only too happy to comply with Arlene's instruction to go to bed and rest – and I mean rest, she had said bossily – for a couple of hours. The walk had taken more out of me than I cared to admit.

On rising, we shared a pot of coffee – it tasted like nectar after the cheap instant of the hospital. At seven o'clock I swallowed a handful of painkillers, kissed Arlene goodbye and went off to make my peace with Sally.

*

We met, for dinner, on neutral territory. A little trattoria in Covent Garden. Decked out as if the owners had ticked a box on an order form (Italian, middle period, rustique) and sent it back to a firm of decor packagers. Red and white check tablecloths. Chianti bottles strung together and hung on the walls.

Large glass fishing globes suspended from the ceiling. Gargantuan, phallic symbol, pepper mills. Despite these inauspicious signs, the staff were genuinely friendly; the food high quality – fish simply cooked and ocean-fresh as if straight from boat to grill.

I asked the waiter for one of the quiet tables tucked away in the secondary dining room at the back. We had the place almost to ourselves: the theatregoers had bolted down their meals and scurried off for the evening performances; another hour would pass before the main throng of night-time revellers arrived.

Tina had been staying with her. She had given me daily reports of Sally's gradual progress on the long haul back from grief towards relative normality. The dark rings under Sally's eyes told me she still had some way to go before she could sleep easily at nights. But her eyes were free of the redness of tears – that stage, thankfully, had past.

Tina had kept her busy. Even taken her shopping. The new outfit bore touches of the student's style. The dress was simple – knee length, navy blue with small white polka dots, plain white belt around the gathered waist – but the trimmings were straight from Tina's collection: blue and white bead necklace, blue teardrop earrings, broad white bangle on each wrist Sally's long blonde hair had been swept back into an intricate plait, leaving just two thin wisps spiralling down in front of her ears.

Sally avoided my attempt to give her a peck on the cheek. Great start! This was going to be even more difficult than I'd feared.

We shared a bottle of Pinot Grigio – light, easy to drink, safe – and ate seafood salad and grilled Dover sole. She chewed as if the food were sawdust in her mouth, sipped as from a poisoned chalice.

I began by offering my condolences. Reminded her I had been through it too. Could feel what she felt. That the wounds of grief would eventually heal – although the scars would always remain. And that was how it should be. We need the memories. Of the good times; the love shared.

She listened impassively, her eyes avoiding mine.

It made the next part even harder. But the truth had to be spoken. I wanted her to understand my reasons – only then might she give her approval.

I told her how truly sorry I was that I had lied, not once but three times, about her brother; kept her in the dark concerning his death solely to further my own ends.

'Collins has explained everything,' she said coldly. 'Told me the story from beginning to end. I don't blame you for what you did, if that's what you want to hear.'

The hardness in her eyes robbed me of any consolation the words might otherwise have provided.

An awkward silence descended upon us.

For something to do, I ordered coffee – cappuccino for Sally, espresso for me. She stared thoughtfully at the white foam, stirred the coffee for an age before finally pushing the cup aside.

'And what about John?' she said. 'What will happen to him?'

It was a question I had hoped she would not ask.

'He won't get away with it, that's for sure.' I paused to try to find a way to break it gently. There wasn't one.

'Collins tells me that John is trying to pull a fast one. He's had a long session with his lawyers. Collins didn't like the look of them: a bent solicitor, one of the less scrupulous barristers and a prim and proper junior – thick spectacles, hair in a bun, you know the type – to give a touch of respectability in court. John is going to plead guilty – but insane.'

I tried to sound reassuring. 'I wouldn't worry. If the jury believes him, he might avoid going to prison but he'll only finish up in one of the "special hospitals" – Broadmoor, Rampton, Moss Side. Given the choice, I'd take Brixton any day.'

I left the rest unsaid. Collins's angry outburst about the system – how John might be released at any time if his 'mental condition' was deemed to have improved to the point where society would no longer be at risk from his 'dangerous, violent or criminal propensities'.

I made the mistake of taking hold of her hand. Tenderly. Just one last gesture of sympathy.

She snatched her hand away as if I were a leper.

'I told you Collins explained everything.' A tear rolled down her cheek. 'Including why John did it.' She looked at me accusingly. The innocence had gone forever. Hate flared from deep within her. 'I can't help thinking about what might have happened. If you hadn't come on the scene. Without you, John would have taken the easy way out. I don't blame you for lying, Nick. But I do blame you for Sam's death.'

*

I turned my jacket collar against the cold wind and hobbled back to the Savoy. The pain in my leg was nothing compared with the one in my heart.

The short, but slow, walk did me good. It gave me time to think. To rationalise Sally's harsh words. She may have been right. I certainly couldn't deny her accusation. Perhaps I had been an unwitting catalyst for John's plans. But I couldn't carry this extra baggage. Who knows, I lectured myself, what fate might have had in store for Sam under different circumstances? I shrugged my shoulders and took refuge in chaos theory. One small, insignificant event can change the course of history. The flapping of a butterfly's wings in the Amazon can establish the conditions for a hurricane five thousand miles away.

By the time I reached the hotel, I had come to terms with the guilt she had tried to lay at my door. I was free again. Sally had been the last responsibility. I was determined to relax now.

The foyer was like a market-place in Babel. Tourists of all nationalities stood jabbering away in front of the reception desk. The Japanese clutched cameras and theatre programmes and made brave, but risible, attempts at pronouncing 'Lloyd Webber'.

A porter shouted indecorously to make himself heard above

the chaos. The sound of my name took me by surprise; stopped my cautious progress through the human obstacle course.

'Good evening, Mr Shannon,' the porter said. 'If you would follow me, sir, the manager would like to see you, sir.'

'What for?' I asked, wondering exactly what I had done now.

'I can't really say, sir. I'm sure it will only take a minute.'

He took hold of my arm like a boy scout trying to help a pensioner cross a busy road, and shouldered his way through the crowd.

In the relative peace of the corridor I told him I could cope without his support.

'If you say so, sir,' he said.

He set off this time with an exaggerated slowness – consideration or umbrage? Eventually we came to a set of double doors. The porter gave three loud knocks and flung the doors wide open without bothering to wait for a reply.

The room was in darkness.

I felt exposed standing there in the doorway, a sharply defined silhouette against the brightness from the corridor.

A sudden blaze of light blinded me. Blinking my eyes, I balanced myself as best I could in preparation for an attack: I waved the walking stick sideways in a threatening scythe-like motion.

Then I heard the shout.

'Surprise!'

This just had to be Arlene's doing.

There she stood in the middle of the group, wearing a silver and black trouser suit.

She tottered towards me on three-inch heels, a wide grin on her lips and a glass of champagne in each hand. The others followed close behind.

Arthur, Norman, Tina. And was that Collins in a smart suit and crisp white shirt, hair neatly trimmed and smelling of Head and Shoulders? They had been right to shout 'surprise'.

There could be no better celebration. And, thanks to Arlene, no better timing.

'All over?' she asked anxiously.

'Yes.' I said. 'All over.'

Arthur, his face already showing a champagne bloom, ushered me across to a ring of easy chairs. 'Take the weight off that leg,' he said. 'No one will mind. You're among friends. You've nothing to prove to us. Come on, drink up.'

'Thanks,' I said. 'To all of you.' I raised my glass to each of them in turn and then slowly drained it so that my glistening eyes were on the ceiling for a while.

'Hey, Arthur,' I said to deflect their attention, 'have you told Arlene how John got the jump on you. She likes a laugh.'

Arthur blushed self-consciously.

Arlene took my hand and squeezed it. 'Well, Arthur?' she said.

'It was coming up to eleven,' he said slowly. 'I'd been in that bleeding car park for hours.' He paused, hoping that we would understand the consequences and spare him the next part of the story. No such luck. 'I needed a Jimmy' he mumbled.

Arlene looked quizically at him.

'A Jimmy Riddle. You know. A Frazer Nash.'

'Do you mean the "little boys' room"?' she asked, milking his embarrassment for all it was worth. 'The "heads"? "A man's gotta do what a man's gotta do".'

'Anyway,' he said. 'I was coming back from the, er, wassname, you know. I turned the corner, and whack. I still don't know how he managed it.'

'The punk must have brought a stepladder,' Arlene said.

The party lasted two hours. Or, rather, that was as long as I lasted. The combination of being able to relax at last, the wine during the meal and then the champagne took a rapid toll of my weakened constitution. As much as I wanted to carry on enjoying the occasion, my tired body had other ideas. Arlene saw the signs and nodded at the other guests.

Collins was the first to make a move.

As he prepared to leave, he pressed a package into my hand. A memento, he said.

Puzzled as to the contents, I eagerly lifted the lid of the small cardboard box.

It contained a perspex cube. Embedded inside were the two cartridge cases from the bullets I had fired at John.

I smiled at him with gratitude. Shook his hand warmly.

'Try and stay out of trouble, Shannon!' he said sternly, trying to cover his embarrassment at the show of sentiment behind the gift.

'And if you can't,' he added, 'then make sure you give me a call.' He landed a playful punch on my shoulder. 'Stay lucky,' he said finally.

Arthur, Norman and Tina said they would stay on to finish the last bottle of champagne. 'No sense wasting it.' They sent me off with a flurry of handshakes, hugs and kisses that left me breathless.

Arlene took charge of me. Led me upstairs to our suite. Told me, with a wink, that it was time for bed – and then for rest.

*

Giggling like a pair of schoolkids, we walked along the corridor. I leaned heavily on the walking stick to keep from stumbling; Arlene teetered equally unsteadily on her high heels. The stooped lady from room service discreetly gave us no more than a sideways glance – in her job she must have presumably witnessed far worse behaviour than ours. She looked like a typical Sicilian peasant woman with her walnut skin, severe scraped-back hairstyle and long black skirt that gave the merest glimpse of a pair of trim ankles. Her hair was that ludicrous shade of copper, black peeking through at the roots, that Latins acquire through using a cheap hairdresser with little imagination. Her accent too was a broad Italian slur as her bespectacled eyes diplomatically addressed the trolley bearing the champagne 'wivva da manager's compliments'.

Once inside, Arlene packed me off to the bedroom while she waited for the refugee from *The Godfather* to open the champagne. My leg was aching badly by now – the price to be paid for too much walking, too soon after leaving the hospital. I was grateful for the opportunity to lie down on the bed, rest a while before Arlene joined me. I heard a thud which sounded like an inebriated Arlene bumping into the coffee table and then the pop of the cork. I closed my eyes in anticipation. Thought of the quirk of fate that had brought Arlene and me together.

We had talked a lot over the last few days – but always skirted round the subject of a joint future. Maybe the tables had turned and Arlene did not want to push me into a commitment – too conscious of the seven missed years where other men would have been sowing their wild oats before settling down to married life. Or was it, for her, just a holiday romance? A story to dine out on, or tell in whispers behind the closed doors of the ladies' room?

Perhaps, for my part, I was unsure of how much the excitement and adventure had contributed to the success of our relationship. How would we cope with the relative boredom of domesticity? Where would we live? She had a good job in America – would she be willing to give that up to come and live in England? Or should I take my chances? Up sticks and retrain as an accountant, grappling as best I could with the very singular rules and regulations of the United States? A little practice in New England had its appeal, I had to admit. Might even do well as an Englishman – novelty value (a lanky Dudley Moore?). And there was nothing to keep me here, after all. A fresh start. A place where the name Shannon did not evoke memories of hypodermic needles filled with morphine.

Moonlight in Vermont – and all that jazz.

What was there to lose?

I couldn't go down on one knee, not in my current condition that was for sure. But I doubted if that would make any difference. Arlene would have her answer ready, be it yes or no, whatever the circumstances of the proposal. Now was the time. The champagne was an omen.

Arlene was taking an age – probably some last minute adjustment to her make-up, or maybe she was slipping off the trouser suit. I couldn't wait any longer. I pushed myself up off the bed with the aid of the stout stick. Walked stiffly, and more than a little painfully, through to the sitting room.

She was lying on the sofa. Breathing slowly. Fast asleep. Had the woman no sense of timing? I had to wake her. Surely she would forgive me. When she heard my question.

I lowered myself next to her. Perched precariously on the edge of the sofa. Ran my fingers lightly through her hair. I felt something sticky. Snatched away my hand in horror. It was covered in blood.

I hurried as best I could towards the phone. Caught a blur of movement at the corner of my eye.

A swirl of black. The long skirt of the room service waitress – emerging from the hiding place behind the settee.

She was stooped no longer. As she charged towards me, a long, thin, needle-sharp stiletto in hand, the truth dawned.

Raised to her full height she was easier to recognise. Take the clips out of her hair. Rinse out the dye. Wash off the heavy fake tan. And what did you have?

Sofia.

Sofia of the mouth-kicking foot.

Now Sofia of the death-dealing hand.

She would have been quicker, more agile than I at the best of times. My leg made me clumsy. It was difficult to turn. Would be impossible to balance sufficiently to repel such a headlong attack.

She saw my plight. Smiled as she stepped to my bad side. Darted in, the point of the knife aimed at my chest.

I had but one weapon. The walking stick. I upended it in an effort to keep Sofia at bay. My leg didn't think much of the idea: in return for losing the cushion of its prop, it took vengeance with a fierce spasm of pain.

Steadying myself as best I could, I swung the crook of the handle, intending to catch her ankles and sweep her feet from under her.

Nimbly, she jumped over it. Didn't wait for the returning double-handed backhand swing. Kicked out at me with all the skill of a Thai boxer.

She chose her spot well. Her foot connected above my knee. Directly on the wound.

It felt like an incendiary bomb detonating in my leg. Somewhere underneath the flames, there was a vague sensation of stitches bursting and a warm river of blood pouring through the broken dam.

My leg buckled under me.

I slumped to the floor, immediately rolling away from the menace of Sofia. I managed only one revolution before her foot crashed into my ribs.

She stood over me, legs apart, as I clutched my side in agony. I could only stare up into those pitiless eyes.

She raised her right foot slowly from the ground, toying with me like a cat with a trapped mouse. She paused to give my imagination a chance to panic over the destination of the next blow. Then brought her foot down hard on my stomach.

The wind rushed from my lips. Starved of oxygen, I was totally defenceless.

Tiring of the game, or aware of the danger from the noise I was making, she acted swiftly now. Jumped into the air. Landed on my body, backside thumping down on my solar plexus. Pushed her feet into my armpits, pinning me to the floor in some grotesque parody of a sexual act.

Sofia raised the knife high in the air, its point aimed at my heart. Her mouth, once so luscious, opened to reveal the bloodthirsty grin of a vampire. She lingered sadistically. Savoured, for a moment, my knowledge of certain death.

And, subconsciously, slightly relaxed the pressure from her feet.

I jerked my right arm free.

Wrestled – with my conscience.

Then did what I had done only once before in my life.

Using my good hand, I stabbed two rigid fingers into her eyes.

The scream sent shivers down my spine.

I felt sick to the very depths of my stomach. I fought back the rising bile in my mouth.

My shocked senses shouted at me. 'Ignore her. Think of Arlene. Get help.'

I manhandled the crazed Sofia off me. Looked away as I saw her stumbling across the floor in agony.

I tried to stand up.

Couldn't make it.

It was a long crawl to the phone.

*

The next twenty minutes can only be described as absolute pandemonium. There was so much noise, so many comings and goings, that it was hard to take it all in.

Other hotel guests, awakened by Sofia's screams, were first to arrive on the scene. Most stood at the door gawping, satisfying their morbid curiosity: two men and one woman plucked up courage to cross the threshold but could do no more than wander helplessly between the three of us. The crew of two ambulances were next to enter, followed closely by Arthur, Norman and Tina (who had heard sirens blaring, and – knowing my propensity for trouble – had feared the worst). Next came two uniformed constables.

The four ambulance men got on with their job as best they could, while everyone else milled around getting in each other's way.

And, all the time, Sofia screamed and screamed.

Lying supine on the floor, I watched shamefully as two ambulance men held her down while a third injected her with a sedative. The decibel level, mercifully, dropped into the bearable zone. In the chaotic jostle to clear a path for her stretcher, Norman slipped and fell to the floor. Arthur left my side to scoop him up. Norman, shaky and breathing hard, left the room mumbling about needing some fresh air. He returned, face flushed, just as Arlene and I were being carried out. Flopping on the sofa, he said he'd see us later.

On the journey to the hospital, Arthur and Tina sat with anxious expressions in the jump seats of the ambulance. Arlene and I were buckled to the platforms on either side of the narrow aisle. By straining against the straps I was just able to touch the tips of her icy fingers. She lay motionless, her breath stuttering from her mouth at worryingly irregular intervals.

All I could do was hope and pray.

CHAPTER THIRTY-ONE

'What are you doing for Christmas?' Norman asked me.

We were sitting, with Arthur, at a table for four in a packed restaurant on its opening night.

Christmas was two weeks away. It was hard to believe that two months had passed since that frantic dash in the ambulance. So much had happened. Yet so little had been resolved.

Collins had come to see me in hospital. I awoke on the third afternoon to find him sitting, deep in gloom, by my bedside. A bunch of red carnations lay in his lap. He stared down at the flowers with unseeing eyes. The wrapping paper rustled at the tightness of his grip and with the slow fidgety way he had, he kept lifting the bouquet up a few inches before letting it fall back on his knees. When he finally spoke, it was with a voice that crackled with emotion.

It was an apology. Sloppy police work, he confessed: on the offchance that she might return to this country, immigration officers at all entry points had been alerted to watch out for Sofia Kalamboukis. But not for Sofia Weston.

John and Sofia had been married in Jamaica. I thought of the photograph in the album. The smiling faces. The white dress. I should have guessed.

She had returned for two reasons – vengeance and greed. The police had found a key on the floor of Arlene's suite: Sofia had booked herself a room at the Savoy – cheekily, just along the corridor from us. When Collins searched her room, he had found the black gown of the barrister's junior who had visited John in his cell. And the official forms, bearing John's signature, ready to send to the Banque Credit de St Gallen: he had authorised the transferral of their joint account into her sole name.

Had John been wise to trust her, I wondered? Or was it simply the price that had to be paid for Sofia's promise to eliminate Nick Shannon – the cause of his capture, the soon-to-be star witness against him? Or had he been too clever for her, after all? When the police finally persuaded the bank to open its books, the cupboard was bare. The account had been cleared. It had the ring of a last laugh about it.

Sofia has taken a leaf from John's book and pleaded insanity. She claims her behaviour, her whole personality, stems from being raped by her father at the tender age of twelve: he held a knife to her face – that's how she got the scar. If what she says is true, it could explain many things. But where Sofia is concerned, who is gifted enough to differentiate truth from lie?

At work I am finding it difficult to deal with the sense of anti-climax. Even the drama of Richard's departure provided only a brief respite from the increasing boredom of the routine which I had once found wholly satisfying. I share an office with Metcalfe. His idea of taking a risk is to order a chicken Madras rather than his usual korma.

Having played the game for high stakes, a return to a penny-a-point existence is proving to be exceedingly difficult to swallow.

'I asked you a question, Nick.' Norman was waving his hand in front of my face in a mocking 'Is-there-anybody-there?' gesture. 'What are you doing for Christmas?'

'Sorry, Norman,' I said, snapping back to the present. 'I'm off to New England. A few days at Arlene's house and then we're off to Boston for the New Year.'

Norman started humming the *Wedding March*: Arthur joined in merrily.

'We're going to be bridge partners, that's all.'

'We believe you. Don't we, Arthur?'

'Can we order, Norman?' I said, changing the subject.

'It's all in hand,' he said, checking his watch.

I took of a sip of the Pomerol that Norman had so extrava-
gantly ordered. Leaned back in my chair. Cast my eyes round
the restaurant to take my mind off my rumbling stomach.

All traces of the previous Indian establishment had disappeared. The red flock wallpaper had been stripped away: in its
place was plain, dark-wood panelling to waist-high, the butter-
cream emulsion above running up to a matt white ceiling. The
wooden tables, set with dark blue napkins and heavy cutlery,
were solid and generously proportioned. The floorboards had
been sanded down and varnished. Running the full length of
one wall was a bar festooned with a dazzling variety of shiny-
new pump handles. The whole place had a no-nonsense,
masculine air about it. It was like Rules without the spooks.

Waiters scurried about, dextrously balancing plates of shell-
fish or char-grilled meats.

The door opened, letting in a brief blast of winter air. And
the well-wrapped figure of Collins.

'Can't stop,' he said, settling into the spare chair at our table.

I looked at Norman. He was trying to wipe a grin off his
face.

'I take it this isn't a chance meeting?' I said to Collins.

'Didn't Norman tell you?' he said.

'I thought it would be better coming from you,' Norman
replied.

'Well,' said Collins, as if Norman's habit had rubbed off on
him. His voice sounded as cheerful as a Chris Rea record. 'I've
been commended for bravery. And promoted to boot.'

He seemed to stress the last word.

'Congratulations,' I said, against the din of alarm bells in my
ears.

'Commiserations are more appropriate. They've transferred
me. Into the bleeding Fraud Squad.'

'And what,' I asked, with a strange sinking feeling, 'has that
to do with me?'

'I had a word with your boss – talk about a new miracle cure for insomnia! Anyway, it seems that your firm is anxious to get back in our good books after all the problems John caused. You're being seconded to me for a while. Part of our panel of outside experts – the Fraud Investigations Group, it's called. Jameson Browns will pay your salary and we'll cover your expenses.'

And why, I wondered cynically, if it was a purely advisory role, should there be any need for expenses?

'Norman,' – Collins gave him a conspiratorial smile – 'said you would only be too glad to give me a hand. In view of past events, that is.'

Christ, he hadn't wasted much time in calling in the debt.

'If I agree,' I said, the familiar scent of blackmail in my nostrils, 'then does that settle our account?'

'Let's call it a downpayment, shall we?' He slid a card across the table. 'Here's my address. Shall we say first thing Monday morning?'

I examined closely the faces round the table.

Collins's brows were knitted together expectantly. Norman stared back at me quizzically. Arthur peered down into his wine glass.

'You scheming bastards set me up, didn't you?'

'Let's face it, Nick,' Norman said. 'You haven't been really happy lately. You're bored stiff. Admit it. This is just what the psychotherapist ordered.'

As always, Norman spoke a lot of sense.

'I pull out any time I want,' I said to Collins. 'Is that perfectly clear?'

'Of course, Nick.' He rose from the table. 'Sure,' he called back as he walked towards the door. 'Any time you want.'

'Satisfied now,' I said to Norman.

He grinned at me.

'Here comes the food,' he said, a note of triumph in his voice.

'With the compliments of the owners,' the waiter said, setting the plate in front of me.

I stared down disbelievingly.

The plate was covered. Not by a silver dome. But by a white chef's hat.

The waiter, with a flourish, whisked the hat away, revealing the dish that had been especially chosen for me.

It was a sirloin steak sandwich.

The starched white apron of the chef appeared at my side.

I didn't need to turn around.

I didn't *want* to turn around.

'Come on,' Toddy said. 'Get that down you before it gets cold.'

I looked Norman directly in the eyes.

'Oh, no,' I groaned. 'You didn't?'

He gave me a wink.

'You did!'

I couldn't stop myself from bursting out laughing.

'You're crazy,' I said to the both of them. 'At your time of lives, too. Partners in bloody crime again.'

I shook my head at Norman. 'What am I going to do with you? You crafty old sod. Need some fresh air, my Aunt Fanny! You found Sofia's room key on the floor, didn't you?'

He gave me the butter-wouldn't-melt-in-my-mouth look of a wronged innocent.

I wasn't to be deflected by cheap tricks.

'How did it go then?' I asked. 'Quick dash down to Reception? "Wonder if you'd mind just running off a quick photocopy of these papers?" Sprint back to Sofia's room to replace the originals? No wonder you were flushed and breathless. Had to collapse on the sofa. Or was that just a convenient cover to drop the key down the back?'

However many uncertainties there were in the world, there was one sure-fire bet. Two months ago, Toddy had suffered a severe attack of writer's cramp.

Only one question remained.

When thinking of a name for their joint venture, how had Norman and Toddy resisted the temptation to call it 'Fake and Chips'?

CRUEL AND UNUSUAL

Patricia Cornwell

Cruel and Unusual won the CWA Gold Dagger Award and takes Patricia Cornwell to even greater heights, confirming the extraordinary range and power of this gifted author.

At 11.05 one December evening in Richmond, Virginia, convicted murderer Ronnie Joe Waddell is pronounced dead in the electric chair.

At the morgue Dr Kay Scarpetta waits for Waddell's body. Preparing to perform a post mortem before the subject is dead is a strange feeling, but Scarpetta has been here before. And Waddell's death is not the only newsworthy event on this freezing night: the grotesquely wounded body of a young boy is found propped against a rubbish skip. To Scarpetta the two cases seem unrelated, until she recalls that the body of Waddell's victim had been arranged in a strikingly similar position.

Then a third murder is discovered, the most puzzling of all. The crime scene yields very few clues: old blood stains, fragments of feather, and – most baffling – a bloody fingerprint that points to the one suspect who could not possibly have committed this murder.

'Chillingly detailed forensic thriller confirming Cornwell as the top gun in this field'
Daily Telegraph

'This book is another dazzler from the woman who has raised crime writing on to a new plateau'
Irish Press

FICTION
0 7515 0168 9

GONE, BUT NOT FORGOTTEN

Phillip M. Margolin

In Hunter's Point, New York several years ago Peter Lake, the owner of a high-ranking law firm, returns home one evening to find his wife strangled and his daughter's neck broken. On the bed lies a black rose, and a note: 'Gone, But Not Forgotten'. They are not the first victims of the so-called 'Rose Killer', but when Hunter's Point police track down their suspect – and he is shot – they expect them to be the last.

Now, on the other side of the continent in Portland, Oregon, the sequence of the roses and the notes and the missing women is occurring again, and when a sharp-eyed officer comes across the similarities between these disappearances and the apparently solved case of years ago, there is a desperate hunt to discover the links between the two.

When the police do stumble upon a connection it seems they have made an appalling error of deduction. Betsy Tannenbaum, a sharp, ambitious attorney, decides to accept the brief to defend the suspect in a case which will make or break her career.

She finds herself unlocking a great many closets to discover the skeletons of a crime that shocks and terrifies her. The 'Rose Killer', whose systematic abductions of women reveal no trace of his identity, is back. Why was the former case hushed up? And who is abducting women again, leaving not a single sign of a struggle – not a hair, not a fibre, not a trace – just a note, a rose . . . and eventually, a victim.

FICTION
0 7515 0377 0

Warner Books now offers an exciting range of quality titles by both established and new authors. All of the books in this series are available from:

Little, Brown and Company (UK),
P.O. Box 11,
Falmouth,
Cornwall TR10 9EN.

Alternatively you may fax your order to the above address. Fax No. 01326 317444.

Payments can be made as follows: cheque, postal order (payable to Little, Brown and Company) or by credit cards, Visa/Access. Do not send cash or currency. UK customers and B.F.P.O.: please send a cheque or postal order (no currency) and allow £1.00 for postage and packing for the first book, plus 50p for the second book, plus 30p for each additional book up to a maximum charge of £3.00 (7 books plus).

Overseas customers including Ireland please allow £2.00 for postage and packing for the first book, plus £1.00 for the second book, plus 50p for each additional book.

NAME (Block Letters) ....

....

ADDRESS ....

....

....

☐ I enclose my remittance for ....

☐ I wish to pay by Access/Visa Card

Number ☐☐☐☐☐☐☐☐☐☐☐☐☐☐☐☐

Card Expiry Date ☐☐☐☐